EXTREME ZOMBIES

EXTREME ZOMBIES

Edited by Paula Guran

PRIME BOOKS

EXTREME ZOMBIES

Copyright © 2012 by Paula Guran.

Cover art by ItsBadBeGood.
Cover design by Telegraphy Harness.

Prime Books
www.prime-books.com

For more information, contact Prime Books:
prime@prime-books.com

ISBN: 978-1-60701-352-5

To David J. Schow,
who knows everything you need to know about zombies
(and practically anything else).

Contents

Introductory Warnings, Cautions & Alerts

Paula Guran

Want an overview of a variety of zombie literature in the twenty-first century?

This is not the book for you. I did that one a couple of years back: *Zombies: The Recent Dead* (ISBN: 978-1-60701-234-4, Prime Books). There's some wonderful introductory material by David J. Schow and some additional stuff from yours truly. Book's got some excellent zombie stories from this century and I like to think of it—we all have our little fantasies—being used as one of the textbooks for a class on the subject at some university.

This anthology?

Possession of the content in *Extreme Zombies* might get you kicked out of most high schools, some colleges, and many families. That's a warning, kids! Don't take chances with dangerous reading material. Even if your teacher loves *The Walking Dead* and your parents encourage you to read, there's stuff in here that's against the rules . . . anybody's rules.

If you are of legal age, be careful to whom you lend this book to. Don't leave it on the coffee table (especially anywhere near the bong). People who might otherwise see you as an acceptable person may change their minds if they read a few of the passages in these stories. Worse, it might attract *really* strange new "friends."

Parents, be responsible. Keep this book out of the hands of young children.

You have been warned.

The zombie archetype, once appreciated only by horror fans, has become firmly entrenched in modern culture. The prevalent ideation is the so-called "Romero" zombie—named *en hommage* to George A. Romero whose 1968 film, *Night of the Living Dead*, depicted reanimated corpses (never referred to in the first *Dead* film as "zombies") attacking the living. These walking, decaying dead mindlessly shamble, forever hungering for and devouring the flesh of humans. Although never exactly spelled out in the movies, zombies evidently were the result of a mutant virus that could be passed on to the living by a bite or some bodily secretion.

Closely associated with this undead icon is the "zombie apocalypse": societal breakdown, usually worldwide, following some type infestation or plague or alien virus or science experiment gone bad, etc. Survivors may struggle alone or band together to defend themselves, perhaps waging all-out war against the undead.

There are numerous variations of the Romero zombie and end-of-the-world scenarios; you'll find some of them here. And, occasionally, as here, the "traditional" zombie associated with the Afro-Caribbean religion of Voudou—a dead or living person stripped of their own will and/or soul who is under the control of a sorcerer—still appears. (If you want to learn more about the evolution of zombies, again, read the introductions to *Zombies: The Recent Dead*.)

Just a few years ago, the zombie a still-meaningful metaphor, a horrific embodiment that replaced the outmoded monsters of the past in our collective psyche. Monsters were merely creatures that might get *you*; the living dead could wipe us *all* out; civilization, at least, was doomed.

As this book was being prepared, the Associated Press reported folks are now responding to incidents of true horror—"a naked man eating most of another man's face . . . a college student telling police he killed a man, then ate his heart and part of his brain . . . a man stabbed himself fifty times and threw bits of his own intestines at police [who] pepper-sprayed him, but he was not easily subdued"—by comparing them to zombies.

These incidents inspire online search terms like "zombie apocalypse" to trend. Evidently, zombies still resonate with our view of the world. Creatures that start off as "us," but become monsters with nothing more than feeding and "surviving" as a goal that continue to shamble and create even more of their emotionless, inexorable kind—with no conscience or morality to stop them.

Apocalyptic doom, we fear, will come from that which we, ourselves, have created but cannot stop. Fears of bioterrorism and new contagions are prevalent, economic depression seems to be forcing us closer to the end of our world as we know it . . . we are losing control.

On the other hand—if you have one—we are also responding to zombies (or maybe our fears) and referencing them with humor.

Is the zombie still really an effective horror icon when it is being spoofed in television commercials to sell cars, snack food, candy, cereal, drinks, and, yes, Microsoft's Windows 7? Will zombies soon be passé as terror? The vampire was tamed into Count Chocula, Muppetized to teach toddlers to count, and romanticized into a young girl's dream beau. Are zombies on their way to similar domestication?

There have already been zombie musicals and attempts at zombie romance. You'll now find more zombie fiction published for kids of all ages—including babies—than can be easily listed. Much of it is either cute or entertainingly edifying. Zombie disguises are popular with young trick-or-treaters. I guess you can't really take the $12.99 Dismember-Me Plush Zombie, a "scary (but cute) zombie plush" that "begs to be torn limb from limb. After all he is a decaying re-animated corpse turned into irresistible cuddly plush . . . " as really designed for kids, but the Doctor Dreadful Zombie Lab ($24.99) is: children seven and older can "concoct a variety of disturbingly delicious experiments . . . brew bubbly brains or zombie skins, and eat them too. . . . Watch in horror as the zombie jaw rips open and he pukes his brains out."

Can whole-grain Zombie Skin Flakes with yummy multi-colored marshmallow bits (pink hearts, purple brains, green guts, yellow toes, blue fingers . . .) be far behind?

The stories in *Extreme Zombies* are, one way or another, not for the children. No marshmallows or safe-to-eat bubbly brains. That doesn't mean they simply "go for the gross-out" or are just prose equivalents of shoot-the-zombie games. None of these stories are bereft of meaning. They were not written merely to induce regurgitation or to exercise your virtual trigger finger. Sure, there's gore and grue and depravity and all that cool stuff, but they also reflect the real word, provoke thought, and comment on just how utterly fucked up mundane humanity is. They can also occasionally provide a glimmer of hope we aren't as screwed up and doomed as we think we are

Maybe that's not your cup of brains. If so, we hope that big red word *EXTREME* (or possibly this introduction) has scared you away. Our menu is not intended for the faint-hearted or squeamish. In fact, we at Prime Books suggest those who easily offended avoid chomping down on this collective brainburger. Go crochet a pastel zombie. We think that's keen, too, we just aren't providing the patterns with this anthology. This time, we're unraveling yarn-like festering intestines and jabbing eyeballs with crochet hooks.

Extremity can be many things; don't make the mistake of equating "extreme" solely with grossness and violence—although I won't deny that disturbing description can be, and often is, part of the equation and graphic violence a given. Sex is often used as an extreme element—carnal relations seem to be eternally shocking, especially to Americans—and so is religion. Emotions—especially love—are part of the mix. If the world belongs not to the living, but to the dead, what is perverse? What happens to faith? What can one still feel?

Some of the stories in *Extreme Zombies* use exceptional situations, an unusual premise, or twists on the expected to make them edgy. Humor, satire, absurdism, the grotesque, the weird, and a touch or two of surrealism also come into play. We even stray from the "modern" zombie and, of course, the scariest creatures portrayed may very well be human and not the rotting walking corpses.

Among the tales collected here are some classics of zombie fiction—they've withstood the test of time and cultural absorption and are still *way* out *there* . . . often farther out *there* than more contemporary samples . . . and their razor-sharp edges still slice to the marrow. If you are an aficionado of zom-fic, you may be familiar with them, but when compiling an anthology that dares to be dubbed *Extreme Zombies*—respect is respect and classics are classics because they can be savored time and again. Plus, there are always new mouths to feed and untouched minds to subvert.

Not that we overlook the fresher fictional meat. There's also plenty of that quivering on the platter: previously published but not widely distributed to the slavering masses on zombie connoisseurs.

In other words, we offer a veritable smorgasbord of extreme zombie fiction for you to gnaw on. Nibble at bits and pieces or devour it all without benefit of mastication.

To quote a story contained herein: *BONE appétit!*

Paula Guran
April 2012

As they drove between the Cadillacs, the sky fading like a bad bulb, Wayne looked at the cars and tried to imagine what the Chevy-Cadillac Wars had been like, and why they had been fought in this miserable desert . . .

On the Far Side of the Cadillac
Desert with Dead Folks

Joe R. Lansdale

1

After a month's chase, Wayne caught up with Calhoun one night at a little honky-tonk called Rosalita's. It wasn't that Calhoun had finally gotten careless, it was just that he wasn't worried. He'd killed four bounty hunters so far, and Wayne knew a fifth didn't concern him.

The last bounty hunter had been the famous Pink Lady McGuire–one mean mama–three hundred pounds of rolling, ugly meat that carried a twelve-gauge Remington pump and a bad attitude. Story was, Calhoun jumped her from behind, cut her throat, and as a joke, fucked her before she bled to death. This not only proved to Wayne that Calhoun was a dangerous sonofabitch, it also proved he had bad taste.

Wayne stepped out of his '57 Chevy reproduction, pushed his hat back on his forehead, opened the trunk, and got the sawed-off double barrel and some shells out of there. He already had a .38 revolver in the holster at his side and a bowie knife in each boot, but when you went into a place like Rosalita's it was best to have plenty of backup.

Wayne put a handful of shotgun shells in his shirt pocket, snapped the flap over them, looked up at the red-and-blue neon sign that flashed ROSALITA'S: COLD BEER AND DEAD DANCING, found his center, as they say in Zen, and went on in.

He held the shotgun against his leg, and as it was dark in there and folks were busy with talk or drinks or dancing, no one noticed him or his artillery right off.

He spotted Calhoun's stocky, black-hatted self immediately. He was inside the dance cage with a dead buck-naked Mexican girl of about twelve. He was holding her tight around the waist with one hand and massaging her rubbery ass with the other like it was a pillow he was trying to shape. The dead girl's handless arms flailed on either side of Calhoun, and her little tits pressed to his thick chest. Her wire-muzzled face knocked repeatedly at his shoulder and drool whipped out of her mouth in thick spermy ropes, stuck to his shin, faded and left a patch of wetness.

For all Wayne knew, the girl was Calhoun's sister or daughter. It was that kind of place. The kind that had sprung up immediately after that stuff had gotten out of a lab upstate and filled the air with bacterium that brought dead humans back to life, made their basic motor functions work and made them hungry for human flesh; made it so if a man's wife, daughter, sister, or mother went belly up and he wanted to turn a few bucks, he might think: "Damn, that's tough about ole Betty Sue, but she's dead as hoot-owl shit and ain't gonna be needing nothing from here on out, and with them germs working around in her, she's just gonna pull herself out of the ground and cause me a problem. And the ground out back of the house is harder to dig than a calculus problem is to work, so I'll just toss her cold ass in the back of the pickup next to the chainsaw and the barbed-wire roll, haul her across the border to sell her to the Meat Boys to sell to the tonics for dancing.

"It's a sad thing to sell one of your own, but shit, them's the breaks. I'll just stay out of the tonics until all the meat rots off her bones and they have to throw her away. That way I won't go in some place for a drink and see her up there shaking her dead tits and end up going sentimental and dewy-eyed in front of one of my buddies or some ole two-dollar gal."

This kind of thinking supplied the dancers. In other parts of the country, the dancers might be men or children, but here it was mostly women. Men were used for hunting and target practice.

The Meat Boys took the bodies, cut off the hands so they couldn't grab, ran screws through their jaws to fasten on wire muzzles so they couldn't bite, sold them to the honky-tonks about the time the germ started stirring.

Bar owners put them inside wire enclosures up front of their joints, staffed music, and men paid five dollars to got in there and grab them and make like they were dancing when all the women wanted to do was grab and bite, which, muzzled and handless, they could not do.

If a man liked his partner enough, he could pay more money and have her tied to a cot in the back and he could get on her and at some business. Didn't have to hear no arguments or buy presents or make promises or make them come. Just fuck and hike.

As long as the establishment sprayed the dead fur maggots and kept them perfumed and didn't keep them so long hunks of meat came off on a man's dick, the customers were happy as flies on shit.

Wayne looked to see who might give him trouble, and figured everyone was a potential customer. The six-foot-two, two-hundred-fifty pound bouncer being the most immediate concern.

But, there wasn't anything to do but to get on with things and handle problems when they came up. He went into the cage where Calhoun was dancing, shouldered through the other dancers and went for him.

Calhoun had his back to Wayne, and as the music was loud, Wayne didn't worry about going quietly. But Calhoun sensed him and turned with his hand full of a little .38.

Wayne clubbed Calhoun's arm with the barrel of the shotgun. The little gun flew out of Calhoun's hand and went skidding across the floor and clanked against the metal cage.

Calhoun wasn't outdone. He spun the dead girl in front of him and pulled a big pigsticker out of his boot and held it under the girl's armpit in a threatening manner, which with a knife that big was no feat.

Wayne shot the dead girl's left kneecap out from under her and she went down. Her armpit trapped Calhoun's knife. The other men deserted their partners and went over the wire netting like squirrels.

Before Calhoun could shake the girl loose, Wayne stepped in and hit him over the head with the barrel of the shotgun. Calhoun crumpled and the girl began to crawl about on the floor as if looking for lost contacts.

The bouncer came in behind Wayne, grabbed him under the arms and tried to slip a full nelson on him.

Wayne kicked back on the bouncer's shin and raked his boot down the man's instep and stomped his foot. The bouncer let go. Wayne turned and kicked him in the balls and hit him across the face with the shotgun.

The bouncer went down and didn't even look like he wanted up.

Wayne couldn't help but note he liked the music that was playing. When he turned he had someone to dance with.

Calhoun.

Calhoun charged him, hit Wayne in the belly with his head, knocked him over the bouncer. They tumbled to the floor and the shotgun went out of Wayne's hands and scraped across the floor and hit the crawling girl in the head. She didn't even notice, just kept snaking in circles, dragging her blasted leg behind her like a skin she was trying to shed.

The other women, partnerless, wandered about the cage. The music changed. Wayne didn't like this tune as well. Too slow. He bit Calhoun's earlobe off.

Calhoun screamed and they grappled around on the floor. Calhoun got his arm around Wayne's throat and tried to choke him to death.

Wayne coughed out the earlobe, lifted his leg and took the knife out of his boot. He brought it around and back and hit Calhoun in the temple with the hilt.

Calhoun let go of Wayne and rocked on his knees, then collapsed on top of him.

Wayne got out from under him and got up and kicked him in the head a few times. When he was finished, he put the Bowie in its place, got Calhoun's .38 and the shotgun. To hell with the pigsticker.

A dead woman tried to grab him, and he shoved her away with a thrust of his palm. He got Calhoun by the collar, started pulling him toward the gate.

Faces were pressed against the wire, watching. It had been quite a show. A friendly cowboy type opened the gate for Wayne and the crowd parted as he pulled Calhoun by. One man felt helpful and chased after them and said, "Here's his hat, Mister," and dropped it on Calhoun's knee and it stayed there.

Outside, a professional drunk was standing between two cars taking a leak on the ground. As Wayne pulled Calhoun past, the drunk said, "Your buddy don't look so good."

"Look worse than that when I get him to Law Town," Wayne said.

Wayne stopped by the '57, emptied Calhoun's pistol and tossed it as far as he could, then took a few minutes to kick Calhoun in the ribs and ass. Calhoun grunted and farted, but didn't come to.

When Wayne's leg got tired, he put Calhoun in the passenger seat and handcuffed him to the door.

He went over to Calhoun's '62 Impala replica with the plastic bull horns mounted on the hood—which was how he had located him in the first place, by his well known car—and kicked the glass out of the window on the driver's side and used the shotgun to shoot the bull horns off. He took out his pistol and shot all the tires flat, pissed on the driver's door, and kicked a dent in it.

By then he was too tired to shit in the back seat, so he took some deep breaths and went back to the '57 and climbed in behind the wheel.

Reaching across Calhoun, he opened the glove box and got out one of his thin, black cigars and put it in his mouth.

He pushed the lighter in, and while he waited for it to heat up, he took the shotgun out of his lap and reloaded it.

A couple of men poked their heads outside of the tonk's door, and Wayne stuck the shotgun out the window and fired above their heads. They disappeared inside so fast they might have been an optical illusion.

Wayne put the lighter to his cigar, picked up the wanted poster he had on the seat, and set fire to it. He thought about putting it in Calhoun's lap as a joke, but didn't. He tossed the flaming poster out of the window.

He drove over close to the tonk and used the remaining shotgun load to shoot at the neon Rosalita's sign. Glass tinkled onto the tonk's roof and onto the gravel drive.

Now if he only had a dog to kick.

He drove away from there, bound for the Cadillac Desert, and finally Law Town on the other side.

2

The Cadillacs stretched for miles, providing the only shade in the desert. They were buried nose down at a slant, almost to the windshields, and Wayne could see skeletons of some of the drivers in the cars, either lodged behind the steering wheels or lying on the dashboards against the glass. The roof and hood guns had long since been removed and all the windows on the cars were rolled up, except for those that had been knocked out and vandalized by travelers, or dead folks looking for goodies.

The thought of being in one of those cars with the windows rolled up in all this heat made Wayne feel even more uncomfortable than he already was. Hot as it was, he was certain even the skeletons were sweating.

He finished pissing on the tire of the Chevy, saw the piss had almost dried. He shook the drops off, watched them fall and evaporate against the burning sand. Zipping up, he thought about Calhoun, and how when he'd pulled over earlier to let the sonofabitch take a leak, he'd seen there was a little metal ring through the head of his dick and a Texas emblem dangling from that. He could understand the Texas emblem, being from there himself, but he couldn't for the life of him imagine why a fella would do that to his general. Any idiot who would put a ring through the head of his pecker deserved to die, innocent or not.

Wayne took off his cowboy hat and rubbed the back of his neck and ran his hand over the top of his head and back again. The sweat on his fingers was thick as lube oil, and the thinning part of his hairline was tender; the heat was cooking the hell out of his scalp, even through the brown felt of his hat.

Before he put his hat on, the sweat on his fingers was dry. He broke open the shotgun, put the shells in his pocket, opened the Chevy's back door and tossed the shotgun on the floorboard.

He got in the front behind the wheel and the seat was hot as a griddle on his back and ass. The sun shone through the slightly tinted windows like a polished chrome hubcap; it forced him to squint.

Glancing over at Calhoun, he studied him. The fucker was asleep with his head thrown back and his black wilted hat hung precariously on his head—it looked jaunty almost. Sweat oozed down Calhoun's red face, flowed over his eyelids and around his neck, running in riverlets down the white seat covers, drying quickly. He had his left hand between his legs, clutching his balls, and his right was on the armrest, which was the only place it could be since he was handcuffed to the door.

Wayne thought he ought to blow the bastard's brains out and tell God he died. The shithead certainly needed shooting, but Wayne didn't want to lose a thousand dollars off his reward. He needed every penny if he was going to get that wrecking yard he wanted. The yard was the dream that went before him like a carrot before a donkey, and he didn't want any more delays. If he never made another trip across this goddamn desert, that would suit him fine.

Pop would let him buy the place with the money he had now, and he could pay the rest out later. But that wasn't what he wanted to do. The bounty business had finally gone sour, and he wanted to do different. It wasn't any goddamn fun anymore. Just met the dick cheese of the earth. And when you ran the sonofabitches to ground and put the cuffs on them, you had to watch your ass 'til you got them turned in. Had to sleep with one eye open and a hand on your gun. It wasn't any way to live.'

And he wanted a chance to do right by Pop. Pop had been like a father to him. When he was a kid and his mama was screwing the Mexicans across the border for the rent money, Pop would let him hang out in the yard and climb on the rusted cars and watch him fix the better ones, tune those babies so fine they purred like dick-whipped women.

When he was older, Pop would haul him to Galveston for the whores and out to the beach to take potshots at all the ugly, fucked-up critters swimming around in the Gulf. Sometimes he'd take him to Oklahoma for the Dead Roundup. It sure seemed to do the old fart good to whack those dead fuckers with a tire iron, smash their diseased brains so they'd lay down for good. And it was a challenge. 'Cause if one of those dead buddies bit you, you could put your head between your legs and kiss your rosy ass goodbye.

Wayne pulled out of his thoughts of Pop and the wrecking yard and turned on the stereo system. One of his favorite country-and-western tunes whispered at him. It was Billy Conteegas singing, and Wayne hummed along with the music as he drove into the welcome, if mostly ineffectual, shadows provided by the Cadillacs.

> "My baby left me,
> She left me for a cow,
> But I don't give a flying fuck,
> She's gone radioactive now,
> Yeah, my baby left me,
> Left me for a six-tittied cow."

Just when Conteegas was getting to the good part, doing the trilling sound in his throat he was famous for, Calhoun opened his eyes and spoke up.

"Ain't it bad enough I got to put up with the fucking heat and your fucking humming without having to listen to that shit? Ain't you got no Hank Williams stuff, or maybe some of that nigger music they used to make? You know, where the coons harmonize and one of 'em sings like his nuts are cut off."

"You just don't know good music when you hear it, Calhoun."

Calhoun moved his free hand to his hatband, found one of his few remaining cigarettes and a match there. He struck the match on his knee, lit the smoke and coughed a few rounds. Wayne couldn't imagine how Calhoun could smoke in all this heat.

"Well, I may not know good music when I hear it, capon, but I damn sure know bad music when I hear it. And that's some bad music."

"You ain't got any kind of culture, Calhoun. You been too busy raping kids."

"Reckon a man has to have a hobby," Calhoun said, blowing smoke at Wayne. "Young pussy is mine. Besides, she wasn't in diapers. Couldn't find one that young. She was thirteen. You know what they say. If they're old enough to bleed, they're old enough to breed."

"How old they have to be for you to kill them?"

"She got loud."

"Change channels, Calhoun."

"Just passing the time of day, capon. Better watch yourself, bounty hunter, when you least expect it, I'll bash your head."

"You're gonna run your mouth one time too many, Calhoun, and when you do, you're gonna finish this ride in the trunk with ants crawling on you. You ain't so priceless I won't blow you away."

"You lucked out at the tonk, boy. But there's always tomorrow, and every day can't be like at Rosalita's."

Wayne smiled. "Trouble is, Calhoun, you're running out of tomorrows."

3

As they drove between the Cadillacs, the sky fading like a bad bulb, Wayne looked at the cars and tried to imagine what the Chevy-Cadillac Wars had been like, and why they had been fought in this miserable desert. He had heard it was a hell of a fight, and close, but the outcome had been Chevy's and now they were the only cars Detroit made. And as far as he was concerned, that was the only thing about Detroit that was worth a damn. Cars.

He felt that way about all cities. He'd just as soon lie down and let a diseased dog shit in his face than drive through one, let alone live in one.

Law Town being an exception. He'd go there. Not to live, but to give Calhoun to the authorities and pick up his reward. People in Law Town were always glad to see a criminal brought in. The public executions were popular and varied and supplied a steady income.

Last time he'd been to Law Town he'd bought a front-row ticket to one of the executions and watched a chronic shoplifter, a red-headed rat of a man, get pulled apart by being chained between two souped-up tractors. The execution itself was pretty brief, but there had been plenty of buildup with clowns and balloons and a big-tittied stripper who could swing her tits in either direction to boom-boom music.

Wayne had been put off by the whole thing. It wasn't organized enough and the drinks and food were expensive and the front-row seats were too close to the tractors. He had gotten to see that the redhead's insides were brighter than his hair, but some of the insides got sprinkled on his new shirt, and cold water or not, the spots hadn't come out. He had suggested to one of the management that they put up a big plastic shield so the front row wouldn't get splattered, but he doubted anything had come of it.

They drove until it was solid dark. Wayne stopped and fed Calhoun a stick of jerky and some water from his canteen. Then he handcuffed him to the front bumper of the Chevy.

"See any snakes, Gila monsters, scorpions, stuff like that," Wayne said, "yell out. Maybe I can get around here in time."

"I'd let the fuckers run up my asshole before I'd call you," Calhoun said.

Leaving Calhoun with his head resting on the bumper, Wayne climbed in the back seat of the Chevy and slept with one ear cocked and one eye open.

Before dawn Wayne got Calhoun loaded in the '57 and they started out. After a few minutes of sluicing through the early morning grayness, a wind started up. One of those weird desert winds that come out of nowhere. It carried grit through the air at the speed of bullets, hit the '57 with a sound like rabid cats scratching.

The sand tires crunched on through, and Wayne turned on the windshield blower, the sand wipers, and the head-beams, and kept on keeping on.

When it was time for the sun to come up, they couldn't see it. Too much sand. It was blowing harder than ever and the blowers and wipers couldn't handle it. It was piling up. Wayne couldn't even make out the Cadillacs anymore.

He was about to stop when a shadowy, whale-like shape crossed in front of him and he slammed on the brakes, giving the sand tires a workout. But it wasn't enough.

The '57 spun around and rammed the shape on Calhoun's side. Wayne heard Calhoun yell, then felt himself thrown against the door and his head smacked metal and the outside darkness was nothing compared to the darkness into which he descended.

4

Wayne rose out of it as quickly as he had gone down. Blood was trickling into his eyes from a slight forehead wound. He used his sleeve to wipe it away.

His first clear sight was of a face at the window on his side; a sallow, moon-terrain face with bulging eyes and an expression like an idiot contemplating Sanskrit. On the man's head was a strange, black hat with big round ears, and in the center of the hat, like a silver tumor, was the head of a large screw. Sand lashed at the face, imbedded in it, struck the unblinking eyes and made the round-eared hat flap. The man paid no attention. Though still dazed, Wayne knew why. The man was one of the dead folks.

Wayne looked in Calhoun's direction. Calhoun's door had been mashed in and the bending metal had pinched the handcuff attached to the arm rest in two. The blow had knocked Calhoun to the center of the seat. He was holding his hand in front of him, looking at the dangling cuff and chain as if it were a silver bracelet and a line of pearls.

Leaning over the hood, cleaning the sand away from the windshield with his hands, was another of the dead folks. He too was wearing one of the round-eared hats. He pressed a wrecked face to the clean spot and looked in at Calhoun. A string of snot-green saliva ran out of his mouth and onto the glass.

More sand was wiped away by others. Soon all the car's glass showed the pallid and rotting faces of the dead folks. They stared at Wayne and Calhoun as if they were two rare fish in an aquarium.

Wayne cocked back the hammer of the .38.

"What about me," Calhoun said. "What am I supposed to use?"

"Your charm," Wayne said, and at that moment, as if by signal, the dead folk faded away from the glass, leaving one man standing on the hood holding a baseball bat. He hit the glass and it went into a thousand little stars. The bat came again and the heavens fell and the stars rained down and the sand storm screamed in on Wayne and Calhoun.

The dead folks reappeared in full force. The one with the bat started though the hole in the windshield, heedless of the jags of glass that ripped his ragged clothes and tore his flesh like damp cardboard.

Wayne shot the batter through the head, and the man, finished, fell through, pinning Wayne's arm with his body.

Before Wayne could pull his gun free, a woman's hand reached through the hole and got hold of Wayne's collar. Other dead folks took to the glass and hammered it out with their feet and fist. Hands were all over Wayne; they felt dry and cool like leather seat covers. They pulled him over the steering wheel and dash and outside. The sand worked at his flesh like a cheese grater. He could hear Calhoun yelling, "Eat me, motherfuckers, eat me and choke."

They tossed Wayne on the hood of the '57. Faces leaned over him. Yellow teeth and toothless gums were very near. A road kill odor washed through his nostrils. He thought: now the feeding frenzy begins. His only consolation was that there were so many dead folks there wouldn't be enough of him left to come back from the dead. They'd probably have his brain for dessert.

But no. They picked him up and carried him off. Next thing he knew was a clearer view of the whale-shape the '57 had hit, and its color. It was a yellow school bus.

The door to the bus hissed open. The dead folks dumped Wayne inside on his belly and tossed his hat after him. They stepped back and the door closed, just missing Wayne's foot.

Wayne looked up and saw a man in the driver's seat smiling at him. It wasn't a dead man. Just fat and ugly. He was probably five feet tall and bald except for a fringe of hair around his shiny bald head the color of a shit ring in a toilet bowl. He had a nose so long and dark and malignant looking it appeared as if it might fall off his face at any moment, like an overripe banana. He was wearing what Wayne first thought was a bathrobe, but proved to be a robe like that of a monk. It was old and tattered and moth-eaten and Wayne could see pale flesh through the holes. An odor wafted from the fat man that was somewhere between the smell of stale sweat, cheesy balls and an unwiped asshole.

"Good to see you," the fat man said.

"Charmed," Wayne said.

From the back of the bus came a strange, unidentifiable sound. Wayne poked his head around the seats for a look.

In the middle of the aisle, about halfway back, was a nun. Or sort of a nun. Her back was to him and she wore a black-and-white nun's habit. The part that covered her head was traditional, but from there down was quite a departure from the standard attire. The outfit was cut to the middle of her thigh and she wore black fishnet stockings and thick high heels. She was slim with good legs and a high little ass that, even under the circumstances, Wayne couldn't help but appreciate. She was moving one hand above her head as if sewing the air.

Sitting on the seats on either side of the aisle were dead folks. They all wore the round-eared hats, and they were responsible for the sound.

They were trying to sing.

He had never known dead folks to make any noise outside of grunts and groans, but here they were singing. A toneless sort of singing to be sure, some of the words garbled and some of the dead folks just opening and closing their mouths soundlessly, but, by golly, he recognized the tune. It was "Jesus Loves Me."

Wayne looked back at the fat man, let his hand ease down to the Bowie in his right boot. The fat man produced a little .32 automatic from inside his robe and pointed it at Wayne.

"It's small caliber," the fat man said, "but I'm a real fine shot, and it makes a nice, little hole."

Wayne quit reaching in his boot.

"Oh, that's all right," said the fat man. "Take the knife out and put it on the floor in front of you and slide it to me. And while you're at it, I think I see the hilt of one in your other boot."

Wayne looked back. The way he had been thrown inside the bus had caused his pants legs to hike up over his boots, and the hilts of both his Bowies were revealed. They might as well have had blinking lights on them.

It was shaping up to be a shitty day.

He slid the bowies to the fat man, who scooped them up nimbly and dumped them on the other side of his seat.

The bus door opened and Calhoun was tossed in on top of Wayne. Calhoun's hat followed after.

Wayne shrugged Calhoun off, recovered his hat, and put it on. Calhoun found his hat and did the same. They were still on their knees.

"Would you gentlemen mind moving to the center of the bus?"

Wayne led the way. Calhoun took note of the nun now, said, "Man, look at that ass."

The fat man called back to them. "Right there will do fine."

Wayne slid into the seat the fat man was indicating with a wave of the .32, and Calhoun slid in beside him. The dead folks entered now, filled the seats up front, leaving only a few stray seats in the middle empty.

Calhoun said, "What are those fuckers back there making that noise for?"

"They're singing," Wayne said. "Ain't you got no churchin'?"

"Say they are?" Calhoun turned to the nun and the dead folks and yelled, "Y'all know any Hank Williams?"

The nun did not turn and the dead folks did not quit their toneless singing.

"Guess not," Calhoun said. "Seems like all the good music's been forgotten."

The noise in the back of the bus ceased and the nun came over to look at Wayne and Calhoun. She was nice in front too. The outfit was cut from throat to crotch, laced with a ribbon, and it showed a lot of tit and some tight, thin, black panties that couldn't quite hold in her escaping pubic hair, which grew as thick and wild as kudzu. When Wayne managed to work his eyes up from that and look at her face, he saw she was dark-complected with eyes the color of coffee and lips made to chew on.

Calhoun never made it to the face. He didn't care about faces. He sniffed, said into her crotch, "Nice snatch."

The nun's left hand came around and smacked Calhoun on the side of the head.

He grabbed her wrist, said, "Nice arm, too."

The nun did a magic act with her right hand; it went behind her back and hiked up her outfit and came back with a double-barreled derringer. She pressed it against Calhoun's head.

Wayne bent forward, hoping she wouldn't shoot. At that range the bullet might go through Calhoun's head and hit him too.

"Can't miss," the nun said.

Calhoun smiled. "No you can't," he said, and let go of her arm.

She sat down across from them, smiled, and crossed her legs high. Wayne felt his Levi's snake swell and crawl against the inside of his thigh.

"Honey," Calhoun said, "you're almost worth taking a bullet for."

The nun didn't quit smiling. The bus cranked up. The sand blowers and wipers went to work, and the windshield turned blue, and a white dot moved on it between a series of smaller white dots.

Radar. Wayne had seen that sort of thing on desert vehicles. If he lived through this and got his car back, maybe he'd rig up something like that. And maybe not, he was sick of the desert.

Whatever, at the moment, future plans seemed a little out of place.

Then something else occurred to him. Radar. That meant these bastards had known they were coming and had pulled out in front of them on purpose.

He leaned over the seat and checked where he figured the '57 hit the bus. He didn't see a single dent. Armored, most likely. Most school buses were these days, and that's what this had been. It probably had bulletproof glass and puncture-proof sand tires too. School buses had gone that way on account of the race riots and the sending of mutated calves to school just like they were humans. And because of the Codgers—old farts who believed kids ought to be fair game to adults for sexual purposes, or for knocking around when they wanted to let off some tension.

"How about unlocking this cuff?" Calhoun said. "It ain't for shit now anyway."

Wayne looked at the nun. "I'm going for the cuff key in my pants. Don't shoot."

Wayne fished it out, unlocked the cuff, and Calhoun let it slide to the floor. Wayne saw the nun was curious and he said, "I'm a bounty hunter. Help me get this man to Law Town and I could see you earn a little something for your troubles."

The woman shook her head.

"That's the spirit," Calhoun said. "I like a nun that minds her own business . . . You a real nun?"

She nodded.

"Always talk so much?"

Another nod.

Wayne said, "I've never seen a nun like you. Not dressed like that and with a gun."

"We are a small and special order," she said.

"You some kind of Sunday school teacher for these dead folks?"

"Sort of."

"But with them dead, ain't it kind of pointless? They ain't got no souls now, do they?"

"No, but their work adds to the glory of God."

"Their work?" Wayne looked at the dead folks sitting stiffly in their seats. He noted that one of them was about to lose a rotten ear. He sniffed. "They may be adding to the glory of God, but they don't do much for the air."

The nun reached into a pocket on her habit and took out two round objects. She tossed one to Calhoun, and one to Wayne. "Menthol lozenges. They help you stand the smell."

Wayne unwrapped the lozenge and sucked on it. It did help overpower the smell, but the menthol wasn't all that great either. It reminded him of being sick.

"What order are you?" Wayne asked.

"Jesus Loved Mary," the nun said.

"His mama?"

"Mary Magdalene. We think he fucked her. They were lovers. There's evidence in the scriptures. She was a harlot and we have modeled ourselves on her. She gave up that life and became a harlot for Jesus."

"Hate to break it to you, sister," Calhoun said, "but that do-gooder Jesus is as dead as a post. If you're waiting for him to slap the meat to you, that sweet thing of yours is going to dry up and blow away."

"Thanks for the news," the nun said. "But we don't fuck him in person. We fuck him in spirit. We let the spirit enter into men so they may take us in the fashion Jesus took Mary."

"No shit?"

"No shit."

"You know, I think I feel the old boy moving around inside me now. Why don't you shuck them drawers, honey, throw back in that seat there and let ole Calhoun give you a big load of Jesus."

Calhoun shifted in the nun's direction.

She pointed the derringer at him, said, "Stay where you are. If it were so, if you were full of Jesus, I would let you have me in a moment. But you're full of the Devil, not Jesus."

"Shit, sister, give ole Devil a break. He's a fun kind of guy. Let's you and me mount up . . . Well, be like that. But if you change your mind, I can get religion at a moment's notice. I dearly love to fuck. I've fucked everything I could get my hands on but a parakeet, and I'd have fucked that little bitch if I could have found the hole."

"I've never known any dead folks to be trained," Wayne said, trying to get the nun talking in a direction that might help, a direction that would let him know what was going on and what sort of trouble he had fallen into.

"As I said, we are a very special order. Brother Lazarus," she waved a hand at the bus driver, and without looking he lifted a hand in acknowledgement, "is the founder. I don't think he'll mind if I tell his story, explain about us, what we do and why. It's important that we spread the word to the heathens."

"Don't call me no fucking heathen," Calhoun said. "This is heathen, riding 'round in a fucking bus with a bunch of stinking dead folks with funny hats on. Hell, they can't even carry a tune."

The nun ignored him. "Brother Lazarus was once known by another name, but that name no longer matters. He was a research scientist, and he was one of those who worked in the laboratory where the germs escaped into the air and made it so the dead could not truly die as long as they had an undamaged brain in their heads.

"Brother Lazarus was carrying a dish of the experiment, the germs, and as a joke, one of the lab assistants pretended to trip him, and he, not knowing it was a joke, dodged the assistant's leg and dropped the dish. In a moment, the air conditioning system had blown the germs throughout the research center. Someone opened a door, and the germs were loose on the world.

"Brother Lazarus was consumed by guilt. Not only because he dropped the dish, but because he helped create it in the first place. He quit his job at the laboratory, took to wandering the country. He came out here with nothing more than basic food, water and books. Among these books was the Bible, and the lost books of the Bible: the Apocrypha and the many cast-out chapters of the New Testament. As he studied, it occurred to him that these cast-out books actually belonged. He was able to interpret their higher meaning, and an angel came to him in a dream and told him of another book, and Brother Lazarus took up his pen and recorded the angel's words, direct from God, and in this book, all the mysteries were explained."

"Like screwing Jesus," Calhoun said.

"Like screwing Jesus, and not being afraid of words that mean sex. Not being afraid of seeing Jesus as both God and man. Seeing that sex, if meant for Christ and the opening of the mind, can be a thrilling and religious experience, not just the rutting of two savage animals.

"Brother Lazarus roamed the desert, the mountains, thinking of the things the Lord had revealed to him, and lo and behold, the Lord revealed yet another thing to him. Brother Lazarus found a great amusement park."

"Didn't know Jesus went in for rides and such," Calhoun said.

"It was long deserted. It had once been part of a place called Disneyland. Brother Lazarus knew of it. There had been several of these Disneylands built about the country, and this one had been in the midst of the Chevy-Cadillac Wars, and had been destroyed and sand had covered most of it."

The nun held out her arms. "And in this rubble, he saw a new beginning."

"Cool off, baby," Calhoun said, "before you have a stroke."

"He gathered to him men and women of a like mind and taught the gospel to them. The Old Testament. The New Testament. The Lost Books. And his own Book of Lazarus, for he had begun to call himself Lazarus. A symbolic name signifying a new beginning, a rising from the dead and coming to life and seeing things as they really are."

The nun moved her hands rapidly, expressively as she talked. Sweat beaded on her forehead and upper lip.

"So he returned to his skills as a scientist, but applied them to a higher purpose–God's purpose. And as Brother Lazarus, he realized the use of the dead. They could be taught to work and build a great monument to the glory of God. And this monument, this coed institution of monks and nuns would be called Jesus Land."

At the word "Jesus," the nun gave her voice an extra trill, and the dead folks, cued, said together, "Eees num be prased."

"How the hell did you train them dead folks?" Calhoun said. "Dog treats?"

"Science put to the use of our lord Jesus Christ, that's how. Brother Lazarus made a special device he could insert directly into the brains of dead folks, through the tops of their heads, and the device controls certain cravings. Makes them passive and responsive—at least to simple commands. With the regulator, as Brother Lazarus calls the device, we have been able to do much positive work with the dead."

"Where do you find these dead folks?" Wayne asked.

"We buy them from the Meat Boys. We save them from amoral purposes."

"They ought to be shot through the head and put in the goddamn ground," Wayne said.

"If our use of the regulator and the dead folks was merely to better ourselves, I would agree. But it is not. We do the Lord's work."

"Do the monks fuck the sisters?" Calhoun asked.

"When possessed by the Spirit of Christ. Yes."

"And I bet they get possessed a lot. Not a bad setup. Dead folks to do the work on the amusement park—"

"It isn't an amusement park now."

"—and plenty of free pussy. Sounds cozy. I like it. Old shithead up there's smarter than he looks."

"There is nothing selfish about our motives or those of Brother Lazarus. In fact, as penance for loosing the germ on the world in the first place, Brother Lazarus injected a virus into his nose. It is rotting slowly."

"Thought that was quite a snorkel he had on him," Wayne said.

"I take it back," Calhoun said. "He is as dumb as he looks."

"Why do the dead folks wear those silly hats?" Wayne asked.

"Brother Lazarus found a storeroom of them at the site of the old amusement park. They are mouse ears. They represent some cartoon animal that was popular once and part of Disneyland. Mickey Mouse, he was called. This way we know which dead folks are ours, and which ones are not controlled by our regulators. From time to time, stray dead folks wander into our area. Murder victims. Children abandoned in the desert. People crossing the desert who died of heat or illness. We've had some of the sisters and brothers attacked. The hats are a precaution."

"And what's the deal with us?" Wayne asked.

The nun smiled sweetly. "You, my children, are to add to the glory of God."

"Children?" Calhoun said. "You call an alligator a lizard, bitch?"

The nun slid back in the seat and rested the derringer in her lap. She pulled her legs into a cocked position, causing her panties to crease in the valley of her vagina; it looked like a nice place to visit, that valley.

Wayne turned from the beauty of it and put his head back and closed his eyes, pulled his hat down over them. There was nothing he could do at the moment, and since the nun was watching Calhoun for him, he'd sleep, store up and figure what to do next. If anything.

He drifted off to sleep wondering what the nun meant by, "You, my children, are to add to the glory of God."

He had a feeling that when he found out, he wasn't going to like it.

5

He awoke off and on and saw that the sunlight filtering through the storm had given everything a greenish color. Calhoun, seeing he was awake, said, "Ain't that a pretty color? I had a shirt that color once and liked it lots, but I got in a fight with this Mexican whore with a wooden leg over some money and she tore it. I punched that little bean bandit good."

"Thanks for sharing that," Wayne said, and went back to sleep.

Each time he awoke it was brighter, and finally he awoke to the sun going down and the storm having died out. But he didn't stay awake. He forced himself to close his eyes and store up more energy. To help him nod off he listened to the hum of the motor and thought about the wrecking yard and Pop and all the fun they could have, just drinking beer and playing cards and fucking the border women, and maybe some of those mutated cows they had over there for sale.

Nah. Nix the cows, or any of those genetically altered critters. A man had to draw the line somewhere, and he drew it at fucking critters, even if they had been bred so that they had human traits. You had to have some standards.

'Course, those standards had a way of eroding. He remembered when he said he'd only fuck the pretty ones. His last whore had been downright scary looking. If he didn't watch himself he'd be as bad as Calhoun, trying to find the hole in the parakeet.

He awoke to Calhoun's elbow in his ribs and the nun was standing beside their seat with the derringer. Wayne knew she hadn't slept, but she looked bright-eyed and bushy-tailed. She nodded toward their window, said, "Jesus Land."

She had put that special touch in her voice again, and the dead folks responded with, "Eees num be prased."

It was good and dark now, a crisp night with a big moon the color of hammered brass. The bus sailed across the white sand like a mystical schooner with a full wind in its sails. It went up an impossible hill toward what looked like an aurora borealis, then dove into an atomic rainbow of colors that filled the bus with fairy lights.

When Wayne's eyes became accustomed to the lights, and the bus took a right turn along a precarious curve, he glanced down into the valley. An aerial view couldn't have been any better than the view from his window.

Down there was a universe of polished metal and twisted neon. In the center of the valley was a great statue of Jesus crucified that must have been twenty-five stories high. Most of the body was made of bright metals and multicolored neon; and much of the light was coming from that. There was a crown of barbed wire wound several times around a chromium plate of a forehead and some rust-colored strands of neon hair. The savior's eyes were huge, green strobes that swung left and right with the precision of an oscillating fan. There was an ear-to-ear smile on the savior's face and the teeth were slats of sparkling metal with wide cavity-black gaps between them. The statue was equipped with a massive dick of polished, interwoven cables and coils of neon, the dick was thicker and more solid looking than the arthritic steel-tube legs on either side of it; the head of it was made of an enormous spotlight that pulsed the color of irritation.

The bus went around and around the valley, descending like a dead roach going down a slow drain, and finally the road rolled out straight and took them into Jesus Land.

They passed through the legs of Jesus, under the throbbing head of his cock, toward what looked like a small castle of polished gold bricks with an upright drawbridge inlayed with jewels.

The castle was only one of several tall structures that appeared to be made of rare metals and precious stones: gold, silver, emeralds, rubies, and sapphires. But the closer they got to the buildings, the less fine they looked and the more they looked like what they were: stucco, cardboard, phosphorescent paint, colored spotlights, and bands of neon.

Off to the left Wayne could see a long, open shed full of vehicles, most of them old school buses. And there were unlighted hovels made of tin and tarpaper; homes for the dead, perhaps. Behind the shacks and the bus barn rose skeletal shapes that stretched tall and bleak against the sky and the candy-gem lights; shapes that looked like the bony remains of beached whales.

On the right, Wayne glimpsed a building with an open front that served as a stage. In front of the stage were chairs filled with monks and nuns. On the stage, six monks—one behind a drum set, one with a saxophone, the others with guitars—were blasting out a loud, rocking rhythm that made the bus shake. A nun with the front of her habit thrown open, her headpiece discarded, sang into a microphone with a voice like a suffering angel. The voice screeched out of the amplifiers and came in through the windows of the bus, crushing the sound of the engine. The nun crowed "Jesus" so long and hard it sounded like a plea from hell. Then she leapt up and came down doing the splits, the impact driving her back to her feet as if her ass had been loaded with springs.

"Bet that bitch can pick up a quarter with that thing," Calhoun said.

Brother Lazarus touched a button, the pseudo-jeweled drawbridge lowered over a narrow moat, and he drove them inside.

It wasn't as well lighted in there. The walls were bleak and gray. Brother Lazarus stopped the bus and got off, and another monk came on board. He was tall and thin and had crooked buck teeth that dented his bottom lip. He also had a twelve-gauge pump shotgun.

"This is Brother Fred," the nun said. "He'll be your tour guide."

Brother Fred forced Wayne and Calhoun off the bus, away from the dead folks in their mouse-ear hats and the nun in her tight, black panties, jabbed them along a dark corridor, up a swirl of stairs and down a longer corridor with open doors on either side and rooms filled with dark and light and spoiled meat and guts on hooks and skulls and bones lying about like discarded walnut shells and broken sticks; rooms full of dead folks (truly dead) stacked neat as firewood, and rooms full of stone shelves stuffed with beakers of fiery-red and sewer-green and sky-blue and piss-yellow liquids, as well as glass coils through which other colored fluids fled as if chased, smoked as if nervous, and ran into big flasks as if relieved; rooms with platforms and tables and boxes and stools and chairs covered with instruments or dead folks or dead-folk pieces or the asses of monks and nuns as they sat and held charts or tubes or body parts and frowned at them with concentration, lips pursed as if about to explode with some earth-shattering pronouncement; and finally they came to a little room with a tall, glassless window that looked out upon the bright, shiny mess that was Jesus Land.

The room was simple. Table, two chairs, two beds—one on either side of the room. The walls were stone and unadorned. To the right was a little bathroom without a door.

Wayne walked to the window and looked out at Jesus Land pulsing and thumping like a desperate heart. He listened to the music a moment, leaned over and stuck his head outside.

They were high up and there was nothing but a straight drop. If you jumped, you'd wind up with the heels of your boots under your tonsils.

Wayne let out a whistle in appreciation of the drop. Brother Fred thought it was a compliment for Jesus Land. He said, "It's a miracle, isn't it?"

"Miracle?" Calhoun said. "This goony light show? This ain't no miracle. This is for shit. Get that nun on the bus back there to bend over and shit a perfectly round turd through a hoop at twenty paces, and I'll call that a miracle, Mr. Fucked-up Teeth. But this Jesus Land crap is the dumbest fucking idea since dog sweaters.

"And look at this place. You could use some knickknacks or something in here. A picture of some ole naked gal doing a donkey, couple of pigs fucking. Anything. And a door on the shitter would be nice. I hate to be straining out a big one and know someone can look in on me. It ain't decent. A man ought to have his fucking grunts in private. This place reminds me of a motel I stayed at in Waco one night, and I made the goddamn manager give me my money back. The roaches in that shit hole were big enough to use the shower."

Brother Fred listened to all this without blinking an eye, as if seeing Calhoun talk was as amazing as seeing a frog sing. He said. "Sleep tight, don't let the bed bugs bite. Tomorrow you start to work."

"I don't want no fucking job," Calhoun said.

"Goodnight, children," Brother Fred said, and with that he closed the door and they heard it lock, loud and final as the clicking of the drop board on a gallows.

6

At dawn, Wayne got up and took a leak, went to the window to look out. The stage where the monks had played and the nun had jumped was empty. The skeletal shapes he had seen last night were tracks and frames from rides long abandoned. He had a sudden vision of Jesus and his disciples riding a roller coaster, their long hair and robes flapping in the wind.

The large crucified Jesus looked unimpressive without its lights and night's mystery, like a whore in harsh sunlight with makeup gone and wig askew.

"Got any ideas how we're gonna get out of here?" Calhoun asked.

Wayne looked at Calhoun. He was sitting on the bed, pulling on his boots.

Wayne shook his head.

"I could use a smoke. You know, I think we ought to work together. Then we can try to kill each other."

Unconsciously, Calhoun touched his ear where Wayne had bitten off the lobe.

"Wouldn't trust you as far as I could kick you," Wayne said.

"I hear that. But I give my word. And my word's something you can count on. I won't twist it."

Wayne studied Calhoun, thought: Well, there wasn't anything to lose. He'd just watch his ass.

"All right," Wayne said. "Give me your word you'll work with me on getting us out of this mess, and when we're good and free, and you say your word has gone far enough, we can settle up."

"Deal," Calhoun said, and offered his hand. Wayne looked at it.

"This seals it," Calhoun said.

Wayne took Calhoun's hand and they shook.

7

Moments later the door unlocked and a smiling monk with hair the color and texture of mold fuzz came in with Brother Fred, who still had his pump shotgun. There were two dead folks with them. A man and a woman. They wore torn clothes and the mouse-ear hats. Neither looked long dead or smelled particularly bad. Actually, the monks smelled worse.

Using the barrel of the shotgun, Brother Fred poked them down the hall to a room with metal tables and medical instruments.

Brother Lazarus was on the far side of one of the tables. He was smiling. His nose looked especially cancerous this morning. A white pustule the size of a thumb tip had taken up residence on the left side of his snout, and it looked like a pearl onion in a turd.

Nearby stood a nun. She was short with good, if skinny, legs, and she wore the same outfit as the nun on the bus. It looked more girlish on her, perhaps because she was thin and small-breasted. She had a nice face and eyes that were all pupil. Wisps of blond hair crawled out around the edges of her headgear. She looked pale and weak, as if wearied to the bone. There was a birthmark on her right cheek that looked like a distant view of a small bird in flight.

"Good morning," Brother Lazarus said. "I hope you gentlemen slept well."

"What's this about work?" Wayne said.

"Work?" Brother Lazarus said.

"I described it to them that way," Brother Fred said. "Perhaps an impulsive description."

"I'll say," Brother Lazarus said. "No work here, gentlemen. You have my word on that. We do all the work. Lie on these tables and we'll take a sampling of your blood."

"Why?" Wayne said.

"Science," Brother Lazarus said. "I intend to find a cure for this germ that makes the dead come back to life, and to do that, I need living human beings to study. Sounds kind of mad scientist, doesn't it? But I assure you, you've nothing to lose but a few drops of blood. Well, maybe more than a few drops, but nothing serious."

"Use your own goddamn blood," Calhoun said.

"We do. But we're always looking for fresh specimens. Little here, little there. And if you don't do it, we'll kill you."

Calhoun spun and hit Brother Fred on the nose. It was a solid punch and Brother Fred hit the floor on his butt, but he hung onto the shotgun and pointed it up at Calhoun. "Go on," he said, his nose streaming blood. "Try that again."

Wayne flexed to help, but hesitated. He could kick Brother Fred in the head from where he was, but that might not keep him from shooting Calhoun, and there would go the extra reward money. And besides, he'd given his word to the bastard that they'd try to help each other survive until they got out of this.

The other monk clasped his hands and swung them into the side of Calhoun's head, knocking him down. Brother Fred got up, and while Calhoun was trying to rise, he hit him with the stock of the shotgun in the back of the head, hit him so hard it drove Calhoun's forehead into the floor. Calhoun rolled over on his side and lay there, his eyes fluttering like moth wings.

"Brother Fred, you must learn to turn the other cheek," Brother Lazarus said. "Now put this sack of shit on the table."

Brother Fred checked Wayne to see if he looked like trouble. Wayne put his hands in his pockets and smiled.

Brother Fred called the two dead folks over and had them put Calhoun on the table. Brother Lazarus strapped him down.

The nun brought a tray of needles, syringes, cotton and bottles over, put it down on the table next to Calhoun's head. Brother Lazarus rolled up Calhoun's sleeve and fixed up a needle and stuck it in Calhoun's arm, drew it full of blood. He stuck the needle through the rubber top of one of the bottles and shot the blood into that.

He looked at Wayne and said, "I hope you'll be less trouble."

"Do I get some orange juice and a little cracker afterwards?" Wayne said.

"You get to walk out without a knot on your head," Brother Lazarus said.

"Guess that'll have to do."

Wayne got on the table next to Calhoun and Brother Lazarus strapped him down. The nun brought the tray over and Brother Lazarus did to him what he had done to Calhoun. The nun stood over Wayne and looked down at his face. Wayne tried to read something in her features but couldn't find a clue.

When Brother Lazarus was finished he took hold of Wayne's chin and shook it. "My, but you two boys look healthy. But you can never be sure.

We'll have to run the blood through some tests. Meantime, Sister Worth will run a few additional tests on you, and," he nodded at the unconscious Calhoun, "I'll see to your friend here."

"He's no friend of mine," Wayne said.

They took Wayne off the table, and Sister Worth and Brother Fred, and his shotgun, directed him down the hall into another room.

The room was lined with shelves that were lined with instruments and bottles. The lighting was poor, most of it coming through a slatted window, though there was an anemic yellow bulb overhead. Dust motes swam in the air.

In the center of the room on its rim was a great, spoked wheel. It had two straps well spaced at the top, and two more at the bottom. Beneath the bottom straps were blocks of wood. The wheel was attached in back to an upright metal bar that had switches and buttons all over it.

Brother Fred made Wayne strip and get on the wheel with his back to the hub and his feet on the blocks. Sister Worth strapped his ankles down tight, then he was made to put his hands up, and she strapped his wrists to the upper part of the wheel.

"I hope this hurts a lot," Brother Fred said.

"Wipe the blood off your face," Wayne said. "It makes you look silly."

Brother Fred made a gesture with his middle finger that wasn't religious and left the room.

8

Sister Worth touched a switch and the wheel began to spin, slowly at first, and the bad light came through the windows and poked through the rungs and the dust swam before his eyes and the wheel and its spokes threw twisting shadows on the wall.

As he went around, Wayne closed his eyes. It kept him from feeling so dizzy, especially on the down swings.

On a turn up, he opened his eyes and caught sight of Sister Worth standing in front of the wheel staring at him. He said, "Why?" and closed his eyes as the wheel dipped.

"Because Brother Lazarus says so," came the answer after such a long time Wayne had almost forgotten the question. Actually, he hadn't expected a response. He was surprised that such a thing had come out of his mouth, and he felt a little diminished for having asked.

He opened his eyes on another swing up, and she was moving behind the wheel, out of his line of vision. He heard a snick like a switch being flipped and lightning jumped through him and he screamed in spite of himself. A little fork of electricity licked out of his mouth like a reptile tongue tasting air.

Faster spun the wheel and the jolts came more often and he screamed less loud, and finally not at all. He was too numb. He was adrift in space wearing only his cowboy hat and boots, moving away from earth very fast. Floating all around him were wrecked cars. He looked and saw that one of them was his '57, and behind the steering wheel was Pop. Sitting beside the old man was a Mexican. Two more were in the back seat. They looked a little drunk.

One of the whores in back pulled up her dress and cocked it high up so he could see her pussy. It looked like that needed a shave.

He smiled and tried to go for it, but the '57 was moving away, swinging wide and turning its tail to him. He could see a face at the back window. Pop's face. He had crawled back there and was waving slowly and sadly. A whore pulled Pop from view.

The wrecked cars moved away too, as if caught in the vacuum of the '57's retreat. Wayne swam with his arms, kicked with his legs, trying to pursue the '57 and the wrecks. But he dangled where he was, like a moth pinned to a board. The cars moved out of sight and left him there with his arms and legs stretched out, spinning amidst an infinity of cold, uncaring stars.

" . . . how the tests are run . . . marks everything about you . . . charts it . . . EKG, brain waves, liver. . . everything . . . it hurts because Brother Lazarus wants it to . . . thinks I don't know these things . . . that I'm slow . . . slow, not stupid . . . smart really . . . used to be scientist . . . before the accident . . . Brother Lazarus is not holy . . . he's mad . . . made the wheel because of the Holy Inquisition . . . knows a lot about the Inquisition . . . thinks we need it again . . . for the likes of men you . . . the unholy, he says . . . But he just likes to hurt . . . I know."

Wayne opened his eyes. The wheel had stopped. Sister Worth was talking in her monotone, explaining the wheel. He remembered asking her, "Why" about three thousand years ago.

Sister Worth was staring at him again. She went away and he expected the wheel to start up, but when she returned, she had a long, narrow mirror under her arm. She put it against the wall across from him. She got on the wheel with him, her little feet on the wooden platforms beside his. She hiked up the bottom of her habit and pulled down her black panties. She put her face close to his, as if searching for something.

"He plans to take your body . . . piece by piece . . . blood, cells, brain, your cock . . . all of it . . . He wants to live forever."

She had her panties in her hand, and she tossed them. Wayne watched them fly up and flutter to the floor like a dying bat.

She took hold of his dick and pulled on it. Her palm was cold and he didn't feel his best, but he began to get hard. She put him between her legs and rubbed his dick between her thighs. They were as cold as her hands, and dry.

"I know him now . . . know what he's doing . . . the dead germ virus . . . he was trying to make something that would make him live forever . . . it made the dead come back . . . didn't keep the living alive, free of old age . . . "

His dick was throbbing now, in spite of the coolness of her body.

"He cuts up dead folks to learn . . . experiments on them . . . but the secret of eternal life is with the living . . . that's why he wants you . . . you're an outsider . . . those who live here he can test . . . but he must keep them alive to do his bidding . . . not let them know how he really is . . . needs your insides and the other man's . . . he wants to be a God . . . flies high above us in a little plane and looks down . . . Likes to think he is the creator, I bet . . . "

"Plane?"

"Ultralight."

She pushed his cock inside her, and it was cold and dry in there, like liver left overnight on a drainboard. Still, he found himself ready. At this point, he would have gouged a hole in a turnip.

She kissed him on the ear and alongside the neck; cold little kisses, dry as toast.

" . . . thinks I don't know . . . But I know he doesn't love Jesus . . . He loves himself, and power . . . He's sad about his nose . . . "

"I bet."

"Did it in a moment of religious fervor . . . before he lost the belief . . . Now he wants to be what he was . . . A scientist. He wants to grow a new nose . . . know how . . . saw him grow a finger in a dish once . . . grew it from the skin off a knuckle of one of the brothers . . . He can do all kinds of things."

She was moving her hips now. He could see over her shoulder into the mirror against the wall. Could see her white ass rolling, the black habit hiked up above it, threatening to drop like a curtain. He began to thrust back, slowly, firmly.

She looked over her shoulder into the mirror, watching herself fuck him. There was a look more of study than rapture on her face.

"Want to feel alive," she said. "Feel a good, hard dick . . . Been too long."

"I'm doing the best I can," Wayne said. "This ain't the most romantic of spots."

"Push so I can feel it."

"Nice," Wayne said. He gave it everything he had. He was beginning to lose his erection. He felt as if he were auditioning for a job and not making the best of impressions. He felt like a knothole would be dissatisfied with him.

She got off of him and climbed down.

"Don't blame you," he said.

She went behind the wheel and touched some things on the upright. She mounted him again, hooked her ankles behind his. The wheel began to turn. Short electrical shocks leaped through him. They weren't as powerful as before. They were invigorating. When he kissed her it was like touching his tongue to a battery. It felt as if electricity was racing through his veins and flying out the head of his dick; he felt as if he might fill her with lightning instead of come.

The wheel creaked to a stop; it must have had a timer on it. They were upside down and Wayne could see their reflection in the mirror; they looked like two lizards fucking on a window pane.

He couldn't tell if she had finished or not, so he went ahead and got it over with. Without the electricity he was losing his desire. It hadn't been an A-one piece of ass, but hell, as Pop always said, "Worse pussy I ever had was good."

"They'll be coming back," she said. "Soon . . . Don't want them to find us like this . . . Other tests to do yet."

"Why did you do this?"

"I want out of the order . . . Want out of this desert . . . I want to live . . . And I want you to help me."

"I'm game, but the blood is rushing to my head and I'm getting dizzy. Maybe you ought to get off me."

After an eon she said, "I have a plan."

She untwined from him and went behind the wheel and hit a switch that turned Wayne upright. She touched another switch and he began to spin slowly, and while he spun and while lightning played inside him, she told him her plan.

9

"I think ole Brother Fred wants to fuck me," Calhoun said. "He keeps trying to get his finger up my asshole."

They were back in their room. Brother Fred had brought them back, making them carry their clothes, and now they were alone again, dressing.

"We're getting out of here," Wayne said. "The nun, Sister Worth, she's going to help."

"What's her angle?"

"She hates this place and wants my dick. Mostly, she hates this place."

"What's the plan?"

Wayne told him first what Brother Lazarus had planned. On the morrow he would have them brought to the room with the steel tables, and they would go on the tables, and if the tests had turned out good, they would be pronounced fit as fiddles and Brother Lazarus would strip the skin from their bodies, slowly, because according to Sister Worth he liked to do it that way, and he would drain their blood and percolate it into his formulas like coffee, cut their brains out and put them in vats and store their veins and organs in freezers.

All of this would be done in the name of God and Jesus Christ (Eees num be prased) under the guise of finding a cure for the dead folks germ. But it would all instead be for Brother Lazarus who wanted to have a new nose, fly his ultralight above Jesus Land and live forever.

Sister Worth's plan was this:

She would be in the dissecting room. She would have guns hidden. She would make the first move, a distraction, then it was up to them.

"This time," Wayne said, "one of us has to get on top of that shotgun."

"You had your finger up your ass in there today, or we'd have had them."

"We're going to have surprise on our side this time. Real surprise. They won't be expecting Sister Worth. We can get up there on the roof and take off in that ultralight. When it runs out of gas we can walk, maybe get back to the '57 and hope it runs."

"We'll settle our score then. Whoever wins keeps the car and the split tail. As for tomorrow, I've got a little ace."

Calhoun pulled on his boots. He twisted the heel of one of them. It swung out and a little knife dropped into his hand. "It's sharp," Calhoun said. "I cut a Chinaman from gut to gill with it. It was easy as sliding a stick through fresh shit."

"Been nice if you'd had that ready today."

"I wanted to scout things out first. And to tell the truth, I thought one pop to Brother Fred's mouth and he'd be out of the picture."

"You hit him in the nose."

"Yeah, goddamn it, but I was aiming for his mouth."

10

Dawn and the room with the metal tables looked the same. No one had brought in a vase of flowers to brighten the place.

Brother Lazarus's nose had changed however; there were two pearl onions nestled in it now.

Sister Worth, looking only a little more animated than yesterday, stood nearby. She was holding the tray with the instruments. This time the tray was full of scalpels. The light caught their edges and made them wink.

Brother Fred was standing behind Calhoun, and Brother Mold Fuzz was behind Wayne. They must have felt pretty confident today. They had dispensed with the dead folks.

Wayne looked at Sister Worth and thought maybe things were not good. Maybe she had lied to him in her slow talking way. Only wanted a little dick and wanted to keep it quiet. To do that, she might have promised anything. She might not care what Brother Lazarus did to them.

If it looked like a double cross, Wayne was going to go for it. If he had to jump right into the mouth of Brother Fred's shotgun. That was a better way to go than having the hide peeled from your body. The idea of Brother Lazarus and his ugly nose leaning over him did not appeal at all.

"It's so nice to see you," Brother Lazarus said. "I hope we'll have none of the unpleasantness of yesterday. Now, on the tables."

Wayne looked at Sister Worth. Her expression showed nothing. The only thing about her that looked alive was the bent wings of the bird birthmark on her cheek.

All right, Wayne thought, I'll go as far as the table, then I'm going to do something. Even if it's wrong.

He took a step forward, and Sister Worth flipped the contents of the tray into Brother Lazarus's face. A scalpel went into his nose and hung there. The tray and the rest of its contents hit the floor.

Before Brother Lazarus could yelp, Calhoun dropped and wheeled. He was under Brother Fred's shotgun and he used his forearm to drive the barrel upwards. The gun went off and peppered the ceiling. Plaster sprinkled down.

Calhoun had concealed the little knife in the palm of his hand and he brought it up and into Brother Fred's groin. The blade went through the robe and buried to the hilt.

The instant Calhoun made his move, Wayne brought his forearm back and around into Brother Mold Fuzz's throat, then turned and caught his head and jerked that down and kneed him a couple of times. He floored him by driving an elbow into the back of his neck.

Calhoun had the shotgun now, and Brother Fred was on the floor trying to pull the knife out of his balls. Calhoun blew Brother Fred's head off, then did the same for Brother Mold Fuzz.

Brother Lazarus, the scalpel hanging from his nose, tried to run for it, but he stepped on the tray and that sent him flying. He landed on his stomach. Calhoun took two deep steps and kicked him in the throat. Brother Lazarus made a sound like he was gargling and tried to get up.

Wayne helped him. He grabbed Brother Lazarus by the back of his robe and pulled him up, slammed him back against a table. The scalpel still dangled from the monk's nose. Wayne grabbed it and jerked, taking away a chunk of nose as he did. Brother Lazarus screamed.

Calhoun put the shotgun in Brother Lazarus's mouth and that made him stop screaming. Calhoun pumped the shotgun. He said, "Eat it," and pulled the trigger. Brother Lazarus's brains went out the back of his head riding on a chunk of skull. The brains and skull hit the table and sailed onto the floor like a plate of scrambled eggs pushed the length of a cafe counter.

Sister Worth had not moved. Wayne figured she had used all of her concentration to hit Brother Lazarus with the tray.

"You said you'd have guns," Wayne said to her.

She turned her back to him and lifted her habit. In a belt above her panties were two .38 revolvers. Wayne pulled them out and held one in each hand. "Two-Gun Wayne," he said.

"What about the ultralight?" Calhoun said. "We've made enough noise for a prison riot. We need to move."

Sister Worth turned to the door at the back of the room, and before she could say anything or lead, Wayne and Calhoun snapped to it and grabbed her and pushed her toward it.

There were stairs on the other side of the door and they took them two at a time. They went through a trap door and onto the roof and there, tied down with bungee straps to metal hoops, was the ultralight. It was blue-and-white canvas and metal rods, and strapped to either side of it was a twelve gauge pump and a bag of food and a canteen of water.

They unsnapped the roof straps and got in the two-seater and used the straps to fasten Sister Worth between them. It wasn't comfortable, but it was a ride.

They sat there. After a moment, Calhoun said, "Well?"

"Shit," Wayne said. "I can't fly this thing."

They looked at Sister Worth. She was staring at the controls.

"Say something, damn it," Wayne said.

"That's the switch," she said. "That stick . . . forward is up, back brings the nose down . . . side to side . . . "

"Got it."

"Well, shoot this bastard over the side," Calhoun said. Wayne cranked it, gave it the throttle. The machine rolled forward, wobbled.

"Too much weight," Wayne said.

"Throw the cunt over the side," Calhoun said.

"It's all or nothing," Wayne said. The ultralight continued to swing its tail left and right, but leveled off as they went over the edge.

They sailed for a hundred yards, made a mean curve Wayne couldn't fight, and fell straight away into the statue of Jesus, striking it in the head, right in the midst of the barbed wire crown. Spotlights shattered, metal groaned, the wire tangled in the nylon wings of the craft and held it. The head of Jesus nodded forward, popped off and shot out on the electric cables inside like a jack-in-the-box. The cables pulled tight a hundred feet from the ground and worked the head and the craft like a yo-yo. Then the barbed wire crown unraveled and dropped the craft the rest of the way. It hit the ground with a crunch and a rip and a cloud of dust.

The head of Jesus bobbed above the shattered ultralight like a bird preparing to peck a worm.

11

Wayne crawled out of the wreckage and tried his legs. They worked.

Calhoun was on his feet cussing, unstrapping the shotguns and supplies.

Sister Worth lay in the midst of the wreck, the nylon and aluminum supports folded around her like butterfly wings.

Wayne started pulling the mess off of her. He saw that her leg was broken. A bone punched out of her thigh like a sharpened stick. There was no blood.

"Here comes the church social," Calhoun said.

The word was out about Brother Lazarus and the others. A horde of monks, nuns, and dead folks were rushing over the drawbridge. Some of the nuns and monks had guns. All of the dead folks had clubs. The clergy was yelling.

Wayne nodded toward the bus barn, "Let's get a bus." Wayne picked up Sister Worth, cradled her in his arms, and made a run for it. Calhoun, carrying the guns and the supplies, passed them. He jumped through the open doorway of a bus and dropped out of sight. Wayne knew he was jerking wires loose, trying to hotwire them a ride. Wayne hoped he was good at it and fast.

When Wayne got to the bus, he laid Sister Worth down beside it and pulled the .38s and stood in front of her. If he was going down he wanted to go like Wild Bill Hickock: A blazing gun in either fist and a woman to protect.

Actually, he'd prefer the bus to start.

It did.

Calhoun jerked it in gear, backed it out and around in front of Wayne and Sister Worth. The monks and nuns had started firing and their rounds bounced off the side of the armored bus.

From inside Calhoun yelled, "Get the hell on."

Wayne stuck the guns in his belt, grabbed up Sister Worth and leapt inside. Calhoun jerked the bus forward and Wayne and Sister Worth went flying over a seat and into another.

"I thought you were leaving," Wayne said.

"I wanted to. But I gave my word."

Wayne stretched Sister Worth out on the seat and looked at her leg. After that tossing Calhoun had given them, the break was sticking out even more.

Calhoun closed the bus door and checked his wing-mirror. Nuns and monks and dead folks had piled into a couple of buses, and now the buses were pursuing them. One of them moved very fast, as if souped up.

"I probably got the granny of the bunch," Calhoun said. They climbed over a ridge of sand, then they were on the narrow road that wound itself upwards. Behind them, one of the buses had fallen back, maybe some kind of mechanical trouble. The other was gaining.

The road widened and Calhoun yelled, "I think this is what the fucker's been waiting for."

Even as Calhoun spoke, their pursuer put on a burst of speed and swung left and came up beside them, tried to swerve over and push them off the road, down into the deepening valley. But Calhoun fought the curves and didn't budge.

The other bus swung its door open and a nun, the very one who had been on the bus that brought them to Jesus Land, stood there with her legs spread wide, showing the black-pantied mound of her crotch. She had one arm bent around a seat post and was holding in both hands the ever-popular clergy tool, the twelve-gauge pump.

As they made a curve, the nun fired a round into the window next to Calhoun. The window made a cracking noise and thin, crooked lines spread in all directions, but the glass held.

She pumped a round into the chamber and fired again. Bulletproof or not, this time the front sheet of glass fell away. Another well-placed round and the rest of the glass would go and Calhoun could wave his head goodbye.

Wayne put his knees in a seat and got the window down. The nun saw him, whirled and fired. The shot was low and hit the bottom part of the window and starred it and pelleted the chassis.

Wayne stuck a .38 out of the window and fired as the nun was jacking another load into position. His shot hit her in the head and her right eye went big and wet, and she swung around on the pole and lost the shotgun. It went out the door. She clung there by the bend of her elbow for a moment, then her arm straightened and she fell outside. The bus ran over her and she popped red and juicy at both ends like a stomped jellyroll.

"Waste of good pussy," Calhoun said. He edged into the other bus, and it pushed back. But Calhoun pushed harder and made it hit the wall with a screech like a panther.

The bus came back and shoved Calhoun to the side of the cliff and honked twice for Jesus.

Calhoun downshifted, let off the gas, allowed the other bus to soar past by half a length. Then he jerked the wheel so that he caught the rear of it and knocked it across the road. He speared it in the side with the nose of his bus and the other started to spin. It clipped the front of Calhoun's bus and peeled the bumper back. Calhoun braked and the other bus kept spinning. It spun off the road and down into the valley amidst a chorus of cries.

Thirty minutes later they reached the top of the canyon and were in the desert. The bus began to throw up smoke from the front and make a noise like a dog strangling on a chicken bone. Calhoun pulled over.

12

"Goddamn bumper got twisted under there and it's shredded the tire some," Calhoun said. "I think if we can peel the bumper off, there's enough of that tire to run on."

Wayne and Calhoun got hold of the bumper and pulled but it wouldn't come off. Not completely. Part of it had been creased, and that part finally gave way and broke off from the rest of it.

"That ought to be enough to keep from rubbing the tire," Calhoun said.

Sister Worth called from inside the bus. Wayne went to check on her. "Take me off the bus," she said. " . . . I want to feel free air and sun."

"There doesn't feel like there's any air out there," Wayne said. "And the sun feels just like it always does. Hot."

"Please."

He picked her up and carried her outside and found a ridge of sand and laid her down so her head was propped against it.

"I . . . I need batteries," she said.

"Say what?" Wayne said.

She lay looking straight into the sun. "Brother Lazarus's greatest work . . . a dead folk that can think . . . has memory of the past . . . Was a scientist too . . . " Her hand came up in stages, finally got hold of her head gear and pushed it off.

Gleaming from the center of her tangled blond hair was a silver knob.

"He . . . was not a good man . . . I am a good woman. I want to feel alive . . . like before . . . batteries going . . . brought others."

Her hand fumbled at a snap pocket on her habit. Wayne opened it for her and got out what was inside. Four batteries.

"Uses two . . . simple."

Calhoun was standing over them now. "That explains some things," he said.

"Don't look at me like that . . . " Sister Worth said, and Wayne realized he had never told her his name and she had never asked. "Unscrew . . . put the batteries in . . . Without them I'll be an eater . . . Can't wait too long."

"All right," Wayne said. He went behind her and propped her up on the sand drift and unscrewed the metal shaft from her skull. He thought about when she had fucked him on the wheel and how desperate she had been to feel something, and how she had been cold as flint and lustless. He remembered how she had looked in the mirror hoping to see something that wasn't there.

He dropped the batteries in the sand and took out one of the revolvers and put it close to the back of her head and pulled the trigger. Her body jerked slightly and fell over, her face turning toward him.

The bullet had come out where the bird had been on her cheek and had taken it completely away, leaving a bloodless hole.

"Best thing," Calhoun said. "There's enough live pussy in the world without you pulling this broken-legged dead thing around after you on a board."

"Shut up," Wayne said.

"When a man gets sentimental over women and kids, he can count himself out."

Wayne stood up.

"Well, boy," Calhoun said. "I reckon it's time."

"Reckon so," Wayne said.

"How about we do this with some class? Give me one of your pistols and we'll get back-to-back and I'll count to ten, and when I get there, we'll turn and shoot."

Wayne gave Calhoun one of the pistols. Calhoun checked the chambers, said, "I've got four loads."

Wayne took two out of his pistol and tossed them on the ground. "Even Steven," he said.

They got back-to-back and held the guns by their legs.

"Guess if you kill me you'll take me in," Calhoun said. "So that means you'll put a bullet through my head if I need it. I don't want to come back as one of the dead folks. Got your word on that?"

"Yep."

"I'll do the same for you. Give my word. You know that's worth something."

"We gonna shoot or talk?"

"You know, boy, under different circumstances, I could have liked you. We might have been friends."

"Not likely."

Calhoun started counting, and they started stepping. When he got to ten, they turned.

Calhoun's pistol barked first, and Wayne felt the bullet punch him low in the right side of his chest, spinning him slightly. He lifted his revolver and took his time and shot just as Calhoun fired again.

Calhoun's second bullet whizzed by Wayne's head. Wayne's shot hit Calhoun in the stomach.

Calhoun went to his knees and had trouble drawing a breath. He tried to lift his revolver but couldn't; it was as if it had turned into an anvil.

Wayne shot him again. Hitting him in the middle of the chest this time and knocking him back so that his legs were curled beneath him.

Wayne walked over to Calhoun, dropped to one knee and took the revolver from him.

"Shit," Calhoun said. "I wouldn't have thought that for nothing. You hit?"

"Scratched."

"Shit."

Wayne put the revolver to Calhoun's forehead and Calhoun closed his eyes and Wayne pulled the trigger.

13

The wound wasn't a scratch. Wayne knew he should leave Sister Worth where she was and load Calhoun on the bus and haul him in for bounty. But he didn't care about the bounty anymore.

He used the ragged piece of bumper to dig them a shallow side-by-side grave. When he finished, he stuck the fender fragment up between them and used the sight of one of the revolvers to scratch into it: HERE LIES SISTER WORTH AND CALHOUN WHO KEPT HIS WORD.

You couldn't really read it good and he knew the first real wind would keel it over, but it made him feel better about something, even if he couldn't put his finger on it.

His wound had opened up and the sun was very hot now, and since he had lost his hat he could feel his brain cooking in his skull like meat boiling in a pot.

He got on the bus, started it and drove through the day and the night and it was near morning when he came to the Cadillacs and turned down between them and drove until he came to the '57.

When he stopped and tried to get off the bus, he found he could hardly move. The revolvers in his belt were stuck to his shirt and stomach because of the blood from his wound.

He pulled himself up with the steering wheel, got one of the shotguns and used it for a crutch. He got the food and water and went out to inspect the '57.

It was for shit. It had not only lost its windshield, the front end was mashed way back and one of the big sand tires was twisted at such an angle he knew the axle was shot.

He leaned against the Chevy and tried to think. The bus was okay and there was still some gas in it, and he could get the hose out of the trunk of the '57 and siphon gas out of its tanks and put it in the bus. That would give him a few miles.

Miles.

He didn't feel as if he could walk twenty feet, let alone concentrate on driving.

He let go of the shotgun, the food and water. He scooted onto the hood of the Chevy and managed himself to the roof. He lay there on his back and looked at the sky.

It was a clear night and the stars were sharp with no fuzz around them. He felt cold. In a couple of hours the stars would fade and the sun would come up and the cool would give way to heat.

He turned his head and looked at one of the Cadillacs and a skeleton face pressed to its windshield, forever looking down at the sand.

That was no way to end, looking down.

He crossed his legs and stretched out his arms and studied the sky. It didn't feel so cold now, and the pain had almost stopped. He was more numb than anything else.

He pulled one of the revolvers and cocked it and put it to his temple and continued to look at the stars. Then he closed his eyes and found that he could still see them. He was once again hanging in the void between the stars wearing only his hat and cowboy boots, and floating about him were the junk cars and the '57, undamaged.

The cars were moving toward him this time, not away. The '57 was in the lead, and as it grew closer he saw Pop behind the wheel and beside him was a Mexican puta, and in the back, two more. They were all smiling and Pop honked the horn and waved.

The '57 came alongside him and the back door opened.

Sitting between the whores was Sister Worth. She had not been there a moment ago, but now she was. And he had never noticed how big the back seat of the '57 was.

Sister Worth smiled at him and the bird on her cheek lifted higher. Her hair was combed out long and straight and she looked pink-skinned and happy. On the floorboard at her feet was a chest of iced beer. Lone Star, by God.

Pop was leaning over the front seat, holding out his hand and Sister Worth and the whores were beckoning him inside.

Wayne worked his hands and feet, found this time that he could move. He swam through the open door, touched Pop's hand, and Pop said, "It's good to see you, son," and at the moment Wayne pulled the trigger, Pop pulled him inside.

JOE R. LANSDALE is the author of over thirty novels and numerous short stories. His novella, *Bubba Ho-tep*, was made into an award-winning film of the same name, as was *Incident On and Off a Mountain Road*. Both were directed by Don Coscarelli. His works have received numerous recognitions, including the Edgar, eight Bram Stoker awards, the Grinzane Cavour Prize for Literature, American Mystery Award, the International Horror Award, British Fantasy Award, and many others. *All the Earth, Thrown to the Sky*, his first novel for young adults, was published last year. His most recent novel for adults is *Edge of Dark Water*.

---

*The teacher always hated this day. Nothing he'd seen on his tour of duty
bothered him half as much as the sight of ten thousand
schoolchildren, all screaming for gore . . .*

The Traumatized Generation

Murray J. D. Leeder

Land sniffed at the air. He felt a kind of peace out here, so different from the
city thick with industrial fumes and soldiers. The prairies sprawled in every
direction, wilder and more overgrown than they had been in more than a
century, and the Rockies were lost in a pink haze to the west. All of it sent
Land back to a childhood spent traipsing around the countryside, when he
didn't need to be worried about what might be hiding in the wheat.

He rapped on the front door. Eventually a woman came to the door in
her nightgown, slightly older than him and glowering at him. She knew
what was happening, and Land's heart sank when he realized what he was
about to do.

"Mrs. March? I'm Michael Land, Paul's homeroom teacher. I'm here to
pick him for today's—" He hesitated. "Today's field trip."

"I didn't give permission for any field trip," she snorted, and Land put
his hand against the door to stop her from closing it.

"I'm afraid the school board doesn't require parental permission when
the field trip has been made mandatory by the government of Canada."

"The government," she said. "You mean the military, don't you?
Either way, I'm not about to send my son away to be traumatized by your
bloodshow."

"Mrs. March," he told her. "In that car is the sergeant they sent to escort
me up here. If Paul doesn't come out of this house in ten minutes, she'll
have to come and talk to you yourself. Nobody wants that."

There was desperation in her voice. "Mr. Land, you and I remember a
time before the military controlled our lives. You're an educator—how can
you stand idly by and . . . "

"Just get your son, Mrs. March. Please. Just get Paul."

Mrs. March breathed in deeply. "Wait here," she said. "I can't believe I'm doing this."

She returned a few minutes later with the round-faced, serious little boy, dressed in unfashionable clothes and shoes that so often made him a target for jeers.

"It's good to see you, Paul," Land said, and the boy half-smiled up at him. Land knew the boy all too well; smart, shy, sensitive, and far too vulnerable for this world. Just like the young Michael Land, back when CNN reported that the dead were rising from their graves.

The car door opened and Sgt. Hazelwood walked over to the door just as Paul was slipping on his coat. She was blond and beautiful but Land disliked her intensely. She was just the kind of rhetoric-spouting career army type that Land had encountered too often during his own tour of duty in Alaska. "All ready to go?" she asked, wearing a false smile that Mrs. March did not return. Ignoring the sergeant's presence, Mrs. March dropped to her knees and embraced her son.

"Remember not to be too scared," she said, and Paul nodded uncertainly.

"Do something for me," Mrs. March said to Land. "Promise me you'll sit by him. Try to keep him from being too scared. He has a weak heart."

Land nodded but before he could speak, Hazelwood interrupted. "Then we'll just have to strengthen up that heart a bit," she said, ushering the trembling boy toward the car.

As Land looked back at Mrs. March, watching the doorway as her son went away. He wanted to look in her eyes and reassure her that everything will go all right, whether or not that was true, but found that he could not.

The huge chain-link fence encircling Calgary was intended to keep the zombies out, which it did, but it also served to keep the people in. The rule of law didn't need to enforce this, for few wanted to leave. Officers waived Sgt. Hazelwood's transport through the military checkpoint at the city's north gate, and they continued down the vacant Deerfoot Trail, bound for the Saddledome. In the distance Calgary's downtown was silhouetted against the morning sky, postcard pristine, like a snapshot from Land's childhood.

Paul was quiet the entire time. His parents certainly taught him to avoid talking to anyone in a uniform. Land felt like he was ferrying a prisoner to an execution. He always hated this day, the worst of any school year. Nothing he'd seen up in Alaska bothered him half as much as the sight of ten thousand schoolchildren, all screaming for gore.

Yellow schoolbuses dotted the Saddledome's parking lot, and Hazelwood weaved through the crowds of kids before they found Mr. Land's grade-seven class. Land hoped they'd arrive first, to spare Paul the humiliation of arriving under military escort, but no such luck. Built for the 1988 Olympics, the Saddledome had served for years as sports arena and concert venue. Now the military had appropriated it and remade it into their modern-day Coliseum.

"You get out here," Hazelwood said. "I'll go park in the barracks and join you inside."

"What?" Land said. "Isn't your duty here finished?"

"No." The sergeant flashed him an unreadable smile. "I'm with you for the whole day."

Land coughed in disgust. She probably thought he'd let Paul slip away from the show at the first occasion. She was probably right.

The rest of the class caught sight of them as they stepped out of the military vehicle. Land saw Bruce Tomasino say something to Jason Barrows, and they sent their whispers all along the line.

"Don't worry about them, Paul," Land said softly. "Just take your place in the line."

His student dutifully shuffled over to the uneven row of students. Land addressed them: "I don't want to see any shoving or shouting. When we get the signal, I want us to go in a straight line inside and take our seats. Any questions?"

"I got a question," asked chubby Jimmy Schwab. "Is it true . . . I mean, we heard a rumor that Zombie Bob will be here."

Please, no, Land thought. That would make it even worse; the presence of a TV celebrity would change this field trip from a military demonstration to a rock concert. Robert Smith Harding went with a camera crew behind the lines in lost cities and in infested countryside, found zombies and inevitably killed them in daredevil ways. His weapons of choice ranged from a jackhammer to a katana. The kids loved him, wore his picture, talked about him constantly. Land watched the boy's face grow grimmer still at this news.

A whistle blew somewhere across the parking lot, and the rows of students started proceeding up the concrete stairs and into the Saddledome itself. A uniformed officer waved Land's class ahead, and he took up the end of the line to watch they kept their course. Amid all the noise of kids gabbing away, he could barely hear Bruce and Jason talking about Paul. He made out one sentence: "That corpse-hugger's going to wet his pants when he sees this."

Land was always impressed by how little the Saddledome had changed since his childhood. This wasn't a real surprise; though the military owned it now, it was still a sports arena of sorts. The floors were still sticky and the plastic seats still painful. The Jumbotron was still there too, left over from hockey games. Now it flashed messages like ENJOY THE SHOW and THIS IS FOR YOU KIDS.

The most visible things changed from the old days were the sideboards. The protective glass now went up much higher than in the old days and needed to be cleaned nightly of splattered blood and brain meat. As usual, the arena was covered with a layer of freshly tilled dirt. At one end there was a raised platform with a few microphones, and at the other there was a black velvet drape, which hid the zombie cage. A trained crew with cattle prods were ready to send them out into the arena on cue.

When the students took their seats, Land called for Paul to come over and sit by him by the aisle. He'd wished he could have done this more subtly—Paul didn't need to be a teacher's pet on top of a zombie-lover—but he'd agreed to sit by the boy. As the other students chatted away, he asked Paul: "What do you think of all this?"

"I don't know," the boy said. "I've never been anywhere like this before."

"Your parents didn't want you to come here," Land said. "You know that."

"But they made you get me."

Land nodded. "The military thinks it's important that you be here."

"Why?"

The question caught Land by surprise. It was a good question—why? Why did one child deserve all this special attention? He stammered, searching for an answer, before one was provided.

"Because someday you'll be called to the service, and we think it's best you know what it's all about." Sgt. Hazelwood stood in the aisle, grinning down on them both. She had changed from her green field outfit into a brown dress uniform that accentuated her curves.

That's not a real answer, Land though, but he couldn't say anything here.

"Got room for one more?" Hazelwood asked.

Land looked at the empty seat next to him and tried to think of an excuse to keep her from sitting there, but could not. "Sure," he said. "Have a seat."

"No." She shook her head. "You sit there, and I'll sit on the other side of Paul."

Land went to protest but thought better of it. He stood, and as she slipped past he felt her body against his, her holstered pistol rubbing against his thigh.

She took her place next to the boy and smiled at him. "Your parents don't let you have a TV, do they?" she asked.

Paul shook his head.

"Then you don't know who Zombie Bob is?"

"Well, I know who he is because the other kids . . . "

"Oh good," she said. "It just so happens that I'm a friend of Bob's, and after the show I could take you to meet him backstage."

"Well," said Paul, "I don't really know if . . . "

"Just you, out of all these kids." She gestured at the thousands of schoolchildren around them. "That could really help you could make friends, Paul. They'll want to know you for sure after that."

Land shot her a disapproving look, but she only grinned. Fortunately, the lights began to dim. He heard Hazelwood whisper ,"We'll talk about this later," as a hush settled over the Saddledome.

A spotlight sprang into life, illuminating a lone figure on the platform. It was a silver-haired man in a brown dress uniform, metals dangling at his pocket. His image appeared, a thousand times larger, on the Jumbotron above.

"Howdy, kids," he said. "I'm Colonel Patrick Simonds. I recently got back from directing the troops on the coast, and the top brass asked me, 'Pat, you've just done such a great job in Vancouver. When you get back, just you name it and it's yours.' And I said, 'I want to be the one who talks to the kids at the Saddledome.'"

The colonel wore the same politician's smile that he was never seen without. Affable and grandfatherly, Simonds was just the kind of public face that the military needed to as it pressed its endless, costly war against an enemy that neither thought nor planned.

"Yup," Simonds, went on, "that's my favorite duty, because it's so important for the future. Once we recapture Vancouver and Toronto, then the real challenges will be open to us. New York, *Lost* Angeles . . . " he paused briefly as some of the audience of the chuckled at the popular pun, "maybe even London, Tokyo. That's where you kids will be fighting the zombies. You should think of this day like a 'thank you' in advance. I think the very least we can do is show you how to do it."

Another spotlight suddenly cut through the darkness, spotlighting the black drape at the other opposite of the arena. Out stumbled a putrescent walking corpse, flailing its arms and awkwardly making its way forward. Its jaw was slack, its tongue lolling out in anticipation of its next meal. A collective sigh filled the arena.

"Look at it," Simonds said. "I bet this is the first zombie most of you kids have ever seen. That says something about how far we've come. It's hard to imagine, but there was a time when zombies even walked the streets of Calgary. But thanks to the vaccine developed right here in Canada, none of us will ever be zombies. Remember that: kill a zombie, and that's one closer to killing them all.

"That disgusting creature you're looking at was somebody's brother or father or son once. I'm not going to lie at you about that. But he isn't no more; in fact, he's not a 'he' at all, but an 'it'!"

The colonel pulled his service pistol from its holster and carefully aimed at the brightly lit target, before firing. It sounded little more potent than a cap gun, but Paul twitched in his seat anyway. The bullet struck the zombie's shoulder, and it barely even noticed as it kept shambling forward.

"Ah, I didn't quite get him, did I?" Simonds said. "I've seen zombies lose all their limbs and keep on going. Their brain and their hunger drives them forward. They want to eat our flesh. That's all they want. And they never hesitate before they strike."

The zombie lurched steadily forward, having made it almost halfway to the podium. Many children clenched their teeth with the tension, but Land knew that it would take a minor miracle for that zombie to actually reach the colonel.

"Now," said Simonds, "there are some who say that because this thing was once our loved ones, that means we shouldn't be able to kill it. We all know people like this. These zombie-lovers say that zombies are trainable, that maybe we can toss them the odd steak to keep them happy and teach them to fetch our slippers. But I challenge anyone to look in the eyes of the dead and see anything worth saving. Fellas, can we focus in on that?"

The Jumbotron zoomed in until the zombie's twisted, drooling face filled the screen.

"No life. No intelligence. In humans we see some kind of spark of life; I don't know what it is, but it's always there. You don't see that in zombies. That's what zombies are: humans minus a certain spark, and that's what makes them a perversion in the face of God. There's only one thing to do to them!"

Simonds fired again. This time it struck the zombie square in the head, a perfect killshot. There was a splash of bright red blood, and the creature fell. The Saddledome erupted with cheers and shrill whistles.

The house lights came up. "Pretty cool, eh?" whispered Sgt. Hazelwood to Paul.

"Now before I bring out a very special friend of mine," Simonds said, "we should all rise for the singing of our national anthem." An organ started up with "O Canada," and, as they stood, Land extended his arm behind Paul's back and nudged Hazelwood.

"Sergeant," he whispered. "We need to share a word outside."

"But Mr. Land, it's disrespectful . . . "

"*Now*," he said, just a little too loud, and he started away from the arena. She placed her drink at her feet and stomped after him. He led her right outside onto the Saddledome's front steps, and there she began to snap at him.

"Who do you think you are that you can—"

"Who do you think you are to mess with my student like that?" Land shouted back at her. "God, a military pick-up, you hanging over his shoulder . . . Do you think this isn't hard enough for him anyway? The other kids will never let him hear the end of this."

"Good," Hazelwood said. "I don't want him to forget today. I want him to be traumatized as hell. He'll thank us for it later."

"When? When will he thank us?"

"When he's been dropped in some hellhole and told to kill." There was an absolute conviction in her voice.

"He'll be a man then, and better equipped to handle it than these kids are," Land argued. "Listen to them: they're whistling and cheering! It's just a show for them. That's just how you want them. They don't consider things. They don't think about things. The military doesn't want them to. I don't know who's more braindead, zombies or soldiers."

"How dare you!" Hazelwood cried, her throat hoarsening. "This isn't our world any more! It's theirs! We let our guard down, and they tear our throats out! Society *must* be prepared, prepared in every way, for war! It is the only way!"

Land shrunk back at the force of her argument. "Do you remember," he said, his voice cracking, "when they used to say that watching violent movies was desensitizing, and that was a bad thing?"

For a long time there was silence, and then Hazelwood said, "You've been wondering why all this special treatment for this one kid? What makes him so important?"

Land nodded.

"That was my idea. When I heard about Paul from your school's liaison office, I thought about the way I was before the zombies. A quiet, rural life. No TV. I'd never even witnessed violence. Then I watched while a zombie tore my father's head off while he was working the fields. You know what I did? I didn't run, I didn't scream—I just shut off. The shock almost killed me. But that made me who I am."

Hazelwood was trembling slightly, and clenched her fists where she stood to steady herself. "Maybe you're a zombie-lover too, but you earned that right by fighting for your country up in Alaska. Mr. and Mrs. March never served, but their son will have to. Maybe it was noble once to be a conscientious objector, but now it's lunacy. The more they shelter Paul, the more they try to protect him, the more harm they do.

"I know you have stories like mine. We all do. We are the traumatized generation. A bit older and maybe we could have been better prepared for what was happening. A bit younger and we'd never have known a world without the zombies. If we are to spare the new generation what we went through, they must grow up impervious to trauma. Understand me. I value innocence. That's what Paul is. But in this world of ours, innocence kills." There were tears in her eyes. "It seems wrong, I know. Sometimes I spend whole nights crying into my pillow. But it's the only way. Let them cheer when zombies die. Better they cheer than they scream."

Land turned away from Hazelwood and gazed at the skyscrapers of downtown Calgary, built so many decades ago and standing there like silent memorials to a dead world. "I wasn't made for these times," he said.

"None of us were," she answered.

Land wiped his eyes and turned back to face her. "They've probably brought out Zombie Bob by now. We should get back to Paul."

"Yes," Hazelwood agreed. "He needs our support."

Inside, the Saddledome pulsed with rock music. Land recognized the Doors' "Peace Frog," which, thanks to the tastes of a certain general, became something of a military anthem. To its steady beat Zombie Bob, dressed in full western garb with a white Stetson, wove his way between ten or so zombies, a roaring chainsaw in his hand.

It was part of Zombie Bob's appeal that it seemed like he could die at any moment.

Colonel Simonds was still on the platform, now protected by a half-dozen guards with submachine guns, offering commentary as Bob played the clown, always making it look like the zombies were just about to get him, before getting them instead.

"Careful Bob, there's a another deadhead behind you," said Simonds. Bob did a cartoon double-take and slid the saw around to his back. Then he slid backwards on the dirt, driving the saw through the hapless zombie's midsection. Bob did a pirouette, slicing the zombie mostly in two before slamming his weapon right through its neck. A thick plume of blood shot out.

Land winced at the display. No one he had known in Alaska would attempt anything remotely like Zombie Bob's antics. He and Hazelwood slid back into their seats on either side of Paul, and Land asked the boy, "How are you doing?"

Paul March sat there in wide-eyed, stunned silence. "I . . . uh . . . " was the best answer he could manage.

"Remember," Hazelwood whispered, "there's glass between you and the zombies. They can't get you."

Zombie Bob's opponents seemed selected for maximum diversity; an old granny, a slender college girl, a middle-aged Chinese man, and so on. All that was missing was a child zombie. The media always shied clear of those.

"Wow, look at that, kids," Simonds said. "Remember, you can see Zombie Bob's adventures every Wednesday at 3:00 p.m. on CBC."

"Peace Frog" ended and the music switched gears to a whimsical country waltz. Bob took a while to forget the zombies and offer a few dance steps, tipping the white hat now splattered with blood. Bob pulled away from zombies for a moment to wave to the crowd, eliciting laughter as the zombies lurched up on him from behind. Then he sprang into motion, running circles around the zombies, causing them to bump into each other, trip over each other, fall down. The crowd roared with laughter.

Paul made fist of his hands and squeezed until his knuckles were white. He was trembling hard, unstoppably. Land put a hand on his shoulder to try and steady him, and he felt the reverberations through to his bones.

In this confusion Bob rushed forward with his chainsaw swinging at chest level. He caught two zombies right next to each other and forced the saw through bone and flesh, slicing through both of them. Their legs collapsed, useless, but their upper torsos were not dead and pulled themselves across the dirt with their strong arms. Bob pulled away, ignoring them for the time.

"Two at once, Bob!" Simonds declared. "You've outclassed yourself this time. I don't see how you can top that."

The crowd went mad, screaming, whistling, stomping their feet, sounds echoing through the Saddledome's steel rafters. For a moment Land felt like he was a kid again, listening to a crowd cheering for a wrestling match or a fight in a hockey game. Paul started making noises like little yelps. Land and Hazelwood looked at each other.

"Are you all right, Paul?" Land asked, looking into the boy's eyes. They were beginning to look glassy. Paul grasped hard onto his forearm and squeezed. Land cried out.

Zombie Bob slipped among his remaining foes, so that they lurched at him from every side. Most weeks on his show, he performed some variant of this, positioning himself directly in the densest collection of zombies and fighting his way out. It was a crowd-pleaser with any weapon, and the chainsaw was best of all. He swung it at the zombie in front of him, smoothly slitting it through the middle. On the Jumbotron they could see smoke billowing out of the chainsaw. As he retrieved, it seemed to sputter and die.

The camera caught the expression on Bob's face. It was real panic. This was not that unusual; the TV cameras often found Zombie Bob running for his life.

"Uh-oh," said Colonel Simonds. "Looks like ol' Bob's got himself in trouble again."

Somebody cut out the music just in time for everyone to hear Bob release a stream of profanity. He threw the dead chainsaw in the face of the closest zombie and dove past it, his Stetson tumbling off his bald head in the process. He kicked up dust as he raced away from the remaining zombies, but had the misfortune of tripped over something, landing face-first in the dirt. Before he could run, a strong zombie hand clamped down on one of his legs. He looked back to see a half-zombie, one of those he'd sliced in two earlier, its entrails dragging through the dirt behind it. It squeezed tighter on his leg, shattering bone and pulling away a handful of flesh. Bob's scream hit the steel roof and resonated through the Saddledome's every corner.

"Fuck!" shouted Simonds into his microphone. There was no doubt now—this was not part of the show.

The smell of fresh blood spurred the other zombies on to greater speed. Zombie Bob tried to pull himself to his feet, but they were on him in no time, ripping, tearing at his clothes and his flesh. The entire Saddledome could hear his screams. Piece by piece they devoured him, stuffing human meat by the handful into their mouths. So here it was at last, the death of Robert Smith Harding. Everyone knew he'd die violently, himself most of all. But nobody expected that it would be witnessed by ten thousand schoolchildren.

This would be remembered as the great trauma of a generation. They weren't screaming in excitement now. They were screaming in terror.

Land felt Paul's hand go limp on his arm.

"Fire! Fire! Fire! Fire!" Colonel Simonds shouted the command like a mantra, and his bodyguards loosed a hail of bullets into the mass of zombies. Many of the bullets struck their targets, but those that didn't impacted the bulletproof glass, ricocheting through the arena and off into the crowd. One of these stray bullets caught Simonds in the chest and he collapsed on stage, barely noticed amid all the pandemonium.

Children and adults alike crawled over each other, fueled by the most primal surge of adrenalin, frantically seeking to escape the danger. Bodies swamped the exits and fell from balconies. Land grabbed Paul, ready to carry him out of the Saddledome, but found him limp and cold. He reached for Paul's jugular but felt no pulse.

He has a weak heart, Mrs. March had told him. She must have meant it. This shock must been too much for poor sensitive Paul, and his little heart gave out. Hazelwood looked at him open-jawed, and amid all this chaos noise and chaos everything suddenly seemed so still and calm.

Then Paul's eyes jumped open.

Thank God I was wrong, Land thought first, but then he saw his eyes. He could never explain this to anyone who hadn't seen it for themselves, but the eyes of the dead were different. Simonds was right; they lacked spark, life. This was true even of the freshest zombies.

Paul sank his teeth into Sgt. Hazelwood's forearm, biting down hard. Her legs kicked involuntarily, knocking against the seat in front of her. Her mouth opened to scream, but no noise came out as her eyes glassed over and she sank back into her chair, growing increasingly inert as Paul gnawed through to raw bone. Land grabbed Paul by the hair and yanked back, but even a child zombie possessed inhuman strength, and Paul wouldn't release his grasp on his prize.

The Marches, Land thought. *They live outside of the city. The inoculation drives must have missed them somehow.*

Damned zombie-lovers—they didn't even inoculate their own kid against becoming one of them! How irresponsible can they be?

Land slid his hand down Hazelwood's thigh to her holster. He pulled out her service pistol, drove it into Paul's chin, and squeezed the trigger.

MURRAY LEEDER is the author of the novels *Son of Thunder* and *Plague of Ice* for Wizards of the Coast, as well as more than twenty short stories. He also holds a Ph.D. from Carleton University and has published academic articles in such journals as *Early Popular Visual Culture*, the *Journal of Popular Film and Television*, the *Journal of Popular Culture*, *Clues: A Journal of Detection*, *Popular Music and Society,* and the *Canadian Journal of Film Studies.*

"It's the dark wave that sweeps over things, son, changing the world, readying for the end times. People, they do evil to each other and it opens the door for more evil. Evil deeds call up evil spirit and its hunger enters the dead, it's a sickness on the land . . . "

Aftertaste

John Shirley

8:45 p.m., Saturday Night, West Oakland, California

Dwayne was sick of hearing Uncle Garland talk. The old man would talk about Essy and he would talk about the dope and he would talk about grindin', about everything but his own goddamn drinking. Sitting in that busted wheelchair at the kitchen table, talking and sipping that Early Times. Talking shit about his angeldreams, too. One more word about the dope . . .

But Dwayne tolerated more than just one more word, because he needed Uncle Garland. He needed a place to stay and some place to run to. So he just sat and listened while he waited for Essy to get up, waited for Essy to get them started again. Essy in the next room, had to crash for a while, been two hours already. Fuck it. Dwayne could taste rock at the back of his tongue; smell it high in his nostrils. All in the imagination.

The TV was on, with the sound turned off. A rerun of a show with that guy used to be in *Taxi*. Tony something.

"You listening to me, Dwayne?" Uncle Garland demanded, scratching his bald pate with yellowed fingers. His rheumy eyes looking at Dwayne and not seeing him. Moving with less life than the TV screen. Blind. The old man was blind, but that was easy to forget, somehow.

"Can't hardly not listen, you talking all the time," Dwayne said.

"The dope killing this town, it be killing our people," Garland was saying. "Killing the black man. I'm fixin' to go the Next World, and I'm glad to be goin', Praise Jesus, with the devil eating this world like a pie . . . " Didn't pause to take a breath.

Uncle Garland's place was an apartment in the Projects, in the shadow of the freeway that collapsed in the '89 earthquake. Used to be you heard the freeway booming and rushing all night. Now it was eerie quiet. Or quiet as it ever got in the Projects.

"Tell you some true now," Uncle Garland said, using the expression that always prefaced a long, long lecture. "These are the end times, that the Lord's truth. In my angel dreams, they come to me and tell me it's so. And it's on the news, about the dead people rising. It's in the Bible, son, when the dead rise it's a Sign that the Lord is coming for Judgment—"

"You see that shit in the *Weekly World News*?"

"Radio news, I heard it. A disease in the air, they said, a radiation. The dead rising and hungry for the flesh of the living, Lord, and they—"

"That's complete shit," Dwayne snorted. Why didn't fucking Essy get up? Maybe he wouldn't help him, get him started on the rock today. Cousin Essy think he's a big Grinder now, selling dope, stylin' like a B Boy, but he got nothing to show for it. Not like he paying the rent here. Some grinders they put their family in a nice house, buy them cars. Essy don't give the old man shit, so don't tell me you're the big Fly. Of course, the old man wouldn't accept the money, he'd know it was dope money . . .

"'Tisn't radiation," the old man said, sucking on the pint bottle. "It's the dark wave, the night wave that sweeps over things, son. It changing the world, readying for the end times. People, they do evil to each other and it opens the door for more evil. Evil deeds call up evil spirit and its hunger enters the dead, it's a sickness on the land . . .

Dwayne couldn't stand it anymore. Fuck Essy. He'd get his materials, one way or another.

He stood up abruptly and headed for the door. Put his hand on the knob. Said, over his shoulder, "Uncle you tell Essy I got tired of waiting. I going to—"

"No p'int in telling Essy shit. He dead."

Dwayne felt a cold wave, like that wave of darkness the old man gabbled about, ripping through his gut. "Bullshit."

"I feel it. He died, maybe an hour ago. Got some p'ison in him."

"Shit," Dwayne said again, and opened the door. He wasn't going to go in and check on Essy. Wake him up when he's crashing, he'd go off on you. Anyway the old man was full of shit.

But as he walked down the hallway he felt like Essy was dead, too.

In the kitchen, Garland sat up straighter on his wheelchair: he heard

Essy stirring. Heard the creak of the bedsprings. Garland had been blind so long he scarcely noticed the darkness anymore. But now, it seemed to take on density and weight; his blindness seemed to thicken about him and chill him like a cloud covering the sun.

Heard the shuffling steps coming. Knew for certain what it was. The dream angels had left him in no doubt.

He reached out, found his cane, forced himself to his feet. He rarely stood anymore, but this time the danger of it, of fracturing one of his porous old bones, didn't matter. He crossed to the broom closet by the old, whirring refrigerator. Moving only a little more slowly than the footsteps coming up behind him from the next room. He felt for the knob, found it, pulled the closet open. Found the old pistol where he kept it under the oily rags on the top shelf and drew it out, his hands shaking.

Then thought: What if the dark wave brings me back too?

It wouldn't be Garland, not really him, but . . .

He heard a dream angel whisper: Not you, nor your old body.

He heard the shuffling nearer. Heard no breathing with it. No breathing, not any.

He raised the gun. Raised it to his mouth, pressed the barrel up against the palate, pulled the trigger.

His last thought was: Leaving a kind of gift for it.

Light.

9:57 p.m., Downtown Oakland

Dwayne knew. He knew even before the white guy got out of his car. You could see it by the way he drove up, the car moving almost spastically, and the way he parked, the sedan slung across two parking spaces outside the liquor store, and the way his head moved around like one of those little dashboard dolls that's got a head wobbling on a spring. The white guy was fucked up, really fucked up, and probably on base. Crack cocaine.'

He was opportunity on the hoof.

The white guy had longish red-brown hair, bright blue eyes, and a little reddish mustache. He was driving a tan Acura, maybe a '95, and he had a gold watch on his right wrist. This was looking better and better.

Hobey saw him too. But Hobey was across the parking lot, trotting up real slow. Hobey was too old, too fat. Didn't smoke, drank Night Train instead. Sold the rock sometimes, but never used, and acted like he was ruff because of it.

Dwayne was leaning into the white guy's passenger side window by the time Hobey got there. "Whus'up," Dwayne said. "What you need, tell me, I help,"

The white guy's mouth was hanging open a little. His eyes dilating, shrinking, dilating, shrinking. A tongue so dry you could almost hear the rasp of it as be licked his lips. Word: it was base.

"Rock," the guy said. "Crack." Things white guys called base cocaine.

"How much?'

"Uh—sixty bucks worth."

Man, he was fucked up. Not supposed to make a deal that way, people rip you off. They sure do.

Dwayne almost laughed. But he said, "Okay, I take you there."

"Get in."

Hobey was coming around to the guy's driver side, "What you need, chief? I get it for you, I find the best—"

"I got it," Dwayne snapped. "I takin' care of it." He gestured briskly to the white guy. "Hobey's a rip-off artist. He gafflin' people all the time. Let's go."

The guy changed gears like a robot and they backed out, nearly plowing into the brick wall on the other side of the lot. Then they were careening down the street, Dwayne hissing, "Yo, chill this thing down, man, you get the cops on us."

The white guy slowed down to a crawl.

10:15 p.m.

This part of San Pablo Avenue was mostly liquor stores; flyblown bars with the light bulbs burned out in their signs; adult video stores where fag hustlers cruised the video galleries. Dwayne had worked the video stores doing the tease thing, as Essy called it. Pretending you were a fag, going into the booth with a real fag. He puts some tokens in the machine, some fag video comes on, he's watching it and you're kind of messing around with his dick with one hand, distracting him, making a lot of noise about it, then lifting his wallet, going through his pockets while his pants are down. Then you say "Oh shit—I think somebody's coming, they checkin' the booths," and you split. It takes them a minute to discover they are ripped off and—

"There it is," Dwayne said, now. "That hotel."

It was an old white wedge of a building, tall and narrow, on a sort of island where three streets almost intersected. The rest of the block was abandoned office space, rickety buildings from the early part of the twentieth century. Doc was standing in the doorway of the hotel, all in white as usual. A white suit, with a pink carnation. His black Jag was parked just a few feet from him where he could keep an eye on it.

"Thas the dude," Dwayne said. "Got him a Jaguar XKE, doing this shit." Dwayne couldn't keep the admiration out of his voice. That Doc had it together.

"Pull up over there," Dwayne said. "No, fuck, don't—shit!"

The guy cut across two lanes with a screeching right angle turn.

"Shit!" Dwayne looked around as the guy parked. No cops. Lucked out again.

"What's your name?" the white guy asked.

"Dwayne."

"I'm Jim. Okay . . . uh . . . " He looked through the window at Doc. Knew he couldn't go over and buy the shit himself. Or thought he couldn't, anyway. Probably could have. Probably didn't need Dwayne.

But Dwayne was banking on Jim White Guy not knowing that. And. in fact, Dwayne could feel he was going to connect good here. Fuck Essy. Dwayne could grind his own business. Essy could come asking Dwayne for a start. (No way Essy was dead, that old man was getting brain damaged from drinking . . . Drinking kill you . . .)

Jim went on, "What you want for this?"

Dwayne said, "A dove."

"Half a dove."

So he knew what a dove was anyway. A forty dollar rock of crack.

"Whatever you wanta do, hey homes, it's okay. I'm not one of these gafflers like Hobey—"

"Yeah, yeah." The guy was getting a weary look as he took a chip of rock out from a jar, broke it in half in his teeth, put one of the halves in a pipe . . . Shit. The pipe was a *pipe*. It was a motherfucking briar pipe. Lighting it with a Bic. Sucking at it.

Dwayne felt his scalp contract, his mouth go dry as he watched. Smelled the oily perfume and insecticide tang of the smoke. "You oughta get yourself a stem, man. What kind of fucking pipe is that?"

"Only one they had left in the store. I'll get a stem later. Here's sixty. Don't cruise on me, you'll be fucking up a good thing." The guy was involuntarily grinning as he said it.

"Gimme a blast," Dwayne said. The guy handed over the pipe and the Bic. Dwayne took a hit. The pipe worked shitty, but good enough for now, except it burned his fingers having to hold the Bic upside down over the bowl. The blast feeling blossomed in him. It rushed through him and instantly he began to work on ways to get more. This guy, no telling how much money he had. Probably had a bank card. Maybe—

"Go on," Jim said, taking the pipe back.

Dwayne folded the sixty bucks into his palm. "Keep that pipe low, watch for cops." Still shaking a little from the blast, he got out and crossed to Doc, thinking: Play this guy carefully.

Saturday Night, 10:50 p.m.

Hobey almost went to sleep on the bus. Last time he did that he slept past his stop, took him half the night to get home. He was tired and when he was tired he noticed the creakiness in his bones more. Fuck that damn little nigger, that Dwayne, he be stepping in every time something should be Hobey's coming down . . . Someone had left an *Oakland Tribune* on a seat. There were headlines on the metro section that said: THREE MORE CRACK DEATHS CORONER DOUBTS OD CAUSE.

"Huh," Hobey said. Some bad shit going around. That kind of shit, that's why he didn't smoke. Shit like that.

The night sky was jet black, looking starless over the glaring anti-crime lights on Martin Luther King, Jr. Way when Hobey got off the last bus.

He turned down Winston Street. There was action over to the parking lot of the 7-Eleven, but Hobey didn't care, he was too tired to fuck with trying to get in on it. Some of those piped-up motherfuckers shoot you, Uzi your guts out soon as look at you. Don't be fucking with it when you're weary.

He stalked past a dirt lot where an old crackerbox house was almost demolished. Hobey used to work in demolition, before he got kicked out of the union, and this mess made him shake his head. The demolition had been subcontracted to some damn non-union crew! Just went after it with crowbars and a rented plow. It looked like a tornado had flattened the house at random, a scattered pile of plasterboard and timbers like a crazy snail shell for the slug of a rotten old mattress left in the house during demolition . . .

Hobey stopped and stared.

The mattress had moved. Had humped up, a little. By itself. Humping up so there was a dark little cave under it. Fringe of wet, mildewed mattress stuffing hanging down over the mattress cave. Like a gooey wig over the face that was coming into the light, showing, now, in the little cave. Something crawling out . . .

Just some homeless nigger, Hobey thought.

So why was he scared to look at it? Why did he feel, at the same time, scared to look away from it?

The fella was about forty feet away, coming out on his hands and knees. All raggedy. Looked beat up, like he'd been tossed in there and stuff dumped on him. Maybe that mattress got dragged from somewhere else to cover him. The man ditched because they thought he was dead, most likely. Hobey bad seen it before. Somebody ODs, the rockhouse doesn't want the body around so they drag it to the nearest river or vacant lot, dump it, cover it up, let the bugs chew it up so nobody knows who it is . . .

Only they thought this guy was dead and he wasn't.

Should stay out of this. But he was feeling kind of low about himself, felt like doing for somebody, give him a lift. This man was lower down than he was . . . Must be getting old.

"You need some help, man. You lookin' poorly," Hobey said, picking his way through the debris toward the man. Didn't recognize him. Black man, maybe was a teenager, not much older. Not standing up straight yet, hunched over. Something hanging off his head, maybe mattress stuff . . .

Ten feet away. Hobey stopped. The man took a shaky step, bringing him into a streak of streetlight shine. Lifting his face toward Hobey.

He had eye sockets full of ants.

His eyes were gone. Ants, instead. Ants in the empty sockets, the ants moving all squiggling and searchingly the way ants do. Seeking and chewing, shiny and restless. No eyes. Ants.

"My Lord, man . . . " Hobey breathed. "What they done to you . . . "

Then he saw the spike. Big rusty metal spike from some concrete support of the house. Bent and blunt. Right through the man's chest.

Right through the motherfucker's heart.

Saturday Night, 10:55 p.m.
White guy on a binge, that's what he was, Didn't smoke most days, but tonight he got mad at his wife or something, he go out on a binge, Dwayne thought. Not used to it, puts him farther out of his head. He's righteous tweakin'.

Dwayne watched Jim White Guy crossing the street. Walking to the bank machine. A little island of light in the dim street: a little high tech sweetness in the concrete and fake marble.

Leaving the keys in the car. Leaving the keys with Dwayne. A complete stranger.

Got to be tweaked to do that.

Now Jim White Guy was standing at the machine, swaying, twitching a little, trying to figure out the buttons. Probably end up leaving his card in the machine. Better check. When Jim Pale come back, they going to need that card. They'd already burned through the dove, and another one, and the guy was making his second run to the bank machine, and he'd left the keys in his Acura, and . . .

The high was buzzing in Dwayne, but the buzz was fading. Time for another hit. He lit up some of the base he'd palmed when Jim White Guy wasn't looking, sucked it up in the stem, the glass pipe he'd picked up on Telegraph Avenue.

There. There it is. Spreading out in him, expanding through his nervous system. The blast. The rush spreading its wings. Wings made of flashpaper on fire. Going up, gone.

Blasts were getting shorter, weaker. Need bigger hits.

Maybe some black tar to go with it, ease the landing.

Maybe take the car now.

But then Jim White Guy was back, sliding in. "I got some money for that pussy, too," the guy said. Thinking he was real street smart talking about pussy that way.

They made a stop at Doc's dope house, Dwayne breaking some of the dove off with a thumbnail, sliding it into his change pocket while he was walking around behind the Acura. Then Dwayne said, "Okay. Left at the corner. If you want ho's."

It was coming together in Dwayne's head. He knew a whore, Joleen, used an empty building up on Martin Luther King and Winston. That the opportunity,

They found Joleen easy. She was a floppy-titted bitch with skinny legs, not getting much work, walking up and down the sidewalk in front of the condemned house. Across the street from the demolition lot where Samson Ramirez had dumped that OD case out of his rockhouse. Joleen, clutching a fake patent leather purse, was moving back and forth like a wind-up toy, marching on broken-down white Adidas gone gray from the street.

Jim White Guy was so high anything with tits looked good to him. Two minutes, and Dwayne had him out of his car, across the sidewalk, making a quick deal for Joleen. Acting like Joleen was going to do them both. Joleen was cheap. Didn't work out of a house or a motel or anything, she couldn't handle the overhead. Bitch just do it right there in your car or wherever was handy. Forty dollars for two. Another time, if he was trying to get some pussy from a toss up, he'd trade some smoke for it. But now he didn't want to waste time in negotiations.

"I got a place back here," Joleen said, leading them up a walkway used for storing garbage cans. The side door had been knocked off its hinges long ago. They stepped through it, went down a stairs, into a furnace room. There was a pile of dirty blankets in the corner; gray light coming through a grimy window from the street.

"Shit," Jim White Guy said, whirling on Dwayne. "You setting me up to rob me? I got some friends, I'll fucking have you killed—anything happens to me, they—"

"Yo, chill out, we here for some pussy. Look, I got my dick out. I usin' my dick to rob you?" Dwayne pulled out his dick, wagged it at Joleen, who dutifully went to her knees. Started sucking. Wouldn't be able to get it hard, after all the base. Not Jim White Guy's dick either. But the man was too piped-up to care.

"I'll take her from behind while she does you," Jim White Guy said. But what he was doing was firing up his pipe.

"All right, I hear you!" Dwayne said, and slapped Jim's side in a companionable way; taking the Acura's car keys from Jim White Guy's jacket pocket as the white guy got his blast.

"Suck the man's dick, Joleen, he payin' for this shit," Dwayne said.

Joleen silently shifted over to the white guy, unzipping his pants, taking his pasty, shriveled thing out in her hands.

"You gonna give me a blast, honey?" she said, playing with his dick.

The guy took out the pipe, put it in her mouth, flicked the Bic onto the glass bowl. Not noticing Dwayne moving off behind him.

"Got to pee," Dwayne muttered.

Then he slipped out the door, out to the car. With luck, the white guy be distracted for a few minutes, long enough for Dwayne to get away with the Acura.

And it worked okay, as far as it went.

Tuesday, 2:05 p.m., Fremont, California

"Are you?" she said. Her tone matched her expression. Brittle.

"Yeah," Jim Diggins said, "I am. I'm sure." Feeling like it was the truth. He was sure he'd never do cocaine again. How could he do cocaine again after all this? (But, yeah, he'd said the same thing before the last binge . . .)

She was angrily taking clothes out of the dryer, putting them directly into her suitcase, hardly bothering to fold them. Jim wouldn't have thought that you could take clothes out of a dryer angrily, but Patty could do anything angrily he'd discovered. She could brush her teeth angrily.

"You're passive-aggressive, you know," she was saying. "This is just another way to express hostility. Getting stoned, getting robbed."

"That's a pretty solipsistic idea of things," Diggins said. Jim Diggins. Jim White Guy. Jim Pale.

He was leaning against the concrete sink next to the washer. A cobweb hung down from one of the old two-by-fours that held up the kitchen floor, feather tickling the back of Diggins' neck. He didn't have the energy to move away from it. He felt like the core had been dug out of him. He might collapse inward, any second. His head fall into his chest. Fold up like the Scarecrow of Oz without straw.

"Jim," his wife was saying, "I heard this crap three times before. You were sure, this time. No more, you said." She was a thin woman, with long straight brown hair hanging to her bony ass. She had violet-blue eyes that everyone thought were her best feature. She wore shorts, which maybe her legs were too skinny for. She looked especially pinched and taut when she was angry.

"This time I'll get counseling."

"You got counseling, Jim."

"I mean, therapy, serious therapy. Maybe Schick Center or something."

"How about a car? Are they going to give you a car at the Schick center?"

"We got insurance."

"We'll still lose money and it'll take a month to get the insurance payoff."

"Look—" He was near tears, crushed by humiliation. "I know I'm a screw-up sometimes but most of the time I work hard for you and Donna . . . "

"I don't want to hear that speech either." She carried the suitcase out of the laundry room to the stairs.

Ten minutes later she was gone. She'd taken Donna, their four-year-old and she'd gone, her sister coming all the way from San Jose to pick her up. Jim doubted this was intended to be permanent. It was some kind of . . . therapy. Patty's way of giving him shock treatment. It was like making him stand in a corner. More humiliation. What really hurt was not being able to hold it against her. Who could blame her? He'd had a drug relapse, and he'd done cocaine again—crack this time, for God's sake. Crack. Which had a nasty street smell about it, the taint of crazies and thieves and whores. And he'd wallowed with all of those—with a thief, with the sleaziest kind of whore (could she have given him AIDS from an unfinished blowjob? could he say for sure she hadn't?), and a crazy. He was the crazy. He'd been totally out of his head. A miracle he'd only had his car stolen. Could have been robbed of his credit cards. Could have been murdered. Could have been killed, driving under the influence of the stuff.

That fucker Dwayne.

Jim thought about it as he got himself a Corona and walked through the house from the kitchen, through the dining room and the parlor, to the front room they never used except as a kind of showplace for the furniture Patty'd picked out. His footsteps sounded loud in the house. Lot of creaking boards he'd never noticed before. He could hear water trickling in the sink of the front bathroom where his little girl had left it running, as usual. He couldn't bring himself to turn it off. He crossed to the window, his hand tight on the beer bottle. Looked between the white curtains at the big, wind-blown oaks in the Barton's front yard, across the street. On the ground beneath the trees, tangled shadows of branches and leaves moved like dark seaweed in a translucent ocean.

That fucker Dwayne had seen him coming. Seen a stoned stupid middle-class white dumbshit.

He drank half the bottle of beer down all at once. The beer was like running cold water on a burn. For a moment it smoothed over some of the pain. The depression.

"You knew it was going to make you depressed afterwards," Patty had said. "When you go on one of these stupid binges you always feel like total shit for a week afterwards. How come you don't think about that before you—?"

"I don't know, hell, I don't know," he'd said. "I just get too stressed out or something and it's like somebody throws a switch, I just turn into a fucking drug robot and I go find it. I mean—I've got it down so it only happens once or twice a year now—"

"Once a decade is too damn much," she'd said. Snapping it.

"I know. I know."

"Christ, don't you think about afterwards at all, Jim?"

"All I can think about is how I'm scared to crash. As long as I keep the drug coming I don't think about it." And he snorted derisively at himself, mumbling, "It's like skydiving with a busted parachute. It's a great ride till you hit the ground."

No sympathy at all from her this time. He couldn't blame her. That came sneering back at him again. Could. Not. Blame her.

For about the five-hundredth time since he'd gotten out of the Crisis Ward of the hospital Sunday afternoon, he thought about killing himself. Get a gun. *Blam*. Brains on the wall. Or maybe use a noose, hang himself. I ought to suffer, he thought,

He thought about killing Dwayne, too.

My car. How dare he touch my car.

The phone rang. He walked in a dream to it. It took an effort of will just to pick it up and say, "Hello?"

"This is the Oakland Police Department calling for Mr. James Diggins."

"That's me."

"You reported a stolen car . . . " He read out the license number, the other specs.

"That's my car."

"The car was found by a patrolman yesterday morning. It's been towed to a lot at . . . "

Tuesday, 3:30 p.m.

Why had they taken only three wheels? he wondered numbly.

The Acura was tilted onto its right side wheel rims and the left rear tire. The car's hood was standing open. Dwayne must have gotten spooked or burned out, Jim decided, after taking three tires. Anything that could easily be detached from the engine was missing. The front seats were missing, too. The trunk had been cleaned out, tools, tire and jack were missing. The headlights were missing. The radio was gone, pried from the dashboard like a rotten tooth.

And the windshield was smashed out by vandals.

The insurance company would want to have the car repaired. It would be expensive, but still cheaper than a new car. It'd take months. Then he'd get to drive around in this reminder of the night he'd had a nasty fight with Patty, gone out and gotten blown away on coke and fucked up royal. Maybe even got AIDS for all he knew.

He stared at the hulk of his car. Stripped. Picked over like a mollusk after the gulls had been there. A lifeless shell.

Shit. He couldn't believe it. He'd let this happen to the family car. It was a ton or so of pure, raw, undiluted symbol. Sitting on the hardened dirt of a tow-away lot.

That fucker Dwayne. It wasn't Dwayne's fault, ultimately, he knew that. It was his own fault. Dwayne was just a drug addict who'd seen an opportunity that Jim Diggins had stupidly dropped in his lap. But, nevertheless, Dwayne had preyed on him. It was like stealing from a blind man. A retarded blind man. Dwayne was raw, undiluted symbol, too.

And Jim wanted to kill him.

Thursday Night, 10:07 p.m., Oakland
A sultry night at Winston Street and Martin Luther King, Jr. Way. Lots of goods going around. Joleen and Binda turning toss-up tricks to get their blasts. Dwayne pacing in front of the rockhouse. Thinking: two hundred forty-five dollars. For all that stuff I got out of that Acura. Could have gone to the joint for stealing a car. Five to ten years in prison for two Cs and forty-five fucking dollars. Nobody wanted to buy a hot car. All that risk for a hour's worth of rock . . .

Then here came Samson Ramirez in a new BMW that looked carved out of a single block of snow and ice. So new it didn't have the plates on it, just a sticker in the windshield.

Samson was half white, half Mexican, but he'd been on the street so long Dwayne thought of him as just another homeboy. He was a hard motherfucker, and getting harder as his biz got bigger. He was supposed to he pulling down even more money than Doc now, which was what his white BMW was about, Dwayne figured, to advertise that.

Samson was pulling up in the white BMW, parking across the street and a ways down, not wanting to associate the car too obviously with the rockhouse. He had long, wavy brown hair in a fancy unisex perm, a brown leather jacket and brown leather pants with just a touch of a Latin flare about them. He was small but good looking, with his white mama's green eyes and his Mexican daddy's perfect white teeth. Perfect, but he'd had an incisor replaced with a gold tooth, to go with his thick gold chains and maybe just for the flash of wealth in his patronizing smile. They said he didn't do his own product, but some combination of crystal meth and Demerol instead. You could see it in the way he moved. Real fast, but real smooth.

Raiders came out of the rockhouse to meet Samson on the sidewalk. Raiders was a tall black man in a red sweat suit he never changed or washed, a gold Raiders' medallion around his neck and a blue waistpack slung around his hips. The pack hung like a scrotum because of the snub-nosed pistol in it. They called him Raiders because when his talk wasn't about grinding it was always about the Oakland Raiders; he held the team in reverence like they were gods.

Dwayne thought: Maybe I do it now. I could walk up to Samson when he's talking to Raiders and ask for the delivery work, talk him up good.

But he didn't have the nerve yet. The man didn't know him.

Dwayne stepped back into a doorway, where he wouldn't be noticed. He waited, listening in.

" 'Nother one died," Raiders was telling Samson, "and 'nother one killed with his head busted in."

"Same as old Hobey?" Samson asked.

"Same as Hobey. Head busted in like a melon."

Dwayne felt a strange contraction in his stomach. Hobey was dead? He hadn't heard. It was never a surprise to hear that someone he knew had died. He'd seen his father beat his mother with piece of pipe and he wasn't surprised when she died in the hospital. And two of his homeboys had died within a year of each other, one fighting over base and the other from heroin. And he had an aunt was a whore, died of pneumonia that was probably from AIDS. But Hobey had seemed like a survivor, like he was too careful to get himself popped.

It was kind of scary, Hobey being dead. Made Dwayne remember what Uncle Garland had said about Essy.

"They think dogs are gettin' into them," Raiders was saying. "Somebody bust their heads in, then wild dogs come along . . . "

"You making me sick, I don't need to hear this," Samson said, grimacing. "What makes you think it was the silver cap that did the other ones?"

"I sold it to them both half-hour before. One of them went right here, died in the house, other one out in the alley."

"You get rid of them?"

"What you think?"

"So what you want me to do about this shit?"

"Maybe it's the bug spray."

"Everybody uses bug spray for bonding."

"Not this industrial shit we been getting. They use Black Flag or something. We oughta go back to it, maybe it's this stuff that's been—"

"Shut up. It's not us, pendajo. Okay? This bug spray I got makes the stuff go farther, people like it, they come back for more, that's bueno."

"Reporters was hanging around the 'hood, 's'afternoon. Nobody told 'em shit. And The Man be coming around. Asking shit."

"They connect it to us?"

"Not yet."

"Then fuck 'em. It's not us anyway." Samson made a dismissive motion, a hummingbird blur of his hand, and started toward the front steps that led up to the old two-bedroom stucco place that was the neighborhood rockhouse.

Dwayne started to go after Samson. Froze when he saw Raiders glare at him. They'd already had a run-in. Come back when you got the green, Raiders had said, we not hiring. You come around with money or we hammer your whole fucking body.

Samson was going into the house. Opportunity walking away. Dwayne rubbed his Bic-thumb callous with a forefinger, could almost feel a dove there, between his fingers. Could picture putting the dove in a pipe, firing up. Could almost taste it.

Once Samson was in his "office" there'd be no getting to see him. Not from where Dwayne was at in the pecking order.

Dwayne smelled base, someone smoking somewhere. Turned and saw Joleen in the front seat of a beat-up van, her head bobbing over some guy's lap. The guy firing a blast in a broken-off stem, the glow pulsing, lighting up a little blue skull tattoo on the guy's cheek, and showing his face. He was a big, dirty yellow-haired white guy, a biker type, with an overgrown beard and matted hair; a biker who'd had to sell his bike for crack.

Dwayne smelled the burning base. Watched the flare of pipe. Heard the biker grunt as the blast rocked him.

Fuck it. Dwayne couldn't stand it. He started up the stairs, after Samson. "Yo, Samson— !" he called after him. "Yo, my bro, wait up—"

But then Jim White Guy stepped out of the bushes with a gun. A .45 automatic. He was grinning. Motherfucker was real proud of himself.

～

10:15 p.m.

"You fucking with me, right?" Samson said.

Raiders shook his head. "While I was out. Ramon told me. Three more dead, just all in the last half hour, right here in this fucking house."

Samson and Raiders were in the pipe room, which had once been someone's living room. Now it was a big box, just a place to sit and smoke crack with a couple of burn-pocked mattresses on the floor and a smell like a shitty diaper from the plugged-up toilet in the bathroom off to one side. Naked bulb, windows double-boarded over, linoleum curling up off the sagging wooden floor. Intricately calligraphed posse graffiti on the walls next to the mattresses. One broken stem in a corner.

Samson swore in Spanish. "What you do with them?"

"Some of the posse taking them to the dumpster behind the Pioneer Chicken place. I fucking don't know. I ain't smoking none of that silver cap."

"You don't be smoking at all around here. I go off on you, I catch you. Don't smoke at work." But he was thinking about something else. "We use up this batch, then maybe we switch to Black Flag for the bonding agent in the stuff—who's making it up?"

"The base? Ramon."

"He get sick?"

"Hard to tell with Ramon."

"Okay, we get rid of the Bug Deth now, but we use up this batch of the cooking. That's forty, fifty thousand dollars, Raiders."

Raiders looked like he was about to argue when Ramon and Buzzy came running in, yelling, and Ramon was missing half his face.

10:18 p.m.

Jim stared at Dwayne. Jim wasn't sure how he was going to do this. Or what exactly he was going to do. Should he really do it, go ahead and kill him? Or maybe just kneecap him? Bust his knees open with a bullet. Fucking change his life for him. Ruin his transportation.

"How much you get for that shit you took off my car, Dwayne? More'n four hundred bucks? Probably less. Pretty pathetic, asshole."

Dwayne just stared back at him. "You got me confused with somebody, man." Maybe if he kept saying it, the guy'd buy it. Just keep saying it, make him doubt himself.

"No. Uh-uh. I was fucked up but I remember you vividly, Dwayne. And

Joleen. I found her, see I figured she wasn't in on it, so I didn't shoot her, and she told me you'd be here eventually."

They were standing in the thick shadows by the dark green bushes, standing amidst dog crap in the balding front yard at an angle where nobody could see them but they could see most everybody. Jim White Guy had picked the spot carefully.

Inside the house. Ramon on his knees clutching his face, blood runneling down his arm, and twining through the links of the gold chain on his chest. Sobbing. Samson trying to get a coherent story from him.

"The bodies in the dumpster what?"

And then the naked, filthy guys came stinking and stumbling into the piperoom and when Ramon saw them he screamed and scurried away on his hands and knees. Samson thought they were some kind of homeless lunatics until he saw that one of them was dragging his guts behind him on the floor.

Outside, Dwayne saying, "You mixed up, man, you piped up or something, got me mixed up wid somebody. It dark out here, too. Let's go in the light, over there, you see if it really me. Come on, put your gun in your pocket." All of this was halfhearted. Dwayne realized he was hoping Jim White Guy would shoot him. Put a hole in the hole.

"You lying sack of shit," Jim Diggins said.

Dwayne took a step back, into the streetlight shine. Jim took a step toward him. Aimed the gun.

Then they heard the screaming from the house, and the gunshots. Three seconds of Dwayne and Jim gaping at the house. Another thirty seconds of uncertainty, staring at one another. Dwayne saying, "We better get the fuck—" That's when the naked, coughing man with brains on his fingers came staggering out of the darkness by the bushes, coming from the back door. Coming at them.

Dwayne knew it was brains on the naked man's fingers, because of the head the dude was carrying under his arm. It was a handsome head with a lot of hair that waved like a jacket fringe as the naked guy moved. A big gouge taken out of the skull. It was Samson's head.

"Oh fuck," Dwayne said. Recognizing Samson's still-twitching face on the severed head. Seeing that the naked motherfucker lunatic had one nasty, filth-caked hand in the hole in Samson's head, was scooping out the brains, eating them, using his fingers like a kid eating the frosting left over in a bowl . . .

Jim and Dwayne stared at the naked guy. A white guy with a bloated stomach and snaggly brown teeth. The naked guy was staring back without blinking, his milky eyes not moving. Standing there, swaying like he might fall over any second.

Jim was making a choking sound down in his throat.

The naked guy dropped Samson's head. Thump. It rolled a little, in the grass. The naked dude thrust his head out a little on his neck, like a cat, and sniffed at them. Sniff. Sniff again. Then he made a croaking sound, his mouth exuding a stink that made Dwayne want to puke. He took a step toward Dwayne. Sniffing. Made another sound. A word this time.

"Base."

He reached his hands up toward Dwayne's head.

Dwayne backed away and fell over. The guy dropped to his knees beside Dwayne and gnashed his teeth at him, reached for his head and . . .

Dwayne hoarsely yelling, "Jim, help me, man!" This wasn't the way to die. Not this way. Uh-uh, no.

Jim hesitated. Then he fired the .45 at the naked guy. *Blam.* The flash strobe lighting up the yard for a tenth of a second, a flame licking out, the dead man staggering—

Oh yes, Dwayne knew it was a dead man.

Staggering, turning toward Jim, all his movements like flinches. The dead man with a hole right through its heart.

Jim felt unreal, looking at the walking dead man. Like he should lean back in his chair and reach for the popcorn and just let things happen on a screen. He fought the feeling, thinking: this is happening to me. Aiming the gun this time as the corpse came at him, aiming at the dead man's head. *Blam*, flash, right between the eyes. It went down like a puppet with its strings cut.

Then it started thrashing, kind of floppy-sideways on the ground, like a landed fish. Making sputtering sounds, shit and blood running down its leg from its butt. One of its eyes swelling up, popping out with yellow and red fluid, as it began to crawl with one arm, pulling itself toward them.

"Base," it rasped. "Crack. Rock. Silver top. Base."

There were three more coming around the other corner of the house. Two more on the street, coming down the sidewalk. Mostly naked. One of them didn't have any eyes, and it had a rusty piece of metal through its middle, its head moving herky-jerky. All of them coming toward Jim and Dwayne.

One of them was carrying Joleen's head. Her head raggedly torn off at the neck. Holding her head up to its face, biting into Joleen's forehead. The naked men coming at them sniffing, snuffling . . .

Dwayne and Jim ran up the stairs, into the house.

Both of them yelling the same thing so much in synch it sounded rehearsed: "FUCK FUCK FUCK FUCK FUUUUUUCK!"

10:35 p.m.

They found two freshly killed women in the front hall, one with her head missing, the other one with her head only half attached. The top gone from that head. Scooped out. Part of the brain. Just part of it. They only wanted . . .

Jim threw up in the pipe room. Samson's body was curled up in one corner, a puddle still spreading out from it, Ramon dead beside it, face down. The back of his head gone. One of the naked guys was clawing feebly at a closet door. Strings of entrails had dragged behind it, leaving a rancid trail on the floor, the top of its head shot off. It was scraping like a cat at the closet door, and they could hear someone sobbing in there, someone hiding in the dark closet.

The naked bulb lit the room brightly, every corner of it. Stark and sharp.

Jim straightened up, feeling like he was going to hyperventilate and walked over to the crawling thing at the closet door (thinking about what it was, with quiet amazement: a human being gone literally rotten, dead meat dragged around by hunger like an empty cart dragged by a rabid horse. It was entropy that could feel hunger; scraping at the door in a tape loop of robotic stupidity, a thing that had once been a person, someone whose picture had appeared in some high school year book . . .) and shot it twice in the back of the head, near the spine. It twitched and slumped, then started moving again—but weak now, like a dying roach. Probably have to incinerate the son of a bitch to really kill him, Jim thought.

Feeling numb, Jim dragged it away by the ankle and shoved it in the bathroom, crammed a board under the doorknob to lock the thing in. It made faint scrabbling sounds behind the door.

Jim went back to the closet. It was a long way across the little room. "Come on out, man, I shot the fucking thing," Jim said to the guy in the closet. He wanted living people around him.

Dwayne was pushing bodies up against the door to the hall. Samson's headless body, Ramon's body. Dwayne was crying without tears, his face contorted like a little kid's. Jim looked at him and thought: He's no more criminal than I am. Just another guy on a street corner. Used to be a kid watching Saturday morning cartoons.

Dragging mattresses up against the door, dumping them on the bodies, now. That wouldn't work for long. Those things could pull people's heads off. They were strong.

Jim opened the closet door. A black dude in a grimy jogging outfit was crouched in there, hugging his knees, shaking. An Oakland Raiders medallion on a heavy gold chain around his neck. There was a little snub-nosed gun on the floor between his feet. Probably used up all the rounds in it.

"Raiders, thas Raiders," Dwayne said.

"There a phone here?" Jim asked Raiders, tasting vomit in his mouth.

"They gone?"

"No. They're outside," Jim said. Fighting panic. Fighting the urge to shove the guy out of the closet and get in it himself. "I said, 'Is there a phone here?' " Don't lose it don't lose it don't lose it . . .

"In the office."

"Where's that?"

"Behind the steel door, down the hall. Give me that fucking gun."

"No way." Jim turned his back on Raiders. Stepped over the corpse. The dead thing made a movement with its whole body like a worm on a hot sidewalk, and then lay still again.

Jim stopped in the middle of the room, his gun in his hand, wanting to scream but not having the energy, still sick to his stomach, thinking that all this should feel dreamlike, but it didn't now, not anymore.

That was because there was a smooth and ordinary continuity between being strung out, crashing on crack, perceiving himself as human vermin . . . and being here, with the dying and the dead who moved around.

It all felt like one, seamless thing, to him. Like the fall of a pebble into a mineshaft was part of the pebble's splashing into slime and mud. It had all led right here.

The hall door heaved inward, cracking down the middle. A black woman's face with milky eyes in the break. Big woman wearing blood-stained designer jeans, but naked above the waist. She had one enormous pendulous breast, the other mostly chewed away. Somehow he knew she'd chewed it away herself. One of her eyes was missing. Her upper lip raggedly absent so that her teeth showed in permanent feral baring. She was pushing through the blocked doorway, pressing the broken wood aside, moving slow as lava over the dead bodies and the mattress blocking her way.

Fumbling, but inexorable, like the motion of a big maggot feeling its way along, as she shoved through the broken door.

Climbing over the dead. The dead climbing over the dead.

"Base," she said, in a croak. "Crack. Rock. Silver top. Base."

"Some kind of poison in the base," Dwayne whispered to himself. He was standing with his back to the wall opposite the door, just looking at her. "Kills them and the dark wave brings them back."

"The dark what?" Jim asked.

"Garland . . . Uncle Garland said—" He shook his head. "It's just too much greed, he said one time. Spills over and changes things . . . "

Dwayne and Jim stared at the woman, and then at the two dead men coming in behind her. They weren't cooperating with her consciously, but shoving in beside her like impatient commuters forcing their way onto a BART train. Two walking dead men, one white, an aging punk rocker, and the other black. Their faces peeling away, One of them missing his eyes.

The light flickered. Jim thought the bulb was going to go out and they'd be in here, in the dark with these things sniffing after them. The light flickered again, but didn't quite go out. The shadows fluttered and shifted, distorting the way things looked. Like the faces on those two living dead men in the hall. Jim thought, in the flickering light, that their faces had changed. Their faces become Dwayne's face, Jim Diggins' face. Mouthing, "Base, Rock. Silver Top. Base."

Jim nodded. Looking at himself dead, face blue, skin peeling away, bone in his throat exposed like the broomstick in a scarecrow. Flies crawling in and out of his nostrils.

And the truly-dead, those that the two living-dead men were crawling over, were Patty and some black woman Jim had never seen, but heard Dwayne mumble, "My aunt . . . "

Dead Dwayne and dead Jim clambering over Patty and the black woman, crawling toward the living Dwayne and Jim; the dead, reaching out for a hit, a dose, a blast: of life.

The light flickered again, and then the men crawling through the doorway were no longer Dwayne and Jim, they were once more men with the faces of strangers, and they were coming on through, stumbling toward them, sniffing, snuffling. Toward Dwayne's head and Jim's head.

Going for the cocaine they smelled in their living brains. Some particular combination of drug residue and brain chemistry. Some semblance of life. In some sense mutated by crack to hunger for crack-rancid brain . . . living brain.

Jim raised his gun—

Raiders stepped up from behind, clouted Jim on the side of the head with the empty snubnose. Jim went to his knees, skull tolling like a cracked bell, and Raiders yanked the gun from Jim's hand, ran at the big dead black woman shrieking "FUCKING FREAK BITCH CUNT!" Firing the gun into her face. She threw her arms around him like a loving mother, then fell backwards, pulling him onto her. The two hungry dead men behind her lunged onto him, biting down on his head. Sharing it, biting into Raiders' skull from both sides. Jim could hear the sound of it, of their teeth in the bone of Raiders' cranium. A squeaking grating sound that seemed louder than Raiders' scream.

Then Raiders was quiet, and there were wet, crunching noises. Dwayne said, "Fuck this," and was dragging a mattress up, holding it like a shield. Jim got up, got behind the mattress with him, and helped him shove it onto the mass of feeding dead blocking the doorway, using the mattress to keep the dead down so Jim and Dwayne could scramble over it and out into the hall. Two more of the dead were swaying in the front door. Dwayne and Jim dodged to the right, down the hall. The office. Through the open steel door

A kitchen. An AK47, without a magazine in it, lay on a old, ornate wooden kitchen table. Next to it was a freezer bag full of base crystal, half spilled onto the tabletop. On a sink to the back was a big, five gallon steel pot crusted with crack cocaine residue. A gallon can of something called BUG DETH: ALL NEW! INDUSTRIAL STRENGTH FOR BIG JOBS! stood on the counter next to the sink. The bonding agent. There was a dead Hispanic boy in the corner, eating something. He had been about twelve. He was eating raw crack from another freezer bag, a sack with blood and brains dripped into it; chewing bloody crack cocaine up like a mouth full of rock candy.

There was a dead man on the floor; missing his head, too. Near the dead man, also on the floor, was a phone off the hook with a mechanical voice coming out of it, small and foolish, saying, "If you are not going to make a call, please hang up the telephone . . . "

Jim almost dove for the phone. Crouched in blood, by the stump of a neck, with an effort of will he made his hands work the touchtone buttons. His heart going off like one of those obnoxious car alarms.

The dead were coming down the hall. Scuffling. Making sniffing sounds. Dwayne scooped up a handful of the base fallen on the table, a big handful of crystals, couple thousand dollars worth. Stared at it hungrily. Jim watched the boy in the corner eating bloody rock cocaine, while he told 911 that there were murders happening here. Not trying to explain more than that. (Thinking, in some twitchy corner of his mind, that it would be easy to get a handful or two of the rock for himself, hide it somewhere, come back after the cops and the things were gone, fuck it, it wasn't like anything mattered anymore—and then he had a flash vision of himself chewing a hole in his own kid's head.) Jim told Dwayne, as he hung up the phone, "The shit's poisonous, Dwayne, even more than usual."

Dwayne looked at the double handful of rock cocaine. Then bent over, dipped the base in a puddle of blood and brains and tossed the whole double-handful through the door, into the hall. Scrabbling, clawing sounds as the dead went for it.

Jim Diggins carried the phone across the small room, and smashed the head of the dead boy eating the cocaine, twice, crushed his skull, very thoroughly, with a corner of the phone, each blow making the phone ring a little.

The boy slumped, twitching, bloody cocaine dribbling from his mouth . . . not dead, you couldn't kill them that easy.

11:30 p.m.
A lot of cops milling around.

The detective in charge was named Johnson, a tall, mild-eyed black guy, a uniformed lieutenant with a college cadence to his talk. Jim had ditched the .45. Didn't tell the cops the background to the story. Johnson listened to the story, as Jim told it, then went to his cruiser, his face flashing in and out of red with the cherry-top light. He spoke into a microphone, something about cocaine-overdose hallucinations and mass murder and hysteria, as the paramedics carted the truly-dead away. Paramedics shaking their heads in weary amazement.

Carrying the dead dead. The others, the ambulatory dead, had crawled out back, when the cops had come. Hid themselves. Still functioning, instinctively, to protect themselves. Still out there, in the city, somewhere, sniffing around. Settling for any kind of living flesh they could find, now, Jim supposed.

But then again, it wouldn't take them long to find more crack heads.

Dwayne and Jim stood to one side. They'd been told to wait, put on the back burner for the moment. Johnson was convinced they were bystanders, not the killers. Jim said, "Shit like this doesn't happen by accident, Dwayne. Something's talking to us. All of us."

Dwayne said nothing. He stared at light on the cop car. The headless bodies being hoisted into the ambulance.

Jim said, "What your Uncle said about a sickness in the air, the dark wave thing . . . Well, shit. I don't know. I mean, I don't know if there's a God, man, but I think we ought to act as if there is one, you know?"

Dwayne still said nothing.

"Dwayne?"

Dwayne said, softly, "I gettin' the fuck out of here."

"Where you going to go?"

"Way different neighborhood."

"Is that right? Hey, Lieutenant Johnson!"

The cop said something more into the mike, then walked over to them. "Yeah?"

"This man here stole my car. A few days ago. I went to talk to him about it when all this happened . . . "

Dwayne said, "He's full of shit."

Jim said, "They dusted the car for prints. I insisted on it. They got your prints, Dwayne. They got evidence of that. Not of anything else." Meaning: no evidence that Jim had been buying drugs.

Dwayne looked at Jim like he was going to bite through Jim's skull himself. "You pale motherfucker."

"Just what I need," Johnson was saying, wearily putting cuffs on Dwayne. "As if I don't have enough to deal with. You have the right to remain silent . . . " He went through the whole thing.

"You don't know what I do for a living, Dwayne," Jim said, later, talking through the half-open window of the car; Johnson had put Dwayne in the back of a cruiser. "I'm a lawyer. I've gotta lot of connections. I can get you remanded to my custody, set you up in drug rehab. Both of us in drug rehab."

"Fuck you, you pale bullshit motherfucker."

"You better hold onto that attitude, you're gonna need it sometime, Dwayne. I'm doing this to help, man. Because I had a choice and you didn't."

"You think you on a Mission? Fuck you, you kneejerk liberal cocksucker!" Dwayne shouted out the car window as Johnson started the cruiser and drove off.

Jim was taken to the precinct in another cop car. After awhile all the rest of the police cars drove off into the night, vanishing into the darkness where the hungry dead were shuffling, sniffing the air.

JOHN SHIRLEY is the author of more than thirty novels. The latest, *Everything Is Broken*, was published earlier this year. His numerous short stories have been compiled into eight collections including *Black Butterflies: A Flock on the Darkside*, winner of the Bram Stoker Award, International Horror Guild Award, and named as one of the best one hundred books of the year by *Publishers Weekly* and, most recently, *In Extremis: The Most Extreme Short Stories of John Shirley*. He has written scripts for television and film, and is best known as co-writer of *The Crow*. As a musician, Shirley has fronted several bands over the years and written lyrics for Blue Öyster Cult and others. To learn more about John Shirley and his work, please visit his website at john-shirley.com.

"S'different," Mama Randolph said. "Different world now. Just adjustin' to cold water is all. Might not want to do it, but sometimes just can't be helped. Gotta survive, after all."

Abed

Elizabeth Massie

Meggie's A-line dress is yellow, bright like a new dandelion in the side yard and as soft as the throats of the tiny toads Meggie used to find in the woods that surround the farm. There aren't many stains on the dress, just some spots on the hem. Mama Randolph, Quint's mother and Meggie's mother-in-law, ironed the dress this morning, and then gave it to Meggie with a patient and expectant smile before locking the bedroom door once more. Meggie knows that Mama likes the dress because it isn't quite as much a reminder of the bad situation as are the other blotted and bloodied outfits in Meggie's footed wardrobe.

From the open window, a benign breeze passes through the screen, stirring the curtains. But the breeze dies in the middle of the floor because there are no other windows in the room to allow it to leave. The summer heat, however, is quite at home in the room and has settled for a long stay.

There has been no rain for the past fourteen days. Meggie has been marking the days off on the Shenandoah Dairy calendar she keeps under her bed. Mama has not talked about a grandchild in almost a month now; Meggie keeps the calendar marked for that, as well. Mama Randolph's smile and the freshly ironed dress lets Meggie know that the cycle has come 'round again.

Meggie moves from the bed to the window to the bed. There is a chair in the corner by the door, but the cushion smells bad and so she doesn't like to sit on it. The mattress on the bed smells worse than the chair, but there is a clean corner that she uses when she is tired. She paces about, feeling the soft swing of her hair about her shoulders as she rocks her head back and forth, remembering the feel of Quint's own warm hair in the sunlight of past Julys and the softness of the dark curls that made a sweet pillow of his chest.

At the window, Meggie glances out through the screen, down to the chain-linked yard below. The weeds there are wild and a tall and tangled like briars in the forest. The fence is covered with honeysuckle. There is the remainder of the sandbox Quint used as a child. It is nearly returned to the soil now, and black-eyed Susans have found themselves a home. Mama says it will be a fine thing when there is a child to enjoy the yard once again. She says when the child comes she and Meggie will clean up the yard and make it into a playground that any other child in Norton County will envy.

Mama had slapped Meggie when Meggie said she didn't know if there would ever be any more children in the county.

On the nightstand beside Meggie's bed is a chipped vase with a bouquet of Queen Anne's lace, sweet peas, red clover, and chicory. Mama said it was a gift from Quint, but Meggie knows Quint is long past picking gifts of wildflowers. Beside the vase is a picture of Meggie and Quint on their wedding day three years ago. Meggie wears a white floorlength dress and clutches a single white carnation. Quint grins shyly at the camera, the new beard Meggie had loved just a dark shadow across his lower face. It would be four months before the beard was full enough to satisfy him, although it never satisfied his mother.

"You live in my house, you do as I say, you hear me?" she had told Quint. And although Meggie believed in the premise of that command, and managed to follow the rules. Quint always had a way of getting by with what he wanted by joking and cajoling his mother. And in the dark privacy of night, while cuddling with Meggie in bed, he would promise that it wouldn't be long before he had saved enough money to build them their own small house on the back acre Mama had given him by the river.

But that was back when Quint worked the farm for his mother and held an evening job at the Joy Food Mart and Gas Station out on Route 146. Back when they had a savings account in the Farmers' Bank in Henford and Meggie happily collected her mother-in-law's cast off dishes to use as her own when the house by the river was built.

And then came the change. Things in Norton County flipped ass over teakettle. Old dead Mrs. Lowry had sat up in her coffin at the funeral home, grunting and snarling, her eyes washed white with the preserving chemicals but her mouth chattering for something hot and living to eat. Then Mr. Conrad, Quint's boss down at the Joy Food Mart and Gas Station, had keeled over while changing a tire and died on the spot of a heart attack. Before Quint could finish dialing the number of the Norton volunteer rescue squad, Conrad was up again and licking his newly dead lips, his hands racked with spasms but his teeth keen for a taste of Quint-neck. Quint hosed him down with unleaded and tossed in his Bic lighter and then cried when it was over because he couldn't believe what had happened.

They all believe now, all-righty.

The dead wander the gravel roads and eat what they may, and everyone in Norton County knows it is no joke because they've all seen one or two of the dead, at least. The newspapers say it's a problem all over now; the big cities like Richmond and D.C. and Chicago got dead coming out of their ears. There is a constant battle in the cities because there are so many. In Norton County it is a problem, and a couple people have been eaten, but mostly the walking dead get burned with gasoline or get avoided by the careful.

A thud in the downstairs hallway causes Meggie to jump and clasp her hands to the bodice of her yellow dress. The permanent chicken bone of fear that resides in her chest makes a painful turn. She presses her fists deep into the pain. She waits. Sweat beads on her arms and between her breasts. Mama

Randolph does not come yet.

Meggie turns away from the wedding portrait on the nightstand and tries to remember the songs she sang in church before the church closed down. But all she can remember are some psalms. She walks to the clean spot on the bed and sits. She looks at the window, at the footed wardrobe, at the stained chair near the locked door. Above the chair is a Jesus picture. If there was some way to know what Jesus thought of the change, Meggie thinks she could bear it. If Meggie truly believed that Jesus had a handle on the walking dead, and that it was just a matter of time before He put a stop to it all, then Meggie would live out her confinement with more faith. But the picture shows a happy, smiling Jesus, holding a little white lamb with other white lambs gathered at His feet. He does not look like He has any comprehension of the horror that walks the world today. If He did, shouldn't He be crashing from the sky in a wailing river of fire to throw the dead back into their graves until the Rapture?

Meggie slips from the bed and kneels before the picture, Jesus' smiling face moves her and His detachment haunts her. Her hands fold into a sweaty attitude of prayer, and in a gritty voice, she repeats, "The Lord is my shepherd, I shall not want . . . "

The crash in the hall just outside the door hurls Meggie to her feet. Her hands are still folded but she raises them like a club. The sound was that of a food tray being carelessly plopped onto the bare hall floor, and of dishes rattling with the impact. Mama Randolph brings Meggie her breakfast, lunch, and dinner every day, but today Mama is early.

Meggie looks at the screened window and wishes she could throw herself to the ground below without risking everlasting damnation from suicide. There is no clock in the room, but Meggie knows Mama is early. The sun on the floor is not yet straddling the stain on the carpet, and so it is still a ways from noon. But Meggie knows that Mama has something on her mind today besides food. Mama's excitement has interrupted the schedule. Mama has been marking a calendar as well. Today, Mama is thinking about grandchildren.

Meggie holds the club of fingers before her. It will do no good, she knows. She could not strike Mama Randolph. Maybe Jesus will think it is a prayer and come to help her.

The door opens, and Mama Randolph comes in with a swish of old apron and a flourish of cloth napkin. The tray and its contents are visible behind her in the hall, but the meal is the last of Mama's concerns. When business is tended, the meal will be remembered.

"Meggie," says Mama. "What a pretty sight you are there in your dress. Makes me think of a little yellow kitten." The cloth napkin is dropped onto the back of the stinking chair, and Mama straightens to take appraisal of her daughter-in-law. There is something in Mama's apron pocket that clinks faintly.

"Well, you gonna stand there or do you have a 'good morning'?"

Meggie looks toward the window. Two stories is not enough to die. And if she died, she would only become one of the walking dead. She looks back at Mama.

"Good morning," she whispers.

"And to you," Mama says cheerily. "Can you believe the heat? I pity the farmers this year. Corn is just cooking on the stalks. You look to the right out that window and just over the trees and you can see a bit of John Johnson's crop. Pitiful thing, all burned and brown." Mama tips her head and smiles. The apron clinks.

Neither says anything for a minute. Mama's eyes sparkle in the heavy, hot air. The dead folks' eyes sparkle when they walk about, but Meggie knows Mama is not dead. The older woman is very much alive, with all manner of plans for her family.

Then Mama says, "Sit down."

Meggie sits on the clean spot on the mattress.

Mama touches her dry lips. She says, "You know a home ain't a home without the singing of little children."

Oh, dear Jesus, thinks Meggie.

"When Quint was born, I was complete. I was a woman then. I was whole; I'd done what I was made to do. A woman with no children can't understand that till she's been through it herself."

Meggie feels a large drop of sweat fall and lodge above her navel. She looks at the floor and remembers what Quint's shoes looked like there, beside hers in the night after they'd climbed beneath the covers. Precious shoes, farmer's shoes, with the sides worn down and the dark coating of earth on the toes. Shoes that bore the weight of hard work and love. Shoes Quint swore he would throw away when he'd earned enough money to build the new house. Shoes that Meggie was going to keep in her cedar chest as a memory of the early days.

Quint doesn't wear shoes anymore.

"You know in my concern for you and Quint, I would do I anything to make you happy." Mama nods slowly. "And if I've got it figured right, you're in your time again. I know it ain't worked the last couple months, but it took me near'n to a year and a half before I was with Quint."

Mama steps over to Meggie. She leans in close. Her breath smells of ginger and soured milk. "A baby is what'll help make some of the bad things right again, Meggie. It's a different world now. And we's got to cope. But a baby will bring Joy back."

"A baby," echoes Meggie. "Mama, please, I can't . . . "

"Hush, now," barks Mama. The smile disappears as quickly as the picture from a turned-off television set. She is all business now. Family making is a serious matter. "Get abed."

The word stings Meggie's gut.

"Abed!" commands Mama Randolph, and slowly, obediently, Meggie slides along the mattress until her head is even with the pillow.

Mama purses her mouth in approval. "Now let's check and see if our timing is right." Meggie closes her eyes and one hand moves to the spotted hem of the yellow dress. In her chest, the bone of pain swells, hard and suffocating. She cannot swallow around it. Her breath hitches. She pulls the hem up. She is naked beneath. Mama Randolph has not allowed undergarments.

"Roll over." Meggie rolls over. She hears the clinking as Mama reaches into her pocket. Meggie gropes for the edge of the pillow and holds to it like a drowning child to a life preserver. Her face presses into the stinking pillowcase.

The thermometer goes in deeply. Mama makes a *tsk*ing sound and moves it about until it is wedged to her satisfaction. Meggie's bowels contract; her gut lurches with disgust. She does not move.

"Just a minute here and we'll know what we need to know," crows Mama. "Do you know that I thought Quint was going to be a girl and I bought all sorts of little pink things before he was born? Was cute, but I couldn't rightly put such a little man into them pale, frilly clothes. I always thought a little girl would be a nice addition. Wouldn't a little girl just be the icing on the cake?"

Jesus help me, prays Meggie.

"Here, now," says Mama. The thermometer comes out and Meggie draws her legs up beneath the hem of the dress. She does to not want to hear the reading.

"Bless me, looks like we done hit it on the head!" Mama is almost laughing. "Up nearly a whole degree. Time is right. My little calendar book keeps me thinking straight, now don't it? I'll go get Quint."

Mama goes out into the hall. Meggie watches her go. Then she falls from the bed and crawls on her knees to the Jesus picture. "Oh dear blessed Lord, You are my shepherd, I shall not want I shall not want." Jesus watches the lambs and does not see Meggie.

Meggie runs to the window and looks out at the flowers and the dead sandbox and the burned cornfield over the top of the joy woods. It was those woods that killed Quint. One second of carelessness that crushed Quint's skull beneath John Johnson's felled tree. Quint had gone to help the neighbor clear a little more land for crops. John and Quint had been best buddies since school, and they were always trading favors. But when Quint went down under the tree trunk, brains and blood spraying, and he died, and when he rose up again, he was through trading favors. He wanted a lot more of John than he'd ever wanted before. And he got it. There wasn't enough of John left to rise with the other dead folks, just some chunks of spine and some chewed up feet.

Mama Randolph found Quint after this meal. He showed no immediate urge to eat her as well, so she brought him home and found he was just as happy eating raw goats and the squealing pigs he had tended as a live man.

Mama is in the doorway again. Behind her is Quint. He is dressed in only a pair of trousers that are gathered to his bony waist with a brown, tooth-marked leather belt.

"Abed!" says Mama. "Let's have this done."

Meggie goes back to the bed. She lies down. She knows what Mama will do next. It is the worst to come.

Quint is directed to stand in front of the old chair. Meggie cannot see Jesus anymore but that is a good thing. What is to happen is not for anyone's eyes, especially the Savior's. Meggie looks at her husband. His hair is gone, as is the flesh of his mouth and the bulk of his nose. There is a tongue, but it is slimy and gray like an old rotted trout. The left side of his head is flattened, with the exposed brain now blackened and shimmering, reminding Meggie of a mushroom she tried to save once in a sandwich bag. The eye on the left is missing, but the right eye is wide and wet. The skin of Quint's abdomen is swollen and it ripples like maggots have gotten inside. One hand has no fingers, but the other has three, and they grope awkwardly for the zipper of his trousers. Quint somehow knows why he has been brought upstairs.

Mama Randolph moves beside Meggie and motions for her to hoist up her dress. Meggie flinches, hesitating, and Mama slaps her. Meggie does not hesitate again.

Mama then rolls up her sleeves. She says, "Quint needs the extra stimulation to do what he has to do. Watching helps him. You know that. So be still and let me do my job."

With the perfunctory movements of someone changing a fouled diaper. Mama coaxes the younger woman's legs open, and parts the private folds so Quint can have a better view. Then she begins to rub Meggie's clitoris slowly, while stroking the sensitive skin of Meggie's inner thighs with the other hand. Meggie will not watch. She digs her fingernails into her sides until the pain sings with the rush of blood to her genitals.

"Quint, do you remember? Do you see Meggie? Her pretty dress?" says Mama. "Look Quint, now isn't this lovely?" She leans her face into Meggie's crotch and licks the whole length of slit. The breath from her nose is warm; the wetness of her saliva is cool. Meggie groans. Shame boils her mind and soul. Pleasure teases her body.

Mama, Quint, Jesus, no! I shall not want I shall not want!

Quint grunts. Meggie bucks her head and shoulders and glances at him. He has opened his fly and has found his penis. It is yellowed and decaying, like a bloated fish on a riverbank. As he pulls, it rises slightly. The pre-cum is purpled.

Mama sucks gently and then with a fury. Meggie's body arcs reflexively. Bile rushes a burning path up her throat and dribbles from the corners of her mouth. When Mama's lips move away for a second, Meggie crashes back to the mattress. The acid rockets upward once more and Meggie gags. Mama brings her tongue to Meggie's spot again, and then thrusts her thumb into the opening. Meggie feels the walls of her vagina gush, betraying her in her ultimate moment of revulsion and horror.

I shall not oh dear God Jesus I shall not!

"Good girl," Mama says matter-of-factly.

Meggie writhes on the bed, enraged tears spilling from her eyes and soaking the mattress. Mama stands up.

Quint has a line of moisture on what is left of his upper lip. One side of his mouth twitches as if it would try to grin.

Mama gestures to her son. "Come now, Quint, Meggie can't wait for you." Quint stares, grunts, then stumbles forward. As he passes his mother, she says, "I'd really love a granddaughter."

Meggie turns her face away. She closes her eyes and tries to remember last summer. Days of light and shadows and swimming and play, days of work and trials and promises of forever. But all she can do is smell the creature climbing onto her. All she can do is feel the slopping of the trout-tongue on her cheek and taste the running, blackened brain matter as it drips to the edge of her lips. He burrows clumsily; his body wriggles as his knees work between her knees, and his sore-covered penis reaches like a dazed, half-dead snake for her center.

Meggie bites her tongue until it bleeds to keep from feeling the cold explosion of semen. And as if in some insane answer to it all, her vaginal walls contract suddenly in a horrific, humiliating orgasm.

It is all over quickly. Mama pulls Quint off, then gives Meggie a kiss on the forehead and tells her to stay abed for at least an hour to give the seed time to find the soil.

Alone, with the door locked and the lunch tray balanced on the smelly chair seat, Meggie lies still, her dress still hunched up. She holds her left hand in her right, pretending the right one is that of a living, breathing

Quint. She puts the hand to her face and feels the tender stroking. And then she lowers the hand to her abdomen, and presses firmly. There will be a new human in there soon, if Mama has her way. There could be one already. This could be Mama's magic moment. Meggie wishes she could know. It is not knowing if or when that brings her mind to the edge of twisting inside out.

She looks at the window. There is no breeze now, only the persistent heat. The edge of sunlight stands on the carpet stain.

"S'different," Mama Randolph had said. "Different world now. Just adjustin' to cold water is all. Might not want to do it, but sometimes just can't be helped. Gotta survive, after all."

Meggie holds herself and closes her eyes. She wonders about the different world. She wonders if there will be a baby to grow and use the playground outside her room. And she wonders if the baby, when it comes, will be cuddly and bouncy and take after his mother.

Or if it will be stillborn, and take after its father.

Two-time Bram Stoker Award-winning horror author, ELIZABETH MASSIE also writes historical fiction for young adults as well as mainstream fiction, media tie-ins, and nonfiction for American history textbooks and educational readers and testing programs. Her first short horror story, "Whittler," was published in 1984. Since then her horror fiction has appeared in numerous magazines and anthologies including, among others, *Best New Fantasy and Horror*, *Best New Horror*, *Splatterpunks*, *Inhuman*, *Grue*, *Hottest Blood*, *A Whisper of Blood*, and more. Massie is also the creator of "Skeeryvilletown," a horror cartoon world featuring creatures and monsters. This short story, "Abed," has been filmed and is now in post-production. Her website is www.elizabethmassie.com.

It looked kind of like a big, fleshy leaf, twice as long as his hand. It was all pulpy and shit, like the inside of a bad melon and it smelled like cat piss, only a whole lot stronger . . .

Chuy and the Fish

David Wellington

Rain came down so hard it was tough to tell the difference between the water and the air. It scoured the esplanade, a million soft explosions a second, and it battered the weeds that pushed up through the cracks in the parking lot asphalt. Chuy couldn't see five feet in front of him. He was on guard against dead people who might crawl up out of the channel and onto Governor's Island. But hell, man, not even the dead wanted to be out on a night like this. He stayed where it was safe and dry like a smart guy, under the covered doorway of an old officer's barracks. He wished he had a cigarette. Too bad there weren't anymore, not since the end of the world and all. His wife—she was gone now, and his little babies, too—she had always wanted him to quit. *Hell of a way for her to get her wish*, he thought, as the curl of her mouth swam up through his memory, the soft, soft hairs at the edges of her eyebrows—

Sound rolled up over him from the water. Sounds were coming up from the harbor all the time, but this one was different. A noise like something slapping metal. Like something hitting the railing. Chuy stared out into the murk. Nothing.

Chingadre, he thought. He needed to check this out. One time a dead guy had actually come up over the railing. His body was all bloated with gases, and he had floated across from NYC. They had lost three people that night before they even knew what was going on. When they finally shot the dead guy, he had lit up like a gas main going off and had knocked down one of the houses in Nolan Park. It had been bad, real bad, and Marisol, the mayor of Governors Island, didn't want it happening again. Nothing for it.

Chuy stepped out into the rain and was instantly soaked.

He ran up the road a ways, water pouring down into his eyes so he had to blink it away. He scanned the street that ran around the edge of the island, studying the iron railing that kept foolish people from falling into the water. Nothing—just some garbage that had washed up against the railing. It looked like a white plastic bag, the kind you got at the grocery. Except there weren't any more groceries.

Not thinking much about it, he stepped closer for a better look. Maybe some garbage that had blown over in the wind from the city. The dead owned NYC now and they didn't do much cleaning. He squatted down and thought about getting dry again, sitting by a fire and maybe drinking some coffee. He had half a jar of instant hid away; he could afford to brew a cup if he was careful, sure.

It wasn't a bag. What it was, he didn't know. "Hey, hey, Harry," he called out. "Yo, big guy, come over here!"

Harry was patrolling a couple of blocks down. He had been a teacher up at CUNY before and knew a lot of things. Maybe he would recognize this. It looked kind of like a big, fleshy leaf, twice as long as his hand. It was all pulpy and shit, like the inside of a bad melon and it smelled like ass. Like cat piss, kind of, only a whole lot stronger. Dead-fish bad, but not the same, only kind of similar. Harry came splashing through the puddles and Chuy bent closer for a better look. It was attached to something, something long and thin that trailed down into the water.

He took the gun out of his belt—Desert Eagle, boy, all nickel-plated and deadly, nice one—and gently poked the thing with the end of the barrel. He didn't want to get that stink on his fingers. The flesh yielded okay. Bubbles squelched up when he applied real pressure. He frowned and turned around to look for Harry.

The fleshy thing moved on its rope—he saw it in his peripheral vision. It lifted up and slapped against his thigh. Chuy grunted in disgust, and then in pain. The underside of the thing was covered in tiny hooks that dug deep into him, tearing at him. "Hells no!" he shouted just when the thing yanked at him hard, pulling him by his leg, slamming him up against the railing.

"Harry! Harry!" he screamed. With a strength he couldn't understand, it tugged at him, trying to drag him down into the water. He wrapped his arms and his free leg around the railing, holding tight against the power that wanted to tear him loose. "Fucking bastard! Harry, get over here!"

Harry Cho slid to a stop a couple feet away and just stood there with his mouth open. His glasses were silvered with rain and his black hair was plastered down across his forehead. He was a short, skinny guy and he wasn't very strong. Dropping to the asphalt he grabbed Chuy around the waist and tried to pull him off the railing. "I don't want to tear it loose," Harry grunted. "It's stuck in there pretty well."

"Fuck that!" Chuy screamed. "Shoot this thing!" He could feel his skin peeling away underneath his pants. The ropy thing had twisted around his ankle and the bones there felt like they might pop. "Shoot it in the head!"

Harry unslung his M4 rifle and leaned over the railing. He shook his head, peering down into the choppy water. "I don't see any . . . I mean there's no . . . "

A second pulpy white thing, a twin to the first, batted at the railing a couple of times and made it ring. "Is that a tentacle?" Harry asked, but Chuy didn't care enough to answer. The club-end of the tentacle stroked the asphalt and then coiled around the railing and pulled. The whole island seemed to shudder as the thing on the other end of the tentacles strained and squeezed and dragged itself up out of the channel, great sheets of silver water sloshing off its back.

Eight thicker arms reared up to grab at the railing. The iron bent and squealed as the main body heaved upwards and into view. Chuy saw diaphanous fins, tattered with rot. He saw its long red and white body thick and heavy with muscles. He saw its beak, like a parrot's, only about ten times bigger. He saw an eye, the size of a manhole cover maybe, clouded with decay, and the eye saw *him*.

"*Orale, tu pinche pendejo!* Enough fucking playing!" Chuy screamed and he brought the Desert Eagle up to point right at that motherfucking yellow eye. He was no *cholo* gangsta (not good old funny guy Chuy; no, he had been a doorman in NYC), but at this range he thought he could score. He hit the safety with his thumb and then he blasted the dripping asshole, absolutely blasted it with three tight shots right in the pupil. The eye exploded, spraying him with a mess of jelly and stinking water. He spluttered—some of that shit went right in his mouth.

"An undead squid! Architeuthis?" Harry asked. He looked dazed. "Or is it—it couldn't be a Colossal. . . . " The ex-teacher brought his rifle around and fired a quick burst into its main body. Bullet holes appeared in a line down its back, big fist-sized holes that didn't bother the fucker at all. You could shoot a dead thing all day and it didn't feel it, not unless you got the head. Harry fired another burst at its head where all the tentacles attached: same result.

Rings of fire bit into Chuy's calf muscle, little round buzzsaws of pain. He bit the inside of his cheek as a wave of nausea and agony jittered through him. His hand twitched, but he couldn't let go of his pistol. No, that would be suicide. "Harry—*Christ!* Get some fucking backup!"

Harry nodded and let his rifle fall back on its strap. He twisted open a flare and tossed it high up into the air. Chuy looked up over at the towers on the ferry dock and saw the lights there flicker in acknowledgement. If he could just hold on—if he could just stay cool—help was on the way.

The railing groaned and the bolts that held it to the esplanade began to squeal.

"Where's its fucking brain?" Marisol demanded. "It's undead, right? You shoot it in the fucking brain and it fucking dies. Where's its brain?" She had a shotgun against her shoulder as she bent to stroke Chuy's hair. He was in a bad way. He'd lost a lot of blood and he could barely hold onto the railing. It had been maybe twenty-five minutes since the squid got hold of him. Gathered around him, the crowd had put dozens of rounds of ammunition into the asshole thing, but it only fought harder. It hadn't come up any farther onto land—it lacked the energy, looked like, to come crawling up any more—but it wouldn't let go, either. Its tentacle—one of the two big feeding tentacles, Harry called them—had wrapped around his leg so many times Chuy couldn't see his foot or his shin.

"That's what I'm telling you! It doesn't have one! It has long axons but they're spread out through the body. There's no central nervous system at all. Nothing to target." Harry looked away. "It has three hearts, if you care."

"I don't." Marisol knelt down next to Chuy. "We'll cut you loose, I promise."

Chuy nodded. They'd already tried that, with fire axes. The tentacle was so rubbery that the axes just bounced off. Marisol had sent somebody to look for a hacksaw.

The squid snapped its beak at Chuy's foot. It couldn't quite reach. It pulled again and he felt his skin coming loose. The pain was bright and hot and white, and it seared him. He screamed and Marisol clutched his head. Somebody came forward and tied a rope around him, anchoring him to the railing.

Nobody talked about chopping off his leg to get him free. There weren't any surgical tools on the island. Worse, there was no penicillin. People didn't survive that kind of injury any more. The tentacle had to go, or Chuy would.

He turned his face up to the sky and let rain collect in his mouth.

Someone set off a white flare and held it over his head. The sputtering light woke Chuy with a start, and his body shivered. He looked down and saw the fucking fish all lit up. It was as big as a school bus and it looked like chopped meat: they had done so much damage to it with their guns, but it wouldn't just die. "How long," he said, his throat dry and cracking.

Down on the rocks, Harry stepped close to the thing, keeping his head down, his hands out for balance. He had a hacksaw in one hand. He moved so slow, so quiet. He was coming up on the squid's blind side, on the side where Chuy had popped its eye. Maybe he thought the fish wouldn't notice when he started sawing through its arm.

"How long was I out?" Chuy croaked.

Somebody behind him—he couldn't see who—answered, "About an hour. Sleep if you can, guy. Ain't nothing for you to do right now."

"*No jodas.*" Chuy tried to clear his throat but the phlegm wouldn't come. Down on the rocks, Harry stepped a little closer. He touched the hacksaw blade to the tentacle as if he was trying to brush off a speck of lint.

The squid's enormous body convulsed and the air filled with the stink of ammonia and dead flesh. Foul black fluid spurted from the holes in its back. Gallons more of it slapped Harry across the face, choking him, sending him flying on his back into the water. Ink—the fucker was squirting ink, Chuy realized. Harry thrashed in the water, the rain washing his glasses clean, but he couldn't seem to get his mouth clear. His arms windmilled and his legs kicked, but he couldn't get back to the rocks. Marisol leaned over the railing and threw him a bright orange life preserver. He grasped it in one hand and slowly got control of himself.

The squid rolled over, yanking Chuy savagely against the bars of the railing. He screeched like a dog, like one of those little dogs the white women used to carry in their purses in NYC.

Down in the water, Harry slid up onto a rock covered in green hairy seaweed. He couldn't quite get a grip. He was still trying when the squid's beak cut right into his ribcage. Harry didn't scream at all. He didn't have time.

Nobody spoke but they all looked, the way New Yorkers used to slow down on the highways to look at accidents. They couldn't turn away as the squid cut Harry into tiny pieces and swallowed them one by one, its whole mantle contracting as it sucked down the bloody chunks of meat.

In his dream, he was with his Isabel again, and she was laid out on the bed, smiling up at him. She was wearing a kind of nightie, only like one you get from Victoria's Secret. Her hair was pulled back in one big ponytail and was spread out across the pillows in ten thick tendrils. Those lips, man, they were like sugar. He jumped on top of her, felt her bones against his, and they smiled together. His gold cross pendant touched the skin above her breasts. It was so sweet, man, only why did she smell so bad? She smelled like something dead. He brought his mouth down and kissed her bony lips hard, so hard he could make her be alive again, like Sleeping Beauty.

His shivering had turned into real convulsions by the time the sky turned blue, the funny blue it gets right before dawn. The sea was a uniform and dull gray. The rain had stopped hours earlier, while he was unconscious.

"He's not tracking," somebody said.

He saw Marisol's face swimming before him. "It's shock, probably. Jesus. I've never seen anybody so pale. Do we just put him out of his misery?"

"Don't even say that. There's got to be a way to get him loose."

Marisol was used to making hard decisions. That was why they made her mayor. Chuy was pretty sure she would figure out what to do.

He saw pink clouds over Manhattan—so beautiful, buzzing with beauty—before he slipped away again.

Hot pain in his leg brought him up. The suckers on the feeding tentacles were rimmed with tiny hooks that tore the long muscles in his thigh. It had more of him than before. It was trying to bring him closer, to its beak. It must have gotten hungry again.

Chuy gritted his teeth. He felt foul—slimy with old sweat.

Something was happening.

He struggled to focus, to look around. He saw people running, some towards him, some away. He felt his leg being straightened, felt his foot being torn loose from his ankle and the pain was enormous, it was real big, but it wasn't like he'd felt before. Maybe he was getting used to it. He lifted his head, looked down at the squid.

It was rising up. Pulling itself up with its eight thick arms. He saw the dripping ugly wound where its eye had been, and he thought, You *serote*, I did that.

It was coming for him. The railing sighed and shook and then started to give way.

"Everybody get back!" Marisol shrieked. A bolt let go with an explosive noise, and a section of railing lifted up in the air, twisted. The squid dragged itself an inch closer. Chuy could see the beak, huge, hard, sharp—he looked over his shoulder and saw people edging away from him. So this was it, huh?

More bolts popped loose. Dust and rain shot out each time. The railing crimped back on itself. Chuy reached down and felt the knot of the rope holding him to the railing. Rain and seawater had soaked through it, made it as hard as a rock. He pushed his thumb into it, tried to wiggle it around.

The free feeding tentacle draped around Chuy's neck and arm. He tried to shrug it off, but it was too strong. Razor-sharp suckers sank into his back and he grimaced. He didn't feel the pain so much, but it made his body stop, just squeal to a stop like a taxi with bad brakes. When that passed, he tried to move his thumb again.

The knot started to come loose. "Somebody get me a grenade!" he shouted.

He'd had time to think about this. About how they were going to remember him. He kept working at the knot.

The squid heaved its body up onto the railing, its great big meaty mass. The iron cried out in distress. Tons it must weigh, the fucker. Whole tons. The railing broke under that weight and the squid started to slide, but it held on to his leg and his back. Its beak wallowed closer to him.

"A grenade!" he shouted again, and instantly it was there, hard and fist-sized and round. Somebody shoved it into his free hand and somebody else—they must have seen what he was doing—reached down and cut the rope with a combat knife. The only thing holding him to the railing then was his arm.

The squid rippled toward him. He could see its good eye now, yellow and black. Glassy. He saw the beak moving silently.

He let go of the railing. The squid pulled him hard and he went right through as it yanked him toward its beak. In the process, it shifted its center of gravity backward, toward the water.

It hit the foam with a splash that rushed across Chuy's chest and face, pummeling him. It was all he could do to keep a hold of his grenade. He fought—fought hard to retain consciousness.

"Good luck, *ese!*" he heard Marisol shout. Marisol was fine, he thought. It was good to have a fine woman cheering you on when you gave your all. Saltwater filled his nose and his eyes and made him choke, and then there was no more sound.

The squid took him down, fast. He felt pressure building up in his ears until they popped so hard blood spurted out of his head. He saw the light fading, the last rays of it reaching down from above but not quite reaching. He saw the seaweed on the rocks give way to gray algae, *colorless* algae, and then he saw the bottom and the dead men looking up at him.

They were little more than skeletons. Dead people who fell in the harbor and couldn't get out again. Exposed bone turned to rock, water-logged flesh turned white and fishy, their hands all missing knuckles and fingers, their feet rooted to the bottom muck. Their eyes were still human. He could see human desires and needs in those eyes. They were hungry. So hungry.

He wasn't going to be one of them.

The fish brought around its beak to nip off his foot, and he couldn't stop it. This was its world, and his lungs were bursting. He pulled the pin on the grenade and offered it up. Here you go, *pez pendejo*. Eat 'em up real good.

DAVID WELLINGTON is best known for his zombie trilogy *Monster Island*, *Monster Nation*, and *Monster Planet*. In 2004 he began serializing his horror fiction online, posting short chapters of a novel three times a week on a friend's blog. Response to the project was so great that Thunder's Mouth Press approached Mr. Wellington about publishing *Monster Island* as a traditional print book. He has also written a series of vampire novels—*Thirteen Bullets, Ninety-Nine Coffins, Vampire Zero, Twenty-Three Hours*, and *Thirty-two Fangs*—as well as two werewolf novels: *Frostbite* (published in the UK as *Cursed*) and *Overwinter* (UK title: *Ravaged*). For more information please visit www.davidwellington.net.

Who would have ever guessed it? Who would've guessed that the walking dead would still want to be entertained? I want my ZTV . . .

Dead Giveaway

Brian Hodge

Every night, without fail, it began like this:

MUSIC: Opening of Gustav Holst's "Mars, Bringer of War."

As dark and brooding a piece of music as ever there was.

Next came the announcer, cheerful, bouncy as a beach ball. Monty didn't know where they'd found the guy, but he was the best Don Pardo soundalike he'd ever heard.

ANNCR, V.O.: "Drop what you're doing—it won't crawl away! Come on! Join us now for the most unpredictable hour on television: *Deaaaad Giveawaaaaay!*"

Every night, without fail. Seven nights a week, live on the air, and no reruns.

When Monty first checked his watch, it was a half-hour to showtime. He slumped a little deeper into the chair in his dressing room. Time on his hands. Time to kill. Would that lead to blood on his hands?

Too late, Monty! It's already there!

So he reached out to the counter before him and plucked his bottle of Chivas Regal from the carpet of dust beneath it. And drank until it burned. Penance. A little later he was comfortably numb. And could live with himself again.

Time was that Monty Olson lived with just about everybody. In image, if not in body. He traveled the airwaves, waltzing into bright sunlit living rooms and bedrooms, borne on the wings of daytime TV. Always a guest, never an intruder, forever welcome. Shows such as *Deal of the Century* and *Bet You A Million* had made him a star. And was he loved? Oh, was he ever . . . because he was the man with the cash, the man with the prizes, the man with the motherlode.

The man with the million-dollar smile.

He found it a little tougher to conjure up that smile these days, the big one that wrapped the corners of his mouth almost back to his wisdom teeth. But he managed. Once a pro, always a pro.

Who would have ever guessed it? he wondered for maybe the billionth time since waking up to find that he and everyone else unfamiliar with the rigors of rigor mortis were in a declining minority. *Who would've guessed that they'd still want to be entertained?*

Monty fortified himself with another character-building gulp of Chivas and reached for his makeup case. He did his own makeup these days, wondering why he bothered. His face may have become a little flabbier, a little looser, with a few more broken veins mapping his nose, but he was still a regular Clark Gable by comparison with the rest of the folks on the show. Monty peered at the lines webbing from the corners of his eyes and mouth and did his best to erase them with pancake.

They still want to be entertained.

It wasn't that crazy a notion, not after you gave it time to sink into your already shell-shocked head. Because back in the days when the dead were suddenly no longer obliged to stay in their holes and their morgue drawers, Monty had found himself wandering the streets. He didn't want much, only to avoid becoming lunch for some newly awakened cadaver, and maybe to link up with someone else whose blood still ran warm. And he'd seen the zombies in their homes—by themselves, in pairs, as entire families—parked in front of their televisions just as before, as if nothing whatsoever had changed. Even when all the networks and independent stations had dropped from the airwaves like fruit from a dying tree, they watched the blank screens anyway. Mesmerized by the static.

The watching dead, waiting to be entertained.

Most of the zombies weren't that bright. Most of them weren't much more than two-legged dinosaurs in search of the nearest tar pit to blunder into. But some of them—perhaps those who'd been the sharpest and shrewdest to begin with—had managed to retain enough intelligence that it was downright scary in itself. You looked into those glassy eyes and found that they weren't quite as dull as you'd thought. Or hoped. The lights were still on and somebody was still at home up there . . . only now the resident's priorities had been turned inside-out.

Such a creature was Brad Bernerd. Here in New York, he'd been a fast-track network executive with a string of hit shows as long as your arm. Some people, before the demise of what Monty was beginning to nostalgically regard as the Old World, had said that Brad Bernerd was going to launch his own network.

It came about a lot differently than expected, but he got his chance after all.

Monty had wandered up to the studio soundstage of *Deal of the Century* one day, a huge and silenced amphitheater where even the echoes of past applause had died. He stood at center stage, where he'd spent nearly half of his forty-three years, feeling the glorious pressure of the lights burning through him . . . and he was ready to blow his brains out and die where he'd lived his finest hours.

Except that Brad Bernerd had chosen that moment to make an entrance.

He didn't look much different than Monty remembered, except for a fist-sized dent in the right side of his head. He moved more slowly, more deliberately, but still managed to carry himself with pride. Even arrogance, after death.

Monty nearly piddled his pants like a three-year-old when he looked into those unblinking eyes and saw that they recognized him.

They stared forever.

"I have a job for you," Bernerd said at last. The voice held little of its old animated enthusiasm. But that didn't mean it had lost its power to persuade.

Hey guy, no reason to cash in your chips now, was what it boiled down to. Not when the show must go on. Not when I can put you back on the air. Not when you can reclaim your rightful place in the limelight.

And thus was born the first television program conceived entirely for zombies. I want my ZTV.

Monty checked his watch one last time, found that the zero hour had just about drawn nigh once again. He suckled a final pull from the Chivas and left it behind when the knock came at the door, right on schedule.

"Time for tonight's show," said Brad Bernerd when Monty opened the door. "It's showtime, my man."

Yeah, like I really need a reminder NIGHT AFTER NIGHT!

Monty wound his way backstage among the skeleton crew that kept the cameras whirring and the lights burning. They still needed to do something about the ventilation, but Monty had gotten used to the week-old roadkill smell months ago. Once a pro, always a pro.

How do you do it? they used to ask him; the admirers, the hangers-on. *How do you manage to seem so on top of the world every single show?*

No sweat, he would tell them. It was simply a matter of knowing the right buttons and what to do with them. Turn ON the adrenaline. Turn ON the smile. The charm. The juice. But just as important, turn OFF the mind. And especially the conscience. After all, how long could you live with yourself if you acknowledged that your mission in life was encouraging people to debase themselves for cash?

The switches were all aligned in their proper ON/OFF positions by the time he strolled over to stage left, behind the three huge doors. The crew was putting the final touches on the displays. Now and again, a foreman would have to restrain an overzealous stagehand from helping himself to one of the prizes.

"I rec . . . recog . . . hey I know you." A weak voice from the cage behind Door Number Three. Since the lights were dimming, it was tough to tell who the voice belonged to. Still warm and breathing, of course, if she was in the cage. Monty was the only live one who walked these particular hallowed halls.

"I *know* you." The voice was thick, but clear.

He was drawn to her voice as a moth to the flame, curious why she was still able to speak coherently. Everyone else in the cage had succumbed to the doses of Thorazine administered earlier. It made the live ones so much more docile, kept them from agitating the audience. *And* the master of ceremonies.

"Please let me out . . . please. . . ?" She knelt on the cage floor, her face framed by long dark hair. She wore a red and white skirt, and a dirty white V-neck sweater with a large red *M* on the front. Her hands clutched the bars so tight they looked albino. "Please?"

All switches in place, all systems go.

"No can do, babe," he said, and just to charm the fear out of her, he gave her a great big Monty Olson smile, one to rival any from the Old World. When you still got it, flaunt it. "The stagehands' union would rip me a new one if I did their job."

"How can you just sell us out like this? You're still one of us." She gestured toward the identically dressed girls sharing the cage with her. "You're not one of *them*." She was beginning to cry, eyes glassy but not yet blank, as she fought an uphill battle against the Thorazine. "How can you sell us out?"

"Look: They'll get you one way or another. They're the ones calling the shots these days. And they're the ones signing my paycheck, as it were: They let me live." Monty knelt close to her, his voice almost fatherly. "Remember Andy Warhol? Hmmm? A long time ago he said that everyone was going to be famous for fifteen minutes. Remember that? Well, this is your night, sweetheart. You're gonna be seen from coast to coast tonight."

She stared at him, clawing for more comprehension, then her fingers opened and trailed down the bars. She stared at the spot they'd been clutching.

"Just make the best of it and give us a good show," he said, and left her. He had a date with a lapel mic.

"Showtime," Bernerd called from the shadows. "Look alive, folks."

Bernerd cued the guy in the soundbooth, a forever-young fellow dubbed DeadHead, since he had perished and was then reborn in a Jerry Garcia T-shirt. DeadHead's job was to play the proper music at the proper cues. He juggled a dozen cartridges and, considering his infirmities, managed a remarkable job of keeping them sorted.

The music: "Mars, Bringer of War," throbbing with menace.

The lights: coming up from dim.

The cameras: red tally lights winking on, lenses focusing, slack gray faces peering into the viewfinders.

The pseudo-Don Pardo: "Drop what you're doing—it won't crawl away! Come on! Join us now for the most unpredictable hour on television: *Deaaaad Giveawaaaaay!*"

Monty cemented that huge smile across his face and came striding onstage, sharp and natty in his slacks and blazer. The bulge under the left sleeve was barely noticeable. Doors One, Two, and Three were at his left, and the enormous Wheel of Opportunity at his right. Down he went, down to the very lip of the stage as the curtain rose, the final barrier removed . . .

And there they were. His audience.

They sat politely, somewhere around a thousand of them, somewhat less than two thousand unblinking eyes staring back at him. Some of them clapped, or tried their best, clumsy hands slapping together like pairs of gutted fish. Others cheered, sounding like contented cattle lowing gently into the evening.

A sea of gray faces, agate eyes. Let me entertain you, let me make you smile.

"Right you are, Don, this is *Dead Giveaway*, and my name's Monty Olson. Good-looking crowd tonight, wow. Well hey! I know you hate waiting for the fun to start about as much as I hate long kiss-ass monologues, so let's just get right down to business, what do you say?"

The studio audience murmured its agreement, mottled gray heads bobbing here and there. He imagined their counterparts at home, doing likewise. Monty went striding back toward the wheel, feeling more vital than he had all day. The lights, the cameras, the smell of makeup . . . he knew no better sustenance.

"Just one thing before we get started. Let's run through the rules, shall we? They're simple enough, in keeping with most of your minds out there. Each contestant gets one spin at the wheel, where they can be an instant winner or loser. If the wheel stops on a number, they'll win one of our big prizes behind the three doors. And trust your generous Uncle Monty, we've got some real goodies stashed behind there tonight. Only one word of warning: Just don't commit the Big No-No. We all know what that is and what that means, don't we, ahahahahahaaaaah!"

As Monty patted the bulge beneath his sleeve, there came from the audience a thick rumbling that was probably laughter.

"So! Now that *that* repetitious bullshit's over with, who's our first contestant tonight?"

DeadHead began playing Roy Orbison's "Pretty Woman" as the announcer introduced the shape beginning to scuttle onstage.

"She's a hometown career girl from mid-Manhattan, a former director of sales and training at a downtown bank. First up tonight on *Dead Giveaway* . . . please welcome Cynthia!"

Again, that dead-fish splatter of applause, while there arose several agitated wheezes that in the Old World might've been wolf-whistles. Cynthia shuffled toward the wheel, tall and angular in the moldering remnants of a pinstriped business skirt and jacket. Her mouth was a harsh red slash of lipstick against a white face the texture of dried-out Play-Doh.

"Welcome, Cynthia, welcome," Monty said. "Damned if you don't sound like a lady who has it all together. So tell me, what do you owe your success to?"

"Brains," she said with a lopsided grin.

Monty dug deep and chortled out a big belly laugh. He had her step up to the wheel and she gripped one of the many handles circling its edge and gave it a good shove. An overhead camera flashed the spinning image onto the studio monitors. Numbers and prizes alike flickered past the marker, a blur at first, then settling into focus as the wheel lost momentum. At last the marker settled on a huge numeral 2.

"How 'bout that! A big winner on the first spin of the night!" Monty boomed. On went the aching wraparound smile. "Tell her what she's won!"

Door Number Two eased upward to reveal a display that resembled the back room of a well-stocked butcher shop anticipating rush hour. Stainless steel tables and white-draped gurneys were loaded nearly to the point of collapse. A groan of envy rippled through the audience.

The studio monitors and home viewers were then treated to stock newsreel footage of a suburban neighborhood reduced to the apparent aftermath of a war zone. Grim-faced rescue workers crawled past mounds of burning rubble, extracting victims whole and in part from wreckage twisted beyond recognition.

"Who'll ever forget last May twenty-third?" said the announcer. "Flight 901 out of O'Hare Airport? It crashed a minute after takeoff, but the nation's third worst airline disaster is *your* gain, Cynthia! Direct to you from cold storage in the Cook County Morgue, it's the last of Flight 901! Courtesy of *Dead Giveaway*."

Whatever remained of Cynthia's professional composure was abandoned where she stood. She went lurching toward Door Two in a stiff-legged hobble, falling toward the nearest table and overturning it in an avalanche of assorted parts. Two cameras zoomed in and caught her delight . . . the sweet taste of victory.

The next contestant was a trim lady wearing a tattered dress belted around the waist and a string of pearls. Earrings showed through the matted filth of once-carefully coiffed hair. Her name was June, a homemaker from Mayfield, Ohio, and she lumbered away an instant winner, the proud owner of the thigh and lower leg of what the announcer said had been a marathon runner.

A Brooklyn construction laborer named Carl was up next, entering to the strains of "Born in the U.S.A." His blue workshirt was stained in numerous places where it puckered into the gellifying flesh of his belly and chest, and his shoulders looked as broad as a freezer door.

"Whoa, Carl, let's be careful, okay?" Monty said, laughing. "That wheel's gotta last us the rest of the season, you know."

Carl grunted, and a low moan escaped the audience as he clutched a handle, staggering when he spun the wheel. Then, with the sound of a large, half-rotten carrot snapping in two, the zombie's arm parted company with his shoulder. The arm slithered out of its sleeve like a great gray worm, the hand still holding fast to the wheel. Carl watched in dumbfounded surprise as his arm spun in broad circles, like the last remnant of a child desperate to remain aboard a merry-go-round. Carl looked up, mouth agape, eyes bovine in their stupidity.

Silence, save for the clattering of the marker.

Then a red beacon and the sound of a buzzer ripsawing through the studio.

"Uh oh, that's it! The Big No-No!" cried Monty. "Self-dismemberment *is* grounds for automatic disqualification!" He reached inside his jacket and pulled out a long-barreled .38 revolver, leveling it at the zombie's head. "Too bad, Carl. That was a good spin, too."

The audience uttered a mournful groan at the gunshot, at the mushrooming of the back of Carl's head into gray and maroon, at the thud of his body on the soundstage floor. A pair of stagehands shuffled out to drag the remains away; one licked his fingers when the job was done. Monty reholstered the .38 and grinned broadly and hunched his shoulders in feigned innocence—whattaya gonna do? Always a laff-a-minute here on *Dead Giveaway*.

And on and on it went, a constant, plodding parade of the undead coming to claim their prizes. Shawn, the California beach bum who still had shards of a surfboard sticking from his chest, walked away with a four-pack of heads of various network executives Bernerd hadn't liked. Millicent, who'd been killed shortly after her debutante coming-out party, won the massive arm of a weightlifter and wore it around her neck like a fine fur stole. And on and on . . .

Until, at last, the final contestant.

"Looks like the old clock on the wall says we're just about out of time," Monty said. "But hey, let's squeeze in one more of you grabby eating machines, what do you say? Who's up next?"

"Well, Monty, he comes to us from the Lower East Side, and his interests are slamdancing and graffiti. Six-foot-two, hair of blue, just call him Fang!"

An imposingly tall figure emerged from offstage, made even taller by the blue spikes of hair exploding from his head at all angles. Beneath a loose black-mesh shirt, his sunken chest was crisscrossed with chains. His upper lip was eaten away entirely up to his nose, giving him a perpetual snarl. Fang took his place at the wheel.

"Last spin of the night, Fang," Monty said. "Let's give 'em a good one."

And good it was. The wheel spun forever, slowing at last with a clattering of the marker blade, until it came to rest on a large 3. The crowd broke into a spattering of applause.

"Whoa ho ho ho, what luck!" Monty roared. The best he could tell, Fang was grinning too. "Another big winner! What have we got for him?"

"They're young! They're nubile! They're fresh from Hollywood! And they're all yours, Fang! The entire female cast of last spring's trash-theater epic, *Cheerleader Party Massacre!*"

Door Number Three was up by now, and behind it sat a cage filled with aspiring starlets in identical red and white outfits. What a shame to have spent years hoping and dreaming for that big break, that shot on prime time TV, and miss out on the moment due to Thorazine. It had kicked in hard and heavy, leaving them as active as a basket of vegetables. Except for . . .

The audience was in, for them, a frenzy of excitement. Some were standing, arms waving like stalks of wheat in a summer breeze. Others stomped their feet to no apparent rhythm. DeadHead cued some new music, angry guitars and shouted vocals. The Dead Kennedys, maybe?

Except for . . .

Fang had amped up into a frenzy of his own, twitching in time with the music like a spastic in mid-seizure. His head bristled like a mace. Several of the earlier contestants wandered back onstage for the party atmosphere of the closing credits: Cynthia, with a good deal of Flight 901 smeared across her face; Shawn and his cooler of heads; Millicent, modeling her new arm. Fang twitched and slammed himself into Cynthia. An ear went sailing across the soundstage like a crinkled little Frisbee.

Yet Monty found himself unable to tear his gaze away from the girl he'd spoken with before the show. She clung to the front of the cage, swimming upstream against the current of a Thorazine haze while the rest of the starlets slumped in catatonic heaps. Her knuckles showed white against the steel bars.

She's not supposed to do that! She's supposed to be OUT of it!

She looked thin, painfully so, and no doubt it had been a good long while since her hair had been washed. Her lips trembled, and her eyes loomed huge against the pale of her face. Eyes that fixed, eyes that accused.

Eyes that started reconfiguring those internal switches. OFF went the smile, OFF went the juice.

"Help me, *please*," she said, though over the racket onstage he couldn't hear her, could only read her lips. "Everybody's got a price—what's yours? Is this it?"

In a pathetic attempt at seduction, she fumbled with one side of her sweater and tugged it upward. Ragged fingernails left red streaks on her skin. And there she stayed, holding the cage bar with one hand and her sweater in the other. Gauging his price.

Monty suddenly wanted to be sick. And not entirely from the prospect of her inevitable fate.

Everybody's got a price—what's yours?

In the absurd simplicity of her offer, she'd managed to show him a truth that had always eluded him before: Greed was the one thing death couldn't conquer. Love would succumb before it, and loyalty. Friendship and honor. Morality and dignity and even humanity. But not greed. Greed had an immortality all its own, and would thrive in the stony soil that could kill the rest.

He gave her the first genuine smile he'd anyone given in years.

Monty reached beneath his jacket to finger the grip of the .38. *At least it'll be the merciful way out. And then a bullet for me, maybe?*

He drew the gun, letting his arm hang by his side. The girl saw, and understood. And in pulling her sweater back down, accepted. Her glazed eyes shut and her face tilted toward an unseen sky. *Make it quick*, she seemed to be saying.

And then a bullet for me . . . ? No, I can't do that, can't do that at all. Because God help me, I need this stage more.

But make it quick? Okay, that much he could do.

Except that by the time he raised the gun halfway, it was plucked cleanly from his hand.

Monty hadn't noticed that Brad Bernerd had sidled over beside him. But now they stood face to rotten face. Bernerd was smarter than he looked, Monty knew that. Apparently he was stronger and quicker, as well.

Before Monty could move, Bernerd pointed the revolver's muzzle at his lower thigh and pulled the trigger.

The thunderclap of gunpowder aside, the effect was much like getting clubbed with a brick. Monty felt his leg suddenly swatted from beneath him, and the next thing he knew he was on his side on the floor, tasting dust.

The gunshot brought everything to a halt—the announcer's closing voice-over, Fang's slamdancing, Millicent's preening. DeadHead even killed the music. Everything stopped except the silent scrolling of the credits on the monitors. Once again, Monty was the center of undivided attention. Struggling at the bottom of a sea of staring eyes.

He propped himself up on one elbow, grunting, chilly sweat trickling from his scalp. The lights didn't feel quite so warm anymore. He gazed up into Bernerd's runny eyes.

"It would've happened anyway," Bernerd said. He slowly cocked his dented head toward Door Number Three. "She didn't matter."

Monty's mouth gaped. He figured that his eyes must finally have been as blank and his brain as empty as everyone else's around him. "Then why?" was all he could say.

"The ratings," Bernerd said. "Time for a retooling. Your ratings are slipping."

And as Monty pondered this great imponderable, Bernerd simply turned and walked away. The credits rolled on, and the rest of them began to move again, closing in as surely as the cameras. They mounted the stage from the amphitheater—by themselves, in pairs, as entire families. Converging on him with unblinking, unsated eyes.

My ratings? Slipping? SLIPPING? The thought was too great, and snapped his already fragile mind with pencil-thin ease.

He felt the first insistent tug at the bullet wound in his thigh, saw the cameras leering in.

But the eyes of the world are on me now! he thought. *And its hands . . . and quite a few teeth . . .*

Audience participation at its finest.

～

BRIAN HODGE is the award-winning author of ten novels of horror and crime/noir, over one hundred works of shorter fiction, and four full-length collections. His most recent collection, *Picking The Bones*, was honored with a *Publishers Weekly* starred review. Works slated for 2012 include a collection of crime fiction, *No Law Left Unbroken*; a novella, *Without Purpose, Without Pity*; and a hardcover edition of his early post-apocalyptic novel *Dark Advent*. His website is www.brianhodge.net.

～

He felt entrenched by the sudden weirdness. This was a coke factory
in the middle of Peru. But as long as he got his order, the drug lord could
have his mystery and his truth and his power and his spirit . . .

Makak

Edward Lee

Casparza was repulsive—a human blob. He couldn't pack the food into his fat face fast enough. *Look at him*, Hull thought, disgusted. *Just another greasy spic blimp.*

But the girl—she was beautiful, and all class. She'd said her name was Janice. *Too old to be squeeze*, Hull decided. *Mid- or late-twenties.* He'd heard all the stories; the fat man was a short-eyes, a kiddie-diddler— anything over fifteen was over the hill. So how did Janice figure into it? She looked like a typical American businesswoman. Come to think of it, Hull had seen lots of Americans milling about the plush villa. What were so many Americans doing *here?* This was Peru.

And the black guy? Hull had noticed him at once. Weird. The guy was just standing there, off by some trees. *What is this? Some voodoo fucking freak show?* Hull thought. The guy had dreadlocks past his shoulders, and he was wearing a dashiki-looking thing with something hanging off the sash. Hull had never seen a black man so black. Like anthracite. And the guy hadn't moved. He just stared at them from afar, blank-faced.

"So, Mr. Hull," Casparza bid. "This is most irregular. We rarely deal direct, especially small-timers. But I know some of your people. They say good of you."

That's nice to hear, you fat shit.

Casparza weighed 400 pounds plus. The grinning face scarcely appeared human—comic features pressed into dough. He wore a preposterous white straw hat, and pants and a shirt that could tarp a baby elephant.

"The goddamn DEA interdictions are killing us," Hull informed him.

"They're killing the major cartels too," Janice pointed out. Her voice seemed reserved, hushed. Perhaps she was Casparza's spokeswoman. She had straight, pretty ash blond hair and wore a rather conservative beige business dress. A tiny pendant hung about her neck, but Hull couldn't make it out. She primly held a lit cigarette, though he had yet to see her take a drag. She hadn't eaten, either. The servants had brought food only to Hull and Casparza: some brown mush called *aji*, a stinky napalm-hot fish stew, and slabs of something the fat man had merely referred to as "Meatroll! My favoreet!" Dessert had been *anticoucho*, collops of fried sheep heart on sticks.

Hull hadn't eaten much.

"And now my amigo would like to buy from me," Casparza went on. His accent hung thick as the rolls of flab descending his chest.

"That's right, Mr. Casparza. Our middlemen are getting blanked out. The Bolivians can't be trusted, and the Colombians are losing 80 percent of their orders to seizures. My whole region is going nuts."

Which was an understatement. Peru had been the number three producer; now it was number one. After the hostage thing, the Tactical Air Command had clobbered the Colombian strongholds and Agent Oranged a hundred thousand acres of their best coca fields. Now there was talk of dropping a light infantry division into Bolivia. This was bad for business; Hull had money to make and customers to please. He needed ten keys a month to keep his region happy, but now he was lucky to see two. The fucking feds were ruining everything. He'd had no choice but to come to see Casparza in person. The fat man had a secret.

"You guarantee delivery," Hull said. "Nobody else does that. You've become a bit of a legend in the states. Word is you haven't lost a single drop to the feds."

"This is true, Mr. Hull." Casparza's huge blackhole mouth opened wide and sucked a piece of sheep heart off a skewer. It crunched like nuts when he chewed. "But my production surplus is no very good."

"The influx of orders is maxing us out," Janice coolly added.

"I understand that." Hull trained his attentions on Casparza, though the girl's strait-laced beauty nagged at him. At first he thought the pendant around her neck was a locket; closer peripheral inspection showed him a tiny bag of something, or a tied pouch. *She's probably some whacked-out New Ager from California,* Hull snidely considered. He *hated* California. *It's probably a pouch full of crystal dust or some shit, to purify her fucking aura.*

But of course that didn't mesh with the rest of her looks—primo, neat as a pin. And there was something about her eyes—just . . . something. "We're a small operation, Mr. Casparza. I only want to buy ten keys a month."

"You know my price?"

"Yes," Hull said. Goddamn right he did. The drug war had jacked prices through the roof. A year ago a kilo of "product" ran for 13.5 a key. Now they wanted 25. Casparza charged 30 and he got it. Nobody knew how he evaded seizure losses, and nobody cared. They just wanted the fat man's shit. Even at 30k per drop the profit margin remained huge considering street value and higher pocket prices. But Casparza was a millionaire. He needed Hull's penny-ante business like he needed another helping of meatroll.

"I can pay 35 a key," Hull finally said. The offer would be taken either as a compliment or a grievous insult. Hull knocked on the table leg.

"Hmmm," Casparza remarked. "Let me think. I think better when I eat."

You must think a lot, ya tub of shit.

Sunlight dappled the huge table through plush trees. Hull could smell the fresh scents of the jungle. He looked at Janice again. Yes, it was a tiny pouch at the end of her necklace. She smiled meekly, but her eyes did not match.

"You remind me of home," she said.

"Where's that?"

She didn't reply. Her eyes seemed to beseech him, yet her face remained composed. Hull thought he could guess her story; a lot of the cartel honchos paid big bucks for white girls. Was that what her eyes were saying? *Her eyes*, Hull thought. They looked sad, barely extant.

Casparza shoveled more fried meat into his face, then chugged down a third tumbler of yarch, which smelled liked sewer water but didn't taste half bad. Hull craned around; the black guy in the dashiki was still standing off by the trees. He couldn't be a bodyguard; he was a stick. Besides, Casparza had more guns than the White House. The black guy hadn't moved in an hour.

"Who's the shadow?" Hull eventually asked.

"Raka," Casparza grunted, cheeks stuffed.

"Mr. Casparza's spiritual advisor," Janice augmented. *Spiritual advisor, my cock*, Hull thought. He didn't believe in spirit. He believed in the body and what the body demanded of the lost. He believed in the simple objectivities of supply and demand. Spirit could go fuck itself. Spirit was bad for business.

"Raka is from Africa, the Shaniki province." Casparza wiped his fat fingers on the tablecloth. "He helps me. He is my guiding light."

You need a guiding light, dumbo. You're so fat you block out the sun.

Hull squinted. The black unresponsive face stared back unblinking. Was he staring *at* Hull, or *through* him? The dreadlocks dangled like whipcords. Hull still couldn't identify the thing that hung off Raka's sash.

Casparza chuckled, jowls jiggling. "You are wondering how I do it, yes? You are wondering how it is that I lose no product while everyone else loses their ass."

Sure, blubberhead. I'm wondering. "That's your affair, Mr. Casparza. I'm just a businessman trying to stay afloat."

Casparza's grin drew seams into his immense face. "Truth is power, and spirit is truth. Think about that, amigo. Think hard."

Hull knew shit when he smelled it. Were they playing with him? The black guy watching his back and Casparza's grinning, porky face in front was about all Hull's nerves could stand. But just as he became convinced that this whole thing was a mistake, Casparza stood up, his shadow engulfing the table. He offered his fat hand.

"We have a deal, Mr. Hull. Ten keys a month at 35 a key."

Hull jumped up. He shook the fat man's hand, suppressing the abrupt gush of relief. "I can't thank you enough, Mr. Casparza. It's an honor to do business with you."

"Just remember what I said"—the fat grin beamed—"about spirit."

Hull could think of no response.

Casparza laughed. His eyeballs looked like marbles sunk in fat. "We make arrangements in the morning. Until then, make yourself at home."

"Thank you, sir."

"Janice will show you around."

The fat man lumbered off. He'd been sitting on a packing crate—Hull noticed now—since no chair on earth could accommodate his girth. Rolls of fat hung off his sides and wriggled like Jell-O.

"Ready for the twenty-five-cent tour?" Janice inquired.

"Sure," Hull said. He was elated. He'd done it; he'd made his deal. But impulse dragged at his gaze. Hull turned his head in tingling slowness.

Raka, the black shadow, was gone.

"You're either very stupid or very desperate," Janice said. She led him past the pool. Several girls—blondes—frolicked nude in the water, while a few more lay back in lounge chairs, taking turns freebasing. None of them could have been older than sixteen.

"I'm probably a little bit of both," Hull answered her. "But what makes you think so?"

Janice lit a cigarette. "You've got balls coming down here. Alone. An independent with a small order."

Hearing this prim and proper woman say *balls* was oddly erotic. "I've got a business to run," Hull pointed out. "A direct deal was my last resort. You wouldn't believe what the states are like since the crackdown. I hate to think how many times I've driven around all night with a suitcase full of hundreds and no one to give it to. But your boss guarantees delivery. I had to give it a shot."

Now the girls who'd been freebasing lay back in grinning stupors. Two more climbed out of the pool for their turns, one so young she scarcely had pubic hair. Hull did not feel even abstractly responsible. Loss was always someone else's gain. Why shouldn't he be in on it? He was just a purveyor to a need. *Supply and demand, kids. It's not my fault the world's a piece of shit. If I don't sell it, somebody else will.*

One of the blondes smiled at him, her white legs spread unabashed on the lounge chair. A blowjob maybe, but there was no way Hull would want to fuck any of the pool girls. Too young; kids weren't his style. *See?* he thought, a comical testament to God. *I've got morals.* A drug marketeer, Hull was no stranger to lots of sex; he liked nothing more than breaking a couple of nuts per day into a nice, hot box. But *seasoned* women were more his bag. Women with experience. Women who knew themselves, and were sure of themselves. Like—

Well, like his escort, for instance.

He tried to catch glimpses of Janice as she led him out of the court. Great figure, great legs. Not age but more like a refinement had crept into her model's face, tightening the mouth, etching tiny lines at the corners of the eyes. *Her eyes,* he contemplated again. They were probably once very beautiful. Now they looked lackluster. How long ago had *she* been one of the girls in the pool? Her eyes showed all the broken pieces of her dreams, but Hull didn't feel particularly guilty about that, either. Why should he?

He wouldn't mind fucking her, though—no, indeed. That would be nice, wouldn't it? Humping a good one off up her slot. He could imagine it in his mind: wet and ready, and a gorgeous dark-blond thatch. Then maybe he'd turn her around and treat her to a second load up the back door. *Hmmm.* A nice thought, at least. He was probably even entitled to now that he was Casparza's client.

But what the hell was that goddamn little thing around her neck?

She took him down the hill. As before she ignored the lit cigarette in her hand. "Here're the works," she said.

Casparza ran an impressive operation. This was no cokehole in the jungle; it was a *complex.* Whole warehouses were devoted to maturation and wash-trenches. Dump trucks one after another roared down from the fields, their beds stacked high with coca leaves. Processors in more warehouses treated and pulped the leaves to new paste. Further treatment and desiccation reduced the paste to purified powder, which would then be distilled to crack once it got to the point people in the States.

Then they passed the camp.

At first Hull thought it must be where the field laborers slept. Rows of camouflaged tents lined the field. In the middle of it all stood a single, much larger tent.

Hull spied several men in business suits walking down the tent rows. They were Americans, obviously.

"What's with all the Americans here?"

"Don't worry about it," Janice told him.

A pair of bent laborers dragged big plastic garbage cans out of the central tent. They disappeared around the side. Standing at the tent's posted entrance was Raka, the black.

"Okay, what's with him, then? What's Raka's story?"

"You ask too many questions, Mr. Hull."

I guess I'll take that as a hint. Hull felt entrenched by the sudden weirdness. Americans in business suits? Some black stoneface in a mojo costume? This was a coke factory in the middle of Peru. But the girl was right; he mustn't make waves. *Don't look a gift blimp in the mouth.* As long as Hull got his order, Casparza could have his mystery. He could have his truth and his power and his spirit.

The tour was over. Evening came early here; the jungle darkened in dusk. "I'm impressed," Hull admitted.

"You should be."

Hull kept looking at the camp. More men in suits filed out of the big tent. He saw women, too, dressed like Janice. All clearly Americans.

"Don't worry about it," Janice repeated. It sounded like a warning. "The world is more diverse than we think, Mr. Hull. It's really not a world at all, but a whole bunch of worlds."

"Meaning?"

"This—this place here—is not *your* world."

Hull stared at her.

"Just remember what Casparza said, Mr. Hull. Remember it well."

Her cigarette had grown an inch of ash. Hull's eyes darted from the pendant at her bust to her eyes, always back to her eyes. For a fractured moment he felt seized, or rather bound. He felt tied up by his own confusion. *Her eyes*, he pondered. There was something about her eyes.

Her eyes looked dead.

Janice fingered the makak; it seemed to give off heat.

But Janice felt cold.

She raised her nightgown and rubbed the jelly into her sex. K-Y, the tube read. She barely felt it. The night air steamed around her, but she barely felt that either. She did not sweat. She looked at her hand and saw the cigarette burns encrusted between her fingers.

Moonlight eddied in through the window. Hull lay asleep on the bed. Janice drifted in, still not sure what she was doing. So much was instinct now—habits that sat perched behind her life like ghosts. She envied Hull in his sleep. *Real sleep*, she thought.

Hull reminded her of home, whatever that was. He reminded her of life.

"Mr. Hull?" she whispered, leaning over his bed. She shook him gently. *What am I doing?* she wondered. *Why am I here?*

Hull stirred, then his eyes snapped open. "What . . . ?" he murmured. A pause ticked like dripping wax. Then: "Janice?"

She queried him with her eyes, as if viewing not a person but a notion or an idea only partially interpretable.

"Come here," he said.

She pulled the sheet off and lay beside him. What could she say? I'm lonely, Mr. Hull? You remind me of things? Her fingers closed around his penis. It grew stiff at once. The reaction pleased her; it made her happy: flesh coming to life at her touch. She flinched when he kissed her. His hands felt her body through the nightgown. Again, she wondered if it was the memory of being touched that registered, or the actual sensation. It was like being touched by a ghost.

"You remind me of things," she whispered.

"What things? Tell me."

Janice wanted to cry. Possibly she was, though tearlessly. She hitched her nightgown up and straddled him. His penis slipped right into her sex—another ghost.

He reached for the nightgown. "Take this off."

"No!" she said too quickly.

"You're a beautiful woman, Janice. I want to see you."

Beautiful. Woman. See you. But she didn't want him to see her. She instead pushed the straps off her shoulders and let the gown slide down to her waist. He began to pump slowly in and out. The makak bobbled between her breasts.

"Christ, your pussy feels good," he panted. But even this crude remark pleased her, complimented her. *My pussy feels good.* It made her feel real.

"I'm gonna come so much in you . . . "

Come. Sperm. Fucking. *Yes, you remind me of things.* What, though? She could remember only in snatches. Each thrust of his penis into her sex pushed a little piece to the surface of her mind. How old had she been? Fourteen? Fifteen? Not an uncommon' story. Her father had raped her, sodomized her for years. Then she'd run away only to be raped by worse people, but by then the drugs held the reins of her life so she didn't really care. She'd been passed back and forth—for anything. Lots of gang bangs and bondage. Lots of fletching. Many times, her man—his name was 'Rome—brought her up for what he called the "Champagne Special." She'd have to blow a roomful of men, spitting each ejaculation into a champagne glass; upon completion, of course, she'd then consume the contents of the glass in one gulp. Dog shows were another regular entertainment for 'Rome's dealer friends. Some of the dogs they brought up were quite large and frisky. "Make Fido happy, Janice," 'Rome had ordered, "or it's no froggie for you." The little white rocks were all the motivation she needed, her treasure at the end of the rainbow, day in, day out. Eventually she'd been sold.

And ended up here.

She'd been sold to Casparza as part of a favor. Casparza liked them young, before they got too beat. He owned many girls. He was too fat to effectively have intercourse, but he liked blowjobs and handjobs. He'd lie on his back and hold his massive belly up as the girls took turns. He also liked tongue baths. "Ah, my little lovers," he'd mutter while several girls slowly licked the greasy sweat off his entire lardacious carriage. Casparza didn't wash much, which made it worse. Sometimes he'd lie on his belly, two girls holding apart his buttocks as others licked his testicles and anus. Occasionally he would defecate on a girl's chest—a squatting human whale—and it always seemed to be poor Janice who received the privilege of eating the spicy excrement.

Once a girl got old—twenty or so—he didn't want them anymore. Many were given to the merc camps that patrolled the fields, others simply disappeared. But the lucky ones were saved for special duties. For Raka.

Raka, she thought, riding up and down.

Hull's rhythm steepened. "You are one hot box, Janice—Christ." Her sex made a wet, crinkly noise, like someone eating food. The sensation of motion, of heat and impact, made Janice feel dully elated. Being penetrated—now—was a transposition of sorts, a crossing of matrixes. It put flesh on her memory, life in the space where her heart used to be.

Hull groped for her; he pulled her down, hugging her, as he ejaculated. She could feel his semen spurt into her sex. It felt warm. It was a warm gift he'd given to her, a deposit from one world to another.

She lay back beside him. His finger traced around her breast, then tapped the makak. "What's this?"

My life, she wished she could say. "A makak—a good luck charm."

"Superstitious, huh? I've seen a lot of people around here with these things. At that camp. What is that place, anyway?" When she didn't answer, he pushed her back. "Let me go down on you. I want to eat your snatch."

"No!" she objected.

He pulled at the nightgown rumpled about her waist.

"No!" she said, grabbing his hands. "Please don't."

"You don't have anything to be self-conscious about."

"Just . . . please . . . don't."

Hull let it rest. He was an attractive man, unabashed in his nakedness. He looked clean-cut and professional. He didn't look like what he was, and she supposed that's why Casparza liked him.

"How does he do it?" Hull asked her.

"Do what?"

"How does Casparza get his shit out? He can't be doing it with boats; the U.S. Navy's all over the coast. And surveillance planes are IRing the major land routes twenty-four hours a day."

"He mules the orders."

Hull leaned up, astonished. "What, commercial air flights?"

"Yes."

"That's *crazy*. Customs checks every plane inside and out, and they fluoroscope and sniff every single piece of luggage and hand-carry on every flight. Casparza's probably moving a thousand keys a month. He can't possibly be muling through airports, not in this day and age. He'd lose everything."

"Just don't worry about it." Her voice was weary. Her hand returned to his penis; it was hard again in moments, hard and hot and pulsing with life.

"Do it to me again," she said.

"Yeah," he said. "I'll do it to you, all right. You'll like it." He turned her over, pushed her on her belly, and spat between her buttocks. Yet another memory, not surprising. Then he plugged his penis into her rectum, humping her hard.

'Rome, Daddy, all those other men—no big deal. It made her feel good because it reminded her of things.

She hung partway off the bed. The moon seemed to bob up and down in the window with Hull's frenetic thrusts. Janice's hair tossed; the makak danced dangling about her neck. Each impact beat more memories into her head, more life. The ferocious sodomy seemed to verify something to her. *This is what people do,* she mused. Hull's penis was proof of life. She wanted him to come in her again; she wished he could come in her forever—every time he did was another validation that she was something more than a shadow, more than a ghost.

He shuddered, moaning. Janice felt happy. The warm spurts felt thinner and hotter this time, spurtling into her bowel, and she was so happy she wanted to cry. But then—

—she froze.

The face bled into her—black as obsidian and utterly blank.

Raka's face.

The priest's voice, an echoic chord, marched across her mind.

Now, it commanded.

Still penetrated, Janice slammed the lamp down on Hull's head.

The warped words oozed, spreading. *Truth is power. Spirit is truth.*

The mist of Hull's consciousness trickled up into the light. His eyes lolled open. Blurred faces hovered like blobs, then sharpened, gazing down. Janice and Casparza. He'd been fucking the girl, hadn't he? Yes, and then . . . then . . .

Goddamn, he thought when the rest of the memory landed.

He tried to get up but he couldn't.

"Ah, Mr. Hull." Casparza's face loomed. "Welcome back, amigo."

Hull glanced around. The fuckers had tied him down to a table. He was nude. The hissing light from a dozen gas lanterns licked about drab canvas walls. *The camp*, he realized. *The tent.*

He was in the big tent.

Janice stood beside the table, wan in her nightgown. Casparza stood opposed, the avalanche of flab straining against his huge shirt.

Standing by a canvas partition was Raka.

"We gain power through spirit, Mr. Hull," Casparza cryptified. "Raka is an Obeah priest, a Papaloi. He was bred to harness the spirit."

The black priest stood in total lack of movement, the staring face bereft of life as a wooden mask. He wore a necklace of human fingers, or perhaps pudenda, and the thing that hung from his sash was a shrunken baby's head. But from his hand something else depended, swaying: one of those little bags on a cord, one of the makak.

"I thought we had a deal," Hull moaned.

"Oh, we do, Mr. Hull," the fat man assured. "But you want to know my secret, don't you?"

"I don't give a fuck about your secret. Just let me loose."

"In time." Casparza's grin seemed to prop up the bulbous face. He nodded to Janice.

I'm fucked, Hull realized. He squirmed against his bonds. It didn't take a genius to deduce that they were going to kill him. But why? He hadn't crossed any lines. It didn't make sense. Had some new mover back home put a contract on him? Had someone fingered him as a stool?

"Look, I don't know what I've done, and I don't know what's going on. Just let me go. I'll pay you whatever you want."

Casparza laughed, fat jiggling.

Janice pushed in a wheeled table like a gurney. *Holy motherfucking shit*, Hull thought, and it was the palest of thoughts, and the least human. His eyes felt stapled open. On the gurney lay a corpse: a man, an American. It was pale and naked.

"Janice will show you," Casparza said. "The power of spirit."

Hull grit his teeth. Janice very deftly slit open the cadaver's belly with a heavy-gauge autopsy scalpel. She plunged her hands into the rive and began to pull things out. First came glistening pink rolls of intestines, then the kidneys, the liver, stomach, spleen. She tossed each wet mass of organs into a big plastic garbage can. Then she reached up further for the higher stuff—the heart, the lungs. It all went into the can. By the time she was done, she was slick to the elbows with dark, oxygen-starved blood.

"We can fit six or eight keys into the average corpse," Casparza informed him.

Hull frowned in spite of his dilemma. "You're out of your mind. That's the oldest trick in the book. Customs has been wise to it for years."

Casparza smiled. Now Janice was packing sealed kilos into the corpse's evacuated body cavity, then stuffed in wads of foam rubber to fill in the gaps and smooth things out. She worked with calm efficiency. Finished, she began to sew up the gaping seam with black autopsy suture.

"You can't smuggle coke into the States in *cadavers*," Hull objected. "Customs inspects all air freight, including coffins, including bodies tagged for transport. Any idiot knows that. The girl said you were muling the stuff."

"That's correct, Mr. Hull. My mules walk right past your customs agents."

Wha— Hull thought. *Walk?*

Janice raised her nightgown. Hull's eyes, in dreadful assessment, roved up her legs, over the patch of pubic hair, and stopped. Across her belly was a long black-stitched seam.

"Janice has been muling for me for quite some time."

My God, was about all Hull could think.

Raka began muttering something, heavy incomprehensible words like a chant. The words seemed palpable, they seemed to thicken amid the air as fog–they seemed alive. Then he placed a makak about the corpse's neck.

The corpse sat up and climbed off the gurney.

My God, my God, my—

Raka led the corpse out.

Casparza held out his fat hands, his face, for the first time, placid in some solemn knowledge. "So you see, amigo, we still have a deal. And you'll get to be your own mule."

Aw, Jesus, Jesus—

The scalpel flashed splotchily in Janice's hand. Hull began to scream as she began to cut.

EDWARD LEE has written more than forty novels. Nominated for a Bram Stoker Award for his story "Mr. Torso," his short stories have appeared in numerous magazines and anthologies, including the award-winning 999. Many have been compiled in his nine collections. A number of Lee's projects have been optioned for film. One, *Header*, has been made was released on DVD in June, 2009.

Death and zombies. The two great equalizers. No one gives a fuck what you did or who you were in life. Eat or be eaten. Fuck or be fucked. Kill or be killed.

Tomorrow's Precious Lambs

Monica Valentinelli

Midnight. The hour when flesh walks and good little children are stashed away like stolen diamonds. The hour when the feast begins: skin-ripping hair-raising bone-cracking crunch, crunch, crunches. The hour when my thunder stick comes out, zap, zap zapping all the way 'til dawn.

Go on down. Down to the ri-ver. Go on down and wash a-way.

One-thirty. Dog tired. Got a call from headquarters. Had to exterminate a nest out by a gas station. Was worried I was going to run out of ammo. Pause. Rewind. That's right. I didn't need to reload. Long battery life. Couldn't use the stick like I wanted. There were too many of 'em and not enough of me. So I introduced them to my best friend and mortal enemy—C4. Crickle-crackle snap, snap, snap. Orange flames licked the corpses, ate their rotting flesh right down to the bone. Smelled like my momma's church picnic. Hungry. Nothing to eat. Found an energy shot. Slammed two of them. Made my belly hurt even more.

Come to the ri-ver. Wash, wash, wash your sins and pray.

Fell asleep at the wheel. Phone woke me up. *Three a.m.* Witching hour. Sergeant's on the line saying something about domestic abuse. Tell her it could wait 'til daylight. Man beats a woman down, that's bad. Man eats a woman's brain? That's the guy I'm coming for.

"Officer Mike . . . " Sergeant's got that disapproving tone in her voice, like she's my mother. My momma was a preacher, but she died in a fire, along with the rest of the parish. Don't know much about Sarge or how she survived. Then I remember. She sticks to the rules, because it's all she's got. It's like her feelings dried up and they were replaced with a pile of useless laws. Like my appendix. Don't know what I need it for, but it's still there.

Maybe the law is all I got, too. "Yes, sir?"

"We got a biter." Fuck. "She's twelve." Double fuck. I've been on this job too long, but not long enough. Three years. Shitty pay. Crappy benefits. Divorced. No kids. That was before the dead rose up out of their graves. Some folk thought it was the Rapture, welcomed the dearly departed back into church with open arms. Then the dead took over, gnawing on people like they were Thanksgiving leftovers. Told myself this had nothing to do with God or Jesus or the devil. This reeked of greed, something man-made, and it was up to me to find out who's responsible.

"I'll be there." Sarge's used to the way I talk. She never says it, but she knows why she needs me. I've lasted longer than any other cop she's known. She wasn't from the precinct, not originally. The army, I think. Sarah? Susan? What the hell's her name? Anyway, Sarge told me once that either I'm a crazy motherfucker or I'm the toughest bastard this side of the river. She said I must be off my nut to be doing what I'm doing, and she's right. "But you owe me. What's the address?"

"1543 Cedar Street."

Trees. Why name a street after a goddamn tree? Do they feel guilty for plowing them down? Always seems like the tree-streets in those neighborhoods are oily, black and perfect. Least it covers up the blood. "I'll take care of it."

"Be careful," she warns me. There's no trace of fear in her voice, but I know she's afraid. "Her family's rich."

Oh, crap. Not another one. To some folk, doesn't matter who lives or dies—as long as it ain't them.

Three-fifteen. I take my sweet-ass time getting over to Cedar Street, drive the long, safe way through the electric fences. Fucking rich people. Dead rising from their graves, people dying in the streets, and what do they do? Bribe people with food to build them a goddamn wall with fucking turrets and video cameras. I know that shit ain't legal, but the law doesn't apply to some people, I guess.

Shit. I don't want to meet the family and I'm too tired to fight. Just want to put a bullet in the girl's head and be done with it. Crap, no bullets. Why do I keep forgetting things? Right. No food. Nothing to fuel my body 'cept my red-hot rage.

Survivors are worse than zombies. They'll say stupid shit like, *"Not my precious baby lamb. She's just sick."* Then I'll say, *"Ma'am, with all due respect, your daughter is a zombie. She may be walking, but she's a corpse."*

Sometimes they'll ask me to leave. When I do, I slap the court order on 'em, quarantine the house, and light it up. Fence or no fence: we can't have their precious lamb eating the neighbors. Wasn't always that way. Used to arrest the fuckers for the good of society and all. Now Sarge orders me to burn 'em to the ground. Take no prisoners, no room for the stupid. If they won't follow the law, then the law won't help them. Right or wrong, that's just the way it is. Save those that want to be saved and put down the rest. Put down the sheep.

Lord, Lo-ord! Lead Your lambs through the val-ley, all the way down to the ri-ver.

Four-thirty. Pull up to a big house all lit up like a tree on Christmas morning. Whole lawn is lush, rigged with sprinklers. These fuckers must have money. Most people can't even get fresh bread or water, these assholes have to manicure their grass. I pull up to the door. Grab my gear: handcuffs, Taser staff, C4 and my badge. Set my staff to maximum. That's all I fucking need. No goddamn shrubbery. Bet these people don't care there's a war on. They have their house and all this shit. Why call me?

Four-thirty five. Ring the doorbell. Fat man comes to the door dressed in a black tuxedo. Tells me to be quiet. Says he's having a dinner party and we don't want to disturb his guests.

"I'm Officer Francis, but you can call me Mike." I stick out a hand just to fuck with the guy. Hope he doesn't shake it. If he does? I'd have to play nice.

He doesn't. Damn, I should've called Sarge to bet on that. Could have won an extra hour of sleep. "Yes, well. No names are necessary. You don't need to know who I am."

I lean in close. Know my breath stinks; ran out of toothpaste. "Yeah, I really do. You see I'm the law around here."

Fat man grunts and looks right into my eyes. His eyes are cold, black. "I can have you fired. Then how are you going to eat, Officer?"

"Motherfucker, you can die for all I care," I hiss. "But I will do my job and put that zombie down."

"My little girl is not a zombie," the fat man screams, trails of spit flying out of his mouth. "Her name is Mackenzie."

Knew that was coming. Fat man's precious lamb-child couldn't possibly be one of *them*. "According to ordnance three dash two point . . . " I give the fat man a present, slap the law on his back.

"You can't do this!" Asshole tries to push me down. Almost works, too. Got a lot of meat on his bones, meat I don't have. "I will sue!"

"Do you want the chance?"

Fat man's eyes blink. Once. Twice. Three times.

"Show me where she is and you can sue me and the whole fucking country for all I care."

"Fine. I'll play your game." Fat man waddles down a long hallway like nothing happened. Strange motherfucker. What's his angle? "Come, Officer Francis," fat man says, snapping his fingers. "This way."

I shake my head. People struggling to survive and this fat fuck acts like he's king. There oughta be a law. Wait. There was supposed to be one, up until some idiot politician threw himself at the press, saying some folk were just too important to be treated like everyone else. Said they were vital to the survival of the human race. We all knew it was bullshit. Some people are just way too scared to die.

Course, not all folk are bad. Some of 'em, once they figured out what was going on, they helped out. Gave up their nice homes and fancy cars. Opened their doors and shared their food before they—or *it*—rotted away. I asked one of 'em why he gave up everything to help his neighborhood. Man told me there was no rich or poor. No numbers to crunch. No papers to file. Until the zombies were put down, everyone has shit and we need more than a prayer to get through tomorrow. He was right, too. Life ain't perfect, but we adapted. Some people used the brains that God gave 'em to give us a fighting chance.

Death and zombies. The two great equalizers. No one gives a fuck what you did or who you were in life. Eat or be eaten. Fuck or be fucked. Kill or be killed.

We come to a door at the back of the house. It's white, clean. Can't remember the last time I saw something so new and shiny. "Don't kill her," the fat man tells me. "There will be consequences if you do. *Severe* consequences."

Check my watch. *Five a.m.* Wasting too much time on this guy but I have to humor him. Damn, I hate my job. "Why's that?"

"She volunteered."

And He'll wash, oh He'll wash . . . His lambs, his pre-cious lambs . . .

Fat man pushes the doors open, waves me into a well-lit lab and shuts the door behind us. Gleaming white, looks likes a dentist's office, or a giant tooth. Never did catch this guy's name. *Asshole*. That's his name. *Mister* Asshole.

"There," Mr. Asshole points to a large metal fridge. "I was trying to feed Mackenzie and she got loose. She's over in that corner."

Something's wrong. I can almost taste the bullshit. "If she's turned, you know what I have to do."

Mr. Asshole snorts. "Not this time, Francis. Like I said. She volunteered."

"Then why'd you call me? Why call the cops?" I want to sucker punch this guy. No one volunteers to become a flesh-eating, animated corpse. No one.

Another grunt from Mr. Asshole. "Wife's idea. She didn't want me getting hurt."

Nice. So there was a *Mrs.* Asshole. More than I had. "Let me guess. She doesn't want her precious daughter getting hurt either."

"That sums it up, yeah."

I stare him down, but he doesn't budge. Guy has balls, I'll give him that. Probably lying, though. Don't trust this penguin. He didn't even bother to ask me if I wanted a muffin. "Fine. Wait outside."

"Suit yourself, Officer. This room is sealed from the outside, so knock twice on this door when you're done."

Down by the ri-ver, drink the deep, deep wa-ter. Bathe in the blood of the Lamb.

Five-fifteen a.m. Find the girl, lock her up and be on my way. Take ten minutes. Hour or two 'til dawn. Maybe I'll douse another nest on my way back to the station. Maybe I'll force Mr. Asshole to ride along. First? The girl.

I check the juice on my staff and sneak to a corner. Still can't shake the feeling I'm not supposed to be here. I keep wondering if this is one of those stories I heard about where a cop winds up in the oven. Sarge said this was a domestic abuse call. "A biter," she'd said. Maybe I'm losing it. I try calling the station but my phone's dead. Not good. Could've charged it, but I didn't. Must've forgot.

"Help me."

The words sound like a dying prayer. I walk over to the gap behind the fridge and see a girl crouched behind it. From what I can tell, she's wearing one of them pink frilly dresses girls do for Easter.

Bathe in the blood of the Lamb and wash your sins a-way.

Don't want to examine her, but I do it anyway. Shit. Her dress is covered with stringy, bloody bits. I tap my thunder stick on the ground in front of her. She looks up, but I don't think she's able to see me. Most of the signs are there—bulging veins and blackened flesh—but her hair was combed and her eyes were milky white, no pupils. Couldn't confirm she was a zombie, but I don't think Mackenzie is human any more either. Can't help but wonder who she's eating.

"Help me."

I hear the words, but they aren't coming from the girl's mouth. Sound is coming from somewhere else. Somewhere close. First things first. I bend over to secure the girl, but I slip on something wet. Hit my head. Bitch comes after me, her arms flailing. Drops of blood drip down on my face. Yep, zombie. Has to be. Don't care whose daughter this was, she's no one's daughter now.

I roll over and kick the girl hard in the chest, then crack a good one upside her head, hoping to stun her. Then I pick her up carefully, just in case Mr. Asshole's watching, and haul her over my shoulder. She won't be out for long. Have to tie her up quick.

"Help me."

I wander around to the back and open a plastic curtain. Jackpot. Four beds, only three of them empty. Skinny, naked woman was all tied up. Hell of a way to treat a woman, but I've seen worse things. I throw the girl down and strap her to the bed. Zap her head a few times for good measure. Sizzle, sizzle. Truth be told, I hope she stays knocked out. Maybe that'll teach Mr. Asshole a lesson. Soon as I touch her legs, though, sweet Mackenzie lamb starts chomping at the bit. Can't see how she got loose. Bed's restraints are pretty thick.

"Please, just end it." The woman gasps.

"Gladly." I grab my stick and ram it into the corpse's mouth. Fry it good, so good it won't move anymore. Fuck, Mr. Asshole.

"Quickly, set me free."

Drink and be free, drink the blood of the Lord.

The woman . . . She was conscious, crying, half-eaten. Her body hadn't been gnawed on; pieces of it had been cut off. She'd been kept alive somehow, though. Not sure what kind of tricks Mr. Asshole was using to keep this woman alive, but when I'm through with him, he'll know what it means to be afraid.

"What's your name?" No reply. I check her pulse and see if she's still breathing. "You okay?"

"Officer Francis, I'd like to show my appreciation for the civic duty you have just performed."

Mr. Asshole. How'd I guess? "Sorry, I don't follow you."

"Turn around."

I back up slowly and wave my thunder stick in the air. Doors are open. Good. "You can't hurt me. I'm an officer of the law."

Lord, protect your precious lambs from those nasty wolves. Be our shepherd and lead us to salvation.

Mr. Asshole laughs. "Hurt you? I want to *feed* you. You're obviously hungry." He pushes a cart in front of me filled with apples, peanut butter, nuts, cheese and sweet bread.

"I don't understand. I thought . . . " Not sure what I thought. Been a long time since someone, anyone other than the Sarge has been that nice to me. My gut tells me I can't trust the fat man. There's gotta be something else going on here. There just has to be. What do I do? Phone's dead. Soon as Mr. Asshole finds that out he might kill me where I stand.

"I believe we got off on the wrong foot. I understand you were responding to a domestic abuse call, but it seems you have the wrong house."

Fuck. Impossible. "1543 Cedar Street?"

"Yes, it is."

"Then I have the right house."

"What suburb?"

I close my eyes. Can't think, can't remember. Sarge never did tell me where I was supposed to go. Just assumed, I guess. All the goddamn houses look the same. "I . . . "

Mr. Asshole pushes the cart of food closer to me. "You made a terrible mistake, Officer, but I understand. You're obviously overworked and exhausted. Have something to eat. You'll feel better."

Five-thirty. Sun'll be up soon. Flesh walking, bone-crunching, brain-sucking monsters will go back to the darkness and the worm-ridden earth they came from. As soon as they do, I'll crawl back to the station and pass out on a cot, praying one of the recovery teams brings me some food. Ain't much, but it's what I know. It's my home. "No thank you," I tell the fat man. Maybe he's not an asshole, after all. Maybe I've just lost my mind.

"Suit yourself," the fat man says. I must be imagining things, because I hear a tinge of compassion in his voice. "You know you could stay here."

I shake my head. "And do what? I already have a job."

"Security. I could pay you with food."

Lead us from temptation, Lord. Help us to see into men's hearts, to know right from wrong and recognize when the Devil is manipulating us.

"When are you going to be straight with me? I may be hungry, but I'm no fool. What do you want?"

The fat man, a.k.a Mr. Asshole, grins at me. "You are smarter than you look, Officer Francis."

"That's what my momma used to tell me."

"Where is she now?"

"Cemetery was next to the church. When the dead rose up, my momma thought Jesus had brought back my daddy from the dead, so she led the lot of them into the church for Sunday service. When I heard her and the other churchgoers screaming, I burned it to the ground."

Fat man pushes the cart a little closer to me. The food smells like someone ripped out a piece of heaven and threw it on a plate. Not sure how much longer I can hold out. Probably poisoned. "You have been looking for me for a long time, haven't you?"

"Not unless you're responsible for millions of people dying."

"What if I told you I was?"

"Then I'd beat you down and feed you to the dogs."

"Then do it," the fat man whispers. "Release me."

I scrutinize the man's face to see if I can find something good and decent in his plump cheeks and beady eyes, but I can't. Grabbing my thunder stick, I lift it over his head.

"I've been waiting all night to do this, Mr. Asshole."

Help us to recognize the tricks of the Devil when he walks among us. Save your precious, tiny lambs.

"Don't!" the naked woman cries. "That's what he wants!"

Fat man roars and charges at me. I step out of his way and let him crash into the wall. Too easy. Fat man's too soft for this old bird.

"Woman, what the fuck are you talking about?"

I turn my head for a second and the fat man grabs my ankle. "Kill me," he yells. "I'm the one you want. I'm responsible."

"He's a necromancer!"

"A what?" Fuck. I try to kick the fat man free, but he won't let go. "The hell he is. Magic ain't real."

"Science! He uses science."

"Shut up, Beatrice. You never could keep your mouth shut." Distracted,

Mr. Asshole loosens his grip. I kick him square in the nose. He yelps in pain. "Goddamn that hurts. Any harder and you would have killed me."

Jumping up, I knock Mr. Asshole off-balance. As soon as his foot lifts off the ground, I sweep my leg out in front of him, tripping the bastard. He falls flat on his pudgy face. "Sir, you have a right to remain silent. You are under arrest for the murder . . . " Breaking out my cuffs, I quickly bind his wrists behind him.

Beatrice cackles. "Your superiors won't let him live."

I tighten the cuffs as much as I can. Yep, they'll hurt, but not as much as I want them to. The woman was right. Boss'd never let this son of a bitch live until tomorrow. Bet Mr. Asshole knows that, too. Starting to feel faint; the energy shot is wearing off. I breathe deep and let the anger of a hundred thousand innocent people fill my belly.

Come and wash, oh come ye precious lambs. Wash away your sins in the river of faith. Bathe in the light of the Lord. Oh, yes. Bathe the light of the Lord and tomorrow you'll be clean.

"You're right, Beatrice." I haul the fat man to his feet and drag him over to the little girl. The corpse is gnashing its teeth. How could a man do such a thing?

Fat man stumbles and I push him on top of her. "What are you doing? No, not to her. You can't possibly . . . "

Uncoiling my rope, I tie the fat man to his daughter so tight there's no room for either of them to breathe. "You . . . you win. Let me go. I'll fix this. I promise!"

Ignoring him, I step over to Beatrice. "Are you going to release me?" she asks me. "I guess I wouldn't, either. I don't know what my husband did to me."

I smile down at her to let her know I don't hate her, just her husband. "My friend will come to set you free," I whisper. "It'll hurt."

"I know."

Brave woman. She was nothing like her whimpering mass-murdering husband. I stick a small block of C4 above Beatrice's head and a slightly bigger one on her husband's back. Sarge would be proud of me. I didn't use my whole stash this time.

"Waste not, want not."

Drink the blood of the Lord. Save our precious, baby lambs from the Devil that begs us to live in darkness.

I salute Beatrice, spit on the fat man, and stuff a bunch of food into my jacket. "Forty-nine, forty-eight . . . " Have to count my steps. Only way I know I'll be safe.

"You'll burn in hell you fucking cop!"

My turn to laugh. "That may be, Mr. Asshole, but the Devil knows your name and he's calling for you. Can't you hear him?"

"You're nuts."

I run out into the hallway, seal the lab and light up Mr. Asshole, his undead daughter Mackenzie and poor wife Beatrice. "On behalf of the entire world, fuck you Mr. Asshole."

Door's getting hot. No time to waste. *Ten minutes past six.* Time for the sun, for God's holy light, to wash my sins away. Time for all the precious lambs to come out of hiding, to know they'll be safe for one more day. Safe until tomorrow.

MONICA VALENTINELLI is a professional author and game designer. Described as a "force of nature" by her peers, Monica has been published through Abstract Nova Press, Eden Studios, White Wolf Publishing, *Apex,* and others. Her credits include a short story entitled "Pie" (published in the award-winning *Buried Tales of Pinebox, Texas* anthology) and *The Queen of Crows.* For more information about Monica, visit www.mlvwrites.com.

*Of all the bright cruel lies they tell you, the cruelest is
the one called love . . .*

Meathouse Man

George R.R. Martin

I

IN THE MEATHOUSE

They came straight from the ore-fields that first time, Trager with the
others, the older boys, the almost-men who worked their corpses next to
his. Cox was the oldest of the group, and he'd been around the most, and
he said that Trager had to come even if he didn't want to. Then one of the
others laughed and said that Trager wouldn't even know what to do, but
Cox the kind-of leader shoved him until he was quiet. And when payday
came, Trager trailed the rest to the meathouse, scared but somehow eager,
and he paid his money to a man downstairs and got a room key.

He came into the dim room trembling, nervous. The others had gone
to other rooms, had left him alone with her (no, *it*, not her but *it*, he
reminded himself, and promptly forgot again). In a shabby gray cubicle
with a single smoky light.

He stank of sweat and sulfur, like all who walked the streets of Skrakky,
but there was no help for that. It would be better if he could bathe first,
but the room did not have a bath. Just a sink, double bed with sheets that
looked dirty even in the dimness, a corpse.

She lay there naked, staring at nothing, breathing shallow breaths. Her
legs were spread; ready. Was she always that way, Trager wondered, or had
the man before him arranged her like that? He didn't know. He knew how
to do it (he did, he *did*, he'd read the books Cox gave him, and there were
films you could see, and all sorts of things), but he didn't know much of
anything else. Except maybe how to handle corpses. That he was good at,
the youngest handler on Skrakky, but he had to be. They had forced him

into the handlers' school when his mother died, and they made him learn, so that was the thing he did. This, this he had never done (but he knew how, yes, yes, he *did*); it was his first time.

He came to the bed slowly and sat to a chorus of creaking springs. He touched her and the flesh was warm. Of course. She was not a corpse, not really, no; the body was alive enough, a heartbeat under the heavy white breasts, she breathed. Only the brain was gone, ripped from her, replaced with a deadman's synthabrain. She was meat now, an extra body for a corpsehandler to control, just like the crew he worked each day under sulfur skies. She was not a woman. So it did not matter that Trager was just a boy, a jowly frog-faced boy who smelled of Skrakky. She (no *it*, remember?) would not care, could not care.

Emboldened, aroused and hard, the boy stripped off his corpse-handler's clothing and climbed in bed with the female meat. He was very excited; his hands shook as he stroked her, studied her. Her skin was very white, her hair dark and long, but even the boy could not call her pretty. Her face was too flat and wide, her mouth hung open, and her limbs were loose and sagging with fat.

On her huge breasts, all around the fat dark nipples, the last customer had left tooth-marks where he'd chewed her. Trager touched the marks tentatively, traced them with a finger. Then, sheepish about his hesitations, he grabbed one breast, squeezed it hard, pinched the nipple until he imagined a real girl would squeal with pain. The corpse did not move. Still squeezing, he rolled over on her and took the other breast into his mouth.

And the corpse responded.

She thrust up at him, hard, and meaty arms wrapped around his pimpled back to pull him to her. Trager groaned and reached down between her legs. She was hot, wet, excited. He trembled. How did they do that? Could she really get excited without a mind, or did they have lubricating tubes stuck into her, or what?

Then he stopped caring. He fumbled, found his penis, put it into her, thrust. The corpse hooked her legs around him and thrust back. It felt good, real good, better than anything he'd ever done to himself, and in some obscure way he felt proud that she was so wet and excited.

It only took a few strokes; he was too new, too young, too eager to last long. A few strokes was all he needed—but it was all she needed too. They came together, a red flush washing over her skin as she arched against him and shook soundlessly.

Afterwards she lay again like a corpse.

Trager was drained and satisfied, but he had more time left, and he was determined to get his money's worth. He explored her thoroughly, sticking his fingers everywhere they would go, touching her everywhere, rolling it over, looking at everything. The corpse moved like dead meat.

He left her as he'd found her, lying face up on the bed with her legs apart. Meathouse courtesy.

The horizon was a wall of factories, all factories, vast belching factories that sent red shadows to flick against the sulfur-dark skies. The boy saw but hardly noticed. He was strapped in place high atop his automill, two stories up on a monster machine of corroding yellow-painted metal with savage teeth of diamond and duralloy, and his eyes were blurred with triple images. Clear and strong and hard he saw the control panel before him, the wheel, the fuel-feed, the bright handle of the ore-scoops, the banks of light that would tell of trouble in the refinery under his feet, the brake and emergency brake. But that was not all he saw. Dimly, faintly, there were echoes; overlaid images of two other control cabs, almost identical to his, where corpse hands moved clumsily over the instruments.

Trager moved those hands, slow and careful, while another part of his mind held his own hands, his real hands, very still. The corpse controller hummed thinly on his belt.

On either side of him, the other two automills moved into flanking positions. The corpse hands squeezed the brakes; the machines rumbled to a halt. On the edge of the great sloping pit, they stood in a row, shabby pitted juggernauts ready to descend into the gloom. The pit was growing steadily larger; each day new layers of rock and ore were stripped away.

Once a mountain range had stood here, but Trager did not remember that.

The rest was easy. The automills were aligned now. To move the crew in unison was a cinch, any decent handler could do *that*. It was only when you had to keep several corpses busy at several different tasks that things got tricky. But a good corpsehandler could do that too. Eight-crews were not unknown to veterans; eight bodies linked to a single corpse controller moved by a single mind and eight synthabrains. The deadmen were each tuned to one controller, and only one; the handler who wore that controller and thought corpse-thoughts in its proximity field could move those deadmen like secondary bodies. Or like his own body. If he was good enough.

Trager checked his filtermask and earplugs quickly, then touched the fuel-feed, engaged, flicked on the laser-knives and the drills. His corpses echoed his moves, and pulses of light spit through the twilight of Skrakky. Even through his plugs he could hear the awful whine as the ore-scoops revved up and lowered. The rock-eating maw of an automill was even wider than the machine was tall.

Rumbling and screeching, in perfect formation, Trager and his corpse crew descended into the pit. Before they reached the factories on the far side of the plain, tons of metal would have been torn from the earth, melted and refined and processed, while the worthless rock was reduced to powder and blown out into the already unbreathable air. He would deliver finished steel at dusk, on the horizon.

He was a good handler, Trager thought as the automills started down. But the handler in the meathouse—now, she must be an artist. He imagined her down in the cellar somewhere, watching each of her corpses through holos and psi circuits, humping them all to please her patrons. Was it just a fluke, then, that his fuck had been so perfect? Or was she always that good? But how, *how,* to move a dozen corpses without even being near them, to have them doing different things, to keep them all excited, to match the needs and rhythm of each customer so exactly?

The air behind him was black and choked by rock-dust, his ears were full of screams, and the far horizon was a glowering red wall beneath which yellow ants crawled and ate rock. But Trager kept his hard-on all across the plain as the automill shook beneath him.

The corpses were company-owned; they stayed in the company deadman depot. But Trager had a room, a slice of the space that was his own in a steel-and-concrete warehouse with a thousand other slices. He only knew a handful of his neighbors, but he knew all of them too; they were corpsehandlers. It was a world of silent shadowed corridors and endless closed doors. The lobby-lounge, all air and plastic, was a dusty deserted place where none of the tenants ever gathered.

The evenings were long there, the nights eternal. Trager had bought extra light-panels for his particular cube, and when all of them were on they burned so bright that his infrequent visitors blinked and complained about the glare. But always there came a time when he could read no more, and then he had to turn them out, and the darkness returned once more.

His father, long gone and barely remembered, had left a wealth of books and tapes, and Trager kept them still. The room was lined with them, and others stood in great piles against the foot of the bed and on either side of the bathroom door. Infrequently he went on with Cox and the others, to drink and joke and prowl for real women. He imitated them as best he could, but he always felt out of place. So most of his nights were spent at home, reading and listening to the music, remembering and thinking.

That week he thought long after he'd faded his light panels into black, and his thoughts were a frightened jumble. Payday was coming again, and Cox would be after him to return to the meathouse, and yes, yes, he wanted to. It had been good, exciting; for once he had felt confident and virile. But it was so easy, cheap, *dirty*. There had to be more, didn't there? Love, whatever that was? It had to be better with a real woman, had to, and he wouldn't find one of those in a meathouse. He'd never found one outside, either, but then he'd never really had the courage to try. But he had to try, *had* to, or what sort of life would he ever have?

Beneath the covers he masturbated, hardly thinking of it, while he resolved not to return to the meathouse.

But a few days later, Cox laughed at him and he had to go along. Somehow he felt it would prove something.

A different room this time, a different corpse. Fat and black, with bright orange hair, less attractive than his first, if that was possible. But Trager came to her ready and eager, and this time he lasted longer. Again, the performance was superb. Her rhythm matched his stroke for stroke, she came with him, she seemed to know exactly what he wanted.

Other visits; two of them, four, six. He was a regular now at the meathouse, along with the others, and he had stopped worrying about it. Cox and the others accepted him in a strange half-hearted way, but his dislike of them had grown, if anything. He was better than they were, he thought. He could hold his own in a meathouse, he could run his corpses and his automills as good as any of them, and he still thought and dreamed. In time he'd leave them all behind, leave Skrakky, be something. They would be meathouse men as long as they would live, but Trager knew he could do better. He believed. He would find love.

He found none in the meathouse, but the sex got better and better, though it was perfect to begin with. In bed with the corpses, Trager was never dissatisfied; he did everything he'd ever read about, heard about, dreamt about. The corpses knew his needs before he did. When he needed it slow, they were slow. When he wanted to have it hard and quick and brutal, then they gave it to him that way, perfectly. He used every orifice they had; they always knew which one to present to him.

His admiration of the meathouse handler grew steadily for months, until it was almost worship. Perhaps somehow he could meet her, he thought at last. Still a boy, still hopelessly naive, he was sure he would love her. Then he would take her away from the meathouse to a clean, corpseless world where they could be happy together.

One day, in a moment of weakness, he told Cox and the others. Cox looked at him, shook his head, grinned. Somebody else snickered. Then they all began to laugh. "What an *ass* you are, Trager," Cox said at last. "There is no fucking *handler!* Don't tell me you never heard of a feedback circuit?"

He explained it all, to laughter; explained how each corpse was tuned to a controller built into its bed, explained how each customer handled his own meat, explained why non-handlers found meathouse women dead and still. And the boy realized suddenly why the sex was always perfect. He was a better handler than even he had thought.

That night, alone in his room with all the lights burning white and hot, Trager faced himself. And turned away, sickened. He was good at his job, he was proud of that, but the rest . . .

It was the meathouse, he decided. There was a trap there in the meathouse, a trap that could ruin him, destroy life and dream and hope. He would not go back; it was too easy. He would show Cox, show all of them. He could take the hard way, take the risks, feel the pain if he had to. And maybe the joy, maybe the love. He'd gone the other way too long.

Trager did not go back to the meathouse. Feeling strong and decisive and superior, he went back to his room. There, as years passed, he read and dreamed and waited for life to begin.

(1) When I Was One-and-Twenty

Josie was the first.

She was beautiful, had always been beautiful, knew she was beautiful; all that had shaped her, made her what she was. She was a free spirit. She was aggressive, confident, conquering. Like Trager, she was only twenty when they met, but she had lived more than he had, and she seemed to have the answers. He loved her from the first.

And Trager? Trager before Josie, but years beyond the meathouse? He was taller now, broad and heavy with both muscle and fat, often moody, silent and self-contained. He ran a full five-crew in the ore fields, more than Cox, more than any of them. At night, he read books; sometimes in his room, sometimes in the lobby. He had long since forgotten that he went there to meet someone. Stable, solid, unemotional; that was Trager. He touched no one, and no one touched him. Even the tortures had stopped, though the scars remained *inside*. Trager hardly knew they were there; he never looked at them.

He fit in well now. With his corpses.

Yet—not completely. Inside, the dream. Something believed, something hungered, something yearned. It was strong enough to keep him away from the meathouse, from the vegetable life the others had all chosen. And sometimes, on bleak lonely nights, it would grow stronger still. Then Trager would rise from his empty bed, dress, and walk the corridors for hours with his hands shoved deep into his pockets while something twisted, clawed, and whimpered in his gut. Always, before his walks were over, he would resolve to do something, to change his life tomorrow.

But when tomorrow came, the silent gray corridors were half-forgotten, the demons had faded, and he had six roaring, shaking automills to drive across the pit. He would lose himself in routine, and it would be long months before the feelings came again.

Then Josie. They met like this:

It was a new field, rich and unmined, a vast expanse of broken rock and rubble that filled the plain. Low hills a few weeks ago, but the company skimmers had leveled the area with systematic nuclear blast mining, and now the automills were moving in. Trager's five-crew had been one of the first, and the change had been exhilarating at first. The old pit had been just about worked out; here there was a new terrain to contend with, boulders and jagged rock fragments, baseball-sized fists of stone that came shrieking at you on the dusty wind. It all seemed exciting, dangerous. Trager, wearing a leather jacket and filter-mask and goggles and earplugs, drove his six machines and six bodies with a fierce pride, reducing boulders to powder, clearing a path for the later machines, fighting his way yard by yard to get whatever ore he could.

And one day, suddenly, one of the eye echoes suddenly caught his attention. A light flashed red on a corpse-driven automill. Trager reached, with his hands, with his mind, with five sets of corpse-hands.

Six machines stopped, but still another light went red. Then another, and another. Then the whole board, all twelve. One of his automills was out. Cursing, he looked across the rock field towards the machine in question, used his corpse to give it a kick. The lights stayed red. He beamed out for a tech.

By the time she got there—in a one-man skimmer that looked like a teardrop of pitted black metal—Trager had unstrapped, climbed down the metal rings on the side of the automill, walked across the rocks to where the dead machine stopped. He was just starting to climb up when Josie arrived; they met at the foot of the yellow-metal mountain, in the shadow of its treads.

She was field-wise, he knew at once. She wore a handler's coverall, earplugs, heavy goggles, and her face was smeared with grease to prevent dust abrasions. But still she was beautiful. Her hair was short, light brown, cut in a shag that was jumbled by the wind; her eyes, when she lifted the goggles, were bright green. She took charge immediately.

All business, she introduced herself, asked him a few questions, then opened a repair bay and crawled inside, into the guts of the drive and the ore-smelt and the refinery. It didn't take her long; ten minutes, maybe, and she was back outside.

"Don't go in there," she said, tossing her hair from in front of her goggles with a flick of her head. "You've got a damper failure. The nukes are running away."

"Oh," said Trager. His mind was hardly on the automill, but he had to make an impression, made to say something intelligent. "Is it going to blow up?" he asked, and as soon as he said it he knew that *that* hadn't been intelligent at all. Of course it wasn't going to blow up; runaway nuclear reactors didn't work that way, he knew that.

But Josie seemed amused. She smiled—the first time he saw her distinctive flashing grin—and seemed to see him, *him,* Trager, not just a corpsehandler. "No," she said. "It will just melt itself down. Won't even get hot out here, since you've got shields built into the walls. Just don't go in there."

"All right." Pause. What could he say now? "What do I do?"

"Work the rest of your crew, I guess. This machine'll have to be scrapped. It should have been overhauled a long time ago. From the looks of it, there's been a lot of patching done in the past. Stupid. It breaks down, it breaks down, it breaks down, and they keep sending it out. Should realize that something is wrong. After that many failures, it's sheer self-delusion to think the thing's going to work right next time out."

"I guess," Trager said. Josie smiled at him again, sealed up the panel, and started to turn.

"Wait," he said. It came out before he could stop it, almost in spite of him. Josie turned, cocked her head, looked at him questioningly. And Trager drew a sudden strength from the steel and the stone and the wind; under sulfur skies, his dreams seemed less impossible. Maybe, he thought. Maybe.

"Uh. I'm Greg Trager. Will I see you again?"

Josie grinned. "Sure. Come tonight." She gave him the address.

He climbed back into his automill after she had left, exulting in his six strong bodies, all fire and life, and he chewed up rock with something near to joy. The dark red glow in the distance looked almost like a sunrise.

When he got to Josie's, he found four other people there, friends of hers. It was a party of sorts. Josie threw a lot of parties and Trager—from that night on—went to all of them. Josie talked to him, laughed with him, *liked* him, and suddenly his life was no longer the same.

With Josie, he saw parts of Skrakky he had never seen before, did things he had never done:

—he stood with her in the crowds that gathered on the streets at night, stood in the dusty wind and sickly yellow light between the windowless concrete buildings, stood and bet and cheered himself hoarse while grease-stained mechs raced yellow rumbly tractor-trucks up and down and down and up.

—he walked with her through the strangely silent and white and clean underground Offices, and sealed air-conditioned corridors where off-worlders and paper-shufflers and company executives lived and worked.

—he prowled the rec-malls with her, those huge low buildings so like a warehouse from the outside, but full of colored lights and game rooms and cafeterias and tape shops and endless bars where handlers made their rounds.

—he went with her to dormitory gyms, where they watched handlers less skillful than himself send their corpses against each other with clumsy fists.

—he sat with her and her friends, and they woke dark quiet taverns with their talk and with their laughter, and once Trager saw someone looking much like Cox staring at him from across the room, and he smiled and leaned a bit closer to Josie.

He hardly noticed the other people, the crowds that Josie surrounded herself with; when they went out on one of her wild jaunts, six of them or eight or ten, Trager would tell himself that he and Josie were going out, and that some others had come along with them.

Once in a great while, things would work out so they were alone together, at her place, or his. Then they would talk. Of distant worlds, of politics, of corpses and life on Skrakky, of the books they both consumed, of sports or games or friends they had in common. They shared a good deal. Trager talked a lot with Josie. And never said a word.

He loved her, of course. He suspected it the first month, and soon he was convinced of it. He loved her. This was the real thing, the thing he had been waiting for, and it had happened just as he knew it would.

But with his love: agony. He could not tell her. A dozen times he tried; the words would never come. What if she did not love him back?

His nights were still alone, in the small room with the white lights and the books and the pain. He was more alone than ever now; the peace of his routine, of his half-life with his corpses, was gone, stripped from him. By day he rode the great automills, moved his corpses, smashed rock and melted ore, and in his head rehearsed the words he'd say to Josie. And dreamed of those that she'd speak back. She was trapped too, he thought. She'd had men, of course, but she didn't love them, she loved him. But she couldn't tell him, any more than he could tell her. When he broke through, when he found the words and the courage, then everything would be all right. Each day he said that to himself, and dug swift and deep into the earth.

But back home, the sureness faded. Then, with awful despair, he knew that he was kidding himself. He was a friend to her, nothing more, never would be more. Why did he lie to himself? He'd had hints enough. They had never been lovers, never would be; on the few times he'd worked up the courage to touch her, she would smile, move away on some pretext, so he was never quite sure that he was being rejected. But he got the idea, and in the dark it tore at him. He walked the corridors weekly now, sullen, desperate, wanting to talk to someone without knowing how. And all the old scars woke up to bleed again.

Until the next day. When he would return to his machines, and believe again. He must believe in himself, he knew that, he shouted it out loud. He must stop feeling sorry for himself. He must do something. He must tell Josie. He would.

And she would love him, cried the day.

And she would laugh, the nights replied.

Trager chased her for a year, a year of pain and promise, the first year that he had ever *lived*. On that the night-fears and the day-voice agreed; he was alive now. He would never return to the emptiness of his time before Josie; he would never go back to the meathouse. That far, at least, he had come. He could change, and someday he would be strong enough to tell her.

Josie and two friends dropped by his room that night, but the friends had to leave early. For an hour or so they were alone, talking about nothing. Finally she had to go. Trager said he'd walk her home.

He kept his arm around her down the long corridors, and he watched her face, watched the play of light and shadow on her cheeks as they walked from light to darkness. "Josie," he started. He felt so fine, so good, so warm, and it came out. "I love you."

And she stopped, pulled away from him, stepped back. Her mouth opened, just a little, and something flickered in her eyes. "Oh, Greg," she said. Softly. Sadly. "No, Greg, no, don't, don't." And she shook her head.

Trembling slightly, mouthing silent words, Trager held out his hand. Josie did not take it. He touched her cheek, gently, and wordless she spun away from him.

Then, for the first time ever, Trager shook. And the tears came.

Josie took him to her room. There, sitting across from each other on the floor, never touching, they talked.

J: . . . *known it for a long time* . . . *tried to discourage you, Greg, but I didn't just want to come right out and* . . . *I never wanted to hurt you* . . . *a good person* . . . *don't worry.* . . .

T: . . . *knew it all along* . . . *that it would never* . . . *lied to myself* . . . *wanted to believe, even if it wasn't true* . . . *I'm sorry, Josie, I'm sorry, I'm sorry, I'm sorryimsorryimsorry.* . . .

J: . . . *afraid you would go back to what you were* . . . *don't Greg, promise me* . . . *can't give up* . . . *have to believe.* . . .

T: *why?*

J: . . . *stop believing, then you have nothing* . . . *dead* . . . *you can do better* . . . *a good handler* . . . *get off Skrakky find something* . . . *no life here* . . . *someone* . . . *you will, you will, just believe, keep on believing.* . . .

T: . . . *you . . . love you forever, Josie . . . forever . . . how can I find someone . . . never anyone like you, never . . . special . . .*

J: . . . *oh, Greg . . . lots of people . . . just look . . . open . . .*

T: (laughter) . . . *open? . . . first time I ever talked to anyone . . .*

J: . . . *talk to me again, if you have to . . . I can talk to you . . . had enough lovers, everyone wants to get to bed with me, better just to be friends. . . .*

T: . . . *friends . . .* (laughter) . . . (tears) . . .

II
PROMISES OF SOMEDAY

The fire had burned out long ago, and Stevens and the forester had retired, but Trager and Donelly still sat around the ashes on the edges of the clear zone. They talked softly, so as not to wake the others, yet their words hung long in the restless night air. The uncut forest, standing dark behind them, was dead still; the wildlife of Vendalia had all fled the noise that the fleet of buzztrucks made during the day.

" . . . a full six-crew, running buzztrucks, I know enough to know that's not easy," Donelly was saying. He was a pale, timid youth, likeable but self-conscious about everything he did. Trager heard echoes of himself in Donelly's stiff words. "You'd do well in the arena."

Trager nodded, thoughtful, his eyes on the ashes as he moved them with a stick. "I came to Vendalia with that in mind. Went to the gladiatorial once, only once. That was enough to change my mind. I could take them, I guess, but the whole idea made me sick. Out here, well, the money doesn't even match what I was getting on Skrakky, but the work is, well, clean. You know?"

"Sort of," said Donelly. "Still, you know, it isn't like they were real people out there in the arena. Only meat. All you can do is make the bodies as dead as the minds. That's the logical way to look at it."

Trager chuckled. "You're too logical, Don. You ought to *feel* more. Listen, next time you're in Gidyon, go to the gladiatorials and take a look. It's ugly, *ugly.* Corpses stumbling around with axes and swords and morningstars, hacking and hewing at each other. Butchery, that's all it is. And the audience, the way they cheer at each blow. And *laugh.* They *laugh,* Don! No." He shook his head, sharply. "No."

Donelly never abandoned an argument. "But why not? I don't understand, Greg. You'd be good at it, the best. I've seen the way you work your crew."

Trager looked up, studied Donelly briefly while the youth sat quietly, waiting. Josie's words came back; open, be open. The old Trager, the Trager who lived friendless and alone and closed inside a Skrakky handlers' dorm, was gone. He had grown, changed.

"There was a girl," he said, slowly, with measured words. Opening. "Back on Skrakky, Don, there was a girl I loved. It, well, it didn't work out. That's why I'm here, I guess. I'm looking for someone else, for something better. That's all part of it, you see." He stopped, paused, tried to think his words out. "This girl, Josie, I wanted her to love me. You know." The words came hard. "Admire me, all that stuff. Now, yeah, sure, I could do good running corpses in the arena. But Josie could never love someone who had a job like *that*. She's gone now, of course, but still . . . the kind of person I'm looking for, I couldn't find them as an arena corpse-master." He stood up, abruptly. "I don't know. That's what's important, though, to me. Josie, somebody like her, someday. Soon, I hope."

Donelly sat quiet in the moonlight, chewing his lip, not looking at Trager, his logic suddenly useless. While Trager, his corridors long gone, walked off alone into the woods.

They had a tight-knit group; three handlers, a forester, thirteen corpses. Each day they drove the forest back, with Trager in the forefront. Against the Vendalian wilderness, against the blackbriars and the hard gray ironspike trees and the bulbous rubbery snaplimbs, against the tangled hostile forest, he would throw his six-crew and their buzztrucks. Smaller than the automills he'd run on Skrakky, fast and airborne, complex and demanding, those were buzztrucks. Trager ran six of them with corpse hands, a seventh with his own. Before his screaming blades and laser knives, the wall of wilderness fell each day. Donelly came behind him, pushing three of the mountain-sized rolling mills, to turn the fallen trees into lumber for Gidyon and other cities of Vendalia. Then Stevens, the third handler, with a flame-cannon to burn down stumps and melt rocks, and the soilpumps that would ready the fresh clear land for farming. The forester was their foreman. The procedure was a science.

Clean, hard, demanding work; Trager thrived on it by day. He grew lean, almost athletic; the lines of his face tightened and tanned, he grew steadily browner under Vendalia's hot bright sun. His corpses were almost part of him, so easily did he move them, fly their buzztrucks. As an ordinary man might move a hand, a foot. Sometimes his control grew so firm, the echoes so clear and strong, that Trager felt he was not a handler working a crew at all, but rather a man with seven bodies. Seven strong bodies that rode the sultry forest winds. He exulted in their sweat.

And the evenings, after work ceased, they were good too. Trager found a sort of peace there, a sense of belonging he had never known on Skrakky. The Vendalian foresters, rotated back and forth from Gidyon, were decent enough, and friendly. Stevens was a hearty slab of a man who seldom stopped joking long enough to talk about anything serious. Trager always found him amusing. And Donelly, the self-conscious youth, the quiet logical voice, he became a friend. He was a good listener, empathetic, compassionate, and the new open Trager was a good talker. Something close to envy shone in Donelly's eyes when Trager spoke of Josie and exorcised his soul. And Trager knew, or thought he knew, that Donelly was himself, the old Trager, the one before Josie who could not find the words.

In time, though, after days and weeks of talking, Donelly found his words. Then Trager listened, and shared another's pain. And he felt good about it. He was helping; he was lending strength; he was needed.

Each night around the ashes, the two men traded dreams. And wove a hopeful tapestry of promises and lies.

Yet still the nights would come.

Those were the worst times, as always; those were the hours of Trager's long lonely walks. If Josie had given Trager much, she had taken something too; she had taken the curious deadness he had once had, the trick of not-thinking, the pain-blotter of his mind. On Skrakky, he had walked the corridors infrequently; the forest knew him far more often.

After the talking all had stopped, after Donelly had gone to bed, that was when it would happen, when Josie would come to him in the loneliness of his tent. A thousand nights he lay there with his hands hooked behind his head, staring at the plastic tent film while he relived the night he'd told her. A thousand times he touched her cheek, and saw her spin away.

He would think of it, and fight it, and lose. Then, restless, he would rise and go outside. He would walk across the clear area, into the silent looming forest, brushing aside low branches and tripping on the underbrush; he would walk until he found water. Then he would sit down, by a scum-choked lake or a gurgling stream that ran swift and oily in the moonlight. He would fling rocks into the water, hurl them hard and flat into the night to hear them when they splashed.

He would sit for hours, throwing rocks and thinking, till finally he could convince himself the sun would rise.

Gidyon; the city; the heart of Vendalia, and through it of Slagg and Skrakky and New Pittsburg and all the other corpseworlds, the harsh ugly places where men would not work and corpses had to. Great towers of black and silver metal, floating aerial sculpture that flashed in the sunlight and shone softly at night, the vast bustling spaceport where freighters rose and fell on invisible firewands, malls where the pavement was polished, ironspike wood that gleamed a gentle gray; Gidyon.

The city with the rot. The corpse city. The meatmart.

For the freighters carried cargoes of men, criminals and derelicts and troublemakers from a dozen worlds bought with hard Vendalian cash (and there were darker rumors, of liners that had vanished mysteriously on routine tourist hops). And the soaring towers were hospitals and corpseyards, where men and women died and deadmen were born to walk anew. And all along the ironspike boardwalks were corpse-seller's shops and meathouses.

The meathouses of Vendalia were far-famed. The corpses were guaranteed beautiful.

Trager sat across from one, on the other side of the wide gray avenue, under the umbrella of an outdoor cafe. He sipped a bittersweet wine, thought about how his leave had evaporated too quickly, and tried to keep his eyes from wandering across the street. The wine was warm on his tongue, and his eyes were very restless.

Up and down the avenue, between him and the meathouse, strangers moved. Dark-faced corpsehandlers from Vendalia, Skrakky, Slagg; pudgy merchants, gawking tourists from the Clean Worlds like Old Earth and Zephyr, and dozens of question marks whose names and occupations and errands Trager would never know. Sitting there, drinking his wine and watching, Trager felt utterly cut off. He could not touch these people, could not reach them; he didn't know how, it wasn't possible, it wouldn't work. He could rise and walk out into the street and grab one, and still they would not touch. The stranger would only pull free and run. All his leave like that, all of it; he'd run through all the bars of Gidyon, forced a thousand contacts, and nothing had clicked.

His wine was gone. Trager looked at the glass dully, turning it in his hands, blinking, Then, abruptly, he stood up and paid his bill. His hands trembled.

It had been so many years, he thought as he started across the street. Josie, he thought, forgive me.

Trager returned to the wilderness camp, and his corpses flew their buzztrucks like men gone wild. But he was strangely silent around the campfire, and he did not talk to Donelly at night. Until finally, hurt and puzzled, Donelly followed him into the forest. And found him by a languid death-dark stream, sitting on the bank with a pile of throwing stones at his feet.

T: . . . *went in . . . after all I said, all I promised . . . still I went in. . . .*

D: . . . *nothing to worry . . . remember what you told me . . . keep on believing. . . .*

T: . . . *did believe, DID . . . no difficulties . . . Josie. . . .*

D: . . . *you say I shouldn't give up, you better not . . . repeat everything you told me, everything Josie told you . . . everybody finds someone . . . if they keep looking . . . give up, dead . . . all you need . . . openness . . . courage to look . . . stop feeling sorry for yourself . . . told me that a hundred times. . . .*

T: . . . *fucking lot easier to tell you than do it myself . . .*

D: . . . *Greg . . . not a meathouse man . . . a dreamer . . . better than they are . . .*

T: *(sighing) . . . yeah . . . hard, though . . . why do I do this to myself? . . .*

D: . . . *rather be like you were? . . . not hurting, not living? . . . like me? . . .*

T: . . . *no . . . no . . . you're right. . . .*

(2) The Pilgrim, Up and Down

Her name was Laurel. She was nothing like Josie, save in one thing alone. Trager loved her.

Pretty? Trager didn't think so, not at first. She was too tall, a half-foot taller than he was, and she was a bit on the heavy side, and more than a bit on the awkward side. Her hair was her best feature, her hair that was red-brown in winter and glowing blond in summer, that fell long and straight down past her shoulders and did wild beautiful things in the wind. But she was not beautiful, not the way Josie had been beautiful. Although, oddly, she grew more beautiful with time, and maybe that was because she was losing weight, and maybe that was because Trager was falling in love with her and seeing her through kinder eyes, and maybe that was because he told her she was pretty and the very telling made it so. Just as Laurel told him he was wise, and her belief gave him wisdom. Whatever the reason, Laurel was very beautiful indeed after he had known her for a time.

She was five years younger than he, clean-scrubbed and innocent, shy where Josie had been assertive. She was intelligent, romantic, a dreamer; she was wondrously fresh and eager; she was painfully insecure, and full of hungry need.

She was new to Gidyon, fresh from the Vendalian outback, a student forester. Trager, on leave again, was visiting the forestry college to say hello to a teacher who'd once worked with his crew. They met in the teacher's office. Trager had two weeks free in a city of strangers and meathouses; Laurel was alone. He showed her the glittering decadence of Gidyon, feeling smooth and sophisticated, and she was suitably impressed.

Two weeks went quickly. They came to the last night. Trager, suddenly afraid, took her to the park by the river that ran through Gidyon and they sat together on the low stone wall by the water's edge. Close, not touching.

"Time runs too fast," he said. He had a stone in his hand. He flicked it out over the water, flat and hard. Thoughtfully, he watched it splash and sink. Then he looked at her. "I'm nervous," he said, laughing. "I—Laurel. I don't want to leave."

Her face was unreadable (wary?). "The city is nice," she agreed.

Trager shook his head violently. "No. *No!* Not the city, you. Laurel, I think I . . . well . . . "

Laurel smiled for him. Her eyes were bright, very happy. "I know," she said.

Trager could hardly believe it. He reached out, touched her cheek. She turned her head and kissed his hand. They smiled at each other.

He flew back to the forest camp to quit. "Don, Don, you've got to meet her," he shouted. "See, you can do it, I *did* it, just keep believing, keep trying. I feel so goddamn good it's obscene."

Donelly, stiff and logical, smiled for him, at a loss as how to handle such a flood of happiness. "What will you do?" he asked, a little awkwardly. "The arena?"

Trager laughed. "Hardly, you know how I feel. But something like that. There's a theatre near the spaceport, puts on pantomime with corpse actors. I've got a job there. The pay is rotten, but I'll be near Laurel. That's all that matters."

They hardly slept at night. Instead they talked and cuddled and made love. The lovemaking was a joy, a game, a glorious discovery; never as good technically as the meathouse, but Trager hardly cared. He taught her to be open. He told her every secret he had, and wished he had more secrets.

"Poor Josie," Laurel would often say at night, her body warm against his. "She doesn't know what she missed. I'm lucky. There couldn't be anyone else like you."

"No," said Trager, "*I'm* lucky."

They would argue about it, laughing.

Donelly came to Gidyon and joined the theatre. Without Trager, the forest work had been no fun, he said. The three of them spent a lot of time together, and Trager glowed. He wanted to share his friends with Laurel, and he'd already mentioned Donelly a lot. And he wanted Donelly to see how happy he'd become, to see what belief could accomplish.

"I like her," Donelly said, smiling, the first night after Laurel had left.

"Good," Trager replied, nodding.

"No," said Donelly. "Greg, I *really* like her."

They spent a *lot* of time together.

"Greg," Laurel said one night in bed, "I think that Don is . . . well, after me. You know."

Trager rolled over and propped his head up on his elbow. "God," he said. He sounded concerned.

"I don't know how to handle it."

"Carefully," Trager said. "He's very vulnerable. You're probably the first woman he's ever been interested in. Don't be too hard on him. He shouldn't have to go through the stuff I went through, you know?"

The sex was never as good as a meathouse. And, after a while, Laurel began to close. More and more nights now she went to sleep after they made love; the days when they talked till dawn were gone. Perhaps they had nothing left to say. Trager had noticed that she had a tendency to finish his stories for him. It was nearly impossible to come up with one he hadn't already told her.

"He said *that*?" Trager got out of bed, turned on a light, and sat down frowning. Laurel pulled the covers up to her chin.

"Well, what did *you* say?"

She hesitated. "I can't tell you. It's between Don and me. He said it wasn't fair, the way I turn around and tell you everything that goes on between us, and he's right."

"*Right!* But I tell you everything. Don't you remember what we . . . "

"I know, but . . . "

Trager shook his head. His voice lost some of its anger. "What's going on, Laurel, huh? I'm scared, all of a sudden. I love you, remember? How can everything change so fast?"

Her face softened. She sat up, and held out her arms, and the covers fell back from full soft breasts. "Oh, Greg," she said. "Don't worry. I love you, I always will, but it's just that I love him too, I guess. You know?"

Trager, mollified, came into her arms, and kissed her with fervor. Then, suddenly, he broke off. "Hey," he said, with mock sternness to hide the trembling in his voice, "who do you love *more*?"

"You, of course, always you."

Smiling, he returned to the kiss.

"I know you know," Donelly said. "I guess we have to talk about it."

Trager nodded. They were backstage in the theatre. Three of his corpses walked up behind him, and stood arms crossed, like a guard. "All right." He looked straight at Donelly, and his face—smiling until the other's words—was suddenly stern. "Laurel asked me to pretend I didn't know anything. She said you felt guilty. But pretending was quite a strain, Don. I guess it's time we got everything out in the open."

Donelly's pale blue eyes shifted to the floor, and he stuck his hands into his pockets. "I don't want to hurt you," he said.

"Then don't."

"But I'm not going to pretend I'm dead, either. I'm not. I love her too."

"You're supposed to be my friend, Don. Love someone else. You're just going to get yourself hurt this way."

"I have more in common with her than you do."

Trager just stared.

Donelly looked up at him. Then, abashed, back down again. "I don't know. Oh, Greg. She loves you more anyway, she said so. I never should have expected anything else. I feel like I've stabbed you in the back. I . . ."

Trager watched him. Finally, he laughed softly. "Oh, shit, I can't take this. Look, Don, you haven't stabbed me, c'mon, don't talk like that. I guess, if you love her, this is the way it's got to be, you know. I just hope everything comes out all right."

Later that night, in bed with Laurel; "I'm worried about him," he told her.

His face, once tanned, now ashen. "Laurel?" he said. Not believing.

"I don't love you anymore. I'm sorry. I don't. It seemed real at the time, but now it's almost like a dream. I don't even know if I ever loved you, really."

"Don," he said woodenly.

Laurel flushed. "Don't say anything bad about Don. I'm tired of hearing you run him down. He never says anything except good about you."

"Oh, Laurel. Don't you *remember*? The things we said, the way we felt? I'm the same person you said those words to."

"But I've grown," Laurel said, hard and tearless, tossing her red-gold hair. "I remember perfectly well, but I just don't feel that way anymore."

"Don't," he said. He reached for her.

She stepped back. "Keep your hands off me. I told you, Greg, it's *over*. You have to leave now. Don is coming by."

It was worse than Josie. A thousand times worse.

III

WANDERINGS

He tried to keep on at the theatre; he enjoyed the work, he had friends there. But it was impossible. Donelly was there every day, smiling and being friendly, and sometimes Laurel came to meet him after the day's show and they went off together, arm in arm. Trager would stand and watch, try not to notice. While the twisted thing inside him shrieked and clawed.

He quit. He would not see them again. He would keep his pride.

The sky was bright with the lights of Gidyon and full of laughter, but it was dark and quiet in the park.

Trager stood stiff against a tree, his eyes on the river, his hands folded tightly against his chest. He was a statue. He hardly seemed to breathe. Not even his eyes moved.

Kneeling near the low wall, the corpse pounded until the stone was slick with blood and its hands were mangled clots of torn meat. The sounds of the blows were dull and wet, but for the infrequent scraping of bone against rock.

They made him pay first, before he could even enter the booth. Then he sat there for an hour while they found her and punched through. Finally, though, finally; "Josie."

"Greg," she said, grinning her distinctive grin. "I should have known. Who else would call all the way from Vendalia? How are you?"

He told her.

Her grin vanished. "Oh, Greg," she said. "I'm sorry. But don't let it get to you. Keep going. The next one will work out better. They always do."

Her words didn't satisfy him. "Josie," he said, "How are things back there? You miss me?"

"Oh, sure. Things are pretty good. It's still Skrakky, though. Stay where you are, you're better off." She looked offscreen, then back. "I should go, before your bill gets enormous. Glad you called, love."

"*Josie,*" Trager started. But the screen was already dark.

Sometimes, at night, he couldn't help himself. He would move to his home screen and ring Laurel. Invariably her eyes would narrow when she saw who it was. Then she would hang up.

And Trager would sit in a dark room and recall how once the sound of his voice made her so very, very happy.

The streets of Gidyon are not the best of places for lonely midnight walks. They are brightly lit, even in the darkest hours, and jammed with men and deadmen. And there are meathouses, all up and down the boulevards and the ironspike boardwalks.

Josie's words had lost their power. In the meathouses, Trager abandoned dreams and found cheap solace. The sensuous evenings with Laurel and the fumbling sex of his boyhood were things of yesterday; Trager took his meatmates hard and quick, almost brutally, fucked them with a wordless savage power to the inevitable perfect orgasm. Sometimes, remembering the theatre, he would have them act out short erotic playlets to get him in the mood.

In the night. Agony.

He was in the corridors again, the low dim corridors of the corpse-handlers' dorm on Skrakky, but now the corridors were twisted and torturous and Trager had long since lost his way. The air was thick with a rotting gray haze, and growing thicker. Soon, he feared, he would be all but blind.

Around and around he walked, up and down, but always there was more corridor, and all of them led nowhere. The doors were grim black rectangles, knobless, locked to him forever; he passed them by without thinking, most of them. Once or twice, though, he paused, before doors where light leaked around the frame. He would listen, and inside there were sounds, and then he would begin to knock wildly. But no one ever answered.

So he would move on, through the haze that got darker and thicker and seemed to burn his skin, past door after door after door, until he was weeping and his feet were tired and bloody. And then, off a ways, down a long, long corridor that loomed straight before him, he would see an open door. From it came light so hot and white it hurt the eyes, and music bright and joyful, and the sounds of people laughing. Then Trager would run, though his feet were raw bundles of pain and his lungs burned with the haze he was breathing. He would run and run until he reached the room with the open door.

Only when he got there, it was his room, and it was empty.

Once, in the middle of their brief time together, they'd gone out into the wilderness and made love under the stars. Afterwards she had snuggled hard against him, and he stroked her gently. "What are you thinking?" he asked.

"About us," Laurel said. She shivered. The wind was brisk and cold. "Sometimes I get scared, Greg. I'm so afraid something will happen to us, something that will ruin it. I don't ever want you to leave me."

"Don't worry," he told her. "I won't."

Now, each night before sleep came, he tortured himself with her words. The good memories left him with ashes and tears; the bad ones with a wordless rage.

He slept with a ghost beside him, a supernaturally beautiful ghost, the husk of a dead dream. He woke to her each morning.

He hated them. He hated himself for hating.

(3) Duvalier's Dream

Her name does not matter. Her looks are not important. All that counts is that she *was*, that Trager tried again, that he forced himself on and made himself believe and didn't give up. He *tried*.

But something was missing. Magic?

The words were the same.

How many times can you speak them, Trager wondered, *speak them and believe them, like you believed them the first time you said them? Once? Twice? Three times, maybe? Or a hundred? And the people who say it a hundred times, are they really so much better at loving? Or only at fooling themselves? Aren't they really people who long ago abandoned the dream, who use its name for something else?*

He said the words, holding her, cradling her, and kissing her. He said the words, with a knowledge that was surer and heavier and more dead than any belief. He said the words and *tried*, but no longer could he mean them.

And she said the words back, and Trager realized that they meant nothing to him. Over and over again they said the things each wanted to hear, and both of them knew they were pretending.

They tried *hard*. But when he reached out, like an actor caught in his role, doomed to play out the same part over and over again, when he reached out his hand and touched her cheek—the skin was smooth and soft and lovely. And wet with tears.

IV
Echoes

"I don't want to hurt you," said Donelly, shuffling and looking guilty, until Trager felt ashamed for having hurt a friend.

He touched her cheek, and she spun away from him.

"I never wanted to hurt you," Josie said, and Trager was sad. She had given him so much; he'd only made her guilty. Yes, he was hurt, but a stronger man would never have let her know.

He touched her cheek, and she kissed his hand.

"I'm sorry, I don't," Laurel said. And Trager was lost. What had he done, where was his fault, how had he ruined it? She had been so sure. They had had so much.

He touched her cheek, and she wept.

How many times can you speak them, his voice echoed, *speak them and believe them, like you believed them the first time you said them?*

The wind was dark and dust heavy, the sky throbbed painfully with flickering scarlet flame. In the pit, in the darkness, stood a young woman with goggles and a filtermask and short brown hair and answers. "It breaks down, it breaks down, it breaks down, and they keep sending it out," she said. "Should realize that something is wrong. After that many failures, it's sheer self-delusion to think the thing's going to work right next time out."

The enemy corpse is huge and black, its torso rippling with muscle, a product of months of exercise, the biggest thing that Trager has ever faced. It advances across the sawdust in a slow, clumsy crouch, holding the gleaming broadsword in one hand. Trager watches it come from his chair atop one end of the fighting arena. The other corpsemaster is careful, cautious.

His own deadman, a wiry blond, stands and waits, a morningstar trailing down in the blood-soaked arena dust. Trager will move him fast enough and well enough when the time is right. The enemy knows it, and the crowd.

The black corpse suddenly lifts its broadsword and scrambles forward in a run, hoping to use reach and speed to get its kill. But Trager's corpse is no longer there when the enemy's measured blow cuts the air where he had been.

Sitting comfortably above the fighting pit/down in the arena, his feet grimy with blood and sawdust—Trager/the corpse—snaps the command/ swings the morningstar—and the great studded ball drifts up and around, almost lazily, almost gracefully. Into the back of the enemy's head, as he tries to recover and turn. A flower of blood and brain blooms swift and sudden, and the crowd cheers.

Trager walks his corpse from the arena, then stands to receive applause. It is his tenth kill. Soon the championship will be his. He is building such a record that they can no longer deny him a match.

She is beautiful, his lady, his love. Her hair is short and blond, her body very slim, graceful, almost athletic, with trim legs and small hard breasts.

Her eyes are bright green, and they always welcome him. And there is a strange erotic innocence in her smile.

She waits for him in bed, waits for his return from the arena, waits for him eager and playful and loving. When he enters, she is sitting up, smiling for him, the covers bunched around her waist. From the door he admires her nipples.

Aware of his eyes, shy, she covers her breasts and blushes. Trager knows it is all false modesty, all playing. He moves to the bedside, sits, reaches out to stroke her cheek. Her skin is very soft; she nuzzles against his hand as it brushes her. Then Trager draws her hands aside, plants one gentle kiss on each breast, and a not-so-gentle kiss on her mouth. She kisses back, with ardor; their tongues dance.

They make love, he and she, slow and sensuous, locked together in a loving embrace that goes on and on. Two bodies move flawlessly in perfect rhythm, each knowing the other's needs. Trager thrusts, and his other body meets the thrusts. He reaches, and her hand is there. They come together (always, *always,* both orgasms triggered by the handler's brain), and a bright red flush burns on her breasts and earlobes. They kiss.

Afterwards, he talks to her, his love, his lady. You should always talk afterwards; he learned that long ago.

"You're lucky," he tells her sometimes, and she snuggles up to him and plants tiny kisses all across his chest. "Very lucky. They lie to you out there, love. They teach you a silly shining dream and they tell you to believe and chase it and they tell you that for you, for everyone, there is someone. But it's all wrong. The universe isn't fair, it never has been, so why do they tell you so? You run after the phantom, and lose, and they tell you next time, but it's all rot, all empty rot. Nobody ever finds the dream at all, they just kid themselves, trick themselves so they can go on believing. It's just a clutching lie that desperate people tell each other, hoping to convince themselves."

But then he can't talk anymore, for her kisses have gone lower and lower, and now she takes him in her mouth. And Trager smiles at his love and gently strokes her hair.

Of all the bright cruel lies they tell you, the cruelest is the one called love.

Now a #1 *New York Times* best-selling author, GEORGE R. R. MARTIN sold his first story in 1971 and has been writing professionally ever since. He spent ten years in Hollywood as a writer-producer, working on *The Twilight Zone, Beauty and the Beast,* and various feature films and television pilots that were never made. Martin also edited the Wild Cards series, fifteen novels written by teams of authors. In the mid-1990s he returned to prose, and began work on his epic fantasy series, A Song of Ice and Fire. In April 2011 HBO premiered its adaptation of the first of that series, *A Game of Thrones,* and he was named as one of *Time'*s most influential people of the year. *A Dance With Dragons,* the fifth A Song of Ice and Fire book, was published last year. He lives in Santa Fe, New Mexico, with his wife Parris.

*Then the noise and stench coagulated into a sight, making substance
from shadow at the tip of my beam, and all hell broke loose . . .*

Charlie's Hole

Jesse Bullington

"Get in the goddamn hole, Private!" Sergeant Reister was bellowing now.

"No, sir," Tosh repeated.

"You miserable piece of panda shit, get in the hole!"

"No, sir."

"I'm giving you to the count of five to get your scrawny ass down there
before I put you there permanently, you disrespectful faggot."

"No, sir."

I felt sure Reister was gonna lay him out right there, put a bullet in his
head or maybe just beat the life out of him, but no—he just stared at Tosh,
loathing emanating from his eyes. All fifteen of us did our best to pretend
not to notice the confrontation, but I'm sure everyone there could see the
score. Tosh had snapped, and Reister didn't give two shits.

"Five," Reister said levelly. "You are not in the hole, Private."

"I am not going down there, sir," Tosh said, as if Reister hadn't heard
right the first nine times.

"Am I to understand you are disobeying a direct order?" Reister
now looked perfectly calm—serene, even. His smooth face glowed in
the sunlight, giving him the look of a warlord, as opposed to a grimy
sergeant.

"That is correct, sir," Tosh said in that monotone voice of his. "I've
gone down six holes in the last month. That's every damn hole we've come
across, and I'm sick of this shit. I'm no goddamn tunnel-rat, and you know
it."

"Do you know what happens if you disobey my direct orders, you yellow
turd?" Reister asked real sweetly.

"Court-martial, the brig," Tosh shrugged. "I don't care anymore. Anything to get the hell away from your crazy ass."

"Court-martial?" Reister grinned. "Court-martial's for a trial. Trivial offenses only, my boy. What you're talking about is sedition."

All the chatter stopped right then, and to my horror I saw Collins slinking toward me. Collins is definitely all right, but he usually thinks with his lips instead of his brain. He might've been the best friend I've had here, but his smart mouth had gotten us the worst goddamn post possible: point. And the last thing this situation needed was a heckler. I tried to scoot away, but where could I go?

"Sedition?" Tosh yelled, finally raising his voice. "I didn't say shit about sedition and you know it!"

"Disobeying my direct orders is incitement to rebellion, and I have authority to neutralize a rebellion by any means necessary," Reister said cheerily. "At sea we'd call it mutiny, plain and simple."

At this all the other grunts ceased their chores to watch things play out, and all pretenses were dropped as Reister's hand folded up to grip the handle of his M-16. Some of the fellas trained their pieces at Tosh. Others leaned forward, puffing their cigarettes. The shit was about to go down.

"Do it, then," Tosh shouted. "Enough of this bullshit!"

"You're going down that hole or you will be one dead dink, I shit you not," Reister spat.

I knew Tosh was gonna bite it right then and there, when Collins leans over to me, never minding the cataclysmic turn events had taken, and opens that goddamn mouth of his.

"Reister's hoping to find a Silver Star down one of these holes," the stupid fuck says as loud as day.

Did I say things were tense before? Shit. I heard a drop of sweat explode louder than a shell as it struck a leaf, and then the silence was broken. Shattered would be a better word.

"Fuckin' goddamn hell!" Reister's full attention had swiveled to Collins and me. "You think there's something funny about the way I run my ship, queerbait?"

He advanced on us through his disciples, and stopped ten feet away. I about shit my pants. I thought I was gonna get it, gunned down by my own sergeant. Reister looked back and forth between Collins and me. I was tempted to put my Colt in my mouth and end it all there, but I didn't.

"Eh?" I saw, with a mix of relief and dismay, that Reister was pleased.

Immensely pleased. "Laugh it up, butt-buddies, 'cause you're going with him."

He turned back to Tosh, calling, "Now you got someone to hold your hand down there."

"More like his dick!" this big gorilla named Frank says, and all the grunts have a good belly laugh at our expense. Reister beamed at us like we'd just won a new car. I looked to the hole, where Tosh stood.

The mouth of the tunnel gaped at me like an open grave. It was an almost predatory opening, a gap in the floor of the jungle. Roots stuck out of its side, and I felt queasy watchin' Tosh stick his head in there. It didn't look so steep, leisurely arcing down into the earth.

I shook like the coward I was as I descended into my first tunnel, Tosh's boots kicking wet dirt into my mouth. Of all the places to lose my VCTS cherry, it had to be this damn hole? The only good thing was that it hadn't been used in a while; the flip side of this being spiders, centipedes, and worse, all on my ass. All I'd brought was my pistol and canteen, and even then it felt tighter than a nun's ass in there. I even forgot my flashlight, so all I could see were shadows cast on Tosh's butt.

With each foot I wriggled, it got worse and worse, claustrophobic as fuck. I felt like I'd reverted to the me of six months ago—freshmeat, a pussy. Of course, we all were. Assholes, dickheads, limpdicks, dickbiters, dicksmokers, faggots, queers, girls, bitches, pussies, pukes, chickenshit motherfuckers; any insult you can think of, Reister had called us. I'd always wanted to stick up for Tosh when Reister fucked with him, but how could I? I'd been in here for twenty-three weeks and five days, and I still got teary every time I went on point. A couple of times I'd nearly collapsed with fear in the jungle, so scared I couldn't breathe.

This felt worse. Much, much worse. I had no idea how far we'd gone, wondering if gunfire would come from ahead or behind. Reister, that psychotic bastard. I suddenly hated Tosh for causing the whole mess, and Collins even more. Then I hated myself for being such a pussy.

On we went, into the mud, into the very ass of Vietnam, until Tosh stopped, and I rammed my skull into his boot.

"It's cool," he said. Twisting his waist, he squirmed forward and disappeared from sight.

I could hardly breathe, and I nearly vomited as Tosh helped me out of the tunnel and into the tiny cave ahead.

"Dead end," Tosh whispered, waving his light around the burrow.

It couldn't have been more than a dozen feet across, and maybe six feet wide, but after that tunnel it felt as spacious as any mess hall. Collins' orange head poked out of the hole and we helped him up.

Even squatting so our asses brushed the soft earth, my head still raked on the ceiling. It was a goddamn miracle this place hadn't caved in.

"Thank God," Collins panted, spitting dirt and pawing his vest.

"Lucky there weren't any snakes in this one," Tosh said as he leaned back and unscrewed his canteen. "Last one Sergeant sent me down had a goddamn pit viper in it."

My breathing had almost returned to normal, when Collins lights up a joint. I swear, that mother can be a right dick sometimes. I started coughing and turned to go back up the tunnel. I felt spooked, nauseous, cramped, and was more than ready to get topside. Tosh grabbed my boot, though, and turned to Collins.

"Put that shit out before you smoke up all our oxygen," he told Collins, as he passed me his canteen.

After a few more puffs, Collins stamped out his Jay and we all just laid back for a second. It stunk like weed and mold down in that cave, and I turned to leave again.

"What's your hurry?" Tosh asked. "This hole's cool—no other tunnels."

"But Reister," I began.

"Fuck 'em," he said. "He'll just have us stand watch or some shit when we get out. Better off down here with the spiders."

"So, Tosh—" Collins said, but Tosh cut him off.

"Toshiro, man. Toshiro," Tosh grinned. "I hate that 'Tosh' shit."

"So what's with you and Reister?" Collins asked him. "He seems eager to get rid of you."

"Why do you think?" Tosh snapped with sudden intensity. "Because in his book I'm just another slope, not a Japanese-American, not an American at all."

We were all quiet for a second, but then Collins, of course, keeps prodding.

"Jesus, why don't you transfer?"

"Why don't you?" Tosh smiled weakly. "No one gets out of this squad without his okay. I've tried, but he's not down. He wants me dead out here, and that's that."

"Bastard," Collins muttered, and began chewing up the remainder of his joint.

"What's his damage?" I thought aloud.

"Former drill sergeant," Tosh answered. "Got tired of being an asshole back home, needed to come be an asshole over here. Wanted to 'see the shit,' he told us once. 'Need to get some gook blood under my fingernails.' Stupid redneck fuck."

I slipped as my boots shifted in the sloppy dirt, and I toppled backward. I didn't hit the wall very hard, but my shoulder sunk in deep, so deep I had to put my elbow in the wall to push myself up.

"So I'm the only guy who thinks Reister's nuts, at least until you guys showed up," Tosh continued while Collins turned his flashlight on me. "I can't get him court-martialed, and even if I did, I'd get fucked up."

"Oh shit," I managed, as the part of wall I'd hit collapsed, and I pitched onto Collins to avoid falling in.

"Shut up, shut up," Tosh hissed, pointing his pistol and flashlight into the gap I'd busted in the wall. Tosh scooted to it and punched out a few more heaps of clay. Between the two beams of light we could see a second tunnel running alongside the wall. It was a little larger than the first, but not by much.

"Must've been a T-intersection they blocked off," Tosh whispered as he flashed his light down the tunnel in either direction. As he did, we all heard a faint rustling, but it went silent before we could get a bead on which way it had come from.

No one spoke, but a decision was made. There was no point in arguing; we were going down there. Not for Reister; not for the greater glory of the USMC; but for our own lives, worthless though they may be. The noise told us Vincent Charles was close, and we stood a much better chance down here than in his jungle later tonight. Splitting up was our only option. If they got behind us, we were fucked.

Tosh went right, Collins and me went left. We were to meet back at the cave in one hour. That seemed a helluva long time to me, but it was slow going in those tunnels. Collins had the flashlight, so I wiggled after him in the darkness. After a few dozen feet, I managed to get around so I could look behind us, but Tosh's light had already vanished. All I could hear was the wheezing of Collins' lungs and the gurgling in my own sorry guts.

The fear washed back over me, and I started to lag behind. Once I tried to tell Collins to wait up, but he shushed me immediately. I had to stop several times to get my breathing sorted out, and I was sure we must've gone too far. After shaking off the willies for the hundredth time, I noticed

Collins had stopped up ahead at an intersection. It was another T, our tunnel dead-ending into it. I scrambled through the tight hole, unable to see anything but the firefly of Collins' flashlight far ahead of me.

I'd calmed down a bit, when my already-strained nerves were snapped by a sudden burst of gunfire somewhere back in the tunnels.

Three shots in quick succession, then silence, then the rest of the clip going off. The possibilities were endless, but none of them were good.

I cupped my hands to call out to Collins, but paused, unsure if I should disturb the tomblike quiet that had again enveloped the tunnel.

Then I heard the screams. The echoing wails came from back the way we'd come, from Tosh. The shrieking got worse and worse, rising in pitch until it cut off suddenly.

For a while I lay still in the tunnel, feeling dizzy all of a sudden. Then Collins was waving his light in my eyes, and I lost it. I began to kick and claw the walls and ceiling, covering myself in mud.

"Get yer ass over here," Collins called out, his voice booming. "Chill the fuck out!"

Getting myself under control, I moved forward once more. Every few yards I'd have to stop and squirm around to glance back down the passage, even though I couldn't see a damn thing. I was getting close to Collins, a scant twenty-five feet away, when I heard it.

There are no words to describe the horror I felt at hearing that sound. I envied the dead as I heard that noise, and froze in mid-wiggle. It was the unmistakable scraping of someone or something pulling itself up the tunnel.

I groaned, trying to scream but too damn scared to do so. Collins must have heard as well, because he hurled his flashlight at me. It thudded off the floor, bouncing to within my reach. I frantically drew my Colt and turned the light down the tunnel. Its beam splashed over the pockmarked burrow, fading out down the passage.

"Come on, get over here," Collins said, his voice drowning out the scrape-scraping.

Then it hit me, a warm breeze fluttering down the tunnel. A sweet, charnel-house smell rode that draft, the odor of southern fried slope. I thought of a guy I'd hated in my last company, and how he'd smelled after the mortar had done its work and left him to the jungle for a few hours. That same, almost erotic smell of raw meat had hung over the crater his remains were spattered about.

The light revealed nothing but an empty tunnel. Still, I knew something lurked just beyond the beam's reach. The noise grew louder and louder, and the smell became worse and worse. I wanted desperately to crawl up the tunnel to Collins, but stayed rooted in place. Then the noise and stench coagulated into a sight, making substance from shadow at the tip of my beam, and all hell broke loose.

The thing didn't crawl so much as slither, its leathery skin sticking to the clay. I'd seen dead bodies on numerous occasions, and more importantly, I'd smelled them.

Even if what came at me out of that pit had a whole face instead of that larvae-infested quilt of rotting skin, even if its chest was intact rather than split open and coated in gore; even then the smell would have been enough for me to know:

The thing was dead.

A dead gook—moving, for God's sake!

Its left arm ended at the elbow, the flesh worn away to reveal splintered bone and the ragged threads of nerve and muscle. The fingers of its other hand were grated and mangled. Yet they pulled its mutilated body forward. As the thing leered fully into the light, I could make out the brainpan through a crack in its decaying face. It came at me out of the darkness, and I went totally fucking apeshit.

The first few shots sank into the side of the tunnel, but the weeping flesh-blossoms opening on its face and shoulders told me I'd hit it a few times. It stopped, but only momentarily, before lurching forward again. I sobbed and spat, pulling the trigger again and again, even after the clip ran dry. Unable to take my eyes off the crawling corpse, I tried to back up, but my legs wouldn't bend.

I chunked my empty gun at the crawling thing, but it fell short. Before I knew what I was doing, I had thrown the flashlight at it, too. That fell short, too, and worse—the light landed pointing into the wall. Most everything went dark, except for a small patch of tunnel wall lit up by the beam. I couldn't see the thing, but knew it was still there. And when the hand grabbed me by the back of my collar, I thought it had gotten behind me somehow—but it was only Collins, pulling me back up the tunnel by my head and flailing arms.

He probably said something, but I all I could hear was the scrape-scraping. And the smell—oh God, the smell! I stopped thrashing as Collins hauled me backward in short jerks. *Scrape, scrape, scrape.* Inspiration hit me, and I fumbled madly at my vest. Just as Collins backed into one of the cross-passages at the intersection, the thing bumped the flashlight and the beam spun around to spotlight that oozing face. Scraps of wet flesh dangled from its mouth, dribbling blood onto the clay.

Screaming, I yanked the pin from a grenade. Collins was screaming then, too, and I side-armed the explosive at the oncoming horror. I badly wanted to see if it would hit, but Collins punched me in the mouth. Then he was shoving me up a tunnel, grinding his back into my folded knees.

The light came next, so bright I could see miles and miles down the empty tunnel in front of me—hundreds of miles of dirt and clay and light—and then I went black.

I awoke to Collins screaming, and hands clawing at my legs. Whimpering, I kicked at the arms and began to pull myself away up the tunnel. It had got us, and I dared not think what kind of shit we were in. Then Collins stopped screaming, and the hands stopped pawing.

"David," Collins gasped from behind me. "David, it's me, oh fuck, it's me, it's me . . ."

He sounded far away down the tunnel. I wanted out of this shit, out of this damn grave I'd crawled into. I thought of the smell, and vomited onto myself.

"David," Collins was saying, "Jesus, David, help me. I can't feel my legs. They're gone—my legs, my fuckin' legs."

He began to cry, and in my delirium I crawled up the tunnel, away from the sobbing. The blast had done a number on me, and I paused to try to get a grip on what had happened. Run, I thought. Get out now. Then I remembered Collins lying fucked up in the dark. Part of me had to keep moving, but just as I resumed my crawling I heard Collins shouting my name. I couldn't leave him.

"David?" Collins whimpered. "Hey, fuckin' say something, man."

"It's me," I mumbled, uncertain how to proceed. I backed up a way, so that I lay awkwardly over Collins and could feel his arms and chest under my legs.

"My lighter," he groaned, and tried to get at his vest, but my knees were in his way. Blind and half deaf, my head grinding into the ceiling, I groped all over his muddy fatigues until I found the bulge of his Zippo. I clumsily pulled it out and squirmed off of him. It took some work, since I was shaking so badly, but I got it lit after a few tries. I fearfully waved it in Collins' direction, and began to laugh. The light was feeble compared to a flashlight, but I could clearly see that Collins lay buried up to his thighs in dirt; the tunnel behind us had caved in on him.

With some work we dug him out, and at finding his feet intact, he began to laugh like it was all some big fucking practical joke. It was miraculous he hadn't broken anything. He seemed a little shook up, but otherwise okay.

"A grenade?" Collins said. "That was fuckin' stupid."

"I'm sorry," I whispered, as those dingy old claws of fear began digging themselves into my heart again, "I'm so sorry. I didn't mean to—oh shit, we are so fucked!"

Collins went silent, and he took his Zippo out of my hands and flicked it closed.

"Turn it on," I begged him.

"No."

"Please, I can't see—I can't—I can't," I stuttered.

"Look," Collins said, his voice a helluva lot sterner than I'd ever heard it before, "we can't get out the way we came. That's obvious."

"But—"

"And if were gonna find another way out, we'll need some light. I don't want to burn the fluid until we really need to see something."

And even though I knew he was right, I couldn't stop shaking.

Buried alive, I kept thinking. *My dumb ass had buried us alive. How far to the surface? Were we going up or down? What was that thing? Seriously, what the fuck was it?*

"Let's get going," Collins said, and I was squashed into the mud as he scrambled over me.

My fear didn't leave, but I beat it into submission, and followed Collins. Every time I moved forward, though, I'd sniff the air and perk my ears a bit. For shit's sake, I was scared.

All I could hear was the sound we made as we went, scraping and squishing. Rather than growing used to the dark, my eyes seemed to tint, the blackness appearing to thicken and harden. Several times we rested, our fingers just as raw and aching as our knees were bruised and sore. Once I thought I smelled the stench again, but immediately realized it was only my own stink of piss and puke and sweat. We encountered no adjoining passages, and I began to lose hope.

I had no grenades, no gun, and no flashlight—only a goddamn jackknife. The death I'd sentenced us to would not be quick. I couldn't stop thinking about the creature, and wanted to know what Collins thought about it, but he wasn't in the mood for conversation.

Collins stopped suddenly after God-knows-how-many hours, and I immediately curled up to get some shut-eye. He kicked me, and I was about to tell him to fuck off when I saw it, too: A speck of light glittered far off down the tunnel, a spot of brilliance in the catacombs.

I heard Collins unholster his Colt, and as quietly as we could, we resumed crawling. My guts jumped about in agitation, and I had to suppress my giggles. We had finally made it, dragged our worn-out bodies through miles of tunnels all night long, and were now about to emerge into the morning jungle. After all the pain and terror and despair, we had made it.

With the light still apparently a long way off down the tunnel, Collins stopped again. I began to ask him what the score was when he kicked me quiet. I heard his Zippo flick open, and everything went white. As my eyes readjusted, I saw why we had stopped.

The passage ended not a foot in front of Collins. A smooth, reddish block—wholly out of place in this world of brown clay—was wedged into the tunnel. A hole no wider than a cigarette passed through the block, which was where the light was coming from. It wasn't sunlight either, not nearly bright enough.

Collins looked pretty rough, with blood caked on his chin and vest. He turned to me and put his index finger to his lips, the pistol concealing his face. Be quiet. No shit, Sherlock.

The tunnel wasn't any broader here, but Collins was small enough that he could swivel around in a fetal position after giving me the lighter, getting his feet in front of him. He clicked the safety off his Colt and pushed at the wall with his feet. Nothing. Killing the Zippo and pocketing it, I leaned into Collins as he gave it another go. The block shifted a fraction of an inch. With a groan, Collins heaved again, and the block moved another half-foot.

Light now trickled in from all four sides of the block. A final kick made it topple forward. Collins scooted into the light. He slid down a little way into what must have been a deeper, wider tunnel beyond the one that had brought us there, though I couldn't see any details yet. The back of Collins' head was in the way.

Suddenly Collins yelled, "Don't move, motherfucker!"

My gorge rose. We weren't alone anymore. Shit.

I nervously crawled to the end of the hole and stopped, paralyzed with awe. Not only were we not outside, we weren't in another tunnel, either. Stretching out above and below me lay an ornate temple, lit with several long candles that cast an unnatural amount of brightness on the room. The ceiling had clearly been carved from the clay, but the four walls all looked like they were made up of blocks similar to the one we had dislodged. The floor below my perch gleamed black and yellow, covered in a thin coating of moss.

I wanted to examine the carved ceiling and what appeared to be a shrine set against the opposite wall, but Collins and his new friend quickly reclaimed my attention. The man wore yellow robes, and stood in the center of the room. He looked old, like ancient fucking old, and rather amused at the pistol being waved in his face by the furious Irishman. It seemed ridiculous, but we'd apparently managed to bust out into the church of some weird gook god.

"David," Collins yelped, his back to me. "David, get down here! Oh shit, don't you fuckin' move, you fuck."

I tried clambering down, but slipped and fell, cracking my shoulder painfully. The moss felt soft and nice, though, and I wanted sleep more than anything in the world, but Collins' boot persuaded me to rise once more. I got up, supporting myself on the loose block I'd narrowly avoided braining myself on.

"Oh, man," Collins said, "what the fuck is this, what the fuck?"

I looked up again at the images etched in the clay ceiling.

It was like I couldn't help myself.

They were kind of a cross between a sculpture and a picture, weird spirals of black clay rearing out of the smooth earth to form miniature people and less identifiable creatures.

The detail seemed flawless, right down to the ribbons of drool hanging from the teeth of the monstrosities that tore their way free of the clay.

My heart beat wildly, and I had to remind myself to breathe.

Then I looked to the shrine—a tiny spring encircled by clay beasts. The spring bubbled out a pathetic stream of black water. The run-off was carried along some tiles into a fungus-coated stone pipe, an aqueduct. Scrawled over the hole where the pipe left the room were a bunch of odd letters, not Vietnamese or Cambodian, but characters from some older, weirder alphabet.

Other than the way we had come and the aqueduct, there seemed to be no exits from the room.

My canteen was dry, so I made my way to the shrine on shaky legs. The idea to do so came to me suddenly, and seemed like a really good one. When I got close, I saw that the spring was only able to sustain the small pool. The run-off barely made it a few feet down the tunnel before moss sopped it up. As I bent to drink, Collins got agitated.

"Hey—hey! What're you doing?" he stammered. "Get the fuck away from there!"

I paused, looking back at Collins and the old man. The geezer had turned so that I could see he was still smiling, but I got real confused then, because I realized that the old guy was about as Charles as me or Collins. He looked—I dunno, Middle-Eastern, maybe—because of his long beard. His scalp was shaved smooth, but it looked like his head was covered by faded tattoos or something—the skin all blue and splotchy. He had the palest green eyes, almost white, and those eyes kept staring at me as if I were the only other person in the room, as if Collins and his gun didn't exist.

"Drink," the old man said, his English clear and precise, despite an almost German accent.

At this, Collins flipped his shit.

"You fuck," he babbled. "You're helpin' us—U.S. Marines, understand? Get us outta here, you—you—hey, how many of you bastards are down here? What the fuck is goin' on, what is this shit, what is this?"

"Relax," the old man said. "Drink. Sit. You are my guests."

As he said this, his eyes sparkled, and I moved away from the pool toward Collins.

"Relax?" Collins shook, wired on fear and confusion. "Dude, you got no fuckin' idea what we been through—what we saw—so shut the fuck up!"

"It's been such a long time," the old man continued, ignoring Collins, "since I've had company. Rest a while."

The old man's tranquility must have been contagious, because Collins calmed right down. "Look," he said, his finger easing off the trigger, "how do we get out? That's all we want."

The old man didn't answer, but his smile broadened. He turned his back on Collins, and went toward the spring. Collins, pissed at the brush off but no longer raging, walked after him. I watched anxiously, feeling lost and tired.

"Hey, you old gook," Collins said. "I said you're gonna help us." And at this the geezer spun around. He didn't look so frail anymore, and his beard stirred as if a wind brushed it, only I felt no wind.

"I am no 'gook,' you wretched Western slug," he intoned, his smile gone, "I care not for your petty squabbling, and will not pick sides in your hollow wars. I did not help the others when they came, and I will not help you." And he turned away to kneel before the spring.

I felt sick, not just tired or scared, but one hundred percent, death's-door ill. So I gazed back up at the ceiling, trying to find a familiar, comforting image among the strange gods. Collins kept pressing though, advancing on the old man; like I said, he never did know when to shut the fuck up. "What others—the VC?" he said. "Where are they? When were they here?"

"When they built that tunnel, they came through the wall. After that, they all left. Most, anyway. There are still a few, I think, in here somewhere." He looked slowly around the walls of the temple, as if peering through the blocks or at something invisible to us.

Removing a clay cup from his robe, he filled it with the dark water. He offered this to Collins, who finally lowered his gun. I was relieved by that. The last thing I wanted was for Collins to shoot the old man. I didn't really know why.

"Came through the wall?" Collins asked, sipping the water.

"They came through," the old man said, "by chance, when they were excavating a tunnel system to hide from you crusaders."

"Crusaders?" Collins snorted, finishing his water and handing me the cup. "We're USMC, not King Arthur's fuckin' knights."

"Wait a second," I said, bending back down to refill the cup. "You said they came through the wall. So you were already here. If they built the tunnel, how did you get down here?"

"Yeah," Collins seconded, moving around the side of the pool. He squinted at something I couldn't see, so I turned away and put the cup to my lips. Sipping the water, I found it to be the sweetest I'd had since home. A little thick, but definitely refreshing.

"I read of a spring in the jungles a long time ago," the old man said, "a small creek mentioned in an ancient tome. Many years had passed since the book was penned, and many more passed before I found the stream. By the time I'd arrived, it had dwindled to a miniscule trickle in the hills, which I followed down into the earth, until I located its source."

He waved his spindly arm at the pool before us.

Collins had reached the wall and, ducking down, leaned over the shrine to look down the aqueduct pipe.

"Hot damn," Collins said excitedly, "bet we could follow this all the way out!"

I looked apprehensively at the narrow exit. If possible, it seemed even smaller than the last two tunnels. But I'd spent more then enough time down in that damn temple, or whatever the hell it was.

"Yes," the old man said, his smile reappearing. "Yes, that leads to the surface."

"Aha!" yelped Collins. He snatched a small leather bag he'd spotted in a crevice by the pool, then tossed it to me. The weight of the thing nearly bowled me over. Collins was waving his gun around again, and for the first time I began to question his sanity. We should not fuck with the old man; that seemed obvious.

"What's in there?" Collins hooted. "If it's supplies or food, it's ours!"

My guts began to thrash around again, and I bent to open the bag. Just as my fingers undid the complex knot, the old man appeared over me, and for no reason I can name, I silently handed him back the bag. But as he took the offering, I distinctly felt movement from the satchel, the leather pushed violently outward by something inside.

"What the shit!" Collins gasped. "David, what the fuck is your problem?"

"We don't need it," I whispered, staring at the pulsating bag.

"What the fuck is in it?"

"Nothing to help you," the old man said. "Old books. They'll do the likes of you no good at all."

"Books?" Collins demanded. "Let's see them."

"There is nothing in them that will allow you to live to see the sunrise," the old man said, and even though I could no longer bring myself to look at his face, I knew he still smiled.

"What?" Collins screeched. "What? Fuck you!"

And Collins—nice, funny, a little dumb but okay Collins—emptied his clip into the old man.

I felt paralyzed, watching him jab his gun into the geezer's robes and blast away. But nothing happened. We all stood still for a moment, silent, waiting. Then Collins dropped his Colt, which skipped away off the moss.

The old man turned to Collins, who looked back at him. Collins even met his gaze—for about a minute. Then he collapsed, wailing and pulling at the old man's robes.

As he bowed before the geezer, whispering apologies through his sobs, the man looked to me again, and try as I might to look away, I found myself peering into those treacherous green eyes of his.

He spun away, depositing his satchel back in the nook and striding to the block we'd knocked down. Then he began to mumble and chant. I hurried to Collins, who was still shaking and moaning, and splashed water onto this face. He looked pale and fever ridden, but he came to his senses enough for us to get our shit together. Retrieving his gun, I ejected the spent clip, found some extra rounds, reloaded it, and tucked it into my belt.

I turned back to the old man, who once more faced us. With stomach-turning horror I realized that the half-ton block was back in place, sealing the room. Collins had stopped crying, but when he looked at that block, I thought he might start up again.

The old man towered over us, and I knew the true meaning of fear. Not the fear that compels the feet to action; but a fear of such magnitude that awe or madness or worship can be the only possible responses to it. This was the fear of God that I had never known. Real terror confronted us in that instant, in the guise of that old man. And when he finally averted his glare, we knew that he owned us, and that, for the moment, he was a merciful master.

"Go," he said disgustedly.

We fled—not out of fright, but out of respect. We walked slowly to the pipe, our eyes fastened on the old man's robes. The farther we moved away from him, the more our wonder turned to dread. Finally, we panicked. As I'm bigger, I managed to push in front and began scrambling with maddened intensity down the narrow confines of the aqueduct.

I should've been too tired to move, let alone pull myself by my fingertips over miles of jagged stone, but I moved with a speed bordering on the supernatural. Our flight must have lasted many hours, but I can barely remember it. Once I must have slept, as Collins woke me with a pinch to the ankle. Sometime later I shit myself, the rancid smell an unwelcome reminder of the thing in the tunnel.

Finally, after losing three fingernails and a boot, I found the rock giving way to clay, and knew we'd made it. The tunnel grew wider, opening into a cave that the aqueduct passed through. The incline leveled off as the night sky came into view up ahead, revealed to us through gaps in the vines that dangled over the cave mouth. Grabbing Collins by the arm, I started to run forward, laughing as I approached freedom. If only I'd thought to use Collins' Zippo, we might have made it.

I didn't even feel the first few strikes, and had collapsed to my knees before I understood what had happened. Collins stepped back screaming, and went down hard.

The moonlight barely reached us in the back of the cave, but I could see well enough to know

I was fucked. Cobras, dozens of 'em, rearing at me out of the darkness, long fangs sinking in and ripping out, over and over and over.

It didn't sting so much as burn, my whole body incinerating from the inside. I felt the snakes writhing underneath me, the fire growing and growing, and they didn't stop. They were all over me, fat coils of scales rubbing, hoods flaring, and the noise—the *shick, shick, shick* of snake sliding on snake—and the screams . . .

After a time, they stopped biting. Every few minutes one would experimentally strike at a twitching limb, but the onslaught had ended. *I should die*, I thought, *any second the fire will cool, and I can rest—sleep—die*. But I didn't. The burning intensified, the sickness so bad I could feel my skin crack and ooze as the venom rotted me alive.

Then I remembered the Colt.

It took me a spell to jam my bloated finger into the trigger guard, and as I raised it, the gun went off. At this the snakes under and on me were striking and thrashing again, but I couldn't care less. In the cave's dimness, I could see Collins' serpent-covered body still convulsing a few feet away, could hear his whimpers, soft but clear. I couldn't get up, so from where I lay I put five round into Collins' back, then put the barrel in my own mouth and pulled the trigger.

Thum-thump. Sleep. *Thum-thump.* Staring at the ceiling, can't sleep. Light enters the cave, snakes everywhere, slithering over and under and through us, out into the sunshine. Watch the light on the wall through my ruined face, feeling cold metal in my throat, hearing the damn heartbeat sound, louder and louder, and I'm dead. But I'm not. Heartbeat getting louder until I can't think, all I want is to die but I can't and it hurts, the fucking thundering heartbeat, and I'm clawing at my chest, digging through purple layers of poisoned meat until I find the bastard and put my fingers through it and tear at it until most of it comes off in my swollen fist and I squeeze until it's dribbling gore—and I realize it's not my heart that's making all the racket. Now I'm moving, ripping at Collins' breast, and he's pushing me away, saying, "Get offa me, get offa me."

I find his heart, the bullet holes making it easy, and I crush the fat, warm thing and I still fucking hear that *thum-thump, thum-thump*, and Collins' moans, "Lie down, we're dead, we're dead," and the burning's only gotten worse, and I watch the light dying away, but the snakes don't come back, only the stars.

"You still awake, David?" Collins asks. I try to answer, but my jaw's blown off, so I only gurgle up blood.

"Reister," Collins whispers after a while, and the starlight glimmers just like the old man's eyes, and I can see fine, even though I'm dead. The burning's finally cooling, but the noise is getting worse with every second. It takes some work, some real fucking work, but I conjure up Reister's face—Reister's damned, damning face—and I remember. Even though it hurts, I remember.

Moving makes it a little better, even though the *thum-thump* is even louder out in the grass on the hilltop, but me and Collins are soldiers again, and even with my legs all dripping and soft I run so fast, so damn fast, it's like I'm swimming through the jungle. I can't hear anything but the heartbeat, coming from everything, from everywhere, getting louder and louder, and we find their footprints, and it's so easy, so many footprints. Collins says things, and I want to answer, but I can't, and "Besides," he says, "they'll be able to kill us for sure, definitely, fuckin' A."

Then the jungle stops, and the *thum-thump, thum-thump* is so loud my ears rupture and bleed, and Collins is screaming. Frank, big Frank never liked us much, and Collins is on him—heh, some guard—and Frank is screaming, too, as he drops his gun and falls under Collins.

Soldiers everywhere, flares blinding me all around, but the *thum-thump* is worse, so terrible it hurts more than any bullet. Then he's right there, all three hundred pounds of throbbing fat and muscle: Reister. I want to show him, to lead him down through the tunnels to behold sights unseen by living men, so he can know, so he can understand. But watching him trip as he turns to run, shoving one of his terrified men between us, I know he already does: better him than you, after all, eh, Reister? Loyalty? Courage? Honor? Bullshit. Survival. Blood, under their fingernails or yours. *Thum-thump.* We run together, me and Reister, and then I'm on him, and then he's wide open, his guts unspooling into my arms in the grass under the stars, and the heartbeat gets a tiny bit softer, and it's fucking glorious . . .

JESSE BULLINGTON is the author of the gritty, darkly humorous historical fantasies *The Sad Tale of the Brothers Grossbart,* and *The Enterprise of Death*, with a third, *The Folly of the World*, released in 2012. His short fiction and articles have appeared in numerous magazines, anthologies, and websites, and he can be found online at www.jessebullington.com.

A not-so-charming little story told from a zombie's point of view.
Snap. Snap. Snap.

At First Only Darkness

Nancy A. Collins

At first only darkness: utter and complete. No beginning or end. Eternal blackness. Thick as tar. Heavy as lead. Filling eyes, ears, nose, throat. Blotting out all light, all breath, all smell. There is no time in the darkness. No past. No future. There is only the unceasing Now.

Something not-as-black moves, turns to almost-black, then to dark gray. The dark gray becomes several gray shapes. Gray blobs grow lighter. With it comes sound, muted and warped, as if heard underwater. It is something to focus on, something to struggle toward.

The gray turns lighter. Dark shapes move inside it. The sound becomes clearer. The gray sloughs away. The sound pulls harder: it is a voice. No; two voices. One pitched low, the other high. The high-pitched voice is keening.

The gray fog melts away. The weight binding the limbs and muffling the senses disappears. With its departure comes the arrival of light, sound, smell, *hunger.*

There is no breath, no pulse, no words, no hot, no cold. But there *is* Hunger. The Hunger is the only sharp thing in a dulled and muted world. The Hunger is all pain, all need, all fear. To be Hungry is to be empty and to be empty is to be in pain, *all* the time. And the time is always Now.

A thing kneels down. It has a face. Eyes leaking liquid, mouth open as it makes the keening sound. It has a smell. A smell that names it:

Food.

The Hunger burns and twists and scorches and slashes. Saliva spills. There is only one thing that will make the agony of Hunger go away: food. To bite food. To chew food.

Snap. Snap. Snap.

The food screams. Spurt of blood. Gobble down the fingers. Flesh is the only good thing ever.

More. More. More.

Some more food shouts and grabs the bleeding food, drags it away.

Rise. Arms flail, fingers clutch and spasm. Unsteady legs churn. Sheets tangle. *Find the food.* The scent of fresh blood makes the Hunger hotter, sharper, more painful. The bleeding food is nearby. The smell of it spreads through the air like fog.

Move forward. Go to the blood-smell. Walk out door. Down the hallway. Red mist floats down stairs. *Step.* Leg muscles groan like timber. *Step.* Faces of things line the stairs. Look like food but don't smell like food. *Step.*

The bleeding food is on the sofa. It is moaning, rocking back and forth. Blood on the floor. *Drip. Drip. Drip.* The food looks up. Mouth opens. Sound comes out. A scream: *Richard.* Means something. But what? No matter. All that matters is the Hunger. Eat. Move fast. Hungry.

Snap. Snap. Snap.

Blood. Flesh. Warm. Hot. Salty. Good. Eat. All of it. Teeth gnash. Jaws clench. Eat. The food screams and struggles and bleeds. Flesh tears away like wet paper. Chew. *More.* Keep chewing.

Something heavy strikes shoulder. Neck too rigid to turn. Turn entire body. The other food is back. Shouting. *Monica.* Means something. But what?

The other food smells good. The smell brings the Hunger. The Hunger burns and stabs and strangles and hurts. Eat. Bite. Flesh and blood. Snap. Snap. Snap. The other food drops its weapon and runs away. Turn back around. The bleeding food moans but doesn't move.

Eat fast. Faster; before not food.

Jaws move. Bite. Tear with teeth and hand. Good. *More.* Crack open bones. Belly full. The Hunger stops. The pain dwindles and fades. Stand and stare. Waiting.

A tiny spark, barely a flicker, struggles against the darkness, then abruptly leaps to life, burning hot and high, throwing light to all corners. Everything cloaked in darkness is revealed in a single searing flash, like pictures taken during a lightning storm.

A mangled female corpse lies sprawled across the sofa. The lips, eyelids, and facial skin have been ripped away. It is unrecognizable, save for the wedding ring—mate to the ring on my hand, which lies attached to the arm lying on the hooked rug at my feet.

The television hisses static in the corner. The ax lies on the floor where my sobbing brother dropped it. The mirror over the fireplace reveals a pale, hollow-eyed ghoul, blood smeared across its face, gobbets of raw flesh stuck between its gnashing teeth, a mangled knob of gristle and gore jutting from its left shoulder. I instinctively recoil in fear at the sight of such a hideous creature in my living room. Then I realize it is the only thing I can see in the mirror.

The pain of the Hunger is nothing compared to the Horror. The howling, shrieking agony that comes from knowing you are not just dead, but truly in Hell. I try to scream, but all that comes out is a low, wheezing moan, like wind rushing down the pipe organ I play at our church.

Oh God! Monica! Jesus, Jesus, Jesus, what have I done? Holy God somebody help me! Help meee!

The darkness returns, for good this time, and snuffs out the flame. The light dies, and the world is once more swallowed by shadow. Better the oblivion of the walking dead than the clarity of damnation.

The bleeding food twitches and begins to rise. It is no longer food. Catch scent of more food. Follow. Leg muscles tight. Hard to walk. Follow smell out of house. Sunlight burns eyes. Shapes up ahead. Many, many shapes. Food? No. The shapes move too slow and smell too bad to be food. The shapes are not-food.

Catch scent of food. Saliva fills mouth. Move toward smell. The not-food follows. Some walk stiff and slow; others move as fast as food.

Hungry. Must get to food. Must get to food *first.*

The food stands on a shiny metal thing. The food holds a stick. Shouting. *Get some, motherfuckers. Get some.* The not-food shuffle and lurch forward.

Hungry. So hungry. Grab the food. Claw at the food. *First.* Eat. Bite. Flesh. *First.* The stick explodes, spraying not-food brains. The blood of the not-food tastes bad. The not-food behind push the not-food up front closer to the food. All hungry. All want first bite. The stick explodes again.

The food screams as the not-food drag it off the top of the shiny metal thing. The screams go louder. Smell of blood. Push forward. The Hunger comes. Grab the food. So many hands. Hard to be first with only one arm. Snatch length of intestine from smaller not-food. The smaller not-food hisses, grabs a piece of liver from a weaker not-food. Eat. The food is quiet. The Hunger stops.

Walk. More walk. Search for food. Bump against not-food. Walk. Follow scent of food. Light turns dark. Walk. Track food. Surprise food. The Hunger comes. *Snap. Snap. Snap.* Teeth sink deep. The food screams. More not-food arrive to feed. Pushed aside. Food torn to pieces. Grab leg. Bigger not-food grabs same leg. Pull. Pull harder. Bigger not-food bites arm. No pain. No blood. No let go. Eat side-by-side. The Hunger stops. Walk. More walk. Dark turns light.

Splash.

Look down. Water. Sand. Water up to ankles. Water goes away. Look up. Blue. Wide, empty blue. No food. No not-food. Just blue. The darkness recedes slightly, allowing a tickle of memory: Running barefoot on the beach.

Monica?

Stand and stare at the blue empty. Water comes up to calf. Light turns dark. Water comes up to thigh. Moon. Water comes up to hips. Water goes away. Float out with water.

Stare down into water. No bubbles. Scrape against sand. Scrape against rocks. Float. Shapes appear. Silver. Clicking sound. Shapes push body. *Food?* Grab at maybe-food. Too slow. Maybe-food disappears.

Big shape appears; *very* big. Circle. *Food?* Big shape moves fast. Teeth sink deep; many, many teeth. Jaws shake back and forth. Black blood fills water. Big shape swims away, trailing bowels and blood.

Float. Stare at sky. Dark turns light turns dark turns light turns dark turns light. Float. Tiny shapes nibble. Feathered shapes scream. Peck at face. *Food?* Bite. Feathered shape squawks in alarm and flies away with eye. Light turns dark turns light turns dark turns light turns dark.

Roll up on beach. Water, sand in mouth and nose. No breath. Tiny, shiny hard shapes come from sand. Pick face with claws. No eyelids. No eyes. No lips. No tongue. Darkness.

Sound. Muted by sand and rot. Voices. One high. One low. The smell of food.

Oh dear god—is that what I think it is?

Be careful.

The Hunger comes. Stabbing, burning, strangling, shooting hunger, even though there is no belly to feed. No respite for the damned.

Don't worry. It's been decapitated.

Snap. Snap. Snap.

NANCY A. COLLINS is the author of several novels and numerous short stories. In addition, she served a two-year stint for DC Comics' Swamp Thing series. She is a recipient of the Horror Writers Association's Bram Stoker Award and the British Fantasy Society's Icarus Award, as well as a nominee for the Eisner Award, the John W. Campbell Memorial Award, and an International Horror Guild award. Best-known for her ground-breaking vampire character, Sonja Blue, Collins's works include *Dead Man's Hand, Knuckles and Tales,* and *Sunglasses After Dark.* Her most recent work is the Vamps series, published by HarperCollins. Collins makes her home in Cape Fear, North Carolina.

Life was so weird. Wormboy felt like the only normal person left.

Jerry's Kids Meet Wormboy

David J. Schow

Eating 'em was more fun than blowing their gnarly green heads off. But why dicker when you could do both?

The fresher ones were blue. That was important if you wanted to avoid cramps, salmonella. Eat a green one and you'd be yodeling down the big porcelain megaphone in no time.

Wormboy used wirecutters to snip the nose off the last bullet in the foam block. He snugged the truncated cartridge into the cylinder of his short-barrel .44. When fired, the flattened slugs pancaked on impact and would disintegrate any geek's head into hash. The green guys weren't really "zombis," because no voodoo had played a part. They were all geeks, all slow as syrup and stupid as hell and Wormboy loved it that way. It meant he would not starve in this cowardly new world. He was eating; millions weren't.

Wormboy's burden was great.

It hung from his Butthole Surfers T-shirt. He had scavenged dozens of such shirts from a burned-out rockshop, all Extra Extra Large, all screaming about bands he had never heard of—*Day-Glo Abortions, Rudimentary Penii, Shower of Smegma, Fat & Fucked Up*. Wormboy's big personal in-joke was one that championed a long-gone album titled *Giving Head To The Living Dead*.

The gravid flab of his teats distorted the logo, and his surplus flesh quivered and swam, shoving around his clothing as though some subcutaneous revolution was aboil. Pasty and pocked, his belly depended earthward, a vast sandbag held at bay by a wide weightlifter's belt, notched low. The faintest motion caused his hectares of skin to bobble like mercury.

Wormboy was more than fat. He was a crowd of fat people. A single mirror was insufficient to the task of containing his image.

The explosion buzzed the floor beneath his hi-tops. Vibrations slithered from one thick stratum of dermis to the next, bringing him the news.

The sound of a Bouncing Betty's boom-boom always worked like a Pavlovian dinner gong. It could smear a smile across his jowls and start his tummy to percolating. He snatched up binoculars and stampeded out into the graveyard.

Valley View Memorial Park was a classic cemetery, of a venerable lineage far preceding the ordinances that required flat monument stones to note the dearly departed. The granite and marble jutting from its acreage was the most ostentatious and artfully hewn this side of a Universal Studios monster movie boneyard. Stone cold angels reached toward heaven. Stilted verse, deathlessly chiseled, eulogized the departees—vanity plates in a suburbia for the lifeless. It cloyed.

Most of the graves were unoccupied. They had prevailed without the fertilization of human decay and were now choked with loam and healthy green grass. Most of the tenants had clawed out and waltzed off several seasons back.

A modest road formed a spiral ascent path up the hill and terminated in a cul-de-sac fronting Wormboy's current living quarters. Midway up it was interrupted by a trench ten feet across. Wormboy had excavated this "moat" using the cemetery's scoop-loader, and seeded it with lengths of two-inch pipe sawn at angles to form funnel-knife style pungi sticks. Tripwires knotted gate struts to tombstones to booby traps, and three hundred antipersonnel mines lived in the earth. Every longitude and latitude of Valley View had been lovingly nurtured into a Gordian Knot of killpower which Wormboy had christened his "spiderweb."

The Bouncing Bettys had been a godsend. Anything that wandered in unbidden would get its legs blown off or become immovably gaffed in the moat.

Not long after the geeks woke up, shucked dirt, and ambled off with their yaps drooping open, Wormboy had claimed Valley View for his very own. He knew the dead tended to "home" toward places that had been important to them back when they weren't green. Ergo, never would they come trotting home to a graveyard.

Wormboy's previous hideout had been a National Guard armory. Too much traffic in walking dead weekend warriors, there. Blowing them into unwalking lasagna cost too much time and powder. After seven Land Rover-loads of military rock and roll, Wormy's redecoration of Valley

View was complete. The graveyard was one big mechanized ambush. The reception building and nondenominational chapel were ideally suited to his needs . . . and breadth. Outfitting the prep room was more stainless steel than a French kitchen in Beverly Hills; where stiffs were once dressed for interment, Wormboy now dressed them out for din-din. There was even a refrigerated morgue locker. Independent generators chugged out wattage. His only real lament was that there never seemed to be enough videotapes to keep him jolly. On the nonfiction front he favored Julia Child.

The binocs were overpriced army jobs with an illuminated reticle. Wormboy thumbed up his bottle-bottom fisheye specs, focused and swept the base of the hill. Smoke was still rising from the breach point. Fewer geeks blundered in these days, but now and again he could still snag one.

That was peculiar. As far as Wormboy could reckon, geeks functioned on the level of pure motor response with a single directive—seek food—and legs that made their appetites mobile. Past Year One the locals began to shun Valley View altogether, almost as though the geek grapevine had warned them the place was poison. Could be that Valley View's primo kill rate had made it the crucible of the first bona fide zombi superstition.

God only knew what they were munching in the cities by now. As the legions of ambulatory expirees had swelled, their preferred food—live citizens—had gone underground. Survivors of what Wormboy called Zombi Apocalypse had gotten canny or gotten eaten. Geek society itself was like a gator pit; he'd seen them get pissed off and chomp hunks out of one another. Though their irradiated brains kept their limbs supple and greased with oxygenated blood, they were still dead . . . and dead people still rotted. Their structural integrity (not to mention their freshness) was less than a sure bet past the second or third Hallowe'en. Most geeks Wormy spotted nowadays were minus a major limb. They digested, but did not seem to eliminate. Sometimes the older ones simply exploded. They clogged up with gas and decaying food until they hit critical mass, then *kerblooey*—steaming gobbets of brown crap all over the perimeter. It was enough to put you off your dinner.

Life was so weird. Wormboy felt like the only normal person left.

This movable feast, this walking smorgasbord, could last another year or two at max, and Wormboy knew it. His fortifications insured that he would be ready for whatever followed, when the world changed again. For now, it was a matchless chow-down, and grand sport.

The ATV groaned and squeaked its usual protests when he settled into its saddle. A rack welded to the chassis secured geek tools—pinch bar, fire axe, scattergun sheaths and a Louisville Slugger with a lot of chips, nicks, and dried blood. The all-terrain bike's balloon tires did not burst. Wormboy kick-started and puttered down to meet his catch of the day.

Geeks could sniff human meat from a fair distance. Some had actually gotten around to elementary tool use. But their maze sense was zero-zero. They always tried to proceed in straight lines. Even for a non-geek it took a load of deductive logic just to pick a path toward Valley View's chapel without getting divorced from your vitals, and much more time than generally elapsed between Wormboy's feedings. Up on this hilltop, his security was assured.

He piloted the ATV down his special escape path, twisting and turning, pausing at several junctures to gingerly reconnect tripwires behind him. He dropped his folding metal Army fording bridge over the moat and tootled across.

Some of the meat hung up in the heat flash of the explosion was still sizzling on the ground in charred clumps. Dragging itself doggedly up the slope was half a geek, still aimed at the chapel and the repast that was Wormboy. Everything from its navel down had been blown off.

Wormboy unracked the pinch bar. One end had been modified to take a ten-pound harpoon head of machined steel. A swath of newly-muddied earth quickly became a trail of strewn organs resembling smashed fruit. The geek's brand new prone carriage had permitted it to evade some of the Bouncing Betty trips. Wormboy frowned. His announcement was pointed—and piqued—enough to arrest the geek's uphill crawl.

"Welcome to Hell, dork breath."

It humped around on its palms with all the grace of a beached haddock. Broken rib struts punched through at jigsaw angles and mangled innards swung from the mostly-empty chest cavity like pendent jewels. One ear had been sheared off; the side of its head was caked in thick blood, dirt and pulverized tissue that reminded Wormboy of a scoop of dog food. It sought Wormboy with bleary drunkard's eyes, virulently jaundiced and discharging gluey fluid like those of a sick animal.

It was wearing a besmirched Red Cross armband.

A long, gray-green rope of intestine had paid out behind the geek. It gawped with dull hunger, then did an absurd little push-up in order to bite it. Teeth crunched through geek-gut and gelid black paste evacuated with a blatting fart noise. *Sploot!*

Disinclined toward autocannibalism, it tacked again on Wormboy. A kidney peeled loose from a last shred of muscle and rolled out to burst apart in the weeds. The stench was unique.

Impatient, Wormy shook his head. Stupid geeks. "C'mon, fuckface, come and get it." He waggled his mighty belly, then held out the rib roast of his forearm. "You want Cheez Whiz on it or what? C'mon. Chow time."

It seemed to catch the drift. Mouth chomping and slavering, eyes straying oft in two directions, it resumed its quest, leaving hanks and clots of itself behind all the way down.

It was too goddamned slow . . . and wasting too many choice bits.

Hefting the pinch bar, Wormboy hustled up the slope. He slammed one of his size thirteens thunderously down within biting range and let the geek fantasize for an instant about what a crawful of Wormboy Platter would taste like. Greedy. Then he threw all his magnificent tonnage behind a downward thrust, spiking his prey between the shoulderblades and staking it to the ground with a moist crunch.

It thrashed and chewed air. Wormy waved bye-bye in its face. "Don't go 'way, now." He let the geek watch him pick his way back down to the ATV. He wanted it to see him returning with the axe. Sweat had broken freely; the exertion already had Wormboy huffing and aromatic, but he loved this part almost as much as swallowing that old time home cookin'.

The axe hissed down overhand. A bilious rainbow of decomposing crap hocked from the neck stump while the blue head pinballed from one tombstone to the next. It thonked to rest against the left rear wheel of the ATV.

Wormboy lent the half-torso a disappointed inspection. Pickings were lean; this geek had been on the hoof too long. Burger night again.

He looked behind him and sure enough, the lone head was fighting like hell to redirect itself. Hair hung in its eyes, the face was caved in around the flattened nose, the whole of it now oozing and studded with cockleburs . . . but by God it tipped over, embedded broken teeth into packed dirt, and tried to pull itself toward Wormy. It was that hungry.

Wormboy went down to meet it, humming. He secured the axe in its metal clip and drew the ballbat.

Busting a coconut was tougher. The geek's eyes stayed open. They never flinched when you hit them. On the second bash, curds of blood-dappled brain jumped out to meet the air.

It ceased moving then, except to crackle and collapse. The cheesy brain-stuff was the color of fishbellies. Wormboy pulled free a mucilaginous fistful and brandished it before the open, unseeing eyes. He squeezed hard. Glistening spirals unfurled between his fingers with a greasy macaroni noise.

"I win again."

He licked the gelid residue off his trigger finger and smacked his lips. By the time he got back to the torso with a garbage bag, the Red Cross armband was smoldering. He batted it away. It caught in midair and flared, newborn fire gobbling up the swatch of cloth and the symbol emblazoned thereon, leaving Wormboy alone to scratch his head about what it might have meant.

Little Luke shot twin streamers of turbid venom into the urine specimen cup like a good Christian, providing. He did not mind being milked (not that he'd been asked); it was a necessary preamble to the ritual. He played his part and was provided for—a sterling exemplar of God's big blueprint. His needle fangs were translucent and fragile looking. Cloudy venom pooled in the cup.

Maintaining his grip just behind Little Luke's jaws, the Right Reverend Jerry thanked the Lord for this bounty, that the faithful might take communion and know His peace. He kissed Little Luke on the head and dropped all four feet of him back into the pet caddy. Little Luke's Love Gift had been generous today. Perhaps even serpents knew charity.

Jerry pondered charity, and so charitably ignored the fact that his eldest Deacon was leaking. Deacon Moe stood in the vestibule, his pants soaked and dripping, weaving back and forth. He was not breathing, and his eyes saw only the specimen cup. The odor that had accompanied him into the tiny room was that of maggoty sausage. He was a creature of wretchedness, without a doubt . . . but was also proof to the Right Reverend Jerry that the myth had delivered at last, and skeptics be damned.

The dead had risen from their graves to be judged. If that was not a miraculous proof, what was? The regular viewers of Jerry's tri-county video ministry had been long satisfied by more pallid miracles—eased sprains, restored control of the lower tract, that kind of thing. Since this ukase had flown down from Heaven, it would be foolish to shun its opportunities.

Jerry savored the moment the dead ones had walked. It had vindicated his lagging faith, dispelling in an instant the doubts that had haunted his soul for a lifetime. There *was* a One True God, and there *was* a Judgement

Day, and there *was* an Armageddon, and there was *bound* to be a Second Coming, and as long as the correct events came to pass, who cared if their order had been juggled a bit? The Lord had been known to work in mysterious ways before.

Once his suit had been blazing white, and pure. With faith, it would shine spotlessly again. Right now he did not mind the skunky miasma exuding from the pits of what had once been a $1500 jacket. It helped blanket the riper and more provocative stench of Deacon Moe's presence. The congregation was on the move and there was little time for dapper grooming in mid-hegira.

Jerry beckoned Deacon Moe forward to receive communion. From the way poor Moe shambled, this might be his last chance to drink of the Blood . . . since none of the faithful had meshed teeth lately on the Body, or any facsimile thereof.

He had visited an abandoned library, and books had told him what rattlesnake venom could do.

In human beings, it acts as a neurotoxin and nerve impulse blocker, jamming the signals of the brain by preventing acetylcholine from jumping across nerve endings. The brain's instructions are never delivered. First comes facial paralysis, then loss of motor control. Heart and lungs shut down and the victim drowns in his own backed-up fluids. Hemolytic, or blood-destroying, factors cause intense local pain. Jerry had tasted the venom he routinely fed his quartet of Deacons. Nothing to worry about, as long as your stomach lining had no tiny holes in it. The bright yellow liquid was odorless, with a taste at first astringent, then sweetish. It numbed the lips. There was so much books could not know.

In walking dead human beings, Jerry discovered that the venom, administered orally, easily penetrated the cheese-cloth of their internal pipework and headed straight for the motor centers of the brain, unblocking them, allowing Jerry to reach inside with light hypnosis to tinker. He could program his Deacons not to eat him. More importantly, this imperative could then be passed among the faithful in the unspoken and mystical way that seemed reserved to only these special citizens of God.

A talent for mesmerization came effortlessly to a man who had devoted years to charming the camera's unblinking and all-seeing eye. Jerry preferred to consider his ability innate, a divine, God-granted sanction approved for the use he made of it. *Don't eat the Reverend.*

Deacon Moe's coated tongue moistened cracked and greenish lips, not in anticipation, but as a wholly preconditioned response. The demarcations of the urine specimen cup showed a level two ounces. Little Luke could be fully milked slightly more often than once per month, if Jerry's touch was gentle and coaxing. The cup was tilted to Deacon Moe's lips and the poison was glugged down *in nomine Patris, et Filii . . .*

"And God waved His hand," Jerry belted out.

"And when God did wave His hand, He cleansed the hearts of the wicked of evil. He scoured out the souls of the wolves, and set His born-agains to the task of reclaiming the earth in His name. The Scriptures were right all along—the meek inherited. Now the world grows green and fecund again. Now the faithful must seek strength from their most holy Maker. The damned Sodom and Gomorrah of New York and Los Angeles have fallen to ruin, their false temples pulled down to form the dust that makes the clay from which God molds the God-fearing Christian. Our God is a loving God, yet a wrathful God, and so he struck down those beyond redemption. He closed the book on secular humanism. His mighty Heel stamped out radical feminism. His good right Fist meted out rough justice to the homosexuals; his good left Fist likewise silenced the pagans of devilspawn rock and roll. And He did spread His arms wide to gather up the sins of this evil world, from sexual perversion to drug addiction to Satan worship. And you might say a *memo* came down from the desk of the Lord, and major infidel butt got kicked doubleplusgood!"

Now he was cranking, impassioned, his pate agleam with righteous perspiration. His hands clasped Deacon Moe's shoulders. His breath misted the zombi's dead-ahead eyes. His conviction was utter. Moe salivated.

"And now the faithful walk the land, brother, as a mighty army. God's legions grow by the day, by the hour, the minute, as we stand here and reaffirm our faith in His name. We are all children of God, and God is a loving Father who provides for his children, yes. Yes, we must make sacrifices. But though our bellies be empty today, our hearts are full up with God's goodness!" His voice was cracking now; it was always good to make it appear as though some passion was venting accidentally. "From that goodness you and I must draw the strength to persevere until tomorrow, when the Millennium shall come and no child of the Lord shall want. Peace is coming! Food is coming! Go forth unto the congregation, Deacon Moe, and spread this good news! Amen! Amen! Amen!"

Deacon Moe wheezed, his arid throat rasping out an acknowledgment that sounded like an asthmatic trying to say *rruuaah* through a jugful of snot. Jerry spun him about-face and impelled him through the curtain to disseminate the Word. He heard Moe's stomach-load of accumulated venom slosh. Corrosion was running amok in there. Any second now, gravity might fill Deacon Moe's pants with his own zombified tripe.

Tonight they were billeted in an actual church. Most of the faithful loitered about the sanctuary. The Deacons led them through Jerry's motions; the response quotient of the total group, twoscore and ten, was about as dependable as a trained but retarded lab rat. Less control, and Jerry would have starred at his own Last Supper months ago. Right now he saw his congregation only as vessels itching to be filled with the prose of the Lord. He tried to keep them fed as best he could manage.

He was most proud of the glorious day he had commenced his cross-country revival. He strode boldly into the murk of a Baton Rouge honkytonk and let God say howdy-do to a nest of musicians calling themselves Slim Slick and His Slick Dicks. Marching right behind him were twenty hungry born-agains. That holy purge, that first big feed with which he had blessed his new congregation, would forever burn brightly in a special corner of his heart. Slim Slick, et al, had seen the light. Some of them had joined the marching ministry, those that had not been too chewed up to locomote.

Like Jesus to the temple, the Right Reverend Jerry came not to destroy, but to fulfill. To fill full.

He poked his snakestick into the hatch of the pet caddy. Nobody buzzed. Nobody could. Rattling tended to upset the faithful, so he had soaked the rattle of each of his four Little wine-makers until it rotted into silence. Little Matthew was disengaged from the tangle of his brothers. Eastern diamondbacks were rightly feared for their size and high venom delivery; full contact bites were almost always fatal. Little Matt was five feet long, with large glands that would effortlessly yield a Love Gift that could convert six hundred sixty-six adults to the cause, and wasn't that a significant coincidence of mathematics? Jerry had to push the figures a smidgen, converting milligrams to grains to ounces. How a lethal dosage was administered was a big variable. But the final number summoned by his calculator was 666, repeating to infinity. That was how many sinners could swing low on three ounces of Little Matt's finest kind. To Jerry, that number was a perfect sign . . . and wasn't that what really counted in the Big Book? Perfection just tickled God green.

Deacon Curly had not come forth to receive communion. Perhaps he had wandered astray?

Back in the days before it had become synonymous with smut, the Right Reverend Jerry had enjoyed comedy. Upon his nameless Deacons he had bestowed the names of famous funnymen. As the ramrods wore out or were retired, Jerry's list of names dwindled. Just now, the Deacons in charge were Moe, Curly, WC. and Fatty. Curly was running late. Tardiness was a sin.

Jerry felt secure that his flock would follow him even without the able assistance of his Deacons. He represented the Big Guy, but his course work with Graham and Hummell pealed just as righteously. His tent-revival roots ran deep and wide, he had always trodden the upward path, and his congregation now burgeoned beneath his loving ministrations.

When he sermonized, the born-agains seemed to forget their earthly hungers. He could not pinpoint why, past his own Rock-solid certainty that the Word held the power to still the restless, and quiet gnawing bellies. There were other kinds of nourishment; these lost ones were spiritually starved as well. Jerry held dear a reverence for awareness and sheer faith, and fancied he saw both in the eyes of his congregation when he vociferated. He Witnessed this miracle in a most hallowed and traditional fashion, during a sermon, when he looked out upon the milling throng and just *knew*. The born-agains depended on him for the Word just as much as the Deacons counted on him to deliver the holy imbibitions. Venom governed the Deacons, but it had to be a new kind of faith that oversaw the members of the marching ministry. Had to be.

They needed saving. Jerry needed to save. Symbiosis, plain, ungarnished, and God-sanctioned as all get-out.

In a most everlasting way, they fed each other. Maybe it was not such a big whodunit, after all.

Still no sign of Deacon Curly in the sanctuary. Jerry motioned Deacon Fatty inside. Fatty's eye had popped out to hang from the stalk again. Jerry tucked it in and brushed the bugs from this Deacon's shoulders, then reknotted the armband which had drooped to the zombi's elbow. Each member of the new congregation wore a Red Cross—it seemed an appropriate symbol for the New Dawn, and Jerry needed a handy way to take quick head counts while on the march.

The sudden, flat *boom* of an explosion not far away made Jerry's heart slam on brakes. Deacon Fatty stood unimpressed, awaiting his communion, insects swimming in his free-flowing drool.

Orthodoxies had spent too long fucking up the world, so Wormboy had obliterated all of them with a snap of his knockwurst fingers. Enough was enough. Idiots fumbled about, living their lives by accident, begging nonexistent gods for unavailable mercies, trusting in supernatural beings and nebulous powers of good and evil that predetermined what breakfast cereal they ate. If there was any evil now, its name was either Starvation or Stupidity—two big items that could make you instant history. True Believers spent their lives preparing to die. Wormboy preferred fighting to live.

His survival ethics might become the first writ of a new doctrine.

Another system would rise in time. Nobody ever really learned a goddamned thing.

He preferred heavy caliber projectile peace of mind. Cordite calm. He had named his M60 Zombo and it was swell. One round made raspberry slush. Vaporize the head and the leftovers could not eat you or infect you with the geek germ.

And spraying on Pam kept them from sticking to the cookware.

Wormboy dumped his dishes in the steel tub sink and relaxed on his Valley View sofa. A basso toilet belch eased him into sleep and he dreamed about the first person he had ever eaten.

Duke Mallett had dubbed him Wormboy because of his obesity and spotty complexion. Which, quoth Duke, indicated that 15th Street Junior High's resident wimp, blimp, pussywhip and pariah sucked up three squares chock full o' nightcrawlers each day, with squiggly snacks between. "Yo, Wormy— wotchagot in your locker? More WORMS, huh?" That was always good for a chorus of guffaws from Duke and 15th Street's other future convicts.'

Duke smoked Camels. His squeeze, Stacy, had awesome boobs and a lot of pimples around her mouth. She used bubblegum flavored lipstick. Two weeks prior to becoming a high school freshman, Dukey wrapped a boosted Gran Torino around a utility pole at ninety. He, Stacy, and a pair of their joyriding accomplices were barbecued by sputtering wires and burning Hi-Test. Paramedics piled what parts they could salvage onto a single stretcher, holding their noses.

Tompkins Mortuary also provided local ambulance service, and when Wormboy caught wind he raced there, to grieve. Old Man Tompkins admired the fat kid's backbone in requesting to view the remains of his classmates. "I have to be sure!" Wormy blurted melodramatically, having rehearsed. Tompkins was of the mind that youngsters could never be exposed to death too soon, and so consented to give Wormboy a peek at the carbonized component mess filling Drawer Eight.

Wormboy thought Tompkins smelled like the biology lab at shark dissecting time. While the old man averted his gaze with a sharp draw of untainted air, Wormboy sucked wind, fascinated. The flash-fried garbage staining the tray and blocking the drains was Duke. Harmless now. The sheer joy of this moment could not hold, so Wormboy quickly swiped a small sample. When Tompkins turned to look, he sheepishly claimed to have seen enough. He lied.

Later, alone, he wallowed.

The piece he had purloined turned out to be one of Duke's fricasseed eyeballs. It had heat-shrunken, wrinkled in a raisin pattern, deflated on one side and petrified on the other . . . but without a doubt it was one of Dukey's baby blues. The eye that had directed so much hatred at Wormboy was now in his very hand, subtracted of blaze and swagger and no more threatening than a squashed seed grape.

It gave under the pressure of his fingers, like stale cheese. He sniffed. It was sour, rather akin to the smell of an eggshell in the trash, with no insides.

Wormboy popped it between his lips and bit down before his brain could say no. He got a crisp bacon crunch. His mental RPMs redlined as flavor billowed across his tongue and filled his meaty squirrel cheeks.

His mom would not have approved. This was . . . well, this was the sort of thing that was . . . just not done.

It was . . . a rush of liberation. It was the ultimate expression of revenge, of power wielded over Duke the dick-nosed shitheel. It was the nearest thing to sex Wormboy would ever experience. It was damned close to religious.

Once Wormboy was old enough, he began to work part time for Old Man Tompkins after school. By then his future was cast, and his extra weight gain attracted no new notice.

At the National Guard armory he had tucked in quite a few Type-A boxed combat meals. The gel-packed mystery meat he pried from olive drab tins was more disgusting than anything he had ever sliced off down at the morgue.

BONE appétit!

Wormboy's wet dream was just sneaking up on the gooshy part when another explosion jerked him back to reality and put his trusty .44 in his grasp quicker than a samurai's *katana*. It was getting to be a busy Monday.

His mountainous gut fluttered. *Brritt.* Lunch was still in there fighting. But what the binoculars revealed nudged his need for a bromo right out of his mind.

Two dozen geeks, maybe more, were lurching toward the front gates of Valley View. Wormboy's jaw unhinged. That did not stop his mouth from watering at the sight.

The Right Reverend Jerry unshielded his eyes and stared at the sinner on the hilltop as smoking wads of Deacon Fatty rained down on the faithful. He'd been in front. Something fist-sized and mulchy smacked Jerry's shoulder and blessed it with a smear of yellow. He shook detritus from his shoe and thought of Ezekiel 18:4. Boy, he was getting mad.

The soul that sinneth—it shall die!

Deacon Moe and Deacon Fatty had bitten the big one and bounced up to meet Jesus. The closer the congregation staggered to the churchyard, the better they could smell the sinner . . . and his fatted calves. The hour of deliverance—and dinner—so long promised by Jerry seemed at hand.

Jerry felt something skin past his ear at two hundred per. Behind him, another of the born-agains came unglued, skull and eyes and brains all cartwheeling off on different trajectories. Jerry stepped blind and his heel skidded through something moist and slick; his feet took to the air and his rump introduced itself to the pavement and much, much more of Deacon Fatty. More colors soaked into his coat of many.

The Right Reverend Jerry involuntarily took his Lord's name in vain.

At the next flat crack of gunshot one more of the faithful burst into a pirouette of flying parts. Chunks and stringers splattered the others, who had the Christian grace not to take offense.

Jerry scrambled in the puddle of muck, his trousers slimed and adherent, his undies coldly bunched. Just as wetly, another born-again ate a bullet and changed tense from present to past. Jerry caught most in the bazoo.

It was high time for him to bull in and start doing God's work.

Wormboy cut loose a throat-rawing war whoop—no melodrama, just joy at what was heading his way. The guy bringing up the rear did not twitch and lumber the way geeks usually did, so Wormy checked him out through the scope of the highpower Remington. He saw a dude in a stained suit smearing macerated suet out of his eyes and hopping around in place with Donald Duck fury.

He wore a Red Cross armband, as did the others. End of story. Next case.

Wormy zeroed a fresh geek in his crosshairs, squeezed off, and watched the head screw inside-out in a pizza-colored blast of flavor. With a balletic economy of motion for someone his size, he ejected the last of the spent brass and left the Remington open-bolted while he unracked his M60. Zombo was hot for mayhem. Zombo was itching to pop off and hose the stragglers. Wormy draped a stretch belt of high velocity armor piercers over one sloping hillock of shoulder. The sleek row of shell casings obscured the Dirty Rotten Imbeciles logo on his T-shirt.

Dusting was done. Now it was casserole time. Zombo lived. Zombo ruled.

The next skirmish line of Bouncing Bettys erupted. They were halfway to the moat. The stuff pattering down from the sky sure looked like manna.

Jerry let 'em have it in his stump-thumper's bray, full bore: "Onward, onward! Look unto me, and ye be saved, all the ends of the earth!" Isaiah 45:22 was always a corker for rousing the rabble.

By now each and every born-again had scented the plump demon on the hilltop. He was bulk and girth and mass and calories and salvation. Valley View's iron portals were smashed down and within seconds, a holy wave of living dead arms, legs and innards were airborne and graying out the sunlight.

"Onward!" Jerry frothed his passion to scalding and dealt his nearest disciple a fatherly shove in the direction of the enemy. The sinner. The monster. *"Onward!"*

The flat of Jerry's palm met all the resistance of stale oatmeal. A fresh cow patty had more tensile strength and left less mess. He ripped his hand free with a yelp and gooey webs followed it backward.

The born-again gawped hollowly at the tunnel where its left tit used to be, then stumped off, sniffing fresh Wormboy meat.

The explosions became deafening, slamming one into the next, thunderclaps that mocked God. In the interstices, Jerry heard a low, vicious chuddering—not a heavenly sound, but an evil noise unto the Lord that was making the faithful go to pieces faster than frogs with cherry bombs inside.

He tried to snap off the maggot-ridden brown jelly caking his hand and accidentally boffed Deacon Moe in the face. The zombi's nose tore halfway off and dangled. Moe felt no pain. He had obediently brought the pet caddy, whose occupants writhed and waxed wroth.

Zombo hammered out another gunpowder benediction and Jerry flung himself down to kiss God's good earth. Hot tracers ate pavement and jump-stitched through Deacon Moe in a jagged line. The pet carryall took two big hits and fell apart. Moe did likewise. His ventilated carcass did a juice dump and the Right Reverend Jerry found himself awash in gallons of zombi puree plus four extremely aggravated rattlesnakes.

He never found out who was the first to betray him. The first bite pegged him right on the balls, and he howled.

Deacon Moe, his work on this world finished, keeled over with a splat. It was like watching a hot cherry pie hit a concrete sidewalk.

Wormboy rubbed his eyes. Zombo had *missed*. It wasn't just the salt sting of sweat that had spoiled his aim. His vision was bollixed. The oily drops standing out on his pate were ice cold.

It was probably someone's something he ate.

Zombo grew too heavy, too frying-pan hot to hold. Zombo's beak kept dipping, pissing away good ammo to spang off the metal spikes crowding the moat. Wormboy gritted his teeth, clamped his clammy trigger finger down hard and seesawed the muzzle upward with a bowel-clenching grunt. He felt himself herniate below his weightlifter's belt. Zombo spoke. Geeks blocked tracers, caught fire and sprang apart at the seams. Those in front were buffaloed into the moat by those behind. They seated permanently onto the pungi pipes with spongy noises of penetration, to wriggle and gush bloodpus and reach impotently toward Wormboy.

Zombo demanded a virgin belt of slugs.

Wormboy's appetite had churned into a world class acid bath of indigestion. This night would belong to Maalox.

It took no time for the air to clog with the tang of blackened geek beef. One whiff was all it took to make Wormboy ralph long and strenuously into the moat. Steaming puke pasted a geek who lay skewered through the back, facing the sky, mouth agape. It spasmed and twisted on the barbs, trying to lap up as much fresh hot barf as it could collect.

Zombo tagged out. Wormboy unholstered his .44 and sent a pancaking round into Barf Eater's brain pan. Its limbs stiffened straight as the hydrostatic pressure blew its head apart into watermelon glop. Then it came undone altogether, collapsing into a pool of diarrhetic putrescence that bubbled and flowed amidst the pipework.

Now everything looked like vomit. Wormy's ravaged stomach said heave-ho to that, too, and constricted to expel what was no longer vomitable. This time he got blood, shooting up like soda pop to fizz from both nostrils. He spat and gagged, crashing to his knees. His free hand vanished into the fat cushion of his stomach, totally inadequate to the task of clutching it.

The Right Reverend Jerry saw the sinner genuflect. God was still in Jerry's corner, whacking away, world without end, hallelujah, amen.

Jerry's left eye was smeared down his cheek like a lanced condom. Little Paul's fang had put it out. Must have offended him. Jerry seized Little Paul and dashed his snaky brains out against the nearest headstone. Then he began his trek up the hill, through the valley of death, toting the limp, dead snake as a scourge. Consorting with serpents had won him a double share of bites, and he knew the value of immunization. He stung all over and was wobbly on his feet . . . but so far, he was still chugging.

This must be Hell, he thought dazedly when he saw most of his congregation sliced, diced, and garnishing Valley View's real estate. Tendrils of smoke curled heavenward from the craters gouged rudely in the soil. Dismembered limbs hung, spasming. A few born-agains had stampeded over the fallen and made it all the way to the moat.

Jerry could feel his heart thudding, pushing God knew how much snakebite nectar through his veins. He could feel the power working inside him. Blood began to drip freely from his gums, slathering his lips. His left hand snapped shut into a spastic claw and stayed that way. His good eye tried to blink and could not; it was frozen open. The horizon tilted wildly. Down below his muscles surrendered and shit and piss came express delivery.

As he neared his children, he wanted to raise his voice in the name of the Lord and tell them the famine was ended, to hoot and holler about the feast at last. He lost all sensation in his legs instead. He tumbled into the violence-rent earth of the graveyard and began to drag himself forward with his functioning hand, the one still vised around the remains of Little Paul.

He wanted to shout, but his body had gotten real stupid real fast. What came out, in glurts of blood-flecked foam, was *He ham niss ed begud!*

Just the sound of that voice made Wormboy want to blow his ballast all over again.

Jerry clawed onward until he reached the lip of the pit. The born-agains congregated around him. His eye globbed on his face, his body jittering as the megadose of poison grabbed hold, he nevertheless raised his snake and prepared to declaim.

Wormboy dragged his Magnum into the firing line and blew the evangelist's mushmouthed head clean off before the mouth could pollute the air with anything further.

"That's better," he ulped, gorge pistoning.

Then he vomited again anyway and blacked out.

Weirder things have happened, his brain insisted right before he came to. None of it had been a dream.

One eye was shut against the dark of dirt and his nose was squashed sideways. Over the topography of regurgitated lunch in front of his face, he watched.

He imagined the Keystone Kops chowing down on a headless corpse. Meat strips were ripped and gulped without the benefit of mastication, each glistening shred sliding down gullets like a snake crawling into a wet red hole. One geek was busily chomping a russet ditch into a Jerry drumstick with the foot still attached. Others played tug-o'-war with slick spaghetti tubes of intestine or wolfed double facefuls of the thinner, linguini strands of tendon and ligaments—all marinated in that special, extra-chunky maroon secret sauce.

Wormboy's own tummy grumbled jealously. It was way past dinnertime. The remaining geeks would not leave, not with Wormboy uneaten. He'd have to crop 'em right now, unless he wanted to try mopping up in total darkness and maybe waiting until sunup to dine.

He saw one of the geeks in the moat squirm free of a pungi pipe. Its flesh no longer meshed strongly enough for the barbs to hold it. It spent two seconds wobbling on its feet, then did a header onto three more spikes. Ripe plugs of rotten tissue bounced upward and acid bile burbled forth.

Wormboy rolled toward Zombo, rising like a wrecked semi righting itself. His brain rollercoastered; his vision strained to focus; what the fuck had been wrong with lunch? He was no more graceful than a geek, himself, now. He put out one catcher's mitt hand to steady his balance against a massive headstone memorializing somebody named Eugene Roach, *Loving Father*. Mr. Roach had himself lurched off to consume other folks' children a long time ago.

What happened, happened fast.

Wormboy had to pitch his full weight against the tombstone just to keep from keeling over. When he leaned, there came a sound like hair being levered out by the roots. His eyes bugged and before he could arrest his own momentum, the headstone hinged back, disengaging from Valley View's overnourished turf. Arms windmilling, Wormy fell on top of it. His mind registered a flashbulb image of the tripwire, twanging taut to do its job.

The mine went off with an eardrum compressing clap of bogus thunder. Two hundred pounds of granite and marble took to the air right behind nearly four hundred pounds of Wormboy, who was catapulted over the moat and right into the middle of the feeding frenzy on the far side.

It was the first time in his life he had ever done a complete somersault.

With movie slo-mo surreality, he watched his hunky Magnum pal drop away from him like a bomb from a zeppelin. It landed with the trigger guard snugged around one of the moat's deadly metal speartips. The firmly impaled Deacon W.C. was leering down the bore when it went bang. Everything above the Adam's apple rained down to the west as goulash and flip chips.

Wormboy heard the shot but did not witness it. Right now his overriding concern was impact.

A geek turned and saw him, raising its arms as if in supplication, or a pathetic attempt to catch the UFO that isolated it in the center of a house-sized, ever-growing shadow.

Eugene Roach's overpriced monument stone veered into the moat. The mushy zombi watched it right up until the second it hit. The fallout was so thick you could eat it with a fondue fork.

Wormboy clamped shut his eyes, screamed, and bellied in headfirst. Bones snapped when he landed. Only the yellows of the geek's eyes were visible at the end. It liquefied with a *poosh* and became a wet stain at the bottom of the furrow dug by Wormboy's tombstone.

All heads turned.

His brain was like a boardroom choked with yelling stockbrokers. The first report informed him that aerial acrobatics did not agree with his physique. The second enumerated fractures, shutdown, concussion, an eardrum that had popped with the explosive decompression of a pimento being vacuumed from an olive, the equitable distribution of slaghot agony to every outback and tributary of his vast body . . . and the dead taste of moist dirt.

The third was a surprise news flash: He had not been gormandized down to nerve peels and half a dozen red corpuscles. Yet.

He filed a formal request to roll back his eyelids and it took about an hour to go through channels.

He saw stars, but they were in the post-midnight sky above him. He lay on his back, legs straight, arms out in a plane shape. What a funny.

Eight pairs of reanimated dead eyes appraised him.

They've got me, dead bang, he thought. For more than a year they've whiffed me and gotten smithereened . . . and now I've jolly well been served up to them airfreight, gunless, laid out flat on my flab. Maybe they waited just so I could savor the sensual cornucopia of being devoured alive firsthand. Dr. Moreau time, kids. Time for Uncle Wormy to check out for keeps.

He tried to wiggle numb fingers at them. "Yo, dudes." It was all he could think of to do.

The zombis surrounding him—three up, three down, one at his feet and one at his head—rustled as though stirred by a soft breeze. They communed.

The skull of the Right Reverend Jerry had been perched on his chest. He could barely see it up there. The blood-dyed and tooth-scored fragments had been leaned together into a fragile sort of card ossuary. He could see that his bullet had gone in through Jerry's left eyebrow. Good shot.

His insides convulsed and he issued a weak cough. The skull clattered apart like an inadequately glued clay pot.

More commotion, among the zombis.

The Right Reverend Jerry had been gnawed down to a jackstraw clutter of bones; the bones had been cracked, their marrow greedily drained. All through the feast, there Wormy had been, mere feet distant, representing bigger portions for everybody. He had gone unmolested for hours. Instead of tucking in, they had gathered 'round and waited for him to wake up. They had flipped him over, touched him without biting. They had pieced together Jerry's headbone and seen it blown apart by a cough. They had Witnessed, all right.

He considered the soda cracker fragments of skull and felt the same rush of revelation he had experienced with Duke Mallett's eyeball. So fitting, now, to savor that crunchy stone-ground goodness.

The eyes that sought him did not judge. They did not see a grotesquely obese man who snarfed up worms and eyeballs and never bathed. The watchers did not snicker in a Duke Mallett drawl, or reject him, or find him lacking in any social particular. They had waited for him to revive. Patiently, on purpose, they had waited. For him.

They had never sought to eat of his lard or drink of his cholesterol. The Right Reverend Jerry had taught them that there were hungers other than physical.

One of his legs felt busted, but with effort he found himself capable of hiking up onto both elbows. The zombis shuffled dutifully back to make room for him to rise, and when he did not, they helped him, wrestling him erect like dogfaces hoisting the Stars and Stripes on Iwo Jima. He realized that if he cared to order them to march into one of Valley View's crematory ovens according to height, they'd gladly comply.

He had, at last, gained the devoted approval of a peer group.

And any second now, some asshole would try to whore up this resurrection for posterity in a big, bad, black book . . . and get it all wrong. He decided that anybody who tried would have a quick but meaningful confab with Zombo.

I win again. He had thought this many times before, in reference to those he once dubbed geeks. Warmth flooded him. *He* was not a geek . . . therefore *they* were not.

What he finally spake unto them was something like: "Aww . . . shit, you guys, I guess we oughta go hustle up some potluck, huh?"

He began by passing out the puzzle pieces of the Right Reverend Jerry's skull. As one, they all took and ate without breathing.

And they saw that it was good.

The *Oxford English Dictionary* correctly credits David J. Schow for coining the term "splatterpunk." A Bram Stoker Award-winner and recipient of the World Fantasy Award his short fiction has been gathered into six collections. Some of his nonfiction was compiled for the International Horror Guild Award-winning *Wild Hairs*. In addition to novels *The Kill Riff*, *The Shaft*, *Rock Breaks Scissors Cut*, *Bullets of Rain*, *Gun Work*, and *Internecine*, he authored *The Outer Limits Companion*. Schow edited anthology *Silver Scream*, the three-volume "Lost Bloch" series, and John Farris' *Elvisland*. Film credits include *The Crow*, *The Texas Chainsaw Massacre: The Beginning*, and *The Hills Run Red*. He has written text supplements for such DVDs as *Reservoir Dogs* and *From Hell*, contributed to several British documentaries, and his expertise is displayed on DVD supplements for such movies as *The Dirty Dozen*, *The Green Mile*, and *Creature from the Black Lagoon*. He co-produced and filmed much of the on-location supplemental material seen on the discs for *I, Robot* and *The Chronicles of Narnia: The Lion, the Witch & the Wardrobe*.

The Herefords were evil looking things with their red skin and white faces.
Black lips pulled back exposing bloody yellow teeth,
all of them had those dark-green eyes . . .

An Unfortunate Incident
at the Slaughterhouse

Harper Hull

Being in England, we wrongly assumed we just had another mad cow on
our hands.

It was Jack who spotted it first; he was putting out the feed in the main
dairy pasture when we heard him shouting out *"B.S.E! B.S.E!"* at the top
of his voice. Will and I, who were on a smoke break in the yard by the
slaughterhouse, sighed and heeled out our Rothmans, ambled around
to the pasture fence, and got ready to give Jack some ribbing. He saw us
coming and gestured wildly towards a large black-and-white Friesian that
was snorting and grunting towards the back of the herd. I immediately
nudged Will in the side, knowing this did not look like your classic mad
cow. The rest of the herd, obviously quite upset, had moved as far away
from the crazed cow as they could, pressing up against the fences and
mooing in agitated, high-pitched tones. The sick Friesian, making noises I
had never heard come from a cow before, began stamping and tripping its
way towards the main part of the herd. It looked as if it was about to fall
over with every step it took, but somehow it kept its footing each time. I
noticed that its eyes looked like they were green around the pupils. Dark
green like seaweed on the beach. Jack took off running, saying he was
going for help. Will and I just watched, quite bewildered at what we were
seeing. This wasn't supposed to happen here.

The farm we worked on was the first organic beef and dairy farm
in the great County of Cheshire. What had once been an old-fashioned
pack, rack, and stack blood-and-guts killing compound was now a state-

of-the-art exercise in modern farming. There were nutritionists and geneticists employed here these days, as well as regular workers like me who took a pride in their job. No more cider-soaked village idiots who would blast a bolt between a cow's ears and cheer while they did it; all the simple, inbred bumpkin bully-boys who had actually enjoyed bleeding out cows, and often made sick games out of it, were long gone. This was a highly monitored operation of organic perfection. Everything was carried out with complete professionalism and to the letter—as written out by the new owners. The idea that something could have diseased one of our pristine cows was unthinkable. We had the finest herd of Friesian milkers in the country, and our beef Herefords were top of their class. With no chemicals, nutrients, or altered genetics, our beef was pure, which is what made Will and me wonder how what we were watching could possibly be happening.

The sick black-and-white milker got into the cornered herd and started attacking the other cows. In a frenzy, they started trying to launch themselves over and through the fences. We ran back, away from the sudden chaos, and watched in static shock as the sick 'un took bites out of its herd mates, causing them to react and nip at those around them. Some cows fell at the fences and were trampled; the sounds they made were awful, the type of sounds you never want to hear from a living creature. As we watched, helpless to intervene, Jack returned with a gang of the other workers, a couple of them lugging rifles with them. After an initial moment of complete disbelief when the entire group of men seemed to run into an invisible wall and just gape, the two blokes with the rifles carefully approached the fence and, finding an angle, took out the sick cow with several shots to the skull. It went down with a thud.

But now several more of the Friesians were acting in the same sick manner. Someone cursed, and more shots were fired, a tattoo of cracks that sent crows scattering from the distant tree-line, until all the infected cows were down on the grass, still and bloody. The main herd—the ones still alive, scared by the guns and sensing safety—stomped back away from the fences leaving the dead sick 'uns and the injured, stampeded animals behind. The wounded cows were dispatched swiftly. Everyone looked around at everyone else.

Someone said we needed the bosses out here, and we all looked at the ground.

Clean-up was quick and efficient. Dr. Bloom—known to us as Dr. Doom, the company boffin—arrived with his small science team, and took away the dead cattle. They also took blood samples from the rest of the dairy herd, promising results by the end of the week. In the meantime we were to halt commercial milk distribution until further notice and dispose of the liquid we pumped. They didn't bother with the beef herd. None of the dairy cows mixed with the red-skinned, white-faced Herefords in any way, so contamination seemed an impossibility. As quickly as that, everything seemed back to normal. The company had lost twelve head of cattle and at least half a week's milk income. Not great, but not the end of the world either.

By the next day everybody seemed to have forgotten about the crazed cow, but I couldn't help but wonder about those tests; unless they found out why the cow had gone batty, I assumed it could happen again.

Friday rolled around without further incident; sweet, glorious Friday with the promise of a late night winding down at the town pub chatting up the local totty and maybe swinging a shag once the days toil was done. I was disposing of the day's milk haul with Jack and Will when we heard a ruckus from the slaughterhouse. It was noisy in there at the best of times, but this was something different and unusual. We stopped our swilling, put down the pails and ran towards the building.

"What the buggery now?" said Will, throwing a worried look my way.

As we approached the slaughterhouse, workers came running out, almost colliding with us. Horrible sounds were still emanating from inside the metal building. We asked the manager, Bonehead, what was going on. He told us to take a look, but be careful as it was the most fucked up thing we would ever see. Then he said he was off to fetch the rifles. We paused at this, but Will then clapped his hands together and said he was going in. Everyone else but Jack and me—Bonehead in the lead, cursing and spitting—took off towards the old farmhouse that now acted as the general office for the facility.

When I was a kid I used to play that game *Doom* on my computer. It scared the shit out of me and actually gave me nightmares. Things behind doors, around corners, making noises that turned my bones to liquid in the dark of my bedroom. The sounds coming from the slaughterhouse took me back to *Doom*; it was as if all my life I'd been moving forward attached to an enormous rubber band that had finally stretched too far and snapped me back. I was completely terrified and looked at my own hands, which were shaking like pink blanc mange. Will opened the door slowly, and peeked inside. He swore once, under his breath, and disappeared inside. I looked at Jack and wondered if my eyes were as plate-like as his were. We breathed deep and followed Will into the building; I fully expected to be face to face with an army of ax-wielding minotaurs based on the grunting, snorting reverberations that were assaulting our ears.

Deep red blood was splattered across the walkways. In the holding pens, a group of Hereford cows were acting just like the crazed milker from earlier in the week—evil looking things they were, with their red skin and white faces. Black lips pulled back exposing bloody yellow teeth, all of them had those dark-green eyes. Their ears lay completely flat against their heads. A number of Herefords were down on the floor of the pen, unmoving. They all had bites, gouges, and wounds; a few were missing meat from their bodies, one seemed to have had its entire face ripped off leaving a single eye still in its socket. The infected cows made a gurgling sound when they saw us three lads and threw themselves against the iron rails of the pen, clumsy yet powerful. I was about to ask Will if he thought it would hold when he pointed down the walkway towards the killing zone, mouth agape. I looked and almost fell to my knees.

"Bloody Hell!" said Jack as he saw it too. "That's plain wrong, that is!"

Three cows were up in the air, suspended upside-down on hooks. Their throats had been slit and they had bled out significantly judging by the amount of claret red running down them. Normally, these animals would have been dead. These three, though, these three were flipping and shaking around as if they were performing seals. The hooks were pulling on the ceiling moorings and I had a horrifying vision of them getting loose and charging us, blood splattering from their smiling throats as their loose heads flopped up and down. Will must have had a similar thought, as he suddenly ran the length of the walkway, almost slipping in the blood outside the holding pen as the crazed cattle lunged at him. He made it to the stunning area before the killing zone and grabbed a captive bolt pistol, weighed it in his hands, and made his way towards the jerking, hanging cows. I realized what he was planning and shouted his name as I started running towards him. As someone who had actually worked in the slaughterhouse, unlike Will who was pure dairy boy, I knew we used stun guns, not penetrative. All he was about to do was piss off the angry beef even more. He gave me a quick look, nodded, then reached over and placed the gun hard against the nearest Hereford, right between the eyes. There was a whoosh and a pop, and the cow made a roaring sound. Will went in again, but this time the cow clamped its jaws around his hand. He screamed, tried to use his free hand to beat off the animal as it crunched down on his wrist, but it had no effect. The cow made a frantic jerk and pulled Will down onto the ground beneath it, his right hand severed and in its mouth. Blood spewed from the cow's mouth, covering Will's upturned face with a sticky crimson mask. Screaming and choking at the same time, Will thrashed on the ground as his damaged arm gushed his lifeblood out. By the time I got there he was silent.

The three hung cows were moving more than before. Sensing the hooks wouldn't hold much longer, I turned tail and ran back to a white-faced Jack, telling him we needed to get the fuck out—now. I felt bad for leaving Will, but I knew he was already beyond saving.

We burst out into the sunlight and looked around for Bonehead and his crew. They should have been back by now with the rifles, but there was no sign of them. Behind us the sound of crazed cattle and hard skulls hitting metal was getting louder and louder. Jack groaned and gestured towards the farmhouse.

"The bastards . . . "

I realized that Bonehead's battered old Land Rover was gone. The filthy cowards had left us.

An engine sounded along the glorified dirt path leading to the main road, and for a second we thought the slaughterhouse lads had returned, but it was a small, red car that came into view. As the car pulled up, we ran to the farmhouse, trying to get as much distance between us and the killer cows as we could.

Dr. Doom stepped out of the vehicle, a terrible look on his face. He heard the awful noise, looked towards the slaughterhouse, dropped his head, and muttered something about being too late.

I grabbed him by the arm and demanded answers, spat out something about Will and zombie cows as I did so.

"I have answers, I do, but let's get inside the office first," he said, then turned to Jack.

"Jack isn't it? Would you take a jog over to the dairy pasture and check on the Friesians for me? Good man, we'll be in here"

With that the doctor led me inside the farmhouse.

Neither of us sat down. We stood in the farmhouse kitchen as he explained what had happened. His team had integrated a new feed supplement nicknamed "Agent J" into the diet of our cows; it was from Japan and was supposed to significantly increase resistance to common disease. Something had contaminated a shipment while still in Japan. They hadn't realized the danger until too late. His tests confirmed that this "Agent J" was responsible for the reactions in the cattle. There had been other reports of infected cows elsewhere, but absolutely nothing as severe as what we were experiencing.

Jack came bounding into the farmhouse, breathing heavily. He got his breath back and told us the dairy cows were breaking through their enclosure. All of them were turned.

I suggested we jump in the good doctor's car and bomb off towards town as quickly as possible, but the Herefords busting out of the slaughterhouse put the scupper on my plan. I spotted them first. Their distinctive white faces, which I once thought quite delightful, were now snarling, sunken-eyed death masks splattered with blood. The one we'd seen dead on the floor with its face ripped off was now among the Hell herd, moving towards the farmhouse with them, its exposed skull and one remaining green eye showing above bared teeth.

Somehow, the zombie Herefords seemed to know we were inside and it was obvious they were coming for us. I pushed the doctor out of the way and asked Jack to help me barricade the door with a small desk. As we carried it across the room we both spotted the mass of dairy cows across the yard; like their beef cousins the freakish Fresians were coming towards us with a disturbingly ungainly trot that made them appear half drunk, half brain damaged. We moved faster, planted the desk, and started looking around for what else we could use to fortify the farmhouse against the onslaught.

While we were trying to turn plastic filing cases and empty milk crates into a reasonable barricade, the good doctor was entranced by the oncoming hordes that his magic ingredient had created. We barely noticed him until the terrible sounds of the demon cattle seemed to be all around us and we spotted him at the window, unmoving, palms pressed flat against the glass, frozen in place, absolutely still, just watching.

The first of the Herefords were already banging their heads and jaws against the glass right in front of him, spraying it with dark blood. Jack shouted that the doctor should move back, but he stayed exactly where he was, leaning against the glass in his weird trance. I could see the windowpane pulsing beneath his hands as the cattle barged into it. As I moved to pull him away, the window shattered. Dr. Doom fell forward; I think he snapped out of his strange stupor in this final moment because he shouted something about being a vegetarian as the infected red and white cattle gnashed at his arms. They pulled him through the window and my last-gasp diving reach only made contact with a notepad in his back pocket as he disappeared from sight, his kicking feet the last thing we saw. They were on him like a swarm of locusts, knocking each other out of the way to get to him. We could hear tearing, cracking, snapping all too clearly to not know he was being devoured by the monstrous bovines.

As the front door started to buckle, Jack suggested we head for higher ground. I slipped the doctor's notebook into my waistband and quickly followed Jack down the hall, up the stairs, and into the front room overlooking the yard where the killer cattle were gathered.

We could now see poor old Dr. Doom. Or what was left of him, which wasn't very much. He'd barely feed a cat now.

"His name was Bernard," Jack said quietly.

Before I had a chance to give the old buggerfurther thought, my eyes were drawn back to the slaughterhouse. Oh no, please don't let this be happening. I poked Jack and pointed. He looked out and started to sob.

Our good friend Will was walking towards the farmhouse. Covered in blood and shit, he was missing a hand and his eyes had the same creepy green color to them as the cattle. His gait was off too, like an over-the-limit driver trying to walk the line for the traffic cop. We both knew he was dead and really wasn't Will anymore. It didn't help.

He staggered up behind the herd from Hell and they made way for him! A pathway to the farmhouse opened up as if the bloody cattle were the Red Sea and he was Moses.

"Attic!" I shouted, and ran, Jack on my heels. After some fumbling with the attic ladder it finally unsheathed and came sliding down; we clambered up it like circus monkeys, the increasing banging downstairs pushing us on.

There was a huge crash below us and we panicked. Jack tried to pull the ladder back up but it jammed. I pushed him aside and attempted it myself, but it was well and truly stuck.

We heard footsteps on the stairs.

Forgetting the ladder I dropped the hatch down on the hole in the attic floor and looked around for a weapon. It was practically barren up there;

no farming tools, no table legs, nothing we could club or stab with. I did see a wooden bookcase and a squat black box over in a cobwebby corner and scooted over to it as fast as I could. The box was an old safe, rusty and obviously unused in a long time. Made from cast iron, the thing was too heavy to lift. I had an idea and started pulling and then pushing it across the floorboards until it sat a few feet in front of the hatch. I explained quickly to Jack and we both got behind the safe, our feet behind it and our legs bent at a sharp angle, knees almost touching our chins.

The footsteps were on the landing below us now. We could hear a moaning, gargling sound as well—it was at the ladder. Our ex-friend the Will-thing was at the ladder. Bracing ourselves, we listened hard and watched the hatch across the top of the iron safe, waiting for the Will-thing. It sounded like it was having trouble navigating the vertical steps, but by trial and error it was making it up, missing hand or not. Slowly, slowly it got closer and finally with a great groan the hatch lifted up and fell back, a stumpy arm pushing it and smearing blood across the wood. We watched in complete disgust as the red-masked Will-thing's head appeared through the hole, its nasty green eyes dull in the barely lit attic. I think we froze for a moment, but then someone (I forget who) shouted out and we pushed our legs forward with every ounce of muscle we had. The safe slid quickly across the door and smacked that face dead on with a satisfying crunch. Will-thing was sent tumbling to the door below with the safe following right behind. I leaned over the hatch and looked down. The initial hit from the safe had smashed the zombie's nose and mouth; it was barely a face at all anymore. The safe had landed on Will-thing's chest, crushing its ribs, and was now sitting inside the pocket the impact had made. But the zombie was still moving. Its legs and arms jerked around and even through its broken face it was moaning and groaning, snarling up at me and spitting pieces of tooth. I sighed, sat on the edge of the hatch, balanced myself and dropped down feet first, landing heavily on the angry face. It finally went silent and stopped moving.

"Jack, mate, it's safe!" I called up into the hatch, and made my way to the top of the stairs to see what carnage awaited us below. The noise was deafening and it was obvious the infected cattle were inside the farmhouse. At least, I told myself, cows couldn't climb stairs.

One of the Herefords was climbing the stairs. It had its legs splayed out at what looked like impossible angles, practically pressing itself against the walls, but it was slowly moving up a step at a time, bloody hoof by bloody hoof. Jack arrived at my shoulder, looked, and went straight back the way he had come from.

As I listened to Jack scrambling back up the ladder and watched a huge undead bull attempt to navigate a staircase, I was struck with a wonderful instance of serenity. I don't know where it came from, but I embraced it like a long-lost lover. Seeing the snail's pace at which the Hereford was gaining higher ground, I sat down on the top step, suddenly and ridiculously feeling completely safe and calm. It's snarling, nipping mouth and bloody horns were mere feet from me, but I didn't care. I felt something poking into my side and pulled Dr. Bloom's notebook from my pants, started to flick through it casually as though I was on a park bench reading a Sunday newspaper. A lot of it made no sense to me—scientific jargon a *little* above my head. One section caught my attention though. As I read it my calmness dissipated, replaced by shock, then anger. I closed the notepad, put it back into my pants and went back to the attic, spitting down onto the horned devil below me as I left.

Jack was sitting in the far corner of the attic. I went over to the one small window that overlooked the approach to the farm, wiped away the cobwebs and dust with my sleeve. I moved the wooden bookcase from the far corner in front of the window, slipped it onto its side and used it to perch against, watching through the window as I rested my buttocks against the wood of the shelving.

"What are you doing?" asked Jack quietly.

"Those things will leave soon," I replied, no tone in my voice. "They can't get to us and they'll head off towards town before long. Maybe that old bastard Bonehead actually alerted the right people and they'll be ready for them, maybe even on their way here now. More likely he went straight to the pub and is telling scary tales to his drunk mates and any pretty lass who will listen. Either way, it doesn't matter."

Jack had moved over and stood beside me, scratching himself nervously.

"So are we going to make a run when they leave?" he asked me. "Take old Doom's car?"

I gave him a quick glance then returned to staring out the window, over the dirt path to the main road that led into town.

"You can, mate, you can. I'm going to stay right here. I found a notepad on the doctor before he died. Interesting reading. Oh look, there they go."

I nodded outside where the stumbling Friesians were starting their ragged march away from the farm towards a denser civilization. The red-skinned Herefords were right behind them. Jack ran to the hatch, peered out and disappeared. He came back a few moments later whooping and whistling.

"The big nasty bad 'un is gone, must have given up or fell arse over tit back down again! Stairs are clear, downstairs is clear, we can get out, mate!"

I pulled the notebook out and flipped to a page near the middle.

"Listen, Jack. The day this 'Agent J' stuff started turning the cattle, they'd been consuming it for two days already. Doom and his crew stopped us shipping the milk that very day. They didn't stop shipping beef though. It still went out. And the Herefords had been getting the stuff in their feed as well."

Jack rubbed his chin; he didn't understand what I was telling him.

"Look at what happened to poor Will," I said, "the stuff got into him either through being bitten or the cow blood going all over his face, in his mouth and nose and eyes. He went over pretty quick didn't he?"

Jack nodded, and I saw that he suddenly understood what I was getting at. He seemed to deflate in front of me; all the hope and relief drained from his face.

"All that beef," he whispered, "all that beef out there, across Cheshire, being eaten, whole families will be turned at once."

I kept my eyes on the undead herd outside as it got to the main road and, by instinct perhaps, turned in the direction of town.

"Yes, mate, all across Cheshire. And then all across England, Wales, Scotland . . . then the rest . . . and I bet we're not the only farm to get it this bad despite what your friend Bernard told me."

I sighed.

Jack made for the hatch, shouting at me to go with him, how we could warn somebody.

"Too late Jack. You go, be a hero. See how far you get."

I could see smoke pluming up into the sky—way off in the distance towards town—and knew that it had already started before the infected cattle could even get there. I didn't tell my friend this.

"I'm bloody out, mate. Please come. What are you going to do here?" Jack shouted as he slid through the hatch.

"All I can do. Sit and watch the world end."

Born and raised in the mystical wastelands of northern England amongst harpies and dragons, HARPER HULL now lives in the sultry, sweaty southern United States with his Dixie wife, fighting off giant spiders and man-eating vultures. He has work published or about to be published on four continents and can't wait to hit that dark, mysterious fifth. He has fallen off a boat, been hit by two cars, literally been scared of his own shadow and traveled in an elevator with Kirsten Dunst. Favorite things include the writings of J.G. Ballard, the music of (the) Pixies, Scapa Flow, tiramisu, winter coats, and microbrews. If you ever read anything he is responsible for he just hopes you enjoy it. More info at harperhull.weebly. com/index.html.

According to wedding vows, a marriage lasts "until death do you part."
For Gina, not even living death could part her from Paul . . .

Captive Hearts

Brian Keene

"Maybe I should cut off your penis next."

Richard moaned at the prospect, thrashing on the bed. The handcuffs rattled and the headboard thumped against the wall, but Gina noticed that his efforts were growing weaker. That was good. Weak was better. She wanted him weak—enjoyed the prospect of such a once-powerful man now reduced to nothing more than a mewling kitten. Even so, she'd have to keep an eye on his condition. She didn't want Richard too weak. He'd be useless to her dead.

"Please, Gina. You can still stop this. No more."

"Shut up."

The room was dark, save for flickering candlelight. The windows had been boarded over with heavy plywood. Gina had done the work herself, and had felt a sense of satisfaction when she'd finished.

Richard raised his head and stared at her, standing in the doorway. He licked his cracked, peeling lips. His tongue reminded her of a slug. Gina shuddered, remembering how it had felt on her skin—the nape of her neck, her breasts, her belly, inside her thighs. Her stomach churned. Sour and acidic bile surged up her throat. Gina swallowed, and that brought another shameful memory.

"Just let me go," Richard pleaded. "I won't tell anybody. There's nobody left to tell."

She studied him, trying to conceal her trembling. He had bedsores and bruises, and desperately needed a bath. Richard's skin had an unhealthy sheen that seemed almost yellow in the dim candlelight. His hair, usually so expertly styled, lay limp and greasy. One week into his captivity, she'd held up a mirror and shown Richard his hair, and asked him if it was worth the ten thousand dollars he'd spent on hair replacement surgery. He'd cursed her so loud she had to stuff a pair of her soiled panties in his mouth just to stifle him.

Gina winced. She could smell him from the doorway. He stank of shit and piss and blood, and with good reason. She'd stripped the sheets from the bed, yanking them right out from beneath him when they became too nauseating to go near, but now the mattress itself was crusted with filth. The bandages on his feet covering the nine stumps where his toes had been were leaking again.

"Where would you go?" she asked.

His Adam's apple bobbed up and down. "They said things were better in the country. The news said the government was quarantining Baltimore."

"Not anymore. It's everywhere, Richard."

"Turn on the news. They—"

"There is no news. The power's been out for the last five days."

Richard's eyes grew wide. "F-five days? How long have I been here, Gina?"

"That's easy. Just count your piggies. How many are missing?"

"Oh God, stop . . . "

"I'll be right back."

She went down the hall. When she returned, she was dressed in rubber gloves, a smock, and surgical mask. The bolt cutters were in her hand. She held them up so that Richard could see. That broke him. Richard sobbed, his chest heaving.

"Don't worry," she soothed. "I cleaned them with alcohol, just like always. We can't have you getting an infection."

Gina retrieved her wicker sewing basket—the last gift her mother had given her before succumbing to breast cancer three years ago—from atop the dresser, and then stood over the bed. Richard tried to shrink away from her, but the handcuffs around his wrists and ankles prevented him from moving more than a few inches.

"Listen, listen, listen . . . " He tried to say more, but all that came out was a deep, mournful sigh.

"We've been over this before," she said. "You won't die. I know what I'm doing."

And she did. While most of her fellow suburbanites had fled Hamelin's Revenge—the name the media gave the disease, referencing the rats that had first spawned it—Gina had remained behind. She'd had little choice. There was no way she'd have abandoned Paul. Richard was already imprisoned by then, so she didn't need to worry about him escaping. She'd ventured out after the last of the looters moved on, armed with the small .22 pistol she and Paul had kept in the nightstand. Gina had never fired the handgun before that day, but by the end of that first outing, she'd become a capable shot. Her first stop had been the library, which was, thankfully, zombie free. Alive or dead, nobody read anymore.

Her search of the abandoned library had turned up a number of books—everything from battlefield triage to medical textbooks. She'd taken them all. Her next stop had been the grocery store. She'd scavenged what little bottled water and canned goods were left, and then moved on to the household aisle, where she'd picked up rubber gloves, disinfectant and as many cigarette lighters as she could carry. Finally, she'd hit the pharmacy, only to find it empty. She'd had to rely on giving Richard over-the-counter painkillers and booze instead. She hadn't thought he'd mind, especially given the alternative.

"I just want to wake up," Richard cried.

Gina positioned the bolt cutters over his one remaining toe. "And I just wanted to provide for Paul."

"But I di—"

"And this little piggy cried wee wee wee—"

CRUNCH.

Richard screamed.

"—all the way home."

He shrieked something unintelligible, and his eyes rolled up into his head. He writhed on the mattress, the veins in his neck standing out.

"You brought this on yourself," Gina reminded him as she reached for a lighter to cauterize the wound.

Richard had been her boss, before Hamelin's Revenge—before the dead started coming back to life.

Gina and Paul had met in college, and got married after graduating. They'd been together three years and were just beginning to explore the idea of starting a family when Paul had his accident. It left him quadriplegic. He had limited use of his right arm and couldn't feel anything below his chest. Overnight, both of their lives were irrevocably changed. Gone were Gina's dreams of being a stay-at-home mom. She'd had to support them both, which meant a better job with more pay and excellent health insurance. She'd found all three as Richard's assistant.

Gina had spent her days working for Richard and her nights caring for Paul. Richard had been a wonderful employer at first—gregarious, funny, kind and sympathetic. He'd seemed genuinely interested in her situation, and had offered gentle consolation. But his comfort and caring had come with a price. One day, his breath reeking of lunchtime bourbon, Richard asked about Paul's needs. When Gina finished explaining, he asked about her own needs. He then suggested that he was the man to satisfy those needs. She'd thought he was joking at first, and blushing, had stammered that Paul could still get reflexive erections and they had no trouble in the bedroom.

And then Richard touched her. When Gina resisted, he reminded her of her situation. She needed this job. The visiting nurse who cared for Paul during the day didn't come cheap, nor did any of his medicines or other needs. Sure, Gina could sue him for sexual harassment, but could she really afford to? Worse, what would such a public display do to her husband? Surely he was already feeling inadequate. Did she really want to put this on his conscious, as well?

Gina succumbed. They did it right there in the office. She'd cried the first time, as Richard grunted and huffed above her. She'd cried the second time, too. And the third. And each time, Gina died a little bit more inside.

Until the dead came back to life, giving her a chance to live again.

She'd called Richard before the phones had gone out, telling him to come over, pleading with him to escape with her. They'd be safe together. They could make it to one of the military encampments. Could he please hurry?

He'd shown up an hour later, his BMW packed full of supplies. He smiled when she opened the door, touched her cheek, caressed her hair and told her he was glad she'd called.

"What about your husband?"

"He's already dead," Gina replied. "He's one of them now."

And then she'd hit Richard in the head with a flashlight. The first blow didn't knock him out. It took five tries. Each one was more satisfying than the previous.

The thing Gina had always loved most about Paul was his heart. Her mother, who'd adored Paul, had often said the same thing.

"You married a good one, Gina. He's got a big heart."

Her mother had been right. Paul's heart was big. She stood staring at it through the hole in his chest. Paul moaned, slumping forward in his wheelchair. She'd strapped him into it with bungee cords and duct tape, so that he couldn't get out. He was no longer dead from the chest down. Death had cured him of that. He could move again.

She moved closer and he moaned again, snapping at the air with his teeth. Gina thought of all the other times she'd stood over him like this. She remembered the times they'd made love in the wheelchair—straddling him with her legs wrapped around the chair's back, Paul nuzzling her breasts, Gina kissing the top of his head as she thrust up and down on him. Afterward, they'd stay like that, skin on skin, sweat drying to a sheen.

Paul moaned a third time, breaking her reverie. She glanced down and noticed that another one of his fingernails had fallen off. She couldn't stop him from decaying, but when he ate, it seemed to slow the process down.

She reached into her pocket, pulled out the plastic baggie, and unzipped it. Richard's piggy toe lay inside. It was still slightly warm to the touch. She fed Paul the toe, ignoring the smacking sounds his lips made as he chewed greedily.

"We'll have something different tomorrow." Her voice cracked. "A nice finger. Would you like that?"

Paul didn't respond. She hadn't expected him to. Gina liked to think that he still understood her, that he still remembered their love for each other, but deep down inside, she knew better.

Eventually, Gina grew tired. Yawning, she went around the house and snuffed out the candles. Richard was still passed out when she examined his newest bandage. She double-checked the barricades on the doors and windows. Finally, she said goodnight to what was left of the man who had captured her heart, while in the other room, her captive awoke and cried softly in the dark.

BRIAN KEENE is the author of over twenty books, including *Darkness on the Edge of Town, Urban Gothic, Dark Hollow, Dead Sea,* and many more. He also writes comic books such as *The Last Zombie* and *Dead of Night: Devil Slayer.* His work has been translated into German, Spanish, Polish, French, and Taiwanese. Several of his novels and stories have been optioned for film, one of which, *The Ties That Bind*, premiered on DVD in 2009 as a critically-acclaimed independent short. Keene's work has been praised in such diverse places as *The New York Times*, The History Channel, *The Howard Stern Show*, CNN.com, *Publishers Weekly, Fangoria*, and *Rue Morgue*. Keene lives in the backwoods of Central Pennsylvania with his wife, sons, dog, and cats. You can communicate with him online at www.briankeene.com or on Twitter at twitter.com/BrianKeene.

May the Lord accept the sacrifice at your hands, for the praise and glory of his name, for our good, and the good of all . . .

For the Good of All

Yvonne Navarro

Fida can hear their moans through the floor.

The boarders are restless and hungry—they're always hungry—but there isn't much she can do about that. Broxton House doesn't do bed and breakfast anymore, doesn't even rent to new boarders. Hell, nobody needs to rent now that a good seventy percent of the city population is gone. If a person wants to move, they move; all you need to do is make sure the new place is empty of both the living and the dead. The law now says if you live in it, you own it, period. Squatting is okay, taking it by force isn't. People work jobs just like before, but they make less money, and there's a clear division in classes. Fida's in the lower class, and that's fine with her. She grows most of her food and has learned to live without the electricity she can't afford anyway. There's a weekly flea market in the parking lot of the abandoned high school two suburbs over, nice and safe within a secure eight-foot iron fence. Someone with a sense of humor dubbed it the "Lock 'n' Swap" and the name stuck; Fida goes over and does small sewing jobs. She picked up the talent from her grandmother (who died decades before this zombie mess) and it earns her money for firewood in the winter, candles, enough gasoline to go to a different church each Sunday, and the few other things she can't make on her own.

Fida is ready when the priest knocks on her door at a quarter to twelve, even though he's fifteen minutes early. She's glad he didn't forget or decide not to come, because when that happens—and it does occasionally—it always shakes up her faith. Faith is all she has, and she mustn't let it waver. Too much depends upon it.

"Good afternoon, Miss . . . " He falters for a moment because she never told him her last name.

"Just call me Fida," she tells him. "Long *e*, rhymes with Rita." She steps to the side and motions at him. "Please, come inside."

He nods and Fida can see the relief in his eyes as he steps over the threshold. His car, a heavy sedan that, like almost everyone's, has mesh soldered over the windows, is parked at the curb. It had probably seemed like a very long way from the sidewalk to her door. No one without an armed escort wants to be outside too long nowadays.

Fida judiciously bolts the door, then leads him into the drawing room. "Make yourself comfortable." He obliges by settling on one of the two floral-printed couches and passing a white handkerchief across his forehead. It's impossible to tell if it's the June heat or fear that makes him sweat. Some people just do.

She's made a simple lunch, homemade flatbread baked pizza-style over a grating in the fireplace of the old-fashioned kitchen, then topped with a sliced tomato and green pepper from her little greenhouse (she's privately called it Lock 'n' Grow since hearing the nickname of the swap meet). She hasn't had mozzarella cheese in years, but a sprinkling of dry Parmesan before it goes over the heat works well. She serves it to him along with a glass of room-temperature water freshened by a small sprig of mint. A good man should have a good meal before he gets on about his business. A man such as Father Stane.

They eat without saying much of anything. After about ten minutes, Fida can see the priest finally relaxing. Even though she's herded the boarders to the far end of the house, they have a tendency to fight amongst themselves and now and then one of them gets loud. Occasionally a snarl sails along the upstairs air currents and drifts through the unused heating vents. The first time this happens, Father Stane visibly twitches; when all Fida does is meet his gaze and shrug, he appears to accept that she has made her home safe. The next couple of noises make him raise an eyebrow, but his deep brown eyes are wise and he knows that the time for discussion isn't long in coming. She can tell by his black hair and heavy bone structure that he is perhaps Slavic or Serbian. A man from the old country, where the faith is ancient and strong. Excellent.

Fida sets the dishes aside and folds her hands on her lap. "I appreciate you coming all this way," she says. "I know it's troublesome to travel alone."

Father Stane tilts his head. "Indeed. You said there was something important you wanted to discuss."

Fida nods, then picks at the rough edges of her fingernails as she considers the phrasing of her question. "Father, do you believe in forgiveness?"

"Of course," he answers without hesitation. "Forgiveness is the core of our faith. Christ died for us, so that we would all be redeemed." He studies her. "You attended my Mass last Sunday, but I won't presume you're Christian."

"I'm Catholic."

"But do you believe? These are difficult times, Fida. Even the strongest man or woman of faith can stumble."

"I do believe, very strongly."

He nods. "Then what is it you wanted to discuss?"

Fida takes a deep breath. "Do you believe in redemption? That souls can be saved?"

"Of course," he says again. He leans forward. "Do you need to make a confession? Is that why you asked me to come here—for privacy?" She shakes her head, but he continues anyway. "These are terrible times, Fida. A lot of people have done . . . questionable things, just to stay alive." He reaches over and gives her a paternal pat on the hand. "Many don't want to be public about it. They feel hypocritical. I understand."

Hypocritical . . . like Jesus and the Pharisees and scribes? No, she does not equate herself with them. "I only try to save people," she replies, and both of them look toward the ceiling at the sound of a faraway thump.

Father Stane sits back. "Ah," he says. "You have . . . " He hesitates, unsure of his terminology.

"Boarders," Fida answers for him. "They all lived here . . . " Another pause. "Before."

The priest's forehead furrows. "They came back?"

She nods. "They came *home*. I don't believe that the living dead are just monsters, creatures without thought or purpose. They have memory. They seek comfort." Her hands are squeezing tightly together now, almost in supplication. "They didn't ask for this. They want to be rescued, to be *saved*."

Father Stane rubs his chin. "Have you considered that their return might just be instinct? There have been studies—"

Fida waves away his words. "You mean the experiment labs, where they're dissected like lab rats, treated with chemicals and used as targets for the security forces to try out their latest and greatest weapons." Heat climbs up her face. "And let's not forget that the science centers are the perfect place for people to drop off their relatives—parents, spouses, *children*, for God's sake—then walk away with a clean conscience, saying that what they're doing is for the good of all. You mentioned hypocrites? *Those* are the hypocrites, Father Stane. Those are the monsters. The ones who won't take responsibility for people they once loved." She crosses her arms so tightly that the muscles in her shoulders spasm. "So much for *until death do us part*. The living dead, Father Stane. The *living* dead."

He takes a drink of water and puts it back on the coffee table, carefully centering it on a coaster. "All right. Let's say they are still alive, after a fashion. Then what?"

"They need to be *saved*," she tells him firmly. "Forgiven, like Jesus forgave us all at the Last Supper. It was his body and blood—"

"Metaphorically," the priest reminds her.

"Obviously, Father. I was about to say 'via the bread and wine.'" Fida squashes her irritation, then picks up again. "That's how mankind was forgiven, through his love and sacrifice. That's how we continue to be forgiven." She rises and crosses the drawing room, lifts a photo album from a mahogany side table next to the fireplace. She brings it back and opens it in front of Father Stane, pointing to the pictures.

"This is Patrick. A good Irish boy, first room at the top of the stairs. He's been out of work so he's a bit behind on his rent." She flips the page. "This is Manuella. She lives . . . *lived* here with her boy, Reynaldo, in the biggest room at the back. Reynaldo's gone, though. He was only six." Father Stane nods his head sympathetically. She taps a fingernail against a picture of a sallow-skinned Asian man; his eyes are thin and mean and a gang tattoo curves around the back of his bald skull. "This is Cade. I have to admit that he tries my patience sometimes." She lifts her chin. "Still, I have hope."

"I see."

"Do you?" Her eyes burn as she flips a couple more pages, locking her voice, determined not to show too much emotion. "Jesse and Tina. They're only sixteen. She's four months pregnant and they're hiding from her father, who told her he was going to kill Jesse." Another turn of the page. "Max is a heroin addict, always trying to kick the habit and always blowing it. He's come back here four times because he knows I'll help him keep on trying. And the last one is Sylvie. She's thirteen and a runaway."

Father Stane frowns at her. "You let a thirteen-year-old runaway stay here?"

Fida's gaze doesn't waver. "Her mother turned her out as a prostitute when she was eleven."

The priest's jaw works but he says nothing as Fida puts the album back in its place. "These are my tenants, Father."

"You talk about them as if things never changed."

"I don't think they have, at least not to them. In their minds, they're just lost." She sits back down and clasps her hands again. "Don't you see? These are *my* family. My responsibility. If I don't care for them, don't keep them safe and try to save them, then *I* will be a hypocrite. No better than so many others."

Father Stane nods and to his credit, she can see him struggling to comprehend her way of thinking. "So why did you call me here, Fida? What can I do to help you with this situation?"

He stumbles a bit on the word *situation* and Fida's stomach twists inside. Does he believe, truly? His faith must be complete. It must be pure. If it isn't, he might as well go on home now.

"Will you do something for me, Father?" On the other end of the couch is a large wicker basket covered with a simple, clean white cloth. She pulls the basket to her side and lifts the cotton; beneath is more freshly baked flatbread, five good loaves of it, and a round crystal decanter of dark red wine. "Bless this bread and wine," she says. "Consecrate it with all your faith and everything you believe in. Like you do the Eucharist at Mass."

"And then what?" he asks sternly. His gaze rolls upward. "You feed it to them? There is no forgiveness without confession. You know that."

She shakes her head. "But we have to *try*. The body of Christ, the blood of Christ. Miracles *have* happened. That the dead can walk is in itself a miracle, don't you think? Who's to say that a—a *reverse* miracle can't occur?"

"And if it doesn't? Will you be the one to stop them?" He glances pointedly at the machete hanging at her belt.

Fida looks at her hands. Sometimes she feels so much sadness she can hardly speak the words. "To kill out of judgment is not my place." He doesn't reply and she turns her hands palm up. "It's a small thing that I'm asking, Father. A sacrifice of symbology. A spreading of the Word, the faith, the Sacrament."

"All right," he says after a few moments, but he sounds tired. Is he doing it because he wants to, or because he feels it's what will be necessary for him to leave and feel as if he's done his best?

He reaches for the basket but she stands and lifts it with her. "Upstairs," she says. "In Patrick's room. They're all down at the end, where Manuella stays." She doesn't add that the Mexican woman, whose skin and eyes have gone as gray as old cement and whose mouth is rimmed with the dried blood of her son, spends most of every day moaning and standing over the daybed where the boy used to sleep.

Fida can tell by the expression on Father Stane's sturdy face that he wants to protest, but he doesn't. This gives her reason to hope; a faithless man would have refused, would have asked how dangerous it was and was she sure that the creatures were safely locked away. But Father Stane is a good man. A faithful man.

He follows her up the stairs and she hands him the basket, then opens the door to Patrick's room. The priest pulls back but the room is empty, the door that joins it to Jesse's closed. The bed is rumpled, as if the boy has slept in it, but she knows it isn't so. She makes it up every morning, even changes the sheets once a week, but the boarders only bump against it, or sometimes fall onto the antique quilt. They never sleep, though, just get up and wander away. There are no mirrors in this room because the living dead version of Patrick doesn't like his reflection and he always breaks them.

Fida takes the basket back and walks inside, then sets it on the dresser across from the door. She lifts the cloth reverently and stares at the contents for several seconds without saying anything, then backs away and looks at the priest. "Will you bless it now?" she asks.

Father Shane clears his throat. "Yes." He takes his place in front of the dresser, bows his head and begins to pray, and Fida relaxes a little as the familiar words coat the air with promises of holiness.

"On the night he was betrayed, he took bread and gave you thanks and praise. He broke the bread, gave it to his disciples, and said, take this, all of you, and eat it: this is my body which will be given up for you." Father Shane holds up one of the loaves and breaks it into two. She smiles and nods when he glances at her, then says in a soft voice. "I'll be right back. I have to get my crucifix. Don't stop."

She feels his gaze as she slips out of the room, but when she leaves the door open, his voice resumes and she hears more confidence in it. Excellent.

"When supper was ended, he took the cup. Again he gave you thanks and praise, gave the cup to his disciples, and said, take this, all of you, and drink

from it: this is the cup of my blood, the blood of the new and everlasting covenant. It will be shed for you and for all men so that sins may be forgiven. Do this in memory of me."

He has spoken only a few words by the time Fida gets to the end of the hallway and Manuella's door. She bends and sweeps aside the soiled clothing that has kept the living dead clustered there all day, then walks quickly back to Patrick's room. She knows just where to step so the floor doesn't creak, along the edges of the baseboards where the nails are strong and the old oak boards haven't sagged in the middle. As she silently reaches out, pulls the door shut and bolts it, she hears another part of the Mass in her head, the words that are always said in preparation of the altar and the gifts. They are out of order, but there is nothing more appropriate.

May the Lord accept the sacrifice at your hands, for the praise and glory of his name, for our good, and the good of all . . .

It takes only about thirty seconds for her boarders, her *family*, to lurch down to Patrick's room, where the final door that separates them from Father Stane is not locked. A few seconds later, the priest begins to scream.

Fida sits on the hallway floor and stares at the crucifix she took off the wall down by Manuella's room, discouragement leaving yet another a bitter taste in her mouth. She was wrong about Father Stane—his faith had *not* been strong enough, he hadn't been truly sacred and believing in the body and soul of Christ. If he had, he would have been spared, and her loved ones would have eaten the blessed bread and wine, and they would have been cured.

She'll just have to try again. There is another Catholic church, Saint Benedictine, about five miles away, and she can drive Father Shane's car there next Sunday. After Mass will ask one of the priests to come to her home and speak to her in confidence.

These days, the priests are always out in the community, ministering and spreading the word of God for the good of all. No one thinks twice when they don't come back.

Yvonne Navarro is the author of more than twenty novels, numerous short stories, and a nonfiction book. The recipient of a Bram Stoker Award for her young adult novel, *Buffy the Vampire Slayer: The Willow Files, Vol.*

2, she was also nominated for a Stoker for novels *AfterAge* and *deadrush*. Novel *Final Impact* won both the Chicago Women In Publishing's Award for Excellence and the "Unreal Worlds" Award from the Rocky Mountain News. Her most recent novels are *Highborn* and *Concrete Savior*. A long-time native of Chicago she now lives in Arizona with her husband, author Weston Ochse, two Great Danes, and two spoiled, over-sociable parakeets. Her website is www.yvonnenavarro.com.

*There's gotta be law, and the law's gotta be blind. Some of the residents of
Ocotillo might be dead, but they were still walking; they were
citizens of a town that took care of its own . . .*

We Will Rebuild

Cody Goodfellow

On the third monthly anniversary of V-D Day, some residents of Ocotillo
still came out to wave or put Old Glory up on their porches as Deputies
Snopes and Bascomb rolled up the nameless main drag in their armored
cruiser, siren blaring to lift the curfew.

"Happy Death Day, suckers," Bascomb hollered.

"Leave 'em alone," Snopes said. "Everybody loves a parade."

Bascomb made V-D Day medals out of Xmas ribbon and teeth for the
occasion, but only Bascomb wore his, along with his Army Purple Heart
and the special citation for the Battle of the Calexico Wal-Mart, two weeks
ago. A Wal-Mart greeter's nametag hung from the ribbon: HI! MY NAME
IS SOLE SURVIVOR.

Verna Schepsi swept the sidewalk in front of the feed store, but it
was a fool's errand. The particles of ash that still rained down out of the
sulfurous yellow sunrise were like downy snowflakes, merging into gray
dust devils battling in the empty street.

Chubby Beckwith lumbered out of the Circle K and waved at them
when he got to the end of his chain. Chubby was a good kid, always kept a
fresh pot of coffee on until they ran out of it, but he got grabby when they
stopped to top off the cruiser once, so they had to chop off his hands. It
was all legal, the papers on file with the judge.

"Wanna go out to the canal and look for deadbeats?" Bascomb was
crocked early and itchy today, because his wife got into it with Taffy, their
Doberman pinscher. Reluctant to put either of them down, he was damned
if he wasn't going to shoot something today.

"Waste of ammo," Snopes replied. "Besides, we got to go out and change the sign."

The sign marking the Interstate 8 off-ramp used to read OCOTILLO; ELEV. 47; FT. POP. 220; GAS FOOD LODGING. As soon as the dust settled after V-D Day, they revised the list of amenities with big stenciled red NO's, and shortwave and CB frequencies to call those inside.

Snopes had the idea to borrow the scoreboard numbers from the little league field. He displayed the number of the alive with the black numbers for the home team, and the number of the dead in the red for the visitors. The score was not encouraging: 32 to 67.

Gabe Gonzalez got bit by his daughter last night, and after they woke the judge up to sign the order, she was put down. Everyone pretty much knew what he was trying to do when he got bit, so no one was overly exercised about it.

Still and all, a pretty normal day . . .

Bascomb wanted to tack a 1 in front of the black number. "If any more gangs come looking for shit, we got to look tough."

"When the Army comes, we got to look meek, so they don't just bomb us. You heard on the radio what the Marines did to them rich dicks in Palm Springs."

Snopes went up the road with his binoculars to check the perimeter. Ocotillo straddled the I-8/S.R.46 junction, snug between the Anza-Borrego mountains, studded with fractured granite boulders and the dusty, drained lake bed of the Imperial Valley.

Nothing alive or dead had come up the 8 or down from the hills in over a week. Gangs and deadbeat stragglers from the conflagration that destroyed El Centro and Calexico still dribbled in from the east, but deadbeats couldn't cross the canal; burnt up with hunger and half-mummified by the desert sun, most of them dissolved like soda crackers in the swift current. Everything on wheels stopped where the deputies had blown the I-8 overpass at the canal, and either turned north on the 46 or abandoned their vehicles.

After that doctor from La Jolla, nobody had successfully pled for asylum in Ocotillo. When they let him in with his wife and three daughters, they thought they'd turned a corner; but three days later, the shitbird gassed himself and his whole family with their propane tank. The house blew up and burned down both its neighbors.

People from the cities couldn't handle desert life, before or after Day Zero. Nothing out here had changed. There had always been laws on the books for dealing with aliens. If they were from outside the town's jurisdiction and had nothing to offer, they had to be treated accordingly.

A couple deadbeats had wandered into the minefield along the highway a while back, and parts of them still tried to crawl through the tumbleweed snarls of razor wire that flanked the interstate and encircled the town. The fields were clearly marked for living and dead alike, cardboard signs and rotting, chattering heads on pikes, but nobody took time to read anymore.

Vultures and crows feuded over the last scraps on the skeletons of the latest live invaders—a small herd of runaway horses that had blundered into the claymores set up between the outbuildings of the abandoned Pernicano ranch. The yard sale scatter of long, elegant bones and stringy flesh looked like the ruins of something built to fly. Sometime ago, he might have seen something sad or beautiful in it, but now the waste of meat just made his mouth water.

In the crisp heat haze of the quickening day, everything seemed to squirm with a tortured thirst for blood and sweat. Snopes went back to the cruiser. With sheet metal and chain-link fence for windows, it was already a sweat lodge inside. Bascomb was in the driver's seat, hooting at the radio like football was back. "Hell yeah!"

Snopes pushed him over and got in, turned back down the off-ramp. Bascomb loaded shells into the shotgun and stuffed the rest of them in his pockets. "Dead wetbacks!"

They passed Chubby again, who waved a stump at them as he chewed on the other, and a couple of boarded-up houses. Mrs. Chesebro wandered her dusty yard in her housecoat, looking for her cats. Next door, Chet Bamberger strained at the end of his leash to get his month-old morning paper. He wore only a wifebeater tanktop—second-skinned to him by yellow seepage, and drizzling maggots out the armpits. His muzzle was splashed with bright red blood, which, since his own was black and clotted in his feet and ass, clearly solved the mystery of the missing cats.

Bamberger was unemployed, and lost his license for a third DUI coming back from the Golden Acorn casino, so he and the deputies knew each other pretty well. He liked to tune up his wife, but she never pressed charges. He beat up Connie in Pal Joey's Bar on V-D Day, and got locked up with some deadbeat tweaker from San Diego who'd crashed a stolen car on the off-ramp. The tweaker bit Chet, who died but got up and ate two of his cellmates.

Chet was one of the first locals to stir, and Snopes put four bullets into his torso that night. He sorely regretted that he didn't know, back then, that you have to shoot them in the head. Order was restored, Connie took him home, and he hadn't attacked anyone since. How they stayed together under one roof with no AC was a mystery to Snopes, but their problems were none of his business, until someone complained.

At the stoplight, Ocotillo showed that somebody really believed it would be a proper town, once. A shabby little bandstand and a pocket park once sat in the middle of the road, but now, the town square was a field of black, greasy ash. A sun-bleached and smoke-blackened banner hung over the street, reminding him to catch the Ocotillo Settlers' Days festival that should have started last weekend.

The town hall was a sturdy whitewashed brick monument to itself, with a sheriff's station, courtroom, mayor's office, basement holding cells, and a broom closet that doubled as a library and civil defense shelter.

V-D Day was mostly peaceful in Ocotillo, until the panicked mass exodus from San Diego swept through, with the dead in its wake. Half the town bugged out for the hills, while the rest hunkered down in attics and cellars, or the town hall building.

Ocotillo was overrun and picked clean. Sheriff Lorber and the deputies holed up on the town hall roof when the remaining civilians fled or went down in the shelter. The dead converged on the town hall, wading into the ankle-deep gasoline pool Sheriff Lorber had drained into the square, and gawking up at them as they tossed road flares.

When the fire died down, the wave had crested and fallen, and the remaining deadbeats were easy to put down or contain.

Judge Dooling came down from his ranch that morning, and since the mayor was dead, he took over and restored order. Painting the town hall white again had been the first order of business.

The people in the shelter weren't so lucky. When the power failed and the water pressure dropped, rats boiled out of the toilets and bit them in the dark. All the rats had feasted on the bodies in the streets, and were rife with the bug that made them walk and eat.

Whatever still knocked around inside was too dumb to work the hatch, but the Judge ordered them to open it. Three deputies had family in the shelter, and at first, they were just happy to have them back. Benedetto got careless, and was bit by his son. He looked happy, when he and his family lurched out of their trailer for the chow wagon. Espinoza ate his gun that night, after executing his deadbeat wife and his mother. Bascomb and his hogbitch wife fought almost every night, so for them, nothing much had changed at all.

In all, they identified seventy-nine walking dead residents, and sixty-three living. Getting the deadbeat locals to go home was easy; once chained down in their houses or at their jobs, most just did more or less what they always had, knocking around aimlessly until chow time, or until live meat got too close. Putting the muzzles on, though, was a king-hell bitch.

Deputy Mark Snopes had no family in town. He came over from the San Diego Police Department two years before, and was damned lucky to have a job. The cop mentality—us versus them, with any civilian more or less one of them—ground on his nerves. He tasered an enormous lady shoplifter when she got aggressive with him. She turned out to be five months pregnant, and miscarried.

In a burg like Ocotillo, it was the same problems, but smaller and simpler. Half the town out of its head on drink or drugs or God, and beating on the other half; shitheads and deadbeats passing through, littering and shooting up the signs; and wetbacks, creeping over the border and eating all the livestock. But it was better than the city. The desert took care of those who couldn't take care of themselves. You knew who the good people were, and the right and the wrong of a situation was writ plain. Now, more than ever . . .

Snopes swung the cruiser into the town hall lot and jumped out. Bascomb called after him, "Fuck you, then, I'm driving!"

Betty Olson saw him coming, and unlocked the door, then locked and bolted it when he barged through the saloon doors that led to the courtroom. "I wouldn't," she whispered. "The generator's out, so he's in a mood."

Snopes didn't knock. The courtroom was darker than the other rooms, with no slits cut into the boards over the windows, and no lamplight. The dark was all violet fireworks until his eyes adjusted to the pinprick spiderwebs of daylight seeping into the courtroom.

In the stifling heat and silence, Snopes believed he could feel something scratching, like claws, on the concrete underneath his feet. Somewhere in the room, the dispatch radio crackled.

"Your Honor, even if there *was* something out there, we got bigger shit—beg pardon, sir—issues, to contend with, and I'm worried about Bascomb—"

"He's worried about you, Deputy."

"I can't see you, Your Honor."

A match flashed and kissed the mantle of a Coleman lamp on the judge's desk. "The dark makes it feel cooler." Only the gavel, drinking glass, revolver, and pale, liver-spotted hands came into view. "If we had gas to spare for the generators . . . but never mind. You wanted to resign, then?"

"You know I don't. I take this job seriously, and since Sheriff Lorber got bit, me and Doug are pretty much the only law left. But this patrol duty isn't going to solve anything. We're just wasting gas."

"Deputy, the migrant illegal traffic through this area is more of a scourge now than ever. You saw, yourself, what they did in Seeley and Calexico. You'd like to see them gather at the wire, I suppose, and overrun us again?"

Snopes couldn't lose his temper with the judge, but the way he tied you up with his questions made his head hurt. "I'd like to clean up the mess *inside* the wire."

"What mess is there? What haven't you been reporting to me?"

Snopes came closer to the light. The outline of Dooling's head floated in the dark above the perfect black of his robe. Hairless, blank as the moon. "Your Honor hasn't been outside in a while, so far as I know, but I have, and I file reports on everything. Five of our people got killed this month in, uh, domestic disputes—"

"*Nine* died this month, don't you mean, Deputy Snopes?"

"No sir, the other four were already—"

"They were citizens of this town, each and every one, never forget that. We take care of our own."

"Sir, we have a responsibility to the living to protect them from the dead . . . don't we?"

Judge Dooling looked Snopes up and down, his bifocals and his dentures winking in the yellow light. "Deputy, do you know why the dead got up last month?"

Snopes felt as if the courtroom at his back was packed with laughing ghosts, laughing at him. "No sir, I don't."

The judge clucked his tongue, a dry baby rattler sound. "Then how can you say you know what will happen tomorrow?"

Snopes headed for the door. "I don't get it, Your Honor."

Dooling's chair creaked. "You are the arm of the law, young man, not its brain. The police have ever had the thankless duty of standing between the citizenry and their own worst impulses."

Your Honor might take a different view of the law if he ever got off his fossilized ass and tried enforcing it. That was what Snopes wished he'd said. Instead, he said, "Yes, Your Honor."

Dooling's voice got higher and louder as Snopes walked away. When Snopes stopped at the door, it went down low, but the superb acoustics of the courtroom delivered it to his ear. "This could be divine retribution, and it could be a disease, Deputy. But tomorrow, if it is a disease, there may be a cure; and if it is the judgment of God, then we will go to our greater reward with our sins against the innocent and ill weighing heaviest in our hearts."

Snopes tried hard not to shout. "Your Honor, Bascomb and I are more than ready to take care of business with a clean conscience—"

"Have him start with his wife, then, would you, Deputy? You haven't lost anyone, so you can't relate. The state can't presume to write the law, but should act to preserve order and normality, until the rest of the world does likewise."

"Right, everything's normal."

"Yes, if we say so, and we do. We have restored order, and we will rebuild our town. Now there's a mob of dead illegal aliens massed somewhere around the fence. See to it."

Snopes left, stopped in the library to get a tripod-mounted M-60 and two extra belts. Judge Dooling was also a retired brigadier general in the National Guard, and had the keys to the armory in Seeley. All the heavy stuff went out to blockade the 8 to the east, to stop the deadbeat armies marching out of Mexico. Nothing came back.

Snopes got blindsided by the daylight when he went outside. He slipped on his shades. Bascomb hung out the window with his arms thrown wide for the machinegun. "Okay, you can drive."

They drove south, down the perimeter to where it swerved east to parallel the interstate. "All clear, shit!" Bascomb growled, and cracked open a blood-hot beer.

Most of the ash came from El Centro, Calexico, and Mexicali, which the Marines torched with fuel-air bombs a week after V-D Day. They boiled over like anthills doused in gas, never-ending waves of deadbeats, scorched black and ravenous. The Marines got eaten or bugged out, and that was the last they saw of any order outside their own fence.

Snopes went up the canal to where the fence picked up at the trailer park at the north end of town. He cut across the back end of Bascomb's yard on the cul-de-sac. Bascomb waved to his wife, who drooled and banged on the bars of their bedroom window.

They followed the fence along the canal and turned north, and were almost back to the main drag when Bascomb called, "Wetbacks!"

Snopes braked on the shingled dirt road beside the abandoned Milbank ranch, which stood half in and half out of the perimeter. Donnie Milbank was a small-time TV minister, and when the Rapture found him still on earth, he packed up the family in the Winnebago and hauled ass for some born-again survivalist enclave in Texas.

Where the fence circled behind Milbank's stables, he saw twenty or thirty ragged scarecrows loping across the dead brown lawn. They shambled jerkily through a gap in the razor wire, where it was trampled flat.

Snopes jerked to a stop. The nearest wetback was inside the fence, not ten feet away, flannel and denim rags caked with mud and dust and blood, greedy claws outstretched, slack jaws snapping in dumb, bottomless hunger. Bascomb jumped out, laid the M-60 across the hood and opened up.

Bascomb hosed them down like leaves off a driveway, walking the spray of lead across their midsections to slash them in half and pile them up against the wire.

Snopes stayed behind the wheel, but opened fire with the shotgun. He saw big scoops of meat lifted out of heads and chests and knew he was connecting; at this range, how could he miss?

It was hard to hear with the atomic-typewriter clatter of the machine gun, but when Bascomb finally stopped to reload, Snopes could see how a few survivors tried to run for the open desert. He could hear how they screamed and cried and prayed.

His stomach filled with nightcrawlers and battery acid. "Stop! Bascomb, Doug, Jesus Christ, stop! *They're not dead!*" He hit the siren and jumped out, ran around the cruiser to knock Bascomb down, because his partner just laughed and kept shooting.

Snopes tore down the gun and shut off the siren. If any got away, he didn't see them moving.

Bascomb got up and dusted off, punched Snopes in the shoulder. "Fuck you thinking, fucker? You wanna die?"

"Didn't you hear that? They were fucking screaming!"

"They were screaming in *Spanish*! They're fucking wetbacks, dude, and they look pretty fucking dead now. Come on, let's clean up."

Bascomb covered while Snopes checked for survivors. There were none, and nothing got up. The bodies lay in mounds like wet laundry in the gap, which they'd made by throwing plywood from Millbank's stables over the wire. There were nineteen of them, as near as he could tell, what with their being blown open and running into each other like a casserole. He saw two women with babies in slings, and another who might've been pregnant.

"Give me a hand, asshole," Snopes said. He turned and vomited into the dust, wrapped a bandana over his face. They rolled out some tarp and got them ready for the chow wagon.

The bodies were pitifully light, skeletal, blistered skin flaking away, but they had walked out of Mexico alive. "We gotta get this shit in the chipper before lunchtime," Bascomb said. "Stiffs'll think it's Thanksgiving."

"Your wife'll be so happy," Snopes said, "she might even let you get some."

"Fuck you, Mark. Least I got something to come home to . . ."

They lifted one by the hands and feet, and were trying to sling it over on the tarp without spilling its innards, when Chet Bamberger came limping across the yard, with his chain and a chunk of drywall dragging behind him.

"Oh fuck," Snopes cried, and let go of the corpse's feet.

Bascomb let go a hair too late, and blundered into the piles of razor wire. He shrieked, "Eeeeyagh!" and jerked up, but the curling steel teeth snagged his uniform and flabby back and dragged him back into the thickest of it.

Like all Ocotillo's registered dead citizens, Chet wore a chain and a leather muzzle with a bike lock on the back, and only a tiny hole for eating. They were fed slurry and carrion from the chow wagon, but said supply had petered out as even the dead stopped coming down the road.

Chet wasn't wearing his muzzle.

Snopes's left hand went out to pull Bascomb free, while his right tried to draw his gun. Neither effort met with much success.

Chet ignored them. He ambled over to the pile of bodies and squatted over one, lifted a neatly bisected hemisphere of a woman's skull and slurped at it like a slice of cantaloupe. Snopes smashed Bamberger's grill in when he put on the muzzle, so the slobbering hole he chewed his food with had no teeth in it.

Somehow, this only made him more repulsive, more threatening. His crumbling gray hide was pocked with burns and brands, and carved words. A Camel Filter butt jutted out of his left ear, and his right ear was melted off. With no TV and no Indian casinos down the road, Connie had been forced to take up a new hobby, but nobody had filed a complaint, so who was he to judge?

The jingling music of the approaching chow wagon echoed through the streets. "Music Box Dancer" today, thank God. Snopes didn't know why, but if he heard "Do You Know the Way to San Jose" one more time, *he* was going to eat somebody's brains.

Chet's eyes were pointed at Snopes, but they were as vital as soft-boiled eggs, and was there any remorse in them, any horror, at what he'd become? Was there any spark of anything worth saving, in the rancid mayonnaise behind those dead eyes? Had there ever been?

Snopes drew his gun and shot Chet Bamberger through the left eye, and then, because it wouldn't close, through the right.

The chow wagon pulled up in a cloud of dust. Something about the old ice cream truck always creeped Snopes out, even when it still sold ice cream. Now, with racks of chainsaws, baling hooks and flamethrowers and a wood-chipper in tow, and all the Rocket Pop and Dove Bar stickers slathered in sun-baked blood and clouds of ecstatic flies, the chow wagon only brought relief; somebody else to clean up this mess.

"Murderer! Fucking murderer!" Fists drummed on Snopes's back, ineffectual against his bulletproof vest, but knocking him off-balance when he tried to help Bascomb get free.

Connie Bamberger kicked Snopes in the crotch. He tripped and fell on the body pile. His hand snagged in a body cavity and half a baby spilled down the back of his neck.

"Murderer! Arrest him, Doug! *I want justice!*"

They grabbed him when he came into the courtroom. It was dark, but he recognized the deep-fried roadkill smell of Torres, who ran the Indian Skillet across the street, and Sturtevant's livestock stink, McBride by the whiskey on his breath. Bascomb unsnapped his holster and took his gun.

Connie Bamberger sobbed uncontrollably on the witness stand. Judge Dooling sat at the edge of the lampglow with his hand on the revolver. "Now, Mrs. Bamberger has given her testimony, and her complaint has been reviewed."

"What is this shit?" Snopes shouted. "Get off me, it was self defense."

"Witnesses say otherwise. Mr. Bamberger was not aggressive, and the illegal aliens' refuse was going to be processed for feed, in any event. You took a citizen's life in cold blood, Deputy. You broke the law, and it is very clear."

"That's not the real goddamned law! It's not murder! Chet was already dead!" Snopes struggled in the arms of the other men, but Bascomb jabbed him in the back with his own gun. As his eyes adjusted to the light, he saw the gloomy courtroom was packed with people, half the surviving town gathered to watch.

"All of us are equal before the law, Mark. I can't sentence you to death, but you've shown that you cannot be trusted to wield force in our defense. We'll have to ask for your badge."

Someone ripped it off his uniform. "Fine, take it and fuck you all."

"Excellent. And now, Doctor, tie off his arms."

Snopes bucked backwards, throwing Sturtevant into Torres, and driving Bascomb back into the door. His gun went off into the ceiling. Snopes jumped for the door, but Bascomb was quicker, and smashed him across the back of the head. The lamplight turned into a golden lava lamp glow, and he collapsed on a plastic tarp.

Dr. McBride was a veterinarian and a drunk, but he was Ocotillo's only medical authority, so he tied Snopes off at the elbows, and pumped him with a syringe that made the trippy light into a pointillist cloudscape.

"Son, I'm sorry as hell," McBride whispered in his ear. "We all know why you did it, but there's gotta be law, and the law's gotta be blind. My son, he's dead, but he's walking, so who's to say he won't get better? If we let you go on like you done—"

Judge Dooling banged his gavel. "Don't badger the prisoner, Walter. Deputy Bascomb, proceed."

Bascomb still bled from divots the razorwire gouged out of his neck, scalp and arms, but he did not hesitate to drag his partner's right arm out across the floor and step on the wrist, heft the axe and slam it into the inside of Snopes's elbow.

From head to toe, he was bathed in lightning. Screaming blood and vomit and streaming tears, Snopes tried to fight, but he couldn't even get the breath to scream for mercy when they tugged the other one away from his chest and chopped it off, as well.

A little blood oozed out of the tourniquets, but Dr. McBride cauterized the stumps with a blowtorch and pronounced him sound.

The gavel banged again. "Court is adjourned. Deputy, leave the defendant where he is. I'd like a word. No, touch nothing—"

Snopes lay there, watching the silhouettes of the people he'd sworn to protect and serve file past the tarp. The sight of his severed arms, splayed out in front of him like spare parts from a model kit, was very unsettling; but he couldn't remember why until he reached out to touch them.

He still couldn't scream, but he found it very easy to cry.

When the courtroom was empty, Judge Dooling rose from the bench, shuffled over to Snopes, and knelt beside him.

"I know you think this is very cruel and unusual, Mark, but we all have to learn to submit to something bigger than ourselves."

Snopes' response was garbled, even to himself.

The judge sighed, touched his shoulder. "You think this is insane, but you are fortunate not to be able to understand. You probably won't remember this, but I wish you would, so you could see how wrong you were, as time goes by, about the risen population of Ocotillo.

"The dead are not wholly incapable of recovery, Mr. Snopes."

Dooling brought his face down closer to the deputy and picked up his severed left forearm. He stroked Snopes's face with his own fingers, then took a bite out of the meaty belly of the exposed muscle, just above the clean cut at the elbow.

"We *are* getting better," His Honor said around a mouthful of flesh. "Order has been restored. We will rebuild our town, and it will be better than it ever was, with equal liberty and justice for *all* its citizens."

Snopes had all but blacked out. His last clear memory was of the Judge: wiping his blood-slick lips, taking the scorched stumps of his arms in his hands, and licking them with his gray, ulcerated tongue, just like a stamp.

But he heard him get up and call for Bascomb. "You're free to go."

CODY GOODFELLOW has written three solo novels and three more with John Skipp. His latest collection of short fiction is *All-Monster Action*. He lives in Los Angeles, where he patronizes the same gas station as Mr. T.

*Everybody she knew got to be a Deadie. Everybody but her. But the
Deadies didn't want Paddy. She stank wrong . . .*

Going Down

Nancy Kilpatrick

Shortly after the Deadies got up to stroll the boards on Manitoulin Island,
Paddy ran out of meds.

She'd been on Largactil for years—brain mangulations, dry gut ruttings,
critical BO. The stuff stripped polish off floors and tasted rat-poison sweet
so her insides undoubtedly resembled the arm of a kid she'd seen gnawed
by a combine. She could've lived with that, though. But when everybody
started coming back from the dead and chomping on everybody else, what
was the point of taking drugs, even if she had any, with so much good film
noir available?

Still, those asphyxiation-blue tabs had propped up everything crumbling
inside her skull. Like the retaining wall that kept water from swallowing
the land, her wall had worked pretty good most of the time. But nothing
aired on TV anymore. Or radio. The movie theater closed. Her retaining
wall was eroding fast.

Paddy opened Daddy's channel changer and twisted the wires so she
could corkscrew holes in her wrist. The vein kept jumping out of the way
and she ended up with ten round oozing bloodeyes. She sucked and tasted
fresh flesh. Shit, she thought, now that the Deadies trudge the pebbles
on the lakefront around the clock, nobody's left to ferry to the mainland.
She'd seen all the videos and DVDs on the island. The pills from the drug
store might be gone, but residue floating in her blood stream still broadcast
too loud and clear. Anyway, the second Marilyn Monroe got back, that
signal would dim. Marilyn would like the Deadies, at least Paddy thought
she would.

God knows, Paddy liked them. She'd tried to join their club before there was a club and if she'd done it right she'd have been a charter member. ODs. Hemp slung over the beam in Daddy's root cellar, where he used to lower his pants and pull down her . . . She'd dropped her eyelids once and the screen went blank. *Marilyn's steady hand plunged the bread knife into her heart.* She missed the projector and Paddy'd been pissed. Her lung felt like badly spliced videotape and that's all. *Marilyn refused to visit Paddy the whole time she was in General Hospital.* Paddy'd thrown a fit until they gave her more drugs and a new flat screen TV.

Life had been *tabula rasa* with no chalk. But then the Deadies started. Right away Paddy saw they were luckier than her. They never worried about getting aced in the butt by stray emissions and they didn't have to memorize lines. Anyway, did they care why they were chained to this rocky poor-reception island or wonder who would rip out their liver this week in 3-D or make them sit in a hair seat and suck in a teen comedy then fuck them doggie style with blurry trailers, or any of the other stuff Paddy worried about all the time? All they thought about was grabbing somebody with their slimy green hands to snack on. She could handle that. She could be a Deadie.

But the Deadies didn't want Paddy. She stank wrong.

"It's an insult," *Marilyn assured her when she finally deigned to visit. She waved a spotless silk hanky in front of her perfect transparent nose. Paddy was hurt until Marilyn said she had an idea.*

"Shove your fingers past their cold black lips, into a living porridge mouth and let things crawl over your skin. Action!" *Marilyn giggled.*

Paddy tried it. No cracked molars clamped. No spoiled tongue licked. The switched-off eyes didn't flicker. "I'm not good enough for them," she whined. *Marilyn slapped her silly and shrieked, "I told you before, diamonds are a girl's best friend."*

Paddy felt iced as the black waters rose. The volume increased. Dense moisture plugged every orifice of her body like giant chilled-wax suppositories and the world slipped away on basic hypodermic steel.

Everybody she knew got to be a Deadie.

Everybody but her.

Meryl Streep, Tom Cruise, those anonymous B-zombie brats with mouse-turded hair and kiss-my-deceased-ass grins. Everybody on the island she hated, and that was everybody but Daddy. *Even Marilyn got to chat with the Deadies at the Bus Stop and they listened like she emitted extra-terrestrial short waves, but she said it was because she was an Icon and closer to them than Paddy could ever be. That made Paddy real mad, especially when Marilyn signaled Daddy.*

Nobody sent signals to her Daddy but her!

Paddy tore Marilyn's white arms and legs and ears off and pulled the blond hairs out of her pube until she stopped broadcasting.

Paddy squatted on a boulder eating a double box of Twinkies and drinking warm Upper Canada Lager from the big tins. Two Deadies lumbered after Rewind, one of the last living dogs left. The collie belonged to the Woods, who used to run the video shop. As the three got closer, Paddy saw it was the formerly living Mr. and Mrs. Woods lunging at their golden-haired pooch. Rewind bounded like he was having fun. So did the Deadie Woods. To Paddy's camera eye, they made a nice nuclear family.

Man, she thought, life is incompletely unfair. All the two dimensionals get everything and people like me who are the truly brilliant and can satellite dish every movie channel are relegated to minor sitcoms. How'd *they* like to be inside out for a living? Life always tunes you out. It's depressing as hell. She swallowed a couple of Tylenol to the third power she'd found in Mrs. Soles' medicine cabinet. At least they had codeine in them and that was better than nothing, almost.

She chucked a pill-shaped stone at the stinky mold-gray water and it skipped the surface. One. Two. Three. Three was the right button. She clicked on a Dolly Parton song, turning up the volume on the old tape player so she could masturbate in peace. The Deadies didn't notice. Mr. Woods had caught Rewind and they were biting each other, which was fun to watch, until Mrs. Woods joined in and blocked Paddy's view.

As Rewind howled, Dolly wailed about never gettin' what you need when you need it. Yeah, don't I know it, Paddy thought. Her body spasmed. Like killing yourself's easy. She wiped sticky fingers on her filthy shirttail and shoved another Twinkie all the way into her mouth. Everybody thinks it is but that just shows you what they know. If it was easy, everybody would have been dead before she was born and Paddy'd have managed it by now too.

Shit! She kicked dirt at Fat Eddie the Deadie as he passed. He ignored her, just like he always had. She wanted to be part of the Deadies more than she'd ever wanted anything. Maybe, when Marilyn came for her next visit, *she* could figure some way for Paddy to get in with them, to make them see Paddy's dead potential. Dolly sang about possibilities. If only

Paddy could be a Deadie, she just knew she'd be happy forever like Miss Dolly Parton. She closed her eyes.

"Take three hundred and twelve: Norma Jean to the Rescue!" Marilyn appeared half naked and boxed Paddy's ears good until she was bored. Finally the sex goddess grabbed the last Twinkie and admitted, "I've been working on a plan."

"It's about time," Paddy said, wiping blood from her ear lobe.

Marilyn tilted backwards and hiked up her full white skirt until her pink lips grinned at the camera. She shoved the Twinkie up inside herself and crooned, "Happy Birthday to You."

Paddy opened her eyes. Rewind, or what was left of him, lay in the background of the shot, a golden prop, much of Mr. Woods' forearm sticking out of his mouth. Suddenly this movie came into sharp focus.

Paddy's daddy wandered home every night by instinct, just the way he used to before he became a Deadie. Not that he needed rest. He never had; he was no different now.

Paddy boarded up the windows. *Marilyn nailed a two by four tornado warning across the door.*

Daddy stared, eyes hungry, same as always. Finally Paddy picked up his mottled hand and hauled him down to the root cellar, the way he'd done with her all her life.

She lit the hurricane lamp. Bushel baskets of rotting potatoes and carrots and cabbage lined the shelves and the floor was littered with broken jars with pickled foods she'd put away she didn't know when. The place stank, but no worse than Daddy.

She positioned him on a Peaches and Cream Corn crate. His glazed, half-rotted eyeballs wandered the room aimlessly, like he didn't recognize anything. Paddy was used to that. All the Deadies resided in Bliss, a drive-in theater she hoped to visit real soon.

Marilyn stood in a corner, legs spread, hands on knees, cleavage scrumptious, waiting for the wind to whistle up her skirt on cue. Paddy nodded. Daddy's head kept bobbing like an antenna in a storm because his neck had snapped so she held it steady and made him look in her direction, but she couldn't get his eyes to stay put. Black mixed media belched from his lips; his digestive juices were working; he must be watching the screen.

Marilyn hiked her skirt and turned. Paddy, skirt lifted, waved her backside at Daddy's oscillating face, the way he always liked. Nothing.

Marilyn peeked over her shoulder and pouted her lips into an 'O'. Paddy planted a movie smooch on Daddy's crisp lips. His rotted nose mashed against her cheek and a chunk with crusty stuff inside broke off. *A blowfly with eyes like Daddy's emerged. "Thanks ever so!" the fly said. Paddy yelled at Marilyn, "Cut!" MM tossed back her platinum hair, thrust out her tits and giggled.*

Paddy glanced down at her nearly flat chest and felt lousy. Daddy had always hungered for her before and now he didn't and now she was truly alone on this set. She plunked down onto the dirt floor and cried, something she hadn't done since way before she started taking the meds she'd run out of. The leak created micro mud puddles between her legs. *The fly dived into one and bathed. He smiled up at her with Technicolor eyes in all his clear iridescent holiness and winked.* Paddy found enlightenment. She saw the solution to all her troubles.

"It's a wrap," she said, but MM refused to vacate the studio. Instead, she straddled a Mason jar of pickled banana peppers and mumbled on and on about misfits and how some of them like it hot. Paddy fast forwarded.

She crawled to Daddy and peeled rotting fabric from his groin. His penis, always so big and full, dangled like a thick black connecting cable with green eyes. The eyes leaked puss-yellow tears that white life forms swam in. *Those baby bugs are joining heads to tails! Paddy realized, astonished. The word LOVE flashed onto the screen and a ball bounced along the letters. Wasn't this what Dolly Parton always sang about, and what Marilyn always got?* Now Paddy knew exactly what everybody meant.

She closed her eyes and opened her mouth.

And bit.

Daddy didn't complain. He didn't seem to miss his cock.

Paddy sat back on her haunches and munched.

Marilyn skipped over with a rotting banana pepper dangling from her wet lips. "When it's hot like this, I store my undies in the ice box."

Made sense to Paddy. She swallowed the last bits of her Daddy, the bits that meant anything to her. He tasted like all the buttered popcorn they ever ate watching movies together.

As his head bobbed her way, he grinned like he used to, and Paddy felt proud. At last she'd landed a part in The Deadie Movie. She would play Daddy's Little Deadie Girl and the movie would run forever, or at least until the reel ran out of film.

Award-winning author and editor NANCY KILPATRICK has published eighteen novels, two hundred short stories, one non-fiction book, and has edited a number of anthologies including *Evolve: Vampire Stories of the New Undead* (2010) and *Evolve Two: Vampire Stories of the Future Undead* (2011). Upcoming books include a graphic novel Nancy Kilpatrick's *Vampyre Theater* (Brainstorm Comics); a new collection of her short fiction and novellas *Vampyric Variations*; and as editor, the anthology *Danse Macabre: Close Encounters With the Reaper* (both from Edge SF&F Publishing). She is currently editing her thirteenth anthology, *Expiry Date*, and writing seven novels at once, because insanity runs in her family! Check her website for details (www.nancykilpatrick.com) and she invites you to join her on Facebook.

What had happened was inexplicable and its scale incomprehensible. In the space of just a few minutes something—a germ, virus, or biological attack perhaps—had destroyed his world.

Home

David Moody

Steninger is less than two hours away from home. He hasn't been this close for almost a month. He hasn't been this close since it happened. Twenty-three days ago millions of people died as the world fell apart around him.

I've been here hundreds of times before but it's never looked like this. Georgie and I used to drive up here at weekends to walk the dog over the hills. We'd let him off the lead and then walk and talk and watch him play for hours. That was long before the events which have since kept us apart. It all feels like a lifetime ago now. Today the green, rolling landscape I remember is washed out and gray and everything is cold, lifeless and dead. I am alone and the world is decaying around me. It's early in the morning, perhaps an hour before sunrise, and there's a layer of light mist clinging to the ground. I can see them moving all around me. They're everywhere. Shuffling. Staggering. Hundreds of the fucking things.

One last push and I'll be home. I'm beginning to feel scared now. For days I've struggled to get back here but, now I'm this close, I don't know if I can go through with it. Seeing what's left of Georgie and our home will hurt. It's been so long and so much has happened since we were last together. I don't know if I'll have the strength to walk through the front door. I don't know if I'll be able to stand the pain of remembering everything that's gone and all that I've lost.

I'm as nervous and scared now as I was when this nightmare began. I remember it as if it was only hours ago, not weeks. I was in a breakfast meeting with my lawyer and one of his staff when it started. Jarvis, the solicitor, was explaining some legal jargon to me when he stopped speaking mid-sentence. He suddenly screwed up his face with pain. I asked him what was wrong but he couldn't answer. His breathing became shallow and short and he started to rasp and cough and splutter. He was choking but I couldn't see why and I was concentrating so hard on what was happening to him that I didn't notice it had got the other man too. As Jarvis' face paled and he began to scratch and claw at his throat his colleague lurched forward and tried to grab hold of me. Eyes bulging, he retched and showered me with blood and spittle. I recoiled and pushed my chair back away from the table. Too scared to move, I stood with my back pressed against the wall and watched the two men as they choked to death. It was over and the room was silent in less than a couple of minutes.

When I eventually plucked up the courage to get out and get help I found the receptionist who had greeted me less than an hour earlier face down on her desk in a pool of sticky red-brown blood. The security man on the door was dead too, as was everyone else I could see. It was the same when I finally dared step out into the open—an endless layer of twisted human remains covered the ground in every direction I looked. What had happened was inexplicable and its scale incomprehensible. In the space of just a few minutes something—a germ, virus or biological attack perhaps—had destroyed my world. Nothing moved. The silence was deafening.

My first instinct had been to stay where I was, to keep my head down and wait for something—anything—to happen. I slowly walked back to the hotel as it was the only nearby place I knew well, picking my way through the bodies which carpeted the streets, staring at each of them in turn and looking deep into their grotesque, twisted faces. Each face was frozen in an expression of sudden, searing agony and gut-wrenching fear.

When I got back the hotel was as silent and cold as everywhere else. I locked myself in my room and waited there for hours until the solitude finally became too much to stand. I needed explanations but there was no one else left alive to ask for help. The television was useless, as was the radio, and the telephone went unanswered. Desperate, I packed my few belongings, took a car from the car park, and made a break for home. But I soon found that the hushed roads were impassable, blocked by the tangled wreckage of incalculable numbers of crashed vehicles and the mangled, bloody remains of their dead drivers and passengers. With my wife and my home still more than eighty miles away I stopped the car and gave up.

It was early on the first Thursday, the third day, when the situation deteriorated again to the point where I began to question my sanity. I had been resting in the front bedroom of an empty terraced house when I looked out of the window and saw the first one of them staggering down the road. All the fear and nervousness I had previously felt instantly disappeared and was forgotten as I watched the lone figure walk awkwardly down the street. It was another survivor, I thought, it had to be. At last, someone else who might be able to tell me what had happened and who could answer some of the thousands of impossible questions I desperately needed to ask. I yelled out to the figure and banged on the window but it didn't respond. I sprinted out of the house and ran down the road after it. I grabbed hold of its arm and turned it round to face me. As unbelievable as it seemed, I knew instantly that the thing in front of me was dead. Its eyes were clouded, covered with a milky-white film, and its skin was pockmarked and bloodied. And it was cold to the touch . . . I held its left wrist in my hand and felt for a pulse but found nothing. The creature's skin felt unnaturally clammy and leathery and I let it go in disgust. The moment I released my grip the damn thing shuffled slowly away, this time moving back in the direction from which it had just come. It couldn't see me. It didn't even seem to know I was there.

Out of the corner of my eye I became aware of more movement. I turned and saw another body, then another and then another. I walked to the end of the road and stared in disbelief at what was happening all around me. The dead were rising. Many were already staggering around on clumsy, unsteady feet whilst still more were slowly dragging themselves up from where they'd fallen and died days earlier.

A frantic search for food and water and somewhere safe to shelter led me back deeper into town. Avoiding the clumsy, mannequin-like bodies that roamed the streets I barricaded myself in a large pub which stood proudly on the corner of two once busy roads. I cleared eight corpses out of the building (I herded them all into the bar before forcing them out the front door) and then locked myself in an upstairs function room where I started to drink. Although it didn't make me drunk like it used to, the alcohol made me feel warm and took the very slightest edge off my fear.

I thought constantly about Georgie and home but I was too afraid to move. I knew that I should try to get to her but for days I just sat there and waited like a useless, chickenshit coward. Every morning I tried to force myself to leave but the thought of going back out into what remained of the world was unbearable. I didn't know what I'd find out there and instead I sat in booze-fueled isolation and watched the world decay.

As the days passed the bodies themselves changed. Initially stiff, awkward and staccato, their movements slowly became more purposeful and controlled. After four days I observed that their senses were beginning to return. They were starting to respond to what was happening around them. Late one afternoon in a fit of frightened frustration, I hurled an empty beer bottle across the room. I missed the wall and smashed a window. Out of curiosity I looked down into the street below and saw that huge numbers of the corpses had turned in response to the sudden noise and were beginning to walk towards the pub. Attracted by the clattering sound (which seemed louder than it actually was in the otherwise all-consuming silence) they began to shuffle relentlessly closer and closer. During the hours that followed I tried to keep quiet and out of sight but my every movement seemed to make more of them aware of my presence. From every direction they came and all that I could do was watch as a crowd of hundreds of the fucking things surrounded me. They followed each other like animals and soon their lumbering, decomposing shapes filled the streets for as far as I could see.

A week went by, and the ferocity of the creatures outside increased. They began to fight with each other and they fought to get to me. They clawed and banged at the doors but didn't yet have the strength to get inside. My options were hopelessly limited but I knew that I had to do something. I could stay where I was and hope that I could drink enough so that I didn't care when the bodies eventually broke through, or I could make a break for freedom and take my chances outside. I had nothing to lose. I thought about home and I thought about Georgie and I knew that I had to try and get back to her.

It wasn't much of a plan but it was all that I had. I packed all the meager supplies and provisions I found lying around the pub into a rucksack and got myself ready to leave. I made crates of crude bombs from the liquor bottles I found behind the bar and down in the cellar and storeroom. As the light began to fade at the end of the tenth day I leant out of the broken window at the front of the building, lit the booze-soaked rag fuses which I had stuffed down the necks of the bottles, and then began to hurl them down into the rotting crowds below me. In minutes I'd created more devastation and confusion than I ever would have imagined possible. There had been little rain for days. Tinder dry and packed tightly together, the repugnant bodies caught light almost instantly. Oblivious to the flames which quickly consumed them, the damn things continued to move about for as long as they were physically able, their every staggering step spreading the fire still further and destroying more and more of them. And the dancing orange light of the sudden inferno and the crackling and popping of burning flesh drew even more of the desperate cadavers closer to the scene.

I crept downstairs and waited by the back door. The building itself was soon alight. Doubled-up with hunger pains (the world outside had suddenly become filled with the smell of roast meat) I crouched down in the darkness and waited until the rising temperature in the building had become too much to stand. When the flames began to lick at the final door separating me from the rest of the pub I pushed my way out into the night and ran through the bodies. Their reactions were dull and slow and my speed and strength and the surprise of my sudden appearance meant that they offered virtually no resistance. In the silent, monochrome world, the confusion that I'd generated provided enough of a distraction to camouflage my movements and render me temporarily invisible.

Since I've been on the move I've learned to live like a shadow. My difficult journey home has been painfully long and slow. I move only at night under cover of darkness. If the bodies see or hear me they will come for me and, as I've found to my cost on more than one occasion, once one of them has my scent then countless others will follow. I have avoided them as much as possible but their numbers are vast and some contact has been inevitable. I'm getting better at dealing with them. The initial disgust and trepidation I felt has now given way to hate and anger. Through necessity I have become a cold and effective killer, although I'm not sure whether that's an accurate description of my new found skill. I have to keep reminding myself that these bloody aberrations are already dead.

Apart from the mass of bodies I managed to obliterate during my escape from the pub, the first corpse I intentionally disposed of had once been a priest. I came across the rancid, emaciated creature when I took shelter at dawn one morning in a small village church. It had appeared empty at first until I pushed my way into a narrow storeroom at the far end of the gray-stone building. I was immediately aware of shuffling movement ahead of me. A small window high on the wall to my left let a limited amount of light spill into the storeroom, allowing me to see the outline of the body of the priest as it tripped towards me. The cadaver was weak and barely coordinated and I instinctively grabbed hold of it and threw it back across the room. It smashed into a shelf piled high with prayer books and then crumbled to the ground, bringing the books crashing down on top of it. Moving its leaden arms and legs incessantly, it struggled to pull itself back up onto its dead feet. I stared into its vacant, hollowed face as it dragged itself into the light again. The first body I had seen up close for several days, it was a fucking mess. Just a shadow of the man it had once been, the creature's skin appeared taut and translucent and it had an unnatural green-gray hue. Its cheeks and eye sockets were sunken and its mouth and chin speckled with dribbles of dried blood. Its black shirt and dog-collar hung loose around its scrawny neck.

For a moment I was distracted by the thing's sickening appearance and it caught me by surprise when it charged at me again. I was knocked off-balance momentarily before managing to grab hold of it by the throat and straightening my arm to keep it at a safe distance. Its limbs flailed around me as I looked deep into its cloudy, emotionless eyes. I used my free hand to feel around for something to use as a weapon. My outstretched fingers wrapped around a heavy and ornate candleholder behind me and to my right. I gripped it tightly and lifted it high above my head before bringing the base of it crashing down on the dead priest's exposed skull. Stunned but undeterred, the body tripped back before coming for me again. I lifted the candleholder and smashed it down again and again until there was little left of the head of the corpse other than a dark and unrecognizable mass of blood, brain and shattered bone. I stood over the twitching remains of the cleric until it finally lay still.

I hid in the bell tower of the church and waited for the night to come.

It didn't take long to work out the rules.

Although they have become increasingly violent as time has gone on, these creatures are simple and predictable. I think that they are driven purely by instinct. What remains of their brains seem to operate on a very basic, primitive level and each one is little more than a fading memory of what it used to be. I quickly learnt that this reality is nothing like the trash horror movies I used to watch or the books I used to read. These things don't want to kill me so that they can feast on my flesh. In fact I don't actually think they have any physical needs or desires—they don't eat, drink, sleep or even breathe as far as I can see. So why do they attack me and why do I have to creep through the shadows in fear of them? It's a paradox but the longer I think about it, the more convinced I am that they attack me because of the threat I pose to them. I'm different and stronger and I think they know that I could destroy them. I think they try to attack me before I have chance to attack them.

Over the last few days and weeks I have watched them steadily disintegrate and decay. Another bizarre irony—as their bodies have continued to weaken and become more fragile, so their mental control seems to have returned. They seem to want to continue to exist at all costs and will respond violently to any perceived threat. Sometimes they fight between themselves and I have hidden in the darkness and watched them set about each other until almost all of their rotten flesh has been stripped from their bones.

I know beyond doubt now that the brain remains the center of control. My second, third and fourth kills confirmed that. I had forced my way into an isolated house in search of food and fresh clothes when I found myself face to face with the rotting remains of what appeared to have once been a fairly typical family. I quickly disposed of the father with a short wooden fence post that I had been carrying with me to use as a makeshift weapon. I smacked the repulsive creature around the side of the head again and again until it had almost been decapitated. The next body—the first corpse's dead wife, I presumed—had proved to be more troublesome. I pushed my way through a ground floor doorway and entered a large, square dining room. The body of the woman hurled itself at me from across the room with sudden, unexpected speed. I held the picket out in front of me and skewered the fucking thing through the chest. Its withered torso and parchment skin offered next to no resistance as the wood plunged deep into its abdomen and straight out the other side. I retched and struggled to keep control of my stomach as the remains of its putrefied organs slid out of the hole I had made in its back and slopped down onto the dusty cream-colored carpet in a greasy crimson-black heap. I pushed the body away expecting it to collapse and crumble like the last one had but it didn't. Instead it staggered after me, still impaled and struggling to move as I had obviously caused a massive amount of damage to its spine with the fence picket. I panicked as it lurched closer. I turned and ran to the kitchen and grabbed the largest knife I could find before returning to the body. It had managed to take a few more steps forward but stopped immediately when I plunged the knife through its right temple into the core of what remained of its brain. It was as if someone had flicked a switch. The body slumped and slid off the knife and dropped at my feet like a bloodied rag-doll. In the silence that followed I could hear the third body thumping around upstairs. To prove my theory I ran up the stairs and disposed of a dead teenager in the same way as its mother with a single stab of the blade to the head.

It is wrong and unsettling but I have to admit that I've grown to enjoy the kill. The reality is that it's the only pleasure that remains to me. It's the only time I have complete control. I haven't ever gone looking for sport, but I haven't avoided it either. I've kept a tally of kills along the way and I've begun to pride myself on finding quicker, quieter and more effective ways of destroying the dead. I took a gun from a police station a week or so ago but quickly got rid of it. A shot to the head will immediately take out a single body, but I've found to my cost that the resultant noise invariably makes thousands more of the damn things aware of my location. Weapons now need to be silent and swift. I've tried to use clubs and axes and whilst they've often been effective, real sustained effort is usually needed to get results. Fire is too visible and unpredictable and so blades have become my weapons of choice. I now carry seventeen in all—buck knifes, sheath knives, Bowie knifes, scalpels and even pen knives. I carry two butcher's meat cleavers holstered like pistols and I hold a machete drawn and ready at all times.

I've made steady progress so far today. I know this stretch of footpath well. It twists and turns and it's not the most direct route home but it's my best option this morning. Dawn is beginning to break. The light is getting stronger now and I'm starting to feel uncomfortably exposed. I've not been out in daylight for weeks now. I've become used to the dark and the protection it affords me.

This short stretch of path runs alongside a golf course. There seems to be an unusually high number of bodies around here. I think this was the seventh hole—a short but tough hole with a raised tee and an undulating fairway from what I remember. Many of the corpses seem to have become trapped in the natural dip of the land here and the once well-tended grass has been churned to mud beneath their clumsy feet. They can't get away. Stupid fucking things are stuck. Sometimes I almost feel privileged to have the opportunity to rid the world of a few of these pointless creatures. All that separates me from them now is a wooden fence and a stretch of tangled, patchy hedgerow. I keep quiet and take each step with care for fear of making any unnecessary noise that might alert them to my presence here. I could deal with them, but it will be much easier if I don't have to.

The path arcs away to the left. There are two bodies up ahead of me now and I know I have no choice but to dispose of them. The second one seems to be following the first and I wonder whether there are any more behind. However many of them there are, I know I'll have to deal with them quickly. It will take too long to try going around them and any sudden movement will alert any others that might be moving through the shadows nearby. The safest and easiest option is to go straight at them and cut them both down.

Here's the first. It's seen me. It makes a sudden, lurching change in direction, revealing its intent. With its dull, misted eyes fixed on me it starts to come my way. Bloody hell, it's badly decayed—one of the worst I've seen. I can't even tell whether it used to be male or female. Most of its face has been eaten away and its mottled, pock-marked skull is dotted with clumps of long, lank and greasy gray-blond hair. It's dragging one foot behind it. In fact, now that it's closer I can see that it only has one foot! Its right ankle ends unexpectedly with a dirty stump it drags awkwardly through the mud. The rags wrapped around the corpse look like they might once have been a uniform of sorts. Was this a police officer? A traffic warden perhaps? Whatever it used to be, its time is now up.

I've developed a two-cut technique for getting rid of corpses. It's safer than running headlong at them swinging a blade through the air like a madman. A little bit of control makes all the difference. The bodies are usually already unsteady (this one certainly is) so I tend to use the first cut to try and stop them moving or at least slow them down. The body is close enough now. I crouch down and swing the machete from right to left, severing both of its legs at knee level with a single swipe. With the corpse now flat on what's left of its stomach I reverse the movement and, backhanded, slam the blade down through its neck before it has time to move. Easy. Kill number one hundred and thirty-eight. Number one hundred and thirty-nine proves to be slightly harder. I slip and bury the blade in the creature's pelvis when I was aiming lower. No problem—with the corpse brought down to its knees by the force of my first strike I lift the machete again and bring it down on the top of its head. The skull splits easily like an egg. It's harder pulling the blade out than it was getting it in.

I never think of the bodies as people any more. There's no point. Whatever caused all of this has wiped out every trace of individuality and character from the rotting masses. Generally they all now behave and act the same—age, race, sex, class, religion and all other previously notable social differences are gone. There are no distinctions, there are only the dead; a single massive decaying population. Kill number twenty-six brought it home to me. Obviously the body of a very young child, it had attacked me with as much force and intent as the countless other "adult" creatures I had come across. I had hesitated for a split-second before the kill but then I did it just the same. I knew that what it used to be was of no importance now—it was dead flesh and it needed to be destroyed. I took its head clean off its shoulders with a hand-axe and hardly gave it another thought.

Distances which should take minutes to cover are now taking me hours. I'm working my way along a wide footpath that leads down into the heart of Stonemorton. I can see bodies everywhere I look. The earlier mist has lifted and I can now see their slow stumbling shapes moving between houses and dragging themselves along otherwise empty streets. My already slow speed seems to have reduced still further now that it's getting light. Maybe I'm subconsciously slowing myself down? The closer I get to home, the more nervous and unsure I feel. I try to concentrate and focus my thoughts on Georgie. All I want is to see her and be with her again, what's happened to the rest of the world is of no interest. I'm realistic about what I'm going to find—I haven't seen another living soul for weeks and I don't think for a second that I'll find her alive, but I've survived, haven't I? There is still some slight hope. My worst fear is that the house will be empty, because then I'll have to keep looking. I won't rest until we're together again.

Damn. Suddenly there are another four bodies up ahead of me. The closer I get to the streets, the more of them there are. I can't be completely sure how many are here as their awkward, gangly shapes seem to merge and disappear into the background of gnarled, twisted trees. I'm not too worried about four. In fact I'm pretty confident dealing with anything up to ten. All I have to do is take my time, keep calm and try not to make more noise than I have to. The last thing I want to do is let any more of them know where I am.

The nearest body has locked onto me and is lining itself up to be kill number one hundred and forty. Bloody hell, this is the tallest corpse I've seen. Even though its back is twisted into an uncomfortable stoop it's still taller than me. I need to lower it to get a good shot at the brain. I swing the machete up between its legs and practically split it in two. It slumps at my feet and I swipe its head clean off its shoulders before it's even hit the mud.

One hundred and forty-one. This one is more lively than most. I've come across a few like this from time to time. For some reason bodies like this one are not as badly decayed as the majority of the dead and for a split second I start to wonder whether this might actually be a survivor. When it lunges at me with sudden, clumsy force I know immediately that it is already dead. I lift up my blade and put it in the way of the creature's head. Still moving forward it impales itself through its right eye and then falls limp as the machete slices through the center of its rotting brain.

My weapon is stuck, wedged tight in the skull of this fucking monstrosity and I can't pull it free. The next body is close now. As I tug at the machete with my right hand I yank one of the meat cleavers out of its holster with my left and swing it wildly at the shape now stumbling towards me. I make some contact but it's not enough. I've sliced diagonally across the width of its torso but it doesn't even seem to notice the damage. I let go of the machete (I'll go back for it when I'm done) and, using both cleavers now, I attack the third body again. The blow I strike with my left hand wedges the first blade deep into its shoulder, cutting through the collarbone and forcing the body down. I aim the second cut at the base of the neck and smash through the spinal cord. I push the cadaver down into the gravel and stamp on its expressionless face until my boot does enough damage to permanently stop the bloody thing moving. For a second I feel like a fucking Kung-fu master.

With the first cleaver still buried in the shoulder of the last body I'm now two weapons down with potential kill number one hundred and forty-three less than two meters away. This one is slower and it's got less fight in it than the last few. Breathing heavily I clench my fist and punch it square in the face. It wobbles for a second before dropping to the ground. I enjoy kills like that. My hand stings and is covered in all kinds of foul-smelling mess now but the sudden feeling of satisfaction, strength and superiority I have is immense.

I retrieve my two blades, clean them on a patch of grass, then carry on my way.

In the distance I can see the first few houses on the edge of the estate. I'm almost home now and I'm beginning to wish I wasn't. I've spent days on the move trying to get here—long, dark, lonely days filled with uncertainty. Now that I'm here there's a part of me that wants to turn around and go back. But I know there's nowhere else to go and I know I have to do this. I have to see it through.

I'm down at street level now and I'm more exposed than ever. Christ, everything looks so different to how I remember. It's been less than a month since I was last here but in that time the world has been left to rot and disintegrate along with its dead population. The smell of death is everywhere, choking, smothering and suffocating everything. The once clear gray pavements are sprouting with green-brown moss and weeds. Everything is crumbling around me. I've walked down plenty of city streets like this since it happened but this one feels different. I know this place, and it's the memories and familiarity that suddenly makes everything a hundred times harder to handle.

This is Huntingden Street. I used to drive this way to work. Almost all of this side of the road has been burnt to the ground and where there used to be a long, meandering row of between thirty and forty houses, now there's just a line of empty, wasted shells. The destruction seems to have altered the whole landscape and from where I'm standing I now have a clear view all the way over to the red-brick wall which runs along the edge of the estate where Georgie and I used to live. It's so close now. I've been rehearsing this part of the journey in my mind for days. I'm going to work my way back home by cutting through the back gardens of the houses along the way. I'm thinking that the back of each house should be pretty much secure and enclosed and I'll be able to take my time. There will probably be bodies along the way, but they should be fewer in number than those roaming the main roads.

I'm crouching down behind a low wall in front of what remains of one of the burnt out houses. I need to get across the road and into the garden at the back of one of the houses opposite. The easiest way will be to go straight through—in through the front door and out through the back. Everything looks clear. I can't see any bodies. Apart from my knives I'll leave everything here. I won't need any of it. I'm almost home now.

Slow going. Getting into the first garden was simple enough but it's not going as easy as I thought trying to move between properties. I'm having to climb over fences that are nowhere near strong enough to support my weight. I could just break them down but I'll make too much noise and I don't want to start taking unnecessary chances now.

Garden number three. I can see the dead owner of this house trapped inside its property, wearing a heavily stained dressing gown. It's leaning against the patio window and it starts hammering against the glass when it sees me. From my position mid-way down the lawn the figure at the window looks painfully thin and skeletal. I can see another body shuffling through the shadows behind it.

Garden number four. Fucking hell, the owner of this house is outside. It's moving towards me before I've even made it over the fence and the expression on what's left of its face is fucking terrifying. My heart's beating like it's going to explode as I jump down and ready myself. A few seconds wait that feels like forever, a single flash of the blade and it's done. The residual speed of the cadaver keeps it moving further down the lawn until it stumbles and falls. Its severed head lies at my feet, face down on the dew-soaked grass like a piece of rotten fruit. One hundred and forty-four.

Garden number five is clear, as is garden number six. I've now made it as far as the penultimate house. I sprint across the grass, scale the fence, and then jump down and run across the final strip of lawn until I reach another brick wall. On the other side of this wall is Partridge Road. The turning into my estate is another hundred meters or so down to my right.

I throw myself over the top of the wall and land heavily on the pavement below. Sudden searing pains shoot up my legs and I trip forward and fall into the road. There are bodies here. A quick look up and down the road and I can see seven or eight of them already. They've all seen me. This isn't good. No time for technique now—I have to get rid of them as quickly as possible. I take the first two out almost instantly with the machete. I start to run towards the road into the estate and I decapitate the third corpse at speed as I pass it. I push another one out of the way (no time to go back and finish it off) and then chop violently at the next one staggering into my path. I manage a single, brutal cut just above its, deep enough to hack through the spinal cord. It falls to the ground behind me, still moving but going nowhere. I count it as a kill anyway. One hundred and forty-eight.

I can see the entrance to the estate clearly now. The rusted wrecks of two crashed cars have almost completely blocked the mouth of the road like an improvised gate. Good. The blockage here means that there shouldn't be too many bodies on the other side. Damn, there are still more coming for me on this side though. Christ, there are loads of the bloody things. Where the hell are they coming from? I look up and down the road again and all I can see is a mass of twisted, stumbling corpses coming at me from every direction. My arrival here must have created more of a disturbance than I thought. There are too many of them for me to risk trying to deal with. Some are quicker than others and the first few are already close. Too close. I sprint towards the crashed cars as fast as I can. I drop my shoulder and barge several cadavers out of the way, my speed and weight easily smashing them to the ground. I jump onto the crumpled bonnet of the first car and then climb up onto its roof. I'm still only a few feet away from the hordes of rabid dead but I'm safer here. They haven't got the strength or coordination to be able to climb up after me. And even if they could, I'd just kick the fucking things back down again. I stand still for a few long seconds and catch my breath, staring down into the growing sea of decomposing faces below me. Their facial muscles are withered and decayed and they are incapable of controlled expression. Nevertheless, something about the way they look up at me reveals a cold and savage intent. They hate me. I want them to know that the feeling is mutual. If I had the time and energy I'd jump back down into the crowd and rip every last one of the fuckers apart.

Still standing on the roof of the car, I slowly turn around.

Home.

Torrington Road stretches out ahead of me now, wild and overgrown but still reassuringly familiar. Just ahead and to my right is the entrance to Harlour Grove. Our road. Our house is at the end of the cul-de-sac.

I'd stay here for a while and try to compose myself if it wasn't for the bodies snapping and scratching at my feet. I jump down from the car and take a few steps forward. I then turn back for a second—something's caught my eye. Now that I'm down I recognize the car I've just been standing on. I glance at the license plate at the back. It's cracked and smashed but I can still make out three letters together: HAL. This is Stan Isherwood's car. He lived four doors down from Georgie and I. And fucking hell, that thing in the front seat is what's left of Stan. I can see what remains of the retired bank manager slamming itself from side to side, trying desperately to get out of its seat and get to me. It's being held in place by its safety belt. Stupid bloody thing can't release the catch. Without thinking I crouch down and peer in through the grubby glass. My decomposing neighbor stops moving for a fraction of a second and looks straight back at me. Jesus Christ, there's not much left of him but I can still see that it's Stan. He's wearing one of his trademark golf jumpers. The pastel colors of the fabric are mottled and dark, covered with dribbles of crusted blood and other bodily secretions that have seeped out of him over the last four weeks. I walk away. Stan doesn't pose any threat to me and I can't bring myself to kill him just for the sake of it.

I jog forward again. A body emerges from the shadows of a nearby house, the front door of which hangs open. It's back to business as usual as I tighten the grip on the machete in my hand and wait to strike. The corpse lurches for me. I don't recognize it as being anyone that I knew, and that makes it easier. I swing at its head and make contact. The blade sinks three quarters of the way into the skull, just above the cheekbone. Kill one hundred and forty-nine drops to the ground and I yank out my weapon and clean it on the back of my jeans.

I turn the corner and I'm in Harlour Grove. I stop when I see our house, filled with a sudden surge of emotion. Bloody hell, if I half-close my eyes I can almost imagine that everything is normal and none of this ever happened. My heart is racing with nervous anticipation and fear as I move towards our home. I can't wait to see her again. It's been too long.

A sudden noise in the street behind me makes me spin around. There are another nine bodies coming at me from several directions. At least six of them are behind me, staggering after me at a pathetically slow pace, and another two are ahead, one closing in from the right and the other coming from the general direction of the house next to ours. The adrenaline is really pumping now that I'm this close. I'll be back with Georgie in the next few minutes and nothing is going to stop me. I don't even waste time with the machete now—I raise my fist and smash the nearest corpse in the face, rearranging what's left of its already mutilated features. It drops to the ground, bringing up my one hundred and fiftieth kill in style.

I'm about to do the same to the next body when I realize that I know her. This is what's left of Judith Landers, the lady who lived next-door but one. Her husband was a narrow-minded prick but I always got on with Judith. Her face is bloated and discolored and she's lost an eye but I can still see that it's her. She's still wearing the remains of the uniform she wore for work. She used to work part-time on the checkout at the hardware store down the road on the way to Shenstone. Poor bitch. She reaches out for me and

I instinctively raise the machete. But then I look deeper into what's left of her face and all I can see is the person she used to be. She tries to grab hold of me but one of her arms is broken and it flaps uselessly at her side. I push her away in the hope that she'll just turn round and disappear in the other direction but she doesn't. She grabs at me again and, again, I push her away. This time her heavy legs give way and she falls. Her face smashes into the pavement, leaving a greasy, bloody stain behind. Undeterred she drags herself up and comes at me for a third time. I know I don't have any choice and I also know that there are now eleven more corpses closing in on me. Judith was a short woman. I flash the blade level with my shoulders and take off the top third of her head like it's a breakfast egg. She drops to her knees and then falls forward, allowing the heavily decomposed contents of her skull to spill out over my lawn.

I have carried the key to our house on a chain around my neck since the first day. With hands tingling with nerves I pull it out from underneath my shirt and shove it quickly into the lock. I can hear dragging footsteps just a couple of meters behind me now. The lock is stiff and I have to use all my strength to turn the key but finally it moves. The latch clicks and I push the door open. I fall into the house and slam the door shut just as the closest body crashes into the other side.

I'm almost too afraid to speak.

"Georgie?" I shout, and the sound of my voice echoes around the silent house. I haven't dared to speak out loud for weeks and the noise seems strange. It makes me feel exposed. "Georgie?"

Nothing. I take a couple of steps further down the hallway. Where is she? I need to know what happened here. Wait, what's that? Just inside the dining room I can see Rufus, our dog. He's lying on his back and it looks like he's been dead for some time. Poor bugger, he probably starved to death. I take another step forward but then stop and look away. Something has attacked the dog. He's been torn apart. There's dried blood and pieces of him all over the place.

"Georgie?" I call out for a third time. I'm about to shout again when I hear it. Something's moving in the kitchen and I pray that it's her.

I look up and see a shadow shifting at the far end of the hallway. It has to be Georgie. She's shuffling towards me and I know that I'll be able to see her any second. I want to run to meet her but I can't because my feet are frozen to the spot with nerves. The shadow lurches forward again and she finally comes into view. The end of the hallway is dark and for a moment I can only see her silhouette but there's no question it's her. She slowly turns towards me, pivoting around awkwardly on her clumsy, cold feet, and begins to trip down the hall in my direction. Every step she takes brings her closer to the light coming from the small window next to the front door, revealing her in more detail. I can see now that she's naked and I find myself wondering what happened to make her lose her clothes. Another step and I can see that her once strong and beautiful hair is now lank and sparse. Another step and I see that her usually flawless, perfect skin has been eaten away by decay. Another step forward and I can clearly see what's left of her face. Those sparkling eyes that I gazed into a thousand times are now cold and dry and look at me without the slightest hint of recognition or emotion. I clear my throat and try to speak . . .

"Georgie," I stammer nervously, "are you . . . ?"

She launches herself at me. Rather than recoil and fight I instead catch her and pull her closer. It feels good to hold her again. She's weak and can offer no resistance when I wrap my arms around her and hold her tight. I press my face next to hers and try my best to ignore the repugnant smell coming from her decaying body. I try not to overreact when she moves and I carefully tighten my grip, letting go again when I feel her greasy, rotting flesh slipping through my fingers.

I don't want to ever let her go. This was how I wanted it to be. It's better this way. I had known all along that she would be dead. If she'd survived she would probably have left the house and I would never have been able to find her but I'd never have stopped looking for her. We were meant to be together, Georgie and me. That's what I kept telling her, even when she stopped wanting to listen.

I've been back home for a couple of hours now. Apart from the dust and mildew and mold the place looks pretty much the same as it always did. She didn't change much after I left. We're in the living room together now. I haven't been in here for almost a year. Since we split up she didn't like me coming around. She never usually let me get any further than the hall, even when I came to collect my things. She said she'd call the police if she had to but I always knew she wouldn't. That was just what he told her to say.

I've dragged the coffee table across the door now so that Georgie can't get out and I've nailed a few planks of wood across it too just to be sure. She's stopped attacking me now and it's almost as if she's got used to having me around again. I tried to put a bathrobe around her to keep her warm but she wouldn't keep still long enough to let me. Even now she's still moving around, walking round the edge of the room, tripping over and crashing into things. Silly girl! And with our neighbors watching too! Seems like most of the corpses from around the estate have dragged themselves over here to see what's going on. I've counted more than twenty dead faces pressed against the window.

It was a shame that we couldn't have worked things out before she died. I know that I spent too much time at work, but I did it all for her. I did it all for *us*. She said we'd grown apart and that I didn't excite her any more. She said I was boring and dull. She said she wanted more adventure and spontaneity and that, she said, was what Matthew gave her. I tried to make her see that he was too young for her and that he was just stringing her along but she didn't want to listen. But where is he now? Where is he with his fucking designer clothes, his city center apartment and his flash car? I know exactly where he is—he's out there on the streets rotting with the rest of the fucking masses. And where am I? I'm *home*. I'm back sitting in *my* armchair drinking *my* whiskey in *my* living room. I'm at home with my wife and this is where I'm going to stay. I'm going to die here and when I've gone Georgie and I will rot together. We'll be here together until the very end of everything.

I know it's what she would have wanted.

DAVID MOODY is the author of the Hater and Autumn book series. He grew up in Birmingham, England, on a diet of horror movies and post-apocalyptic fiction. He started his career working at a bank, but then decided to write the kind of fiction he loved. His first novel, *Straight to You*, had what Moody calls "microscopic sales," and so when he wrote *Autumn*, he decided to publish it online. The book became a sensation and has been downloaded by half a million readers. He started his own publishing company, Infected Books. A film adaptation of *Autumn* was made in Canada in 2008 and starred Dexter Fletcher and David Carradine. Film rights to *Hater* were acquired by Mark Johnson (producer of the Narnia films), and Guillermo del Toro. Moody lives in Britain with his wife and a houseful of daughters, which may explain his preoccupation with Armageddon.

Providing for his family's needs gave him a purpose in life beyond driving a traveling crematorium. Not much of a purpose, maybe, but it was something . . .

Provider

Tim Waggoner

"Looks like we got a flopper over there," Kenny said.

Robert nodded. He put Smoky Joe into low gear and pressed on the brake. The truck juddered to a stop—damn thing was overdue for a tune-up—in front of 3298 Chestnut Avenue. There was a large oak tree in the yard. Its branches stretched out over the street and its leaves, while still green, were tinted gold, red and brown. Not quite ready to start drifting to the ground yet, but almost. Fall was Robert's favorite time of the year. It made him think of beginnings, much more so than January first. There was the first day of school, and the start of football season, of course. And given the way stores advertised, it was the unofficial start of the Christmas season, too.

At least, that's the way it had been, back when the word *dead* meant a corpse that didn't move, didn't walk, didn't try to sink its teeth into the living.

Robert put Smoky Joe in park, but he didn't turn off the ignition. They needed to leave the truck running so the furnace would keep burning. If it went out, it was a bitch to get started again, and if the temperature in the back got too low, the furnace wouldn't be able to do its job effectively. He opened the door, and stepped down the street. He removed his gloves from the pocket of his coveralls and put them on while he waited for Kenny to come around and join him.

Kenny walked around the front of the truck. He never walked around the back if he could avoid it, and Robert couldn't say as he blamed the man. Kenny already had his gloves on, and his clear plastic facemask, too.

"I can't believe you still wear that goddamn thing. You've been on the job six months now."

"Five," Kenny corrected. "And I don't care if I'm still doing this stinkin' job five *years* from now, I'm still gonna wear my mask, and I don't give a shit what anyone says about it." Kenny's breath caused condensation to mist the inside of the mask around his mouth.

Robert thought the breath-fog made him look kind of stupid, but he didn't remark on it. No one commented on basic biological processes anymore, whatever they were, not even burping or farting. They were signs that you were alive, and no one made fun of that.

Kenny was a skinny middle-aged man with a scraggly white mustache and wispy white hair that brushed the tops of his shoulders. He had long, tapering fingers (hidden by his work gloves at the moment) that constantly trembled. Robert didn't know if that was due to stress or whether Kenny had a drug or alcohol problem. Though these days the real problem for users was getting hold of recreational chemicals.

Greasy black smoke curled forth from the chimney pipe atop the truck, and flecks of ash drifted through the air. In addition, a nauseating odor somewhat like a backed-up sewer filtered through the neighborhood. Not so many years ago, people would've complained like hell about the pollutants and the stench Smoky Joe pumped out. But that was in the old world. Today, there weren't any such things as environmental protection laws. Well, not unless you counted the kind of work people like Robert and Kenny did.

"Let's go take a look," Robert said.

Kenny grunted assent, though he didn't look too pleased.

They walked up to the oak tree and examined the flopper bound to the trunk. It was held fast against the bark by strong rope, but whoever had put it out hadn't slipped a muzzle on it. The thing gnashed its teeth at them, straining forward, eager to bite off a hunk of flesh. Robert looked into the corpse's eyes but they might as well have been made out of glass for all the emotion they displayed. They were fish eyes, dead eyes.

"Fresh one," Robert commented. No visible wounds, no sign of rot. "Probably died of a heart attack or a stroke last night."

"I don't give a shit what killed him," Kenny said. His voice held a strained edge to it, as if he were on the verge of hysteria. He always sounded like this when they had to deal with a flopper. "I hate it when they tie them up like this."

The preferred method of preparing someone for pick-up was to put a plastic muzzle over their mouth so they couldn't bite, then to bind their wrists, ankles and legs with plastic ties. Prepackaged kits were readily available and free to any resident. Robert and Kenny had a bunch stashed under the seat of their truck. They'd handed out four kits so far today during their rounds.

"Some people can't bring themselves to truss up their friends and family like a bag of trash," Robert said. Though once they Went Bad, as the euphemism went, that's exactly what they were. A scene from an old Monty Python comedy flashed through his mind then, John Cleese pulling a wooden cart through the muddy streets of a medieval village, ringing a bell and shouting, *Bring out your dead!* He wondered how long it had been since he'd seen a movie. Years, he supposed.

"And *this* is any better?" Kenny nodded toward the flopper who was straining more vigorously against his bonds. He started making a high-pitched keening sound in the back of this throat. It was the sound deaders made when they were hungry—and they were always hungry. Luckily, deaders weren't any stronger than the living, and no matter how hard the flopper struggled, he wasn't going to get out of those ropes. Whoever had tied him up had done a good job of it.

He looked to be—to have been—in his early thirties, thin (most everybody was thin these days, since food wasn't nearly as plentiful as it used to be), black hair, clean-shaven. He was dressed in a blue suit, white shirt, maroon tie and polished black shoes. Sometimes relatives dressed them up, like they used to do when the dead stayed still and were buried in boxes beneath the ground.

"Why couldn't they have done us a favor and bashed his skull in?" Kenny asked. Robert noticed his hands were trembling again, so hard it looked as if he might vibrate right out of his work gloves. Rumor had it that before he'd gone to work as a pick-up man, Kenny's girlfriend had Gone Bad, and he'd had to put her down. Robert had never asked—it wasn't the kind of thing you *could* ask—but if it were true, he wondered why Kenny would do this kind of work. As a way of expunging his guilt, maybe? Or perhaps he was one of those people who was drawn to that which terrified him, like a moth to the flame.

"It's not easy to desecrate the body of a loved one, even when you know its going to Go Bad soon," Robert said. The only sure ways to kill a deader were to destroy its brain or burn the damn thing to ash. Not too many folks could bring themselves to do either to the remains of someone they cared about.

Kenny didn't respond. He glared at the deader, fear and disgust mingling in his gaze. "Fuckin' zombie," he muttered.

Robert didn't respond. Instead, he turned and walked back to Smoky Joe. He opened the toolbox bolted to the side of the truck and pulled out a rusty crow bar. He walked back to the oak tree, his thick work boots thump-thump-thumping on the ground.

"Oh, man," Kenny whined. "Can't we use the gun?"

"He's an easy target. No need to waste the ammo." He held out the crow bar to Kenny. "Would you like to do the honors this time?"

"Hell, no. I got the last one."

Kenny hadn't gotten the last one, but Robert decided not to make an issue of it. "Better step back then." *Too bad this fellow's family didn't truss him up right,* Robert thought. If they had, then Kenny and he could've popped the flopper into Smoky Joe's furnace without having to "kill" him. Ah, well. Every job had its shitty side, he supposed.

He glanced at the house. The blinds were closed, and he didn't see anyone peeking out. Good. It was easier when relatives weren't watching. Robert took aim and swung the bar at the deader's head. Metal struck hair, flesh and bone with the same sickening sound as a sledgehammer smashing a watermelon. The deader jerked and shuddered with the first blow, but it took three more before the damn thing finally stopped moving.

When he was finished, Robert lowered the crow bar. His arm was tired and he was breathing heavily. He needed to get more exercise. He wiped the crow bar off in the grass, then held it out to Kenny.

"No way am I touchin' that fuckin' thing, man."

Robert was starting to lose his patience. "You're a pick-up man, damn it. Do your job."

Kenny looked as if he might protest further, but in the end he grabbed the crow bar and headed back to the truck.

"Get a knife out of the toolbox while you're at it, will you?" Robert called over his shoulder. "These knots look pretty tight, and I don't feel like messing with them."

"Yeah, yeah," Kenny muttered.

Robert looked down, saw that the front of his coveralls was splattered with blood. He checked his gloves, saw a few more splatters. Despite razzing Kenny for wearing his facemask, Robert now wished he'd taken the time to put his on. No one was really sure why the dead came back, or why their bite could make someone living Go Bad. He'd heard lots of theories over the years—a genetic weapon cooked up by one government or another, microbes brought back by a space probe, even a mutation of the AIDS virus. But whatever the reason, they did know one thing: it was infectious as hell, and if you weren't careful, you could Go Bad too.

He removed his right glove, reached up to touch his face . . . and found it dry.

Robert let out a breath he hadn't known he was holding. Looked like he was going to stay human another day. He put his glove back on, grabbed hold of the corpse under the armpits, and began dragging it toward Smoky Joe.

Come lunchtime, Robert and Kenny sat at a wooden bench in the park. Smoky Joe was parked nearby, engine idling, furnace chugging away, doing its best to reduce Blue Suit to a sooty smear. It wouldn't take long.

Joe was expensive to operate, especially these days when fuel was difficult to come by. But the town council thought Joe was worth it. The truck might not be as efficient as gathering deaders in the back of a pick-up and taking them outside of town and burning them en masse—something the hunting patrols did whenever there wasn't enough fuel to run Joe—but it was more psychologically comforting. Joe was like a slice of life from the time before, when cities and towns were able to provide trash service, recycling and yard waste pick-up. That's why they'd given the truck a nickname, to make it friendlier. The kids in the town had even come up with a song which began *Here comes old Smoky Joe, huff-puffing down the street . . .*

Robert knew they couldn't keep the truck going forever. The fuel would run out eventually, and so would replacement parts. But as long as Joe still rolled, Robert intended to be behind the wheel, huff-puffing along.

Both men had brought their food in plastic grocery bags; they could be used over more often than paper ones. Kenny had a hunk of coarse bread, an apple, a bit of cheese, and a bottle of water. Robert had the same, with the addition of a small piece of jerky.

Kenny made a face as Robert bit into the dried beef. "I don't see how you can eat that with the truck so close by. I can barely choke down my food as it is with that smell in the air, but there's no way I could keep down any meat."

Robert shrugged. "Man's got to keep his strength up. Besides, it doesn't have much taste anyway." He held out the rest of the jerky. "Want to try it?"

Kenny paled and held up a hand. "Hell, no!"

"Suit yourself." Robert took another bite and chewed methodically. He liked eating lunch in the park. Not only was it pleasant—though since the place hadn't been kept up for years, the grounds had become overgrown with weeds and bushes—but it was safe. At least, relatively so. There weren't as many roaming deaders as there used to be, thanks to the efforts of the hunting squads who patrolled the town day and night, executing any deaders they saw. Pick-up men like Kenny and he helped, too, disposing of the deaders the patrols left in their wake, along with those put out at the curb by individual residents. But if you were going to be out in the open for any length of time, it was only smart to pick a place where you could see around you in all directions, so you could spot a deader before it got too close. They usually moved slow enough that you could avoid them if you saw them in time. *If.*

Robert looked at a nearby swing set. There were two regular swings, and one baby swing. Kenny noticed where he was looking.

"Thinking about your kid?"

Robert nodded. "It'd be nice to be able to take him to a park so he could swing, go down the slide, play in the sandbox . . . "

"Maybe someday. They have to find a cure eventually, right?"

"Sure." But Robert didn't believe it. Supposedly there was some semblance of a government in D.C. again, but since there were no network broadcasts anymore, just a few local radio channels that transmitted infrequently, news was hard to come by. If there was a government again, he guessed they probably were working on a cure, but that didn't mean they'd ever find one. Maybe whatever it was that brought the dead back *couldn't* be cured, not by science anyway.

"How's he doing? Your kid, I mean. What's his name again? Bobbie?"

"Yeah. He's fine. Just started crawling last week."

Kenny frowned. "I thought he was already crawling. I remember when we first started working together, you said—"

"Walking," Robert interrupted. "I meant he just started walking."

Kenny looked at him for a long moment, his expression unreadable. Finally, he said, "Sure, man," and turned his attention back to his lunch. After several minutes, he said, "There's gonna be a dance in the basement of the Methodist Church Saturday afternoon." Not at night; nothing took place at night anymore. "You think you'n Emily might come?"

"I doubt it," Robert said. "Emily doesn't like to go out much. She doesn't feel safe outside the house, you know?"

"Yeah. Too bad, should be a good time."

They continued to eat in silence, and when they were finished, they climbed back in Smoky Joe and resumed their rounds.

It was closing in on dusk by the time Robert turned onto Mapleview, the street where he lived. It felt as if his bike were harder to pedal than usual, and he made a mental note to put some air in the tires before he left for work tomorrow. He had a small bag of groceries in the basket attached to the handlebars—nothing vital: a couple light bulbs, some more jerky, a mason jar full of moonshine—and he cursed himself for taking the time to stop at the general store set up in the city building. He should've waited until his day off to go shopping. Now he was still out as the sun dipped toward the horizon. Deaders, while active twenty-four hours a day, were harder to see at night, and therefore that much more dangerous.

He pedaled harder, passing houses with boarded-up windows and lawns wild with tall grass. Deaders could break through glass, and lawnmowers needed gasoline, which no one would dare waste on something so frivolous as cutting grass. As he rolled by the houses, he wondered how many of them were still occupied. He realized he had no idea. People tended not to leave their houses anymore unless they absolutely had to. He hadn't seen some of his neighbors for months, a few not for years. The only ones he knew for sure were gone were those he had picked up during his rounds and fed to Joe's furnace.

He turned into his driveway, stopped, and got off. He carried the bike up the front walk and onto the porch. His windows, too, were boarded up, and not for the first time he thought what a depressing sight they were to come home to. Like his house had long ago been abandoned, and he a ghost come to haunt it.

He unlocked the door, carried the bike and his groceries inside, then closed and locked the door quickly. No one let doors stay open and unlocked for longer than they had to, not anymore. He propped the bike against the wall next to the door, then moved through the gloom to the dining room. He lit the oil lamp that sat in the middle of the dining table, and turned the flame low. Deaders were attracted to light, probably because they knew that light meant live folks were about. Robert was confident deaders couldn't break into his home, but he didn't want to take a chance, so he made sure to keep the lights to a minimum at night.

He walked into the kitchen and put the plastic grocery bag—the same one he had carried his lunch in—on the counter. He heard a soft, high-pitched sound, not unlike the one that had issued from the throat of Blue Suit this morning. But it was muffled and he was able to ignore it. He opened a cupboard, took down a plastic jug of water, and poured himself a glass. Water was distributed at the high school once a week, and going to fetch his share was one of the few times Robert drove his car.

He got a baggie of dried peaches, took them, some jerky and his water into the living room. He set his dinner, such as it was, onto the coffee table. Then he walked to the entertainment center and turned on the battery-powered stereo. First he tried to see if any of the few remaining radio stations were broadcasting, but none was. He switched the stereo to CD and put in a David Sanborn album. He kept the volume low, of course, and returned to the couch to eat his supper.

He listened to the music, closing his eyes to concentrate on the sound of Sanborn's sax more fully. He wondered if the musician were still alive, wondered if he were playing somewhere right now, knew there was no way he'd ever know. He considered breaking out the shine he'd picked up today, maybe getting a little mellow before bedtime, but the thought of alcohol (especially the paint stripper that passed for booze these days) didn't sound good just then, so he just sat and listened to Sanborn play.

As the music continued, he became aware of another sound intruding: that soft keening, almost like the sound a cat might make, but higher, more . . . human. He tried to shut it out, even risked turning up the volume on the stereo, but no matter what he did, he couldn't ignore it. Finally, he switched off the stereo in frustration, which in the end was probably a good thing since it would extend the life of the batteries. He walked into the kitchen and stopped at the basement door. He hesitated for a moment, then put his ear against the wood and listened.

At first, he didn't hear anything, and he began to hope that maybe tonight he'd be able to pretend there was nothing in the basement. But then the keening started again, louder this time. That meant they were closer to the door.

He went into the kitchen, fetched a flashlight from a drawer, and returned to the door. There was a small panel set at eye level, and he undid the latch and slowly opened it. He took a step back—he *always* did—even though there wasn't any need. Before he'd installed the panel, he'd removed the basement stairs. There was no way they could get to the door. Not unless they stacked boxes to climb on. There were all sorts of boxes down there, junk they'd never gotten around to unpacking when they'd moved. But he wasn't especially worried; deaders' bodies still worked, after a fashion, but their brains stayed dead. They retained enough instinct to hunt for food, and to hide from the patrols, but that was about it.

Still, taking a step back didn't hurt, did it?

He waited a moment, and when greenish-gray skinned hands did not thrust through the open panel, he stepped forward, clicked on the flashlight, and shined it through the opening. As always, his nostrils detected a faint odor that reminded him of a reptile house at the zoo. It was the stink of seasoned deaders, ones that had been around for a while, and kept in an enclosed space. It was the stink of his family.

Emily stood directly beneath the door, looking up at him. Her dead eyes didn't reflect the flashlight's illumination. She wore the tatters of a flower-print dress he had gotten her for one birthday or another; he couldn't recall which one. Once or twice he'd tried tossing down different outfits for her to put on, knowing it was foolish but unable to help himself. She ignored them, of course. Her mold-colored flesh was dry and tight against her bones, and she had lost several fingers on each hand over the years. They'd snapped off, like dried twigs. For some strange reason her blond hair had retained its color, though it was now tangled and matted. Her face . . . He didn't like to look at her face too long.

She reached her hands up toward him and took a couple feeble swipes. Sometimes he fantasized that she was beckoning to him, that in some dim recess of her rotted brain, she recognized him, missed him. Wanted them to be together again, as husband and wife. But he knew better: if Emily got hold of him, she'd tear into his flesh like a starved Rottweiler. Her keening grew louder, and though he wasn't certain her dead eyes could actually see him, he had no doubt she knew he was there. More, that she knew his presence meant it was feeding time. Scattered on the floor around her were small bones and clumps of fur, evidence of past meals.

He heard a second, softer keening in the darkness behind her, and he knew he shouldn't do it, but he shined the flashlight in its direction. A small green-gray thing lay on the basement floor, tiny arms and legs flailing, mouth opening and closing like a fish gasping on dry land. His son, Robert

Anthony Tollinger, Jr. His son who had never known human life, who'd been miscarried during the seventh month of his wife's pregnancy and who'd actually Gone Bad inside her womb. Bobbie (as Robert had come to think of him) hadn't been able to do any real damage without teeth, but he had been connected to Emily by his umbilical cord, and through that conduit or by some other means, he had managed to infect his mother before her body expelled him.

There had been no hospital to take Emily to at the time. Now there was a makeshift one set up in the city building, but Robert knew the lone doctor who practiced there wouldn't have been able to do anything for Emily even if he had set up shop before she changed. There was no cure, no way to halt or reverse the process once it had started.

Robert had been a pick-up man then, though he'd been new to the job, not much more experienced than Kenny. He had known what to do. But like so many others, he couldn't bring himself to do it. Instead, he'd used the hours before they Went Bad to take them down to the basement, bring down some furniture and some toys for Bobbie, though he knew damn well they'd never be used. Then he dismantled the stairs, tossed the wood into a corner of the basement, and hauled himself out. He locked the door, but he didn't barricade it, even though that would have been the sensible thing to do. It would've been too much like he was putting them in a cage, as if they were nothing more than animals. He installed the panel opening right away, finishing it just as his wife and unborn child began to stir. That had been three years ago.

He knew keeping his family like this made him a hypocrite, and worse, that it prolonged their travesty of an existence. Or rather non-existence. He often lay awake at night, wondering if on some level they were aware of what they had become, of what they had once been, what they had lost. And if so, somewhere within the dead lumps of flesh that used to be their minds, did they suffer? Did they long for release?

If so, it was a release he was too weak to grant them. He needed them if he were to keep his sanity in this hellish nightmare the world had become. Providing for his family's needs gave him a purpose in life beyond driving a traveling crematorium. Not much of a purpose, maybe, but it was something.

He turned away from the door, turned off the flashlight, and stuck it handle first in the back pocket of his worn jeans. He walked into the kitchen and opened the refrigerator. There was no light inside because there was no electricity. There hadn't been any for years. He didn't use his fridge to keep things cold, though. He used it because it sealed tight when it shut, holding in the odors of the provender he gathered for his wife and child.

The stench was rank, worse than what he had to put up with on the job. But he didn't care; he'd gotten used to it by now. He reached into the fridge and pulled out a plastic garbage bag. Inside were the remains of a dog he had found two days ago on his bike ride home from work. Deaders preferred human flesh above anything else, but when they couldn't get it—and people had gotten pretty damn good at learning how to avoid getting munched since the plague or whatever it was first struck—they turned to animals. Some deader or other had taken a few bites out of the dog, but not many. Either the deader had been satisfied with what it had taken, or more likely, something had scared it off. Perhaps a hunting patrol cruising the streets.

At any rate, Robert had picked up the dog, which had been relatively fresh then, put it in his bike basket and brought it home. He hadn't given it right away to his family, though. He didn't like to feed them too often. It made them more active and restless, Emily especially. Besides, dog was a treat. Most dogs were wild now, and hard to catch. Normally he fed his family squirrel or rabbit caught in snares he'd rigged in the backyard, though the animals weren't as easy to come by as they had been before the deaders appeared.

He took the dog to the basement door, feeling something squirm through the plastic. Maggots, most likely; the dog *had* lain out for a while before he'd picked it up. While he'd seen and done too many things since the world changed to be squeamish, he'd rather not touch maggots if he didn't have to. So he left the dog in the bag, though he did untie it. He squeezed the animal, bag and all, through the panel opening. It was a tight fit, but he managed to get it through.

He heard the rustle-thud of the bag hitting something, and then another, louder thud. He realized with horror that the dog had struck Emily and knocked her down. He shined the flashlight through the opening and confirmed his guess. Emily lay on the ground, arms and legs waving in the air like a turtle that had rolled onto its back. Her nostrils flared, and she turned her head toward the plastic-wrapped dog. Quick as a crab, she righted herself and scuttled over to her prize. As she began tearing at the plastic, Robert was amazed anew at how fast normally slow and awkward deaders could move when they were starved and within striking distance of meat.

She pulled the dog out of the bag, lowered her head to its maggot-covered body, and took a bite. As she chewed, worms fell from her lips, pattering to the basement floor like fat, white raindrops. The baby, scenting meat, shrieked, the sound so near to that of a living infant as to bring tears to Robert's eyes.

Emily looked at the baby as if she'd never seen it before and couldn't quite figure out what it was. Then she bit off another hunk of dog and crawled on hands and knees toward little Robbie Jr. Once she reached the baby, she chewed for a moment, then lowered her face to the baby's and kissed its mouth.

Back when there had been TV to watch, Robert had seen a documentary on human evolution that claimed kissing began when mothers chewed up food to feed their infants. He wondered if Emily was following a basic maternal instinct so deeply hard-wired into her genes that not even death could alter it.

The sight should've sickened him, but it didn't. Yes, it was an obscene mockery of a mother's tenderness, but it still touched him. He'd never had the chance to hold his son, not alive at any rate. He knew Bobbie wasn't a living being, that his movements were due to whatever force—mystic curse or perverted science—animated his dead flesh. But he wished he could touch his boy, just once. Wished he could be a father to Bobbie, a *real* father, and not just a man who threw down dead animals for him to eat. Food he could provide, no problem. But if his wife and son still had any emotional needs (and didn't their keening cries always seem to hold a touch of sadness and loneliness mixed in with the hunger?) there was nothing he could do for them.

He'd tried talking to them on and off over the years, but the sound of his voice always enraged them. They only grew calm when they were fed—or, in Bobbie's case, on those rare occasions when his mother remembered he existed and touched him, sometimes even cradling him in her arms and stroking the dry, dead flesh of his forehead. Robert had often wondered if he would be able to soothe them with his touch, had even contemplated making the attempt once or twice, but he knew he'd never survive it.

He'd even considered going down and letting them have him, purposefully allowing himself to become infected. At least that way the three of them would be together. But he knew from his time on the job that if a human body was savaged badly enough by deaders—especially if the heart and brain were damaged, or for that matter, devoured completely—it wouldn't return to life. He'd thought about opening the basement door and then committing suicide elsewhere in the house, maybe by slitting his wrists so his body would remain intact. But once he changed, how could he be assured that he'd remember his wife and son in the basement—and if he did, that he'd still want to join them? More likely he'd try to get outside and go hunt for live meat. And even if by some miracle he found his way to the basement, there would be no one to bring them food. They wouldn't starve, but they would remain hungry. Forever.

No, there was no way they could be together again, not as a family. He could keep Emily and Bobbie trapped in the basement and feed them like animals, but that was all. It would have to do.

He turned off the flashlight, closed the panel and latched it. There was enough meat on the dog to keep them busy—and quiet—for a while, maybe all the way until morning. That was good. He didn't think he could stand to listen to their plaintive, lonely keening anymore tonight.

The next morning he biked to the city building to find out whether they were going to send Smoky Joe out again. He hoped Joe was going to stay in the garage; he didn't feel like dealing with any deaders today. But no such luck. The hunting squads had been especially busy last night, and during their patrol, they'd counted a half dozen more bodies put out by townsfolk for Joe to pick up.

Kenny was already there, looking a bit more nervous than usual, but Robert was in too much of a funk to care why, so he didn't ask. They fired Joe up and chugged out of the garage and headed for the first house on the list the hunters had given them. They had an easy morning of it. The first two deaders they stopped for had been killed by whoever put them out—one by a bullet through the brain, another by a brick or a large rock to the head—and they had no problem tossing them into Joe's furnace.

The third stop was different. Not because of the deader; she was inanimate, too, and so petite either of them could have carried her one-handed to the truck. No, the problem occurred when Kenny, who had been silent all morning, finally decided to speak.

"We're partners, right?"

They stood behind Joe, watching the petite woman burn. She was so tiny, Robert didn't think it would take long for her to fall away to ash.

"We work together, if that's what you mean," he replied, not taking his eyes off the flames.

"Yeah, right, but I mean we look out for each other and stuff. You know, like you wouldn't let a deader take a bite out of me, and I wouldn't let one get at you. Right?"

Robert nodded, wondering where Kenny was going with this. "Sure."

"Well, see, the thing is, I got a problem."

Robert glanced sideways at him. Kenny had taken his gloves off and tucked them in the pockets of his coveralls. He had his mask off, too, and beads of sweat had erupted on his forehead, were beginning to trickle down the sides of his face. Maybe the sweat was due to the heat from Joe's furnace, but Robert didn't think so. Kenny was trembling all over, but his hands were the worst. They were vibrating so fast they actually blurred a little.

"You probably heard that my girlfriend Went Bad and I . . . took care of her."

Robert didn't say anything, but he turned to face Kenny.

"I had to do it, right? I mean, I know that's what she would've wanted me to do, but afterward . . . shit, I kept having these *dreams,* you know? Really fucked-up ones. So I started drinking." A nervous chuckle. "I mean, I always drank. Who doesn't, right? But I started in big-time, mostly at night, so I could sleep. If I drink enough, I don't dream."

Kenny fell silent and they watched the flames for a time. Robert decided to let the man continue in his own time.

"I hate this job. Hate it like fucking poison, but it pays well. Damn well ought to, shit we have to do. I mean, who the hell in their right mind would do this kind of work?" A pause. "No offense."

Robert nodded for him to go on.

"Five ration slips a week is pretty good pay these days. I mean, it's more than just about anyone else gets, except for the hunters and the doctor at the city building."

"But five slips aren't enough for you anymore, are they?"

Kenny shook his head. "I guess my body's soaked up too much alcohol for it to work on me the same way. That, or maybe the shiners aren't making their stuff as strong as they used to. I use most of my slips for booze, hardly eat much anymore, but I can't seem to get drunk enough to get to sleep. Even when I do, I hardly ever sleep through the night. Those dreams . . . "

"Why are you telling me this?" Robert asked softly.

Kenny shrugged, a little too nonchalantly, Robert thought.

"I figure you might be able to help me." A nervous smile. "I know about your secret. I mean, you don't have to be a fuckin' genius to put it together. Your wife and kid never leave the house . . . half the time you can't remember how old your boy is. They're deaders, ain't they? And you've got them stashed in your house somewhere. The garage, maybe, or the basement. Because you're just like all these poor sonsofbitches." He made a sweeping gesture to take in the neighborhood. "You can't stand to say goodbye to your loved ones either. The only difference is, you're around deaders all the time, and you ain't afraid of them. You know how to handle them, so while no one else has the balls to keep their family members once they've Gone Bad, you do."

Kenny stopped, a smug expression on his face, as if he were proud of his deductive prowess.

Robert felt a cold twisting in his gut, but he worked to keep his voice level. "So you know. What are you going to do about it?"

"Nothing, *partner*. Not as long as you give me three of your ration slips every week. Otherwise, I'll tell the hunting squad about Emily and little Bobbie, and they'll be over at your house before you can finish singing the first stanza of 'Smoky Joe.' "

Robert said nothing.

"Look, I know this makes me a real prick, but I can't help it, man. I *need* those slips! I gotta get me some sleep!"

A few more seconds went by before Robert finally said, "All right."

"Really? You mean it?" Kenny sounded surprised, as if he hadn't expected his threat to work.

"Yes. But make it two slips a week."

"Uh-uh, no way." He sounded emboldened now. "It's three or bye-bye family."

"All right. Three. But I don't have any on me. You'll have to wait until we get paid."

"That's only a couple more days. I can wait. But if you stiff me, you'll regret it."

"Don't worry. I'll pay. Now let's get back to work. We have at least two more stops to make today, and if we don't keep burning deaders, neither one of us is going to get paid."

Kenny smirked. His expression was easy for Robert to read: he figured he had his partner by the balls now, and he was no longer low man on this team. "What do you mean, *we*? I'll ride along, but I ain't getting out.

I'm never gonna touch another fuckin' deader as long as I live. You do the burnin' from now on, got it?"

"Got it. Now let's go."

Another smirk, and Kenny turned and started heading for Joe's cab—and that's when Robert punched him in the back of the neck. Kenny collapsed like a marionette whose strings had been severed, and once he was down, it was an easy matter for Robert to keep him there. He was, after all, thin and weak from malnutrition. Robert clamped his hands around Kenny's neck and squeezed. Kenny kicked his feet and slapped his hands on the asphalt, but Robert kept squeezing until his partner's struggles lessened and finally stopped altogether.

When it was finished, he climbed off Kenny's corpse and stood looking down at it.

Robert wasn't worried that any of the residents of this neighborhood had seen, and even if they had, who would they report it to? There were no police anymore. Just the hunting squads—and pick-up men like him. Of course, he'd have to make up a story for his bosses at the city building. He supposed he could always tell them Kenny had said he'd had enough of the job and quit in the middle of today's route, but if no one ever saw him again, they might get suspicious. No, better to say that Kenny got careless, let a deader bite him, and had to be put down. He wouldn't be the first pick-up man that had ended up that way. That decided, the only thing left to do was feed Kenny's body to Joe.

Robert bent down, intending to do just that, but as he reached toward Kenny, he hesitated. It seemed an awful waste to just toss him into the fire. He could still be . . . useful.

Robert walked into the kitchen, a heavy plastic bag clutched in his hand. Their keening was especially loud today; it had been almost a week since he had last fed them.

"Hold on, it's coming."

He got the flashlight and opened the basement door panel, taking his usual step back and waiting a moment before stepping forward again and shining the light inside. There was Emily, hands clawing the air, and little Bobbie, wailing and writhing on the floor behind her. But now there was a third one in the basement, much fresher than the other two and wearing a pair of coveralls. He stared up at the light with a blank, unseeing gaze, his mouth opening and closing hungrily.

Robert smiled. "I really appreciate you helping me out like this, partner. It means a lot to me."

The male moaned, as if in response to Robert's words, but he knew the thing was just hungry. He lifted his find—a possum that he'd managed to hit while out in Joe earlier that day—and stuffed it through the opening. The possum struck the floor, and Emily and Kenny fell on it like starving dogs.

Bobbie screamed for his share, and this time it was Kenny who took a mouthful over to the baby, feeding the boy with a gentle kiss.

Robert felt no jealousy. Not only had he provided food for his wife and child, he'd found a way to be down there with them, if only through a surrogate. Still, they were truly a family again, in every way, and that was all that mattered.

Robert watched them for a while longer, then he closed the panel and put the flashlight away. Time for bed; he had to get up early for work tomorrow. Not only did he have a new partner to break in, he had a family to feed.

TIM WAGGONER's novels include the Nekropolis series of urban fantasies and the Ghost Trackers series written in collaboration with Jason Hawes and Grant Wilson of the *Ghost Hunters* television show. In total, he's published over twenty-five novels and two short story collections, and his articles on writing have appeared in *Writer's Digest* and *Writers' Journal*, among others. He teaches creative writing at Sinclair Community College and in Seton Hill University's Master of Fine Arts in Writing Popular Fiction program. Visit him on the web at www.timwaggoner.com.

What good is life—or even half-life—if you can't get near a woman?

Zombies for Jesus

Nina Kiriki Hoffman

I was thinking about women, live ones, dead ones, and in between.

"Ante is one finger joint," said Slim. "Any finger joint."

I put my hands in my lap, ready to sit this one out. I'd already lost a finger this game and didn't feel like playing anymore. There was a few clicks and some mushy thuds as the others anted up.

The flies was loud in the afternoon stillness, drifting here and there, feasting, lazy in the hot amber light coming through the canvas of the tent. I brushed one off my nose. Most of the boys didn't bother, as their nerves was mostly dead and they had no interest in personal hygiene any longer.

Prettyboy Pritchard stood looking out the tent flap. He was the newest revival, the most whole-looking besides me, and he refused to join us at the poker table; didn't want to lose anything and spoil his pretty wholeness; hadn't settled into the bit-part business of the afterlife yet.

Brownie, down to one finger and one thumb, both of which he needed to hold his cards, said, "Can I use a toe? I got extras. I gotta stay in, Slim. I gotta win some parts back, I really gotta."

"Aw, nobody wants toes," Slim said. "I got thirteen already. You got anything else?"

"Zeke," Brownie said to me, "can you loan me a finger or two?"

"Nope," I said. Last time I loaned him something he lost three of my toes, and it took me six games to get them back, and some pinching in the night, because one of the other guys didn't want to give his up. My body parts were different from most of the others'. I was one of the Reverend Thomas's first Born Agains, before he got the Elixir of Life refined. I figured I got some secret ingredients none of the other zombies had, 'cause most of my body parts had a life of their own, and when the Rev punished us by withholding our zombie pickles, I never got so weak and wobbly as the others did.

I went over to join Prettyboy at the tent flap. Only one thing about him interested me, his still-alive wife. Prettyboy was staring toward the main tent. Faint on the heavy afternoon air, the "Amens!" and "Praise Jesus!" of the meeting sounded like a distant game show.

"It's almost time, isn't it, Zeke?" asked Prettyboy.

"You know one of the angels will be over to fetch you when it's time, Prettyboy."

"But it's almost time, isn't it?"

"Settle down and play some poker, will you?" Slim yelled from over to the table. "We're sick and tired of your whining. All of us what has ears, anyway."

Except me, maybe. Prettyboy's noise didn't bother me. He was the fifth or sixth whiner I'd seen since achieving the hereafter. Like a constant drip in a sink, he'd drive you nuts if you paid attention to him, didn't bother you none if you just ignored him.

"Will Caroline be there?" Prettyboy asked, pulling on my shirttail. "Will she be there, Zeke?"

I was hoping she would be. She was the most devoted wife I'd ever seen, hung on far longer than most. Most spouses stopped coming to meeting when things went to pieces, figuring that death had them parted and they wasn't required to stay by and watch their exes rot.

"She'll be happy to see me, won't she?"

I glanced at him and doubted it. Any live woman with the sense God gave her would run the other direction, with how Prettyboy looked and smelled now—not that I could smell him; my senses had changed after death—but so many flies couldn't be wrong. If the Rev didn't hold a revival meeting pretty soon and find himself a new prettyboy, business was going to fall off something wicked.

Edging away from Prettyboy, I settled on the ground and made my silent whistle. The finger I had lost to Artie crept off the table and wriggled back to me. I held out my hand and it hooked right up with its own stump, not needing glue at all. I hauled my way up to my feet again by gripping the canvas, and thought about Final Death. The Rev had threatened to chop me up and burn me a couple times, but I threatened right back—said I'd left some facts about his activities somewhere and if I died again somebody would see the news got to a reporter. I knew the Rev when he was still a prison doctor doing his own secret research, and if his Reverendness came from God, then I had never been on death row for murder.

Lately, though, I'd been brooding more and more about Finals. What good was life or even half-life anyway if you couldn't get near a woman? Might as well see if the Big Nothing was better than what I had now.

The Rev had some Born Again women, but he kept them locked up except for services, when they acted as angels so long as they weren't too obviously fallen-apart women. The Rev didn't rightly know how the Elixir of Life worked, and he didn't want to find out if those of us who still had the equipment could breed. He tried to keep us quiet by telling us there was no sex in Heaven.

One of the angels, all blond hair and white robe, came over from the meeting tent. She was pretty recent, looked pale but not too unhealthy except for the big dark circles under her eyes. Just as I was wondering what she died of, she held out a hand to Prettyboy and I saw the slash across her wrist. It was puckered and ugly. Somebody must have loved her, though, to bring her in to the Rev for revival.

"It's time, brother," she said to Prettyboy. Her voice was nice and gentle. I wondered if they played knuckle poker over to the women's tent, and doubted it, somehow.

"I'm ready," said Prettyboy. He glanced at me. One of his eyes was ready to ooze. I thought, Prettyboy, you should've joined the poker game before this. Show a good enough spirit, and you could be a tent zombie until you fell to pieces or got too weak to cart furniture around; tent zombies got to travel, and see places, even if it was only at night. In the tents, we all knew what to expect of each other; we'd seen it before. Not like the relatives of the Born Agains. Sometimes, if the relations wailed and hallelujahed enough, and the Born Agains agitated for it, the Rev left Born Agains with their folks, and got out of town before corruption set in. Sometimes I speculated on what happened to them all, wondering who screamed first when something dropped off.

The only other thing Prettyboy had to look forward to if he didn't straighten up and be a good tenter was Finals, which looked like the road he was traveling. No sense in him, no fellowship, and too much whine. How'd he ever get a wife like Caroline?

"Are you Zeke?" the angel said to me. She stood there holding Prettyboy's hand. I wished it was mine. My nerves was pretty iffy, but my vision still worked fine, and just knowing she was touching me would have meant a lot.

"Yes ma'am," I said.

"The Reverend told me to tell you there's going to be a revival meeting tonight."

Goodbye Prettyboy. "Yes, ma'am," I said. The Rev would be needing me to make the beginning preparations with the Elixir none of the other zombies knew about.

The angel nodded to me, her eyes bright blue in their nests of bruises. She led Prettyboy off across the browning grass, under the blanket of sun. In all that light, Prettyboy looked terrible even from behind. The skin on his arms was yellow and patchy, and clumps of his hair was coming out. I ambled after them, figuring to go to the supply tent beyond the meeting tent and get the Elixir mixing.

Caroline waited by the back flap of the meeting tent. Every time I had seen her she was wearing skirts and blouses that covered all of her except hands, face, and feet, no matter how hot it was. This time the blouse was white and the skirt was gray, and inside them she was shaped like a woman in a girlie magazine. She wore her red hair twisted in a knot at the back of her neck. Sweat made her forehead shine.

She smiled at Prettyboy. "Walter," she said, holding out a hand.

I looked down at my hands. Right now I had all my fingers and thumbs and most everything else. My skin was yellowish, but it looked all of a piece, and had some vitality to it.

Just before the angel lifted the meeting tent's back flap to usher Prettyboy and Caroline inside, I veered over to them. "Walter," I said to Prettyboy, "you look sickly."

Caroline stared at me. "Are you dead?" she asked.

"Born Again, ma'am," I said. I had watched her before. She clung to Prettyboy like she really loved him, even when some of him came off in her hand. I thought about my wife. Of course, she died before I did, but even when we was alive together, she never liked to touch me unless we was in bed.

Caroline put her hand out toward me. I stood still, and thought, there's something wrong with this one. Maybe the right kind of wrong. She touched my arm. I felt my skin twitch. It had been a long time. I gave her my best smile. I still had most of my teeth.

"Zeke, I want to go in. I want to tell them about the glories of being born again," said Prettyboy.

"Pret— Walter, you don't look so hot. I think you better go lie down." I buttoned up my shirt, rolled down the sleeves, and tucked in the tails. I hadn't been a prettyboy since the Rev's early tenting days, though I could have kept the job forever if I had been more worked up about it. Right now I wanted it more than anything I had wanted since I woke to the afterlife.

The angel looked from Prettyboy to me, her eyes troubled. She patted Prettyboy's hand. "Brother, you do look weary," she said.

"But—but—" His shoulders sagged.

"Go back to the tent and lie down, Walter," I said, as if rest would do him any good.

He turned and shuffled away.

I looked at Caroline. She slid her arm through the crook in mine. It was like the first jolt in the chair. I knew I liked it, and wanted more; didn't mind dying to get it. "You're really dead?" she said.

"Ma'am."

We went through the tent flap together, walking up the back of the dais between two wings of the choir, which, decked out in white and blue satin, looked like a low cloud. They were mostly alive, and not allowed to talk to us. Caroline and I came up beside the pulpit. "Praise the Lord," cried the Rev, not missing a beat, "see what the power of the Lord Jesus can do, and not just in Heaven, but right here on Earth. The age of miracles is upon us again. He who raised Lazarus, He who raised Jairus's daughter, He can raise your dead too. Praise the Lord!" He gripped my shoulder as Amens swept the tent. "Look on a wonder! This man stands before you, a testimony to God's greatness, born again into eternal Life, reunited with his wife. Praise the Lord!"

"Praise the Lord!" The noise was like a wind against us.

"I was lost, but now am found," I yelled. "I was blind but now I see. I was dead to life, a sinner in Satan, but now I am alive again through the power of Jesus." The words came back easy. Caroline's hand stroked my side as I spoke, and I felt her touch through my shirt. I felt it. Her fingernails slid along my ribs. "Born again to be with my beloved, praise the Lord!" Rib of my rib. Dust of my dust.

When all the singing and sobbing and carrying on was over for the afternoon, and Caroline had gone out to talk to some of the women and tell them about the miracle rebirth of me or Prettyboy, the Rev sidled up to me. "Zeke?" he said.

"What?"

"That was the best performance you ever gave. How come you came back into the fold, boy?"

"I want that woman, Rev. She wants me. Give me the night off and I'll prettyboy for you again tomorrow."

He tapped his fingers on his vest and stared off, considering. "You wouldn't run out on me, now would you?"

"You're the man with the special pickles," I said. Most food wouldn't stay down, and without food, we weakened and fell apart even faster. At least, most of us did. The Rev thought those pickles were the only thing that satisfied our appetites, and he kept them locked up.

"Have a nice night," he said.

She had a car, a beat-up blue Chevette. It felt strange sitting in a passenger seat watching a woman drive only a foot away. Oncoming headlights flickered across her face. Who was she, and why did she cling to her husband so long? If she believed in Jesus and his miracles, and the sanctity of her marriage, how come she was taking me home with her?

She parked the car at a cheap motel on the fringe of town. She led me inside, flicking on the light.

The door had hardly closed behind me when she reached for the buttons at the throat of her blouse, staring at me all the while. Then she pulled the pins out of her hair and shook it out. It was long and heavy. Her eyes watched me as all her clothes and things came off. I felt the life rising in me then. Whether it was the life God gave or the Rev's blasphemous version, I neither knew nor cared. Caroline had skin so white the veins showed through, little rivers of life.

When she finished undressing herself, she came for me. I blessed the providence that made me wash that morning, as if I hadn't been doing it every morning since I first saw Caroline hanging on Prettyboy's arm. She leaned so close her hair swung to touch my face as she unbuttoned my shirt, and then her hand was flat on my chest, warmer than the sun. Her eyes met mine and slid away.

"Lie back," she said, pressing me down on the bed. She unlaced my workboots, let them drop, and pulled my pants off. She climbed onto the bed beside me and reached for the light switch.

In the darkness, she said, "I killed him." She let about an acre of silence go by while I thought about that. "He don't even know it. I killed him, and when I heard about the Reverend—I thought if only I had Walter brought back, it would make everything all right, but it didn't. How can he forgive me for something he don't even know I done?"

I thought about my wife, the last time I saw her. White clothes staining red, eyes lost in bruises. I had watched the color seep out of her face, and listened to her last breath.

I slid my arm around Caroline's shoulders.

She leaned over me in the darkness. Her tongue touched my chest. I thought, maybe I'm wrong. Maybe there is a Heaven.

NINA KIRIKI HOFFMAN is the author of adult, middle-school, and young-adult novels, and many short stories. Her first novel, *The Thread that Binds the Bones*, won a Stoker award, and her short story, "Trophy Wives," won a Nebula Award. Her novel, *Fall of Light*, was published by Ace in 2009. Her latest series is Magic Next Door: *Thresholds*, published in 2010; and *Meeting*, published in 2011. Her recently published collection of short fiction, *Permeable Borders*, garnered a starred review in *Publishers Weekly*. Hoffman lives in Eugene, Oregon, with several cats and many strange toys and imaginary friends. For a list of her publications, see: ofearna.us/books/hoffman.html.

Nowadays sometimes talking to yourself is the only way to stay sane.
If you can even use that word any longer.

Viva Las Vegas

Thomas S. Roche

I cruise the blackened city in the primer-gray Caddy, all-steel construction carving a path of blood and bone as I search the faces of the living dead. I stalk the streets like nightmares on a pale horse with a 390 pre-smog, radials and a big ugly hood ornament of a woodpecker or something, the air conditioning on high and the Beretta across my lap. I drive the Strip with its shattered neon lights and fragments of plate glass windows, silver dollars and poker chips and hundred-dollar bills forming drifts like the desert sands across Las Vegas Boulevard. I look into the desperate eyes of the rotting, watching them claw at the windows of the Caddy, and I put my shades on.

Emily is nowhere in sight.

But I hold on to the faith that's kept me on the highway since I started. It's a small burning coal at the pit of my stomach that tells me one day very, very soon I'm going to have my Emily back and then not even Manny Pearlman can take her away again. Off in the distance, I hear the howl of a dog.

I park the Caddy in the parking lot of a Mister Doggy and light an unfiltered Black Lung. I sit there, smoking and thinking about the way Emily's eyes are going to light up when she sees me. It's been a long time coming, pedal-to-the-metal in the Caddy, burning up the road to this place, and every time I look into the face of Death, he is a brainless zomboid drooling green muck on his shirt. Every time I get cornered and try to speak words of wisdom to the great unwashed (which has gotten particularly unwashed of late) I find myself face to face with a greater kind of pinhead, occupant of a brave new and even stupider TV nation looking for a rather unwilling TV dinner—namely, me. Every time I point nine millimeters of death at the brain of the New Regular Joe, his jaws just clack and his hands claw to get a grip on my arm and peel off a succulent morsel.

But none of that matters worth ratshit. I know, *know* in my heart, in my soul, that when I finally lay my hands on Emily I'm gonna take her in my arms and she's gonna see me, recognize me, remember everything we had together. That's when her eyes'll brighten and I'll see those beautiful shining tears of hers, and at long last I'll have my Emily back from the hands of Death.

Then all at once I see them. Two dead hippies, one short and one tall, wearing tie-dye shirts with skull logos, have just walked up to me like they're trying to sell me some weed and now they're coming at the Caddy's side windows with a couple of Louisville Sluggers. No time to get the car in gear. I open the door fast so the short guy takes the bottom edge in the knee, the bat goes flying. I lean out of the car just enough to point the Beretta at his head; the gun barks and brains spray over the second hippy as he comes at me.

I see tie-dye and Jerry Bear on the guy's shirt: "Forever Dead." Christ, could I make this shit up?

I fire again but miss the second hippy's head and the bat comes down on me once, twice; I see stars and tumble back into the Caddy. He starts climbing in, his jaws already working, his hands grabbing for me. I've still got the Black Lung in my mouth and I quickly put it out in the hippy's eye. Not that it hurts the bastard but it seems to slow him down just a hair. That gives me just the chance I need to get the Beretta in his mouth and to spray his brains all over the inside of the Caddy's door. The first bullet takes the guy out something fierce, but you know how it is with those goddamn Berettas, once you get started it's kind of hard to stop, so next thing I know the clip is empty and hot cartridges are rattling around the inside of the Caddy like pinballs in the Hot Rod Derby machine down at the Boardwalk in Santa Monica, and the guy's head isn't just blown open but *gone*, which is maybe how I like it. The Beretta makes a hollow click over and over again as pull the trigger, then with a "Yech," I kick the headless body out into the Mister Doggy parking lot, slam the door, and get the car in gear.

Wetwork never used to be this wet.

Both of the hippies crunch under my radials as I swing a tight turn out of the parking lot and just barely miss the giant dog with the obscene wiener which used to flash neon-red like a goddamn blood sausage. The back end of the Caddy scrapes loud as I crank another turn and get going onto Tropicana, flooring it. Cruising in the fast lane, I shake out another cigarette and get it into my mouth with trembling hands. It doesn't do much to kill the smell of the guy's rotting insides drizzling down the inside of the Caddy's door.

I curse, telling myself not to daydream like that.

"Easy," I whisper around the butt of the Black Lung. "It's a war for the future, don't ever forget that. She's out there and it's your job to take her away from them." Nowadays sometimes talking to yourself is the only way to stay sane. *If* you can even use that word any longer.

I stop in the middle of the street to reload the Beretta and move the pump-action Remington .410 to the front seat. I check the weight of the two .32s in my jacket pocket. Can't be too careful.

There—under the burned-out neon palm tree—

I spot her in the shadows of a shambling horde on the corner of Paradise. There's got to be thirty, maybe forty of them, wandering with arms outstretched, uttering the faintly whining battle-cry of the eternally hungry. I take it slow, creeping forward until the horde, as one, sees me, and—as one—turns toward me.

It's her.

I put the Caddy in "Low" and click the safety off the Beretta.

She's there—in the middle.

The 390 roars like a demon; I'm halfway to sixty when I get there. I see her face and I know I'm cutting it close, maybe too close, but it's the only way to be sure. I hit the brakes at the last possible second, yank the wheel to the left, slam into the mass of rotting flesh and splatter bodies over the front end of the Caddy. She's there, arms out, clawing at the Caddy, only a foot away—I could have nailed her but I missed her, just. The bodies under the wheels are pulped, but heads and arms are still writhing, groping for me. Jaws clack and goo-choked pieholes make wet sounds. I open the driver's side door and slam it into the press of bodies; then I've got the Remington out and I'm standing there surrounded by them, pulling the trigger as fast as I can pump the action until there's gore everyfuckingwhere and the spent shells rain down on me like a plague of locusts. Then it's out with the Beretta, and I've got a path cleared in five shots, heads cracked open all around me. I jump on the hood of the Caddy and take out the two on either side of her, then she's clawing at me and trying to get her teeth latched on to my arm. But it's her: it's my Emily. I almost lose it, almost can't hit her as hard as I need to. I get her in a headlock and all she tries to do is snap her teeth down on my flesh, but she misses and I get her onto the pavement with my knee in her back. I have to blow away three more of them with the Beretta while I'm holding Emily down—not the easiest task in the world—and then I see the group of them crawling over the Caddy. The Beretta makes hollow clicks in my hand. I barely manage to drop it and get the first .32 out before this rotting guy missing one arm comes down on me—lucky shot, one bullet right into the mouth, upward angle. Under me Emily is writhing and shrieking, clawing for me, trying to close her mouth on my thigh. I empty the .32 and pick Emily up in sort of a bastard Full Nelson, swinging her like a pair of nunchucks, knocking a couple of the rotting bastards down. "I'm sorry, baby, I'm sorry—" I mutter as I get the trunk open. Emily claws at my face, her jaw working, her throat uttering an inhuman shriek. Then I slam her into the trunk just as a priest gets his arms around my throat and tries to drag my face into his wide-open mouth. Crap—there's a church just across the street; I'm a Catholic, I hate this shit. Screaming, I try to swing him around and get him down on the pavement so I can slam the trunk closed, but Father Zombie's teeth are shutting hard just an inch from my nose and I know he'll fucking bite it off if he gets half a goddamn chance. His mouth is oozing green puss from sores or infections all over and I'm about to puke from the smell. Ten or twelve more of them are closing in, they'll be here in a few seconds. Holding the priest against the tail fin of the Caddy I hammer down with my knee as he gropes for me, I feel the tail fin piercing his back, maybe severing his spine, but they don't feel pain like the living, which maybe is something to look forward to since my throat is hurting something awful just now. I push the friendly Monsignor harder down on the tail fin but he won't let go of me. I manage to get the second .32 out as I pull him up off the Caddy's tail fin, but I can't bring the gun into line with his face. The Caddy's trunk goes slick with blood and oozing gray-green rot. I put two bullets in his stomach but all it does is send little sprays of blood out his mouth and over my face. And he's still groping and biting at me. Now the other group of them are all around me and I know they're gonna drag me down into their midst any second. I come down hard on top of the priest, wedging my knee into his groin and then into his chest, then standing up with my foot on his throat. I point the .32 at his quickly working mouth and sneer down at him.

"Forgive me, Father, for I have sinned," I say, and put two in his head.

By then they're all around me—a postal clerk, two cops, a showgirl, a bus driver, two strippers, four or five card dealers, a lounge singer, half-a-dozen cocktail waitresses, ten or twelve guys in Hawaiian shirts—Jesus, here come the nuns. A longhair Jimmy Buffet type swings his Strat like a club—I should have brought the chainsaw. The .32's almost empty and as I turn I see that Emily has gotten out of the trunk, is crawling over the bumper holding my tire iron. "Sorry, baby, I'm sorry," I tell her as I take away the tire iron and hit her hard in the chest, pushing her back into the trunk just as three more of the fuckers come up behind me. Emily totters and then falls back into the trunk and I slam the lid down. A butcher has his arms around my leg and is going for it like it's a turkey leg. I bring the tire iron down three times as a rotting traffic cop goes for my waist. I put the last .32 slug in the oinker's head and hammer the butcher till he lets go.

They're all over the car, and in it. There's a lady construction worker searching the back seat for consumables.

Oh no they don't. Not now that I've got her. *No.*

I jump into the car and slam the door on the hand of a blue-skinned cocktail waitress coming after me. There are four of them inside now, and they're coming to get me. No time to reload the Remington. I go at it with the tire iron, aiming for the heads, taking their claws and scratches across my face and arms as I beat them until their heads start to crack open. Then I pop the box of shotgun shells as they lay there whining and clawing for me. I get the Remington loaded just as I hear the glass shattering.

They're covering the Caddy now. They've picked up garbage and rocks and are battering the windows trying to get in. The back window cracks and a bald cashier forces his head through, congealed blood oozing onto the upholstery and covering the lady construction worker.

I push broken limbs and smashed heads out of the way and try to put the Caddy in gear, sobbing like I have never done. This is *not* happening. The Caddy sticks in "Park."

The cashier is forcing his shredded body through the window, trying to claw his way toward me amid the shattered writhing corpses in the back seat. That's when I hear the sound he's making. "Meeeat," he wails, "meeeeaaaaat—"

I don't think I like that. I've never heard them *talk* before.

I hear the tranny grinding, whining, choking as I try to force it into gear. The shift won't budge.

The Caddy is covered with the groping corpses of the living dead, hammering at the car windows. The Caddy's windows are a spiderweb of bloody nightmares, and I'm caught.

And mama spider's coming for me, whispering "Meat."

There are so many squirming bodies crawling over the car that they blot out the sun. It's pitch black inside the Caddy, black as the grave except for a few sunlight streamers shining through somebody's putrefied guts.

I can hear Emily pounding from the inside of the trunk.

I close closing my eyes as I get a firm hold on the shift. The cashier is up to his waist. "Mmmeeeat!"

This is the city of dreams, I tell myself. This is the city of miracles. Viva Las Vegas. *Viva.*

I pull the shift and the tranny grinds and screams; the car pops into drive and lurches forward. I floor the accelerator and the 390 roars with the sound of a terrible authority. I can hear the crunching of bones underneath as the radials grind through the mass of flesh. I can't see a fucking thing so I slam on the brakes and the sun comes tearing through as bodies go flying. Many of them are still hanging on, though. A nurse, garbed in filthy whites, is impaled on the hood ornament, squirming and groping for me. I hit the gas again and grind more of them under the tires. Now I can see, I'm pointed right for a wall of metal garbage cans. I slam into them at full speed and hear the headlights shatter. The windows are almost all cracks, and darkened with the viscous fluids of the undead. The windshield disintegrates all around me as the nurse goes rolling back over the roof of the car, wailing. The lady construction worker and the others are writhing and spewing in the back seat, and there's that—thing—in the front seat making wet noises.

"Mmmmmmeeeeeaaaaat—" comes the screeching sound behind me, and I just about fucking lose it. It's the fucking cashier, up to his groin and covered in gore, missing half a leg but still hanging on and trying to get at me. Cursing uncontrollably and incoherently, I slam on the brakes and haul out the Remington. The cashier is reaching out for my head and he gets his skinny little fingers on my face. I get a shell into the Remington and put the barrel in his mouth.

"I'd like to cash out," I tell him, and pull the trigger, blowing a hole in the Caddy's roof.

The shattered remains of one of the nuns claw for my crotch. I hit her hard on the wrist with the butt of the Remington and then load a shell. I push the nun up against the far door so as not to have to put a load of buckshot through the floor of the Caddy and take the chance of hitting the gas tank—they don't explode, like in the movies, but that doesn't make a gas leak any more fun.

I put the shotgun in her mouth, too, and blow her almost totally out the window. Almost, but not quite. Her bottom jaw working looks kind of freaky in the absence of a top jaw. I shove with the butt and she goes wet and gooey down the side of the car. She makes hissing sounds as she slides.

They're coming after me, up the alley off of Flamingo—and another crowd racing up Paradise. Those fuckers really can move—faster than I've ever seen them move before. Competition must be getting fierce out here—natural selection and all that.

Things are getting serious.

I put it in reverse and floor it, mowing down some, impaling a couple on the tail fins. I hear Emily shrieking and carrying on in the trunk. "Sorry, baby, I'm so sorry," I whisper, as if she can hear me, and then I hit the brakes and get the Caddy in "Drive" again. It doesn't stick this time.

Then I'm out onto Flamingo with the pedal down, tearing like nobody's business. It's just open road in front of me. I almost make it to the Strip before I hear something bumping on the passenger's side; I stop in mid-street and lean out and scream. Part of the nun is glued to the Caddy, her bug-eyes and top jaw regarding me from a thing that does not look like it could once have been a skull, inside a thing that must once have been a habit. For a second it looks like the eyes are moving, but that's got to be my imagination.

I am way past puking. I smack the remains of the nun's face with the butt of the Remington and she goes slick and slidey down the side of the Cad, hitting Las Vegas Boulevard with a slurp—like so many of us.

The headless cashier I just leave there; he's not bothering me. He finally falls off, taking the back window with him, as I hit the on-ramp to 15 a little too fast, the tires squealing. "Mmmeaaaaat," I mumble to myself, sort of a private little in-joke, and that's when I realize that the lady construction worker is still squirming around in the back seat where I left her. I pull over to the side of the freeway and drag her out by her shattered legs, then I just sort of leave her there, since I'm not coming back this direction and I guess I've done enough violence for one day.

I know that sounds crazy, but sometimes it just seems like bullshit to keep killing just because they're there to kill. Occasionally I think I'm in the wrong business.

The sun is going down.

I take a long bath. I'm pretty used to the cold water by now so it doesn't bother me like it used to. I run my hands all over my body and check every inch of my skin that I can get to. I'm covered in cuts and bruises but not a single one looks like it's got tooth marks that broke the skin. *You've got a guardian angel looking out for you*, Mom used to say; she was old school, and thought God maybe loves us. I'm about to find out if she was right: I know Emily will recognize me. I *know*.

I do everything I can to wash the stink of the dead off my body. None of it seems to come off.

I've got her tied to the metal bed frame upstairs. She's still raving and drooling, she hasn't said a single word. Not even "meat." I looked into her eyes and they were blank, the pupils dilated, the whites turned pink with congealed blood. Her eyes did not light up. Her lips didn't whisper my name. Her teeth came together mechanically, rhythmically, as if working on an imaginary meal.

I swear to God if I can make her understand me everything will be all right. This whole apocalypse will be worth it if I can have Emily back. If this one woman can rise from the dead and come back to me, if I can somehow make her the woman she once was so I can love her like I did, everything that happened will be worth it.

I've been living in this place for a couple of weeks while I cruise the streets of the city. It used to be the tower of a church, the steeple. It was up for grabs when I got here. The churchyard is locked up pretty good and I barricade the doors. There's an alarm system and everything, and I was able to jerry-rig it with power from a dozen car batteries. Sometimes they climb the fence, and once or twice they've made it into the sacristy. I've stockpiled a whole lot of ammo, and the altar is looking somewhat worse for wear.

You get into the steeple by going through a door behind the baptismal font. Once I'm above the bottom level I feel pretty safe, all things considered. It's kind of like an old warehouse inside, with stained glass windows and high ceilings. I dragged a bed from the rectory up here and a bunch of candles from the sacristy, since of course there's no power for the lights. And I guess one of the nuns or priests used to grow roses, because there was a whole overgrown rose garden back there. So I clipped some of the red ones them and brought them up here in bunches for Emily, scattering them around the room. They've started to dry out and flake by now. I never was much of an interior designer but I figure if Emily comes to her senses she'll think I did all right. She always did like roses.

I put on a new suit, Armani from a boutique on Fremont Street. Some part of me thinks I should be dressed as nice as possible for Emily. I make myself a drink, Johnnie Walker from the pastor's liquor cabinet. Straight up, since of course there's no ice. I'm starving but I can't bring myself to eat after what I just dealt with. I bring the bottle and go up the many tiny stairs, locking the door to the steeple behind me. I go into what passes for the bedroom.

I've got some soft piano music going on one of those little battery-powered players, just thinking maybe that'll help Emily to sleep and when she wakes up she'll be just like she was, when she was my Emily so long ago.

But she's not. She's not asleep. The dead don't sleep. She's tied to the bed squirming and making these whining, gurgling noises, her lips and tongue and jaw working and clacking as she chomps her teeth together.

She's still wearing the cocktail dress she was buried in, that gorgeous number she always loved so much. It's black, with sequins. The sequins sparkle and dance in the flickering candlelight. Her hair, ratted and tattered, was bleached platinum blonde when she died. Now it's mottled and half-black in ruined streamers. I remember old Marty the undertaker telling me that your hair and fingernails keep growing long after you croak, which turned out to be bullshit; this is just age, age and chemical deterioration. Em's fingernails are still painted red. Her skin is white and pasty, her lips blue-black. Her tongue, an unnatural shade of grayish-pink, lolls out as she makes her little grunts and gasps of hunger. The dress has gotten pulled down a little while she squirmed, and I can see the swell of her breasts and the twin suppurated bullet holes between them. I reach over toward her. Emily strains her neck, trying to bite me as I pull the front of the dress closed and then button it.

I wish I could have given her a bath, but she was shrieking and trying to rip off chunks of my flesh and eat them. A nice relaxing soak wasn't much of an option. So I just wiped her down with rags as I could, apologizing. It didn't help much. She's still filthy.

Emily's throat emits a wild, deafening scream of hunger.

The roses don't do much to offset the other smell.

I look into her twisted face. Her eyes are empty, soulless. Her face is sickly white, tinged with blue, but I don't care about any of that; she's gorgeous. Her lips are almost black but I want more than anything else to kiss them, to tease that purpled tongue out of her mouth and feel it against mine. I try to tell myself that there's some sort of hope, that Emily is going to wake up from this any second, she'll be mine again. I sit down on the side of the bed and that's when the tears come. It just hurts too much to see her like this, more than I thought it would. I climb into the armchair I dragged over by the bed. It's been a long day. I'm asleep before I even finish the Johnnie Walker.

It always comes back to me when I'm wiped out. It makes it that much worse because I know it's real, it's as real as what's happening now.

It was right after I did the hit in the Cleve on Manny Pearlman's kid. Old JT had set things up so I could be on a plane before the cops even made the scene. I went through four airports on different flights under different names, impossible to trace. I landed in Vegas maybe twelve hours after I pulled the trigger, and Emily was waiting for me at the gate.

She wore a brand new dress, pink and white with those big poofy buttons. She had just done her hair, and she looked like a million bucks. She was driving an old Mercury and man, was it cherry. Fifty-six, baby-blue, the chrome polished till it gleamed; it had one of those sweet 292s with a stock Holly Haystack carb—hell on wheels. She even had fuzzy dice hanging from the rearview. JT knew Mercs, all right; he had kept all his promises to me and Em. "You do this for me, I'll set you up right. You'll be free and clear—we'll set you up on that retirement plan you and I talked about. You and Emily both. We'll get you married and get you a house in Vegas. None of this suite bullshit: a *house*. The job gets done, Pearlman never finds out who did it, you get a new life in the 'burbs, everybody's happy." Sounded like heaven.

So I did the job, a little reluctantly. I just didn't think it was right—but, hell, what's right any more? These days no one can say what the moral high ground is. We all make compromises and it's a sick ugly world out there. But I was gonna have my slice of Paradise. I knew Emily and me were gonna be the happiest couple of the face of the Earth.

Emily looked at me with those gorgeous brown eyes and smiled a broad smile. "You should see the house—it's like a dream! Dishwasher and everything! The bed has this motor that makes it jiggle and—Tony, oh, you don't even have to put a quarter in to make it go!" I swear, there were tears in her eyes. "We're gonna be so happy there! Hey, Tony, you must be totally wiped out after your flight."

"Nah," I said, lighting a Black Lung, double filter.

"Then hey, you wanna go out tonight? Jack says we can go anywhere and they'll treat us like royalty!" She seemed so excited about that fact, like it meant she'd finally made it in life. "We'll catch dinner and a show! Freddy Valentine is singing at the Castle—I've got a new dress and I think you'll like it . . . "

And I did. It was a tight little cocktail number in black sequins, cut short, just the way I liked it. Emily was a beautiful girl. There wasn't a lady in the world better looking than my Emily, that was for goddamn sure. We ate like King Tony and Queen Em at the Steaming Plate and cruised over in the Merc to the Castle. Emily had called JT and he had valet parking, the boys in red waiting for us and greeting us by name.

"Don't fuck with the fuzzy dice, punk," I told the parking attendant, a freckle-faced kid. I slipped him a twenty and winked at him.

"Oh, I won't, Mr. Stinson!" He smiled a big broad dopey smile and I patted him on the arm. I was feeling like a million bucks. I even had a brand new Armani on, double breasted. As we went in I reached over and gave Emily a squeeze on the ass.

"Tony!" she giggled, swatting my shoulder.

"Sorry, Em. Just can't control myself. The way you walk in this thing, you make me wanna tear it right off of you."

I leaned down and kissed her, and Emily giggled some more. "*Later*, Tony! Don't forget about the bed—"

"I got a pocket fulla quarters," I snickered.

"No, silly, you don't need quarters for this one!"

"Well I got 'em!" I laughed, and then I winked at Emily. She blushed a deep red and hid her mouth behind her pocketbook as she giggled.

Em mouthed, "I love you" at me with those kissable shiny-pink lips of hers. It was a good thing I'd got the Armani in a full-cut.

Inside, JT had the best table in the place reserved for us, even though the mayor was sitting about two tables back. I walked by the mayor and nodded. He just gave me a tight-lipped smile. The Castle was JT's club, and I was number one on JT's payroll for what I'd done, and I was getting paid back in spades. Not even the mayor got the kind of treatment I did. The rule was usually "lay low" after a job like that, but who could touch me? Vegas was JT's town. The man owned Paradise.

I pulled out Emily's chair for her, and she sat down daintily. The lights went down just as we ordered—rum and Coke for me, brandy Alexander for Em.

"Don't make it too strong," she said to the cocktail waitress. "I don't want this big strong hairy man to take *advantage* of me later."

The waitress floated off and Em gave my knee a squeeze under the table.

The club went dark. In the box, the band began to play. It was a big group with trumpets and trombones and a double-bass and three guys playing maracas, and then Freddy Valentine took the stage, lit up in a single white spot.

Now there's a man with class, I thought. He had on this understated purple velvet tux—exquisite. Black satin on the lapel, with a white carnation in the buttonhole, and a classy white tux shirt and a silver bow tie. Now there's a performer, I thought to myself. There's a man I can admire. He does what he does and he does it with balls. Freddy started into a rendition of "Viva Las Vegas" that was more like velvet than his tux.

"Isn't he dreamy?" whispered Emily into my ear, her breath warm and her lips touching my earlobe.

"Hey—" I started.

She laughed. "Don't worry, Mr. Big Shot. He's no competition for you. You're the only man I want *that* way."

I smiled, satisfied, and put my arm around Emily. She snuggled closer.

Freddy followed up Viva with "Luck Be a Lady"—gorgeous. Emily and I applauded and she even whistled like she was at a baseball game. Em was from Brooklyn.

"We've got a very special couple in the audience tonight," Freddy said between songs. "They're a wonderful coupla cats, gonna—that's right, you know it—tie the knot day after tomorrow, on Valentine's Day." There was a little chorus of "Awwwws" from the audience. "That's right. We all know about the power of eternal love." Freddy nodded to Em and me. "Let's hear a big round of applause for the soon-to-be happy couple Mr. and Mrs. Tony Stinson—!"

The applause started and Em and I did some waving. Em was blushing something fierce there in the half-light and she wore it well. Freddy went on. He got a very serious look on his face.

"That's right, cats. We all know about the power of eternal love. About the bond that happens between a man and a woman who are totally—and I do mean totally—in love. And when I say they're in love, I do mean love, L-U-V." There was a faint spray of laughter. "But all kidding aside, I'm not joking around here, folks. Love. It's serious business. And that's why I'd like to dedicate this next song to Tony and Emily, the very special couple here tonight."

There was more applause.

"Oh, Tony," said Emily, snuggling up against me, and I saw that she was crying mascara tears down her pale cheeks. I fished my handkerchief out of the pocket of the Armani and dabbed at them, smearing black all over the handkerchief.

Freddy started in with "Just Can't Help Falling in Love With You." Emily turned to kiss me in the darkness. When Freddy was done there wasn't a dry eye in the house, including mine. That's how great this guy was, total class, the best crooner in the business. I'm not kidding here. He knew it was time to liven things up so that's why the band started playing a perky island beat.

"All right, folks, there's love and then there's love. That's why we'd like to do a little number for you—" he seemed to think about it for a minute— "Maybe on a cheery note. Got a song they sing down Jamaica way, in a place called the Caribbean, see they've got stories they like to tell about a creature called the 'zombie.'" Some people in the audience laughed a little. "Hey, this is serious," said Freddy. "Hey, I think this audience is a buncha zombies. Heh heh. That's why I think it's time—how 'bout we have a special on zombies? Can we do that, Barry?" Freddy pointed at the bartender, who gave a big nod and a grin. "All right, then. Zombies, half off. Get out there, ya no-good cocktail girls. So now here's a little song, hey, pick up the tempo, guys, a little song they sing down in the Caribbean, something I like to call 'Zombie Love.'"

Freddy started singing. The song was something special, something happy and fun, about how "Zombie love, it ain't what it's cracked up to be—" a cheery, happy song, and that's why I almost forgot myself there in the darkness smoking my Black Lung double-filter. That's why I ordered another drink when the applause rippled through the audience and Freddy was taking a bow for his happy little song called "Zombie Love." And maybe there in the darkness I fell in love with Em all over again, like we were sixteen and horny, like we were just finding out what it's all about. And that's why

I maybe drank a little too much and maybe so did Emily. So when we made our way out to the car park and the freckle-faced kid brought the car around I didn't see the look in the punk's eyes until it was way too late.

The freckle-faced kid grinned his wide grin as I fumbled in my pocket for a bill to hand him. He gave me the keys and I groped after them. That's when his other hand came up holding the .38.

"Manny Pearlman sends his most heartfelt salutations on the happy occasion of your wedding, asswipe," the kid said, quickly, and pulled the trigger twice.

Emily just gasped, like she didn't realize what was happening. But the front of the black-sequined cocktail dress blossomed and red sprayed over her face. Now the kid was gone and I was on my knees screaming.

Em was looking up at me, her eyes suddenly glassy, her breath coming short. I looked into her face with sudden terror, sudden rage as I took her in my arms and whispered, "Em?"

"He seemed like a nice kid—" she told me, and then she was gone.

War for the future: No question about it. This was a new kind of war, and there were no fucking prisoners.

JT taught me that phrase when he was trying to talk me into nailing that little punk Donny Pearlman. I didn't really want to hurt a man by killing one of his relatives, a non-combatant. Just didn't seem to fit in to the code I had grown up with. It just didn't seem right.

"There is no code," JT had told me. "The stakes are too high. The world is a different place than it was, Tony. This is a war for the future. There are no rules."

JT's men had promised me revenge on Manny Pearlman. I didn't want revenge. Way I saw it, nothing mattered anymore. Me and Manny were even, and if he and JT wanted to even up some bullshit score they had between them, that was their own problem. I just wanted out. I hooked up with an outfit, doing security on oil rigs up in Alaska. Maybe I thought the cold would freeze some of the hurt out of my soul. I buried Emily in that cocktail dress she was so proud of, and I wept behind my shades as I scattered Vegas dirt across the red roses on her coffin. Maybe she was the only fucking thing that mattered to me but at least I knew that had been real. JT was right. It was a war for the future, and everybody had lost.

Sometimes I think I went a little nuts up there in Alaska. Maybe the cold froze out my brain, instead of my heart. When it started happening— when the dead started hauling their sorry maggot-eaten asses out of the grave—I realized that there was a chance, a tiny, tiny chance, that I might find my Emily, and she might welcome me with open arms.

Open arms is pretty close to the mark. But it's not exactly what I had in mind.

Roses. Dead roses. Everywhere.

I come to my senses with her hands all over me. She's clawing and scratching, biting and tearing, uttering a nightmare wail like fingernails on the chalkboard of the damned. Or something. She's got her body up against mine and her legs spread around me, grinding her crotch against mine, and so help me I've got a hard-on even though I'm bleeding all over. The Johnnie Walker is spilled across my suit. I'm pressed against the bed and Emily has got the tie pulled tight, strangling me. Somehow she's gotten loose from the bonds. I feel her teeth closing on my throat and it seems like she's ripping me open. That's when I see her wrist, and I know in a flash what she's done. She got free from the ropes by gnawing all the flesh off her wrist. And then using that mangled hand to free the other. Goo smears across my face. I hit her hard but she won't budge. I reach out blindly for the night stand, manage to pop open the top drawer. I feel the butt of the .45 and haul it out, thumbing off the safety. The Armani's come loose and Emily gets her teeth closed on a chunk of my neck, ripping it out with a shred of my shirt. I scream as I feel the flesh tearing. While she's chewing that one I get the barrel of the .45 into her mouth amid the pulpy mass of my skin.

"I'm sorry," I tell her as I pull the trigger.

One ankle is still tied to the bottom of the bed frame, so she flies halfway out of bed and sprawls there ruined and dangling. The pain in my shoulder is overwhelming, it's throbbing and blood is running all over the bed. I look down at Emily and I start to think I should cry, but I just don't feel like it anymore. I kneel over her, amid the scattered rose-petals and upended candleholders, and look into Emily's ruined face.

"Flights of angels, baby," I say. It's hard not to cry.

Sadly, I bend down and kiss the gaping mass that was her mouth a minute ago. One last kiss, tortured and romantic. She tastes like chorizo.

Far below, I hear the sound of breaking glass.

I go to the window. Below, bleached in the white glare of the full moon and mingled with my reflection, stretching out as far as I can see across the moonlit desert, is a sea of the dead, garbed in Hawaiian shirts and Bermuda shorts, black peg pants and dealer's vests, tuxedos and cocktail dresses, plaid and crepe and pinstripe: all the freaks in Vegas; a rotting ocean of shambling bodies come at midnight to church to claim one of their own.

The front of the Armani is caked with gore. My shoulder is torn open and my flesh shows. I pull the jacket off, grunting from pain, and set it on the bloodied bed. I peel off my shirt and look down my shoulder, with its missing chunk of flesh where Emily gave me her final, insistent, kiss. The wound glistens wetly in the candlelight. I turn back to the window, where the dead burbling pricks are mounting the walls.

"Guess the war's over," I say to nobody, or to my reflection.

I feel the dull dead weight of the .45 in my hand.

Downstairs, the dead are climbing.

―◄―

Thomas S. Roche is a widely published writer of erotica, horror, and crime fiction short stories, and also blogs on organized crime, sex, science, and international politics. His books include the story collections *Dark Matter*, *His*, and *Hers*, as well as the military-noir-gonzo zombie novel *The Panama Laugh*, for which nominated for the Bram Stoker Award from the Horror Writers Association. Roche has also been a finalist for the John Preston Short Fiction Award from the National Leather Association. His crime story "Hell on Wheels" was recently adapted into an audio program broadcast on BBC 4, and his short fiction has been translated into French, German, Italian, Danish, Dutch, Turkish, and Russian. You can find him at his personal website, www.thomasroche.com, as well as at his crime fiction blog, boiledhard.com.

―◄―

*It was hard to see the drug as anything but a curse that
had destroyed everything . . .*

Romero's Children

David A. Riley

*Senator Hardy launched an attack tonight against the widespread
use of the age-retarding drug OM (Old Methuselah), in which he
condemned black market sales. "No one today knows what its long
term results will be. It may halt aging in the short term, but it will
be years, perhaps decades before anyone can say that its usage is safe
or does not have possible side effects which no one at this time can
predict. People take this drug with the hope of a longer, healthier life,
but they do not know if this is all they will get."*

—One of the last newspaper reports
ever published in the United States

The old man could hear them scratching and clawing at the outside door
two floors below, trying to get in. He'd been able to hear them for the last
few nights as he lay in bed, trying to keep warm on the thin mattress of the
old cast iron bedstead, with its well-worn blankets and hard pillow. But
the door was strong. It would take months for them to wear it down and he
felt secure enough to lie listening to them without any fear. Let them waste
their energies. He was safe, if neither comfortable nor warm.

The next morning, his joints aching, Jack climbed out of bed and put
on his clothes. Although the sun rose several hours ago, it was wintry
and pale and gave off little heat, and the cold of the threadbare carpets,
scattered like rugs on the bare floorboards, chilled his feet as he trod
across them. He rooted out his boots from where he discarded them last
night when he drunkenly made his way to bed, and tugged on the socks

he'd stuffed inside them, then the boots themselves. He yawned, scratched for a minute or two, then padded across to the window. Its dusty panes looked down onto the street.

They'd gone. Romero's children nearly always disappeared when the sun came up. They preferred the night, with its darkness and shadows. In daylight they were easily seen and picked off. Even their dim minds were aware of this, self-preservation kicking in to make them hide.

Jack put on his padded outer jacket and slipped on his gloves. Snow was on its way, though he didn't need that to appreciate how cold it was. He reached for the rifle propped against the wall, safety catch on, one shell in the breach. Although he felt secure up here at night, there were always accidents—and enough survivors had been complacent in the safety of their homes that they ended up as meat.

Less than twenty years had passed since OM made its first appearance and still they were paying for it. And would till long after he turned into maggot food, Jack thought as he set about unlocking the series of doors that led down the stairwell to the street. He had installed them at the top of each flight, with spy holes through which he could see if any of *them* had gotten inside the building. That had only happened once so far. One night he had been too tired—or drunk, if truth were known—and left the door onto the street ajar. There was a large piece of wood still screwed to the last door at the bottom of the stairs to cover the hole he'd blasted through it—and through the head of the thing mewling on the other side, its beautiful, youthful, dirt-stained face visible through the fish-eye lens.

OM. It was hard to remember it now as anything but a curse that had destroyed everything. Brought an end to all the calamitous fears of global warming too, since few cars, factories or anything else mechanical or electrical had functioned for years. Yes, we sure put a stop to that all right, Jack thought to himself ironically. Something to be proud of, at least.

He pushed an eye against the spy hole of the outside door and peered onto the street. It was a rarely needed precaution. And as usual there was nothing there. Just the permanently parked cars, their ti tyres res long since flattened, while rust ate at their bodywork. There were streaks of ice along the road. And the inevitable debris.

With a sigh, Jack unlocked the door and pulled it open. It was heavy, and shut behind him with a resounding thud, before he locked it again. He swung the rifle from his shoulder and took a careful look in every direction.

In the distance three figures were running towards him. The nearest was a girl. He recognized Candice Roe at once, a hard-bitten seventeen year old from the settlement. And a damned good shot with a rifle. Which puzzled him. Why was her gun clenched in one hand when she was being pursued? It wouldn't be like Candice to have run out of ammo. Like most people these days she would carry at least a dozen rounds, stuffed in bags or in her pockets—anywhere they would fit. Ammo meant survival. Especially against stinkers.

Jack hurried towards her. He could see she was tiring and it looked as if the creatures were gaining on her. They were a man and a woman, their unwrinkled faces gray with years of accumulated dirt, dried food and blood like flaking masks of mud.

Dropping to one knee, Jack aimed his rifle at the nearest, centering the cross-wires of the telescopic lens on one eye. He eased back the trigger. The shot took away most of the upper cranium in a spray of brains, bone and discolored blood. He took out the other a few seconds later. Both lay twitching on the street when Candice reached him, gasping for breath.

"My rifle jammed otherwise I'd have taken them myself," she panted. "Must have run over a mile before I saw you. Gave me a second wind."

"Good job you did. Looked to me as if they were gaining ground."

"Persistent bastards. Comes from not having brains enough to know when you're exhausted."

Jack chuckled. "Stands to sense there must be some compensation for being brain dead psychos. That's just one of 'em."

Candice scowled. "Glad it amused you, Jack."

"It'll amuse you too as soon as you've got your breath back."

"And forgotten how close I came to becoming meat for those bastards."

"And that," Jack added, his humor dying a little. It was a danger all of them had to live with, and one that no one took lightly. They'd all seen the aftermath too often for that.

"How come you're out here by yourself?" Jack asked.

Candice regarded him edgily. "You're a fine one to ask that."

"That's my choice. One I've lived with for years. Wouldn't suit everyone, 'specially these days. But you're not a sad, dried-up old loner like me."

"No." Candice gazed down the empty street, with its stone-clad apartments, shops and offices, all of them derelict. "I just needed some time by myself for a while, that's all."

Deducing it was probably something to do with a boy and none of his business, Jack shrugged. "Okay by me. You can hunker down here for a while if you like. Leastways, I can help fix your rifle. And lend you a handgun. You should always have one as backup. Me, I have a Colt automatic. Stops 'em dead in their tracks every time. I'm not much of a shot with it, mind, but at close range I don't need to be."

"I usually have something. I just wasn't thinking today."

"Not thinking is what gets you killed." Jack gazed down the street, aware suddenly the cold had begun to sink into his bones. "I'm off after some fresh stores. D'you want to lend a hand?"

"Suppose that's the least I could do," she said, an uncertain smile twitching about her lips. "What's it today? Wal-Mart?"

"As always. Canned section."

They walked down the street in silence for a while till they turned onto the car park at the nearest store, with its abandoned cars and the skeletal remains of several hundred bodies, a grim reminder of just how turbulent times had been when the aftereffects of OM showed themselves.

"How come you never took OM?" Candice asked as they passed the first of the bodies. "There aren't many people your age around these days. Almost everyone of your generation took it. Why didn't you? Religious reasons?"

Jack shook his head. "My wife. We were both in our fifties when OM hit the headlines. She'd already started with Alzheimer's by then. What good is a drug that'll retard ageing to someone with that? Putting off old age indefinitely isn't much of a lure for someone whose brains are turning to mush. Me, I couldn't take it while Rachel was like she was. Didn't seem hardly fair somehow. An extra forty or fifty years of life didn't appeal to me then. Hell, even suicide wasn't far from my mind when Rachel passed on, that's how bad I felt."

"You were lucky."

"You could say that, though I don't reckon as I would necessarily agree. This isn't exactly how I saw my Golden Years." Jack gazed across the car park. "It was bizarre how greedy folks were for it," he said a moment later. "It was never licensed by the government, you know. Most of it was sold on the black market—a black market that became huge quickly, the demand was so big. Things went insane. Everyone wanted it, especially those who'd passed their thirties. Made the profits during Prohibition small potatoes, believe you me. Made some criminal empires enormous. For a while, at least."

"Till its aftereffects destroyed them too."

"Destroyed everything—almost. There'd been warnings, of course. Some scientists spoke out against OM. But they were ignored. Immortality was too big an incentive for anyone to wait till all the tests had been completed—tests that would take years. Too many years for most folk. Hell, if OM had come along earlier, when Alzheimer's was something that happened to other people, not to us, I expect that me and Rachel would have taken it too. Why not? We'd have leapt at the chance of putting a stop to ageing and gaining all that extra time."

"And you'd have ended as stinkers too."

"Without a doubt. Never heard of anyone who took OM without that kicking in seven, eight years down the line. Made Alzheimer's look like a dose of flu. You think we've got it bad, girl, you should have seen what it was like when there were millions of the bastards going off the rails. Looking back, it's hard to imagine how any of us survived. If'n they hadn't been such dumb bastards I don't suppose we would. Luckily, they were more often as interested in tearing each other to pieces as attacking us. Cut their numbers down a lot in the first year till some of them started working together, those that were left. The *smart* ones."

"I can't remember any of that," Candice said. "I was only a baby then. Lucky for me, Mom was only eighteen when she had me and hadn't thought about taking OM then. Before she could, it all went to Hell."

"How is your mom?"

"Okay. Feeling her age these days."

"If she's feeling her age, imagine what I'm feeling." Jack gave her a sideways grimace, then tucked the rifle under his arm, ready to fire. They were only a few yards from the main entrance to the abandoned store. Its doors had long since been reduced to splinters. The dark interior was a vast array of tumbledown shelves and scattered produce, filled with shadows. "I don't expect to come across any stinkers here. They tend to prefer somewhere less well-trodden to hang out during the day, somewhere less likely to get them shot."

"They know that well enough," Candice said sourly.

"Those that've survived this long know it. There were a lot in the early days too dumb for that. I suppose it was survival of the fittest. The dumbest were culled early on."

"So we've the brightest, eh?" Candice laughed. It was a sound that helped to lighten Jack's spirit somehow. He hated scavenging through derelict stores for the few undamaged cans of food still left in them. It depressed him. Candice's presence helped take away some of his gloominess. Perhaps he'd made too much of his preference for solitude. Now he was getting older perhaps it was time to enjoy some company for a change; maybe even join the settlement. They'd asked him often enough over the years.

You can't do penance for having outlived her forever, he told himself as he looked back on the last few days of Rachel's life. Ironically, her passing had coincided with the first of the stinkers. Romero's children.

If only they'd known how widespread it was going to be, all those politicians and scientists who had appeared on television, discussing the first cases of violence wreaked by the stinkers. The irony was that most of these people became stinkers too in the next few months.

Romero's children had sounded like a joke at first. Except these creatures weren't movie zombies. Not the shambling, ugly, walking corpses the great director had portrayed them as. They were neither shambling nor ugly. Nor dead. Far from it, Jack thought. But they were deadly all right. Just as deadly as anything ever dreamt up in Hollywood.

"Careful," Jack cautioned as they stepped inside the store. He eased some of the tension from his trigger finger as he scanned the poorly lit interior. He had been here often in the past. Knew almost every untidy pile of moldering food that had been spilled onto the floor from burst bags and ruptured packets. In a few years there'd be nothing left worth scavenging. The alcohol went long ago. Fortunately he had another source for that. One no one else had stumbled on yet.

Something scuffled deep inside the store, and Jack swore softly as he automatically fell into a crouch, gun at the ready, his eyes scanning the gloom.

"What was it? A rat?" Beside him, Candice held a knife in one hand.

Jack shook his head. "I don't know. There are enough vermin about. But that didn't sound like a rat to me." He passed her his Colt, then crept along the aisle, his head twitching from side to side. If there were stinkers present, he was confident of taking two or three of them easily enough. But there was always the chance a nest of them had decided to camp here. He had on occasion come across a dozen or more—though that was rare. The sensible thing would have been to get help. But that wasn't Jack's way. He'd been a loner too long to break old habits easily. And with Candice as back up, he felt sure they could handle up to four, maybe five between them without breaking into a sweat.

"Over there," Candice whispered. She jerked two fingers leftwards. "Behind the freezers. I saw something there. It's watching us."

Which was damnably odd behavior for a stinker, Jack thought.

"You sure it's watching us?"

"Looked like it to me," Candice whispered back. He could tell she was disturbed. She had been brought up dealing with creatures like this and probably knew their behavior as well as him. "Perhaps it isn't a stinker."

Jack didn't know. Could be someone else scavenging for supplies. But why hide? It would have been obvious who Candice and he were the moment they stepped inside the store. For a start off Stinkers didn't carry guns. Stinkers didn't talk either.

Coming to a decision, Jack stood up and advanced towards where Candice had pointed.

"If'n you're one of us step out," he said. "I'll hold my fire. We only shoot stinkers."

Even though the face had recently been washed, Jack could not mistake what hesitantly stepped out of the shadows in front, its hands above its head in an awkward gesture of surrender. It would take more than a few wipes with a wet rag to remove the years of ingrained grime from the creature's face.

For a moment Jack faltered. He knew he should aim and fire. He could have done that in a split second. Instinct tugged at nerve endings, urging him on. But he didn't. He couldn't.

He waved Candice's weapon down when she stepped up beside him.

"Why?" Her question was half bewilderment, half accusation.

Jack shook his head, uncertain. "Something odd about this thing," was all he could think to say as he stepped towards it, his finger still hooked about the trigger of his gun, aimed at waist level ahead of him.

"Who are you?" he asked.

Her clothes were tatters, held together by grease and dirt, which clung like a grimy, obscene skin to her scrawny body. The woman took a cautious step from where she had been hiding. Her fingers were black with crusts of blood and grease, the accumulated debris of a thousand meals eaten raw. She was a stinker all right. Jack was certain of that. But her face, especially her eyes, was wrong. There was fear in her eyes. And confusion.

"You hold it right there," he told her. "One more step and, like it or not, I'll fire."

The woman came to an unsteady halt. She was trying to speak. Jack was certain about that. But her tongue and jaw muscles moved awkwardly as if from lack of practice.

"What the fuck is it doing?" Candice asked.

"Damned if I know." Jack squinted through the gloom. Like every stinker he had ever seen she looked youthful. However old she may have been when she first took OM it had stopped the years from gaining on her, even though nearly two decades had passed since she took it. The drug may have messed up her brain, but beneath all the accumulated filth her body was as perfect as the day she took it.

"Awake . . . " The woman spoke in a stutter, her voice thick, as if her tongue was too large—or unaccustomed to the motions it was being forced to make. "Night . . . mares . . . gone . . . "

"You're the fucking nightmare," Candice grumbled, her eyes venomous as she stared at the woman. "We should cap that thing."

Gently, Jack touched the girl's arm. "Easy now," he said. "Stinkers don't talk."

"Then what is she if she isn't a fucking stinker?"

"That I don't know," he said. "But stinkers don't talk. I know that, if I know nothing else."

The woman swayed. She looked as if she hadn't eaten in days.

"Awake . . . " she repeated.

While Jack heaved a sack of canned goods onto his shoulder, most of their labels unreadable, Candice led the woman back to his place. The stinker's hands had been tied together in front of her. Jack had relented on this precaution. If he hadn't he suspected Candice would have used the slightest excuse—an unsteady step or an odd movement—to open fire and kill the thing.

"You're taking one hell of a risk taking this thing back to your place," Candice grumbled.

"We'll see," Jack said, unsure why he trusted the woman. But somehow, though, he did. Perhaps it was the pain, the confusion and the look of horror in her eyes that convinced him. He didn't know. Less than an hour after discovering her, though, she was sitting in a bath of warm water in Jack's apartment. Apathetically, she let Jack, and then Candice set to work scrubbing decades of grime from her thin body. For the most part the woman was placid, either through exhaustion or fear or both. After a short time she looked almost human again. Or would have except for the fact she was unnaturally youthful and too mature at the same time despite the tiredness and fear on her face. The woman's hands, especially her fingers, had blackened lines of grease and blood that would take more than soap to remove. Like Lady Macbeth, Jack thought to himself, her sins would haunt her in her hands for years to come.

He gave her a pair of trousers and a jumper to replace the shreds of clothing they had peeled like layers of diseased flesh from her body. The mess had reeked so much Jack had been forced to open one of the windows and toss them out into the street, though the apartment still had the unmistakable stench of Romero's children. They weren't called stinkers for nothing, he thought.

"What next?" Candice asked after the woman had been led into one of the bedrooms to rest.

Jack shrugged. "See if she'll eat some of our food. That's the ultimate test. Stinkers aren't interested in normal food."

"Just off the bone with the pulse still pumping," Candice said, more than a trace of bitterness in her voice.

"Never seen one eat cooked food, even when it was available."

"So if she does, she's cured? Is that what you think?"

"Maybe."

"Would you trust her then?" Candice glanced at the closed door to the bedroom the woman was in.

"I don't know," he said. "I'd have to hear her talk. Hear her story. See what she's got to say for herself. Weigh it up."

It was dark by the time they were sat about the table. Jack had prepared a thick stew from some tinned potatoes, beans, and meat they'd brought back from the store. He placed a bowl of it before the woman, along with a spoon. There was a feeling of tension as she stared at it for several moments, and Jack saw Candice's hand stray towards the Colt still tucked inside the belt of her jeans. Uncertain, the woman grasped the spoon. It shook in her fingers as she awkwardly held it between her fingers, then dipped it in the bowl, before slowly lifting it towards her mouth, spilling half its contents. She stopped as the edge of the spoon touched her lips, as if she was struggling to remember what came next. Then she pushed the spoon into her mouth. Some of the stew spilled down her chin but she barely seemed to notice that. For a moment what was left of the food rested inside her mouth, and it looked to Jack as if she was tasting—or testing—the oddity of it. Or trying to recall when she last had food like this. Cooked food. Seventeen, maybe eighteen years was a long time to remember. Could he remember what the food he ate back then was like?

After gulping what remained on her spoon, the woman surprised him by going on to clear her bowl with an appetite that made Jack wonder how long it was since the last time she ate, though he tried not to think what that meal might have been. That was her past. This was her present. Her different present, he hoped.

When they'd finished eating, Jack eased his chair back from the table and regarded the woman. Her complexion looked better now—more normal, he thought. Almost.

"Do you recall your name?" he said.

Though physically she looked no more than thirty, Jack knew she had to be fifty at least. Nearly twenty lost years of madness lay between the last time she'd used her name and now. It was easy to forget this when looking at her youthfulness.

"They—they called me—Lucy—once."

It was painful to hear that voice. It jarred with her face. A fractured, husky whisper, it made Jack's hair rise on the nape of his neck. He could see the same reaction in Candice. Which was worrying, he thought. Maybe practice would ease a more acceptable sound into the woman's voice.

Jack nodded to Candice. He introduced her to the woman. "My name is Jack."

Lucy repeated their names as if to memorize them.

"How long have you been back with us?" Jack asked. "Since the nightmares ended, I mean."

"Days—nights. I was—frightened. I hid."

"What do you remember?"

She closed her eyes and shuddered. "Nightmares. On and on . . . endless . . . nightmares."

"Before then, before the nightmares started?"

For a moment Lucy opened her eyes. She stared at him as if struggling to search back through the decades, then burst into tears. They streamed down her face unchecked. Even Candice looked concerned.

"Easy now," Jack said, quietly. "No need to struggle. If you can't remember, it doesn't matter. If those memories are there they'll come back with time."

"If you want them too," Candice said.

That night, while they lay in separate rooms, Jack heard the scratching outside again. Lucy might have come through whatever Hell she had been to, but others were still living it.

Eventually, though, he slept.

It was three, perhaps four in the morning when he awoke, aware the sounds outside had stopped. Realized they were wasting their time, he thought, though those bastards had time enough to waste, he thought to himself, aware of the irony.

He felt a chill in the air, and he wondered if the window had slipped open. But he was reluctant to leave the warmth of his bed and walk to it, knowing how bitterly cold the air would be. He opened one eye and was surprised to see how light it was. It had snowed overnight, and the building across the street was coated with piles on every ridge and window ledge, reflecting moonlight into his room. It was then he heard something move. Instantly he was wide-awake. He reached for the rifle he had left against his bed. It was gone. Prickles of alarm shivered through his body as his hand reached into emptiness. He moved his head and scanned the room. He saw a figure by the doorway, staring at him. It was Lucy. He recognized her even in the gloom. She was holding something in one hand. It was dark and round. In her other hand he saw the glint of a blade. It was broad like one of the high-tech butcher knives from his kitchen. His breath caught in his throat as his eyes adjusted to the gloom. Beyond her he could see two other figures in the open doorway. At the same time he recognized the smell that wafted from them. Had she gone downstairs and opened the bottommost door to let them? Her fellow "children." Down the front of her clothes Jack saw the vomit that had begun to dry, of the stew she must have thrown up as she lay in bed as the nightmares came and took her again.

Jack swung out of bed, though he had little hope without his rifle. But in the top drawer by the window he kept a handgun. If he reached it he would have a chance. But the thing, that had briefly been Lucy again, flung the object she held in her hand across the floor at his unshod feet, tripping him. Sprawled helplessly on his back, Jack cried out as he recognized Candice's face staring up at him from between his feet.

Lucy moved towards him, her grease-stained fingers hooked like claws.

DAVID A. RILEY has had stories professionally published in numerous anthologies including *The Eleventh Pan Book of Horror Stories, New Writings in Horror & the Supernatural, The Year's Best Horror Stories, Zombies: A Compendium of the Living Dead, The Mammoth Book of Terror,* and *The Black Book of Horror,* as well as in such magazines as *Aboriginal Science Fiction, Fantasy Tales, Fear, Whispers, World of Horror,* and *Dark Discoveries.* One of his stories, "The Lurkers in the Abyss" was recently republished in *The Century's Best Horror Fiction,* edited by John Pelan, published by Cemetery Dance earlier this year. His first collection of short stories, *The Lurkers in the Abyss,* will soon be published by Noose & Gibbet Press as a limited edition hardback in the UK.

He doubted there were many other suntanned zombies
besides Kara North, last year's Miss December . . .

In Beauty, Like the Night

Norman Partridge

The beach was deserted.

Somehow, they knew enough to stay out of the sun.

Nathan Grimes rested his elbows on the balcony and peered through his binoculars. As he adjusted the focus knob, the smooth, feminine mounds that bordered the crescent-shaped beach became nets of purslane and morning glory, and the green blur that lay beyond sharpened to a crazy quilt of distinct colors—emerald, charcoal, glimpses of scarlet—a dark panorama of manchineel trees, sea grapes, and coconut palms.

Nathan scanned the shadows until he found the golden-bronze color of her skin. Naked, just out of reach of the sun's rays, she leaned against the gentle curve of a coconut palm, curling a strand of singed blonde hair around the single finger that remained on her left hand. Her fingertip was red—with nail polish, not blood—and she thrust it into her mouth and licked both finger and hair, finally releasing a spit curl that fought the humid Caribbean breeze for a moment and then drooped in defeat.

Kara North, Miss December.

Nathan remembered meeting Kara at the New Orleans Mansion the previous August. She'd posed in front of a bountifully trimmed Christmas tree for Teddy Ching's centerfold shot, and Nathan—fresh off a plane from the Los Angeles offices of *Grimesgirl* magazine—had walked in on the proceedings, joking that the holiday decorations made him feel like he'd done a Rip Van Winkle in the friendly skies.

Nathan smiled at the memory. There were several elegantly wrapped packages under the tree that August day, but each one was empty, just a prop for Teddy's photo shoot. Kara had discovered that sad fact almost immediately, and they'd all had a good laugh about her mercenary attitude while Teddy shot her with a little red Santa cap on her head and sassy red stockings on her feet and nothing but golden-bronze flesh in between.

Empty boxes. Nathan shook his head. He'd seen the hunger in Kara's eyes when the shoot was over. A quick study, that one. Right off she'd known that he alone could fill those boxes in a finger-snap.

And now she knew enough to stay out of the sun. They all did. Nathan had been watching them for two days, ever since the morning after the accident. He wasn't worried about them breaking into the house, for his Caribbean sanctuary was a Moorish palace surrounded by high, broken-bottle-encrusted walls that were intended to fend off everyone from prying *paparazzi* to anti-porn assassins. No, the thing that worried him about the dead Grimesgirls was that they didn't act at all like the zombies he'd seen on television.

Most of those miserable gut-buckets had crawled out of the grave and weren't very mobile. In fact, Nathan couldn't remember seeing any zombies on the tube that bore much of a resemblance to their living brethren, but that could simply be chalked up to the journalistic penchant for photographing the most grotesque members of any enemy group. It was an old trick. Just as they'd focused attention on the most outrageous members of the SDS and the Black Panthers in order to turn viewers against those groups way back when in the sixties, the media would now focus on the most bizarre specimens of this current uprising.

Uprising. It was an odd word to choose—once such a hopeful word for Nathan's generation—but it seemed somehow appropriate, now stirring images not of demonstration but of reanimation. Cemeteries pitted with open graves, shrouds blowing across empty boulevards . . . midnight glimpses of a shadow army driven by an insatiable hunger for human flesh.

Nathan wondered what the network anchors would make of Kara North. All theories about media manipulation aside, he doubted that there were many other suntanned zombies besides last year's Miss December. Stateside, the victims of an accident such as the one that had occurred on Grimes Island would have been devoured by predator zombies before reanimation could occur. That hadn't happened here, because there weren't any predator zombies on the island when Kara and the others had perished. So something different had happened here, maybe something that hadn't happened before, anywhere.

Kara raised her good hand in what might have been a feeble wave.

"Freaks," Nathan whispered, unable to fight off his signature wry smile. "*Zombie* freaks." He set down the binoculars—an expensive German product, for Nathan Grimes demanded the best in everything—and picked up his pistol, a Heckler & Koch P7M13, also German, also expensive.

The sun inched lower in the sky. The waves became silver mirrors, glinting in Nathan's eyes. He put on sunglasses and the glare flattened to a soft pearly glow. As the horizon melted electric blue and the shadows thickened beneath the coconut palms, Kara North, Miss December, shambled toward the glass-encrusted walls of Nathan's beachfront palace. Again, she curled a lock of blond hair around her finger. Again, she sucked the burned strands wet.

Strange that she could focus on her hair and ignore her mutilated hand, Nathan thought as he loaded the Heckler. His gut told him that her behavior was more than simple instinct, and he wondered just how far her intelligence extended. Did she know that she was dead? Was she capable of posing such a question?

Could she think?

The curl drooped, uncoiled, and again Kara went to sucking it. Nathan remembered a Christmas that had come in August complete with the holiday smells of hot buttered rum and Monterey pine, the sounds of the air-conditioner running on HIGH COOL and seasoned oak crackling in the fireplace. He recalled Kara's dreams and the way she kissed and her red nails slashing through wrapping paper as she opened gifts he'd originally intended for Ronnie. And then, when he was fully ready to surrender to his memories, the shifting July winds brushed back across Grimes Island, carrying the very real stink of scorched metal and charred rubber.

The scent of destruction.

Nathan covered his nose and raised the pistol.

Two days ago, Nathan had the situation under control. Certainly, considering the circumstances, the arrangements for evacuating the Grimesgirls from the United States had been maddening. Certainly, such arrangements would have been completely impossible if Nathan hadn't had the luxury of satellite communications, but such perks went hand in hand with network ownership.

Two days ago, he was, in short, a completely satisfied man. After all, the foresight which some had dubbed paranoia was paying off, and his contingency plan to end all contingency plans was taking shape: he had his own island fortress, adequate provisions, and a plan to sit out the current difficulties in the company of twelve beautiful centerfold models.

So, two days ago, he didn't worry as the hands of his Rolex crossed past the appointed hour of the Grimesgirls' arrival, for the dangerous part of the evacuation operation had already been carried out with military precision. In rapid succession, a trio of Bell JetRanger choppers had touched down on the roof of the New Orleans Mansion, and the Grimesgirls had been transported without incident to a suburban airfield where a private security force was guarding Nathan's Gulfstream IV. Needless to say, takeoff had been immediate.

Of course, the operation was costly, but Nathan considered it a wise investment. He expected that there would be a real shortage of attractive female flesh by the time the government got things under control. The public, as always, would have an immediate need for his services, and he figured that the people he laughingly referred to as his "readers" wouldn't mind looking at last season's models, at least until the competition got into gear.

If there was any competition left. Nathan got himself a tequila—half listening for the Gulfstream, half watching the latest parade of gut-buckets on CNN—and soon he was imagining his chief competitors as walking corpses, one with gold chains circling his broken neck and an expensive toupee covering the gnaw marks on his skull, the other with his trademark pipe jammed between rotted lips, gasping, unable to fill his lungs with enough oxygen to kindle a blaze in the tar-stained brier.

Nathan grinned, certain that he'd never suffer such a humiliating end. He was a survivor. He had plans. And he would get started on them right now, while he waited.

He found a yellow legal pad and started brainstorming titles. GRIMESGIRLS: OUR ISLAND YEAR. No, too much fun in that one. GRIMESGIRLS: FROM HELL TO PARADISE. Better. He'd have to search for the right tone to stifle those who would accuse him of exploitation. And Teddy Ching's pictures would have to match. Hopefully, Teddy had shot lots of nice stuff during the evacuation—decaying faces mashed against the windows of the Mansion, the French Quarter streets clogged with zombies—shots that stank of danger. Pictures like that would make a perfect contrast to the spreads they'd do on the island.

GRIMESGIRLS: NATIONAL TREASURES SAVED. Nathan stared at what he'd written and smiled. Patriotic. Proud. Words as pretty as dollar signs.

Wind from the open door caught the paper, and Nathan trapped it against the table. For the first time he noticed the darkness, the suffocating gray shroud that had come long before sunset. The plane was horribly late. He'd been so caught up in planning the magazine that he'd lost track of time. Jesus. The Gulfstream could be trapped inside the storm, fighting it, low on fuel . . .

The storm rustled over the coconut palms with a sound like a giant broom sweeping the island clean. Rainwater guttered off the tile roof. It was only five o'clock, but the darkness seemed impenetrable. Nathan sent Buck and Pablo to the landing strip armed with flares. He put on a coat and paced on the balcony of his suite until the thrashing sounds of the approaching Gulfstream drove him inside. He stared into the darkness, imagining that it was as thick as pudding, and he was truly startled when the explosion bloomed in the distance. Ronnie (Miss October three years past) tried to embrace him, but he pushed her away and rushed from the room. It was much later, after the rain had diminished to a drizzling mist, that he stepped outside and smelled the wreck for the first time.

Buck and Pablo didn't return. The night passed, and then the morning. Nathan didn't go looking for the boys. He was afraid that they might be looking for him. He hid his pistol and the keys to his Jeep, and he slapped Ronnie when she called him a coward. After that she was quiet, and when she'd been quiet for a very long time he played at being magnanimous. He opened the wall safe and left her alone with a peace offering.

Downstairs, he hid the yellow legal pad in a desk drawer that he rarely opened. He closed the drawer carefully, slowly, without a sound.

That was how it began, two days ago, on Grimes Island. Since then, the living had moved quietly, listening for the footsteps of the dead.

The Heckler was warm, and as Nathan reloaded it he wished that his talents as a marksman were worthy of such a fine weapon. He set the pistol on his dresser and went downstairs, fighting the memory of the purple-gray mess that Kara North's forehead had become when one of his shots—the fifth or the sixth—finally found the mark.

That wasn't the way he wanted to remember her. He wanted to remember Miss December. No gunshots, only Teddy's camera clicking. No blood, only a red Santa cap. Sassy red socks. And nothing but golden-bronze flesh in between.

Nathan took a bottle of Cuervo Gold from beneath the bar. When it came to tequila he preferred Chinaco, but he'd finished the last bottle on the night of the crash and now the cheaper brand would have to do.

"I saw what you did." Ronnie confronted him the way a paperback detective would, sliding the Heckler across the mahogany bar, marring the wood with a long, ugly scratch. "You should have asked Kara in for a drink, made it a little easier on the poor girl. That was a damn rude way to say goodbye, Nate."

Nathan filled a glass with ice, refusing to meet Ronnie's patented withering stare, but that didn't stop her words. "She looked so cute, too, worshiping you from a distance with those big blue eyes of hers. Did you see the way she tried to curl her hair?" Ronnie clicked her tongue against her teeth. "It's a shame what a little humidity can do to a really nice *coiffure*."

Nathan said nothing, slicing a lime now, and Ronnie giggled. "Strong and silent, huh? C'mon, Nate, you're the one who blew off the top of her head. Tell me how it felt."

Nathan stared at the tip of Ronnie's nose, avoiding her eyes. Once she'd been an autumnal vision with hair the color of fallen leaves. Miss October. She'd had the look of practiced ease, skin the color of brandy, and large chocolate eyes that made every man in America long for a cold night. But Nathan had learned all too well the October power of those eyes, the way they could chill a man with a single frosty glance.

He pocketed the Heckler. He'd have to be more careful about leaving the gun where she could get at it. Coke freaks could get crazy. He poured Cuervo Gold into his glass and then drank, pretending that the only thing bothering him was the quality of the tequila. Then he risked a quick glance at her eyes, still chocolate-brown but now sticky with a yellow sheen that even Teddy Ching couldn't airbrush away.

Ronnie picked up a cocktail napkin and shredded its corners. "Why her? Why'd you shoot Kara and not the others?"

"She was the first one that came into range." Nathan swirled his drink with a swizzle stick shaped like the cartoon Grimesgirl that ran on the last page of every issue. "It was weird. When I looked into Kara's eyes, I had the feeling that she was relieved to see me. Relieved! Then I raised the gun, and it was as if she suddenly realized . . . "

Ronnie tore the napkin in half, then quarters. "They don't realize, Nate. They don't think."

"They're not like those things on TV, Ronnie. You noticed the way she looked at me. Christ, she actually waved at me today. I'm not saying that they're geniuses, but there's something there . . . something I don't like."

Bits of purple paper dotted the mahogany bar. Ronnie fingered them one by one, lazily reassembling the napkin. Nathan sensed her disapproval. He knew that she wanted him to strap on his pistol and go gunning for the Grimesgirls as if he were Lee Van Cleef in some *outré* spaghetti western.

"Look, Ronnie, it's not like they're acting *normal*, beating down our walls like the things on TV do. We just have to be a little careful, is all. There are eleven of them now, and sooner or later they'll all wander close to the gate the same way that Kara did. Then I can nail them with no problem. And then we can go out again . . . it'll be safe."

"Don't be so sure." He made the mistake of sighing and her voice rose angrily. "They didn't fly in by themselves, you know. There was a pilot, a copilot . . . maybe even a few guards. And Teddy. That's at least five or six more people." Now it was her turn to sigh. "Not to mention Buck and Pablo."

"You might be right. But who knows, the others might be so crippled up that they can't get over to this side of the island fast, or at all. Or they could have been incinerated in the explosion. Maybe that's what happened to Buck and Pablo." Nathan looked at her, not wanting to say that the boys might have been someone's dinner, and she pursed her lips, which was a hard thing for her to do because they were full and pouty.

"Hell, maybe the boys got away," he said, realizing that he was grasping at straws. "Took a boat or something. I can't see the docks from here, so I can't be sure. It could be that they reasoned with the girls, tricked them somehow—"

"Are you really saying that zombies can think? That's crazy! If they're dead, they're hungry. That's it—*that's* what they say on TV. And Kara North sucking a little spit curl doesn't convince me otherwise."

Nathan cut another slice of lime and sucked it, appreciating the sharp tang. It was the last lime on the island, and he was determined to enjoy it. "Maybe the whole thing has something to do with the crash," he said, taking another tack. "I can't figure it. I saw the explosion, but all the girls seem to be in pretty good shape. Kara was missing a few fingers and her hair was singed, and a few of the others are kind of wracked up, but none of them is badly burned, like you'd expect."

"We could drive out to the plane and see what happened for ourselves," Ronnie offered. "They can't catch us in the Jeep." She touched his hand, lightly, tentatively. "We might be able to salvage some stuff from the wreck. Someone might have had a rifle, maybe even one with a scope, and that would be a much better weapon than your pistol."

Nathan considered her argument, then jerked his hand away as soon as he realized what lay behind it. "Who was bringing it in for you? C'mon, Ronnie . . . you know what I'm talking about. Who was your mule this trip?"

She tried to look hurt. Did a good job of it. "You think you're quite a detective, don't you? Well, round up the usual suspects. Ronnie's a coke freak waiting on a mule. Buck and Pablo pulled a Houdini, or maybe they had a powwow with Kara and her pals, the world's first intellectual gut-buckets. C'mon, Nate, put it together for me, but do it before those things out there turn nasty and come after us." She grabbed the remnants of the napkin and flung purple confetti at his face. "Wake up, boss. The party's over. Me, you've got figured, but them . . . they're dead, and they're hungry, and that's that."

She let the words hang there for a minute. Then she rose and walked to the stairs, gracefully, like brandy pouring from a bottle. *With fluid elegance,* he thought wryly. He watched her calves flex, enjoyed the way she swung her ass for him. Eagerly, he ran his thumb over the little plastic breasts on the cartoon-inspired swizzle stick.

"Me, you've got figured." She did the measured over-the-shoulder glance that she'd used three years ago in her Grimesgirl centerfold, then turned and ran long fingers over her naked breasts, along her narrow hips. Nathan's thumb traveled over the cute swizzle-stick ass; he pressed down without realizing it, and the plastic snapped in two.

Ronnie laughed, climbing the stairs, not looking back.

After he'd come, Nathan kicked off the satin sheets and opened the wall safe. He cut three lines on a vanity mirror and presented them to Ronnie, then hurried downstairs because he hated the sound of her snorting. In the kitchen, he popped open a Pepsi and took a box of Banquet fried chicken out of the freezer. He chose two breasts and three thighs, placed them on a sheet of Reynolds Wrap, and fired the oven.

While he waited for the chicken, he turned on the television and fiddled with the satellite controls until he found something besides snow. Immediately, he recognized the Capitol dome in the upper right-hand corner of the screen, just below the CNN logo. It was a favorite camera setup of Washington correspondents, but there was no reporter standing in frame. There wasn't a voiceover, either.

A gut-bucket in a hospital gown staggered into view, then lurched away from the light. Another followed, this one naked, fleshless. Nathan watched, fascinated. It was only a matter of time before one of the zombies knocked over the camera or smashed the lights. Why didn't the network cut away? He couldn't figure it out.

Unless he'd tuned in some kind of study. Unless the camera had been set up to record the zombies. Bolted down. Protected. That kind of thing.

But to send it out on the satellite? It didn't make any sense. Then Nathan remembered that all satellite broadcasts weren't intended for public consumption. He might be picking up a direct feed *to* CNN instead of a broadcast *from* CNN. In the past he'd enjoyed searching for just such feeds with his satellite dish—on a location to network feed, you could pick up all the nasty remarks that reporters made about the government gobbledygook they fed to the American public, and you could find out what really went on during the commercial breaks at any number of live events.

Nathan stared at the CNN logo superimposed in the corner of the screen. Was that added at the network, or would a technician in a mobile unit add it from location? He wished he knew enough about the technical end of broadcasting to decide. He switched channels, searching for another broadcast. When he was sure he'd exhausted all possibilities, he tried to return to the CNN transmission.

He couldn't find it.

It wasn't there anymore.

A blank hiss filled the room. Nathan hit the mute button on the remote control. A few minutes passed before he noticed the burning chicken, but he couldn't bring himself to do anything about it, didn't want to look at it. Images coiled like angry snakes in his mind, ready to strike, ready to poison him. The explosion, the fleshless zombie on TV, Kara North's mutilated hand.

The snakes struck, and Nathan lurched to the sink and vomited Pepsi.

First he heard her shouts, and he was up off the couch and almost to the stairs before he remembered that he'd left the gun on the kitchen sink. He pivoted too quickly at the foot of the stairway, lurched against the wall, and then ran to the gun, Ronnie's insistent cries still filling his ears.

He returned to the staircase just as she began her descent. "He was calling me," she said, her eyes wild, unfocused. "Outside. I heard him. I went out onto the balcony but I couldn't see . . . But I talked to him, and he answered me! Christ, we've got to let him in!"

"You mean someone's alive out there?"

Ronnie nodded, naked, shivering, her hair a sweaty tangle. Nathan didn't like what he saw any better than what he'd heard. Maybe she was just strung out. Maybe she'd been dreaming. Sure.

One of the gut-buckets had pounded on the gate and she'd imagined the rest.

Or maybe someone had indeed survived the crash.

"We're not opening up until I check things out," Nathan said. "Just stay here. Don't move." He squeezed her shoulders to reinforce the order.

Upstairs, he punched several buttons on the bedroom wall before stepping onto the balcony. Deadwhite light spilled across the compound, glittering eerily over the glass-encrusted walls and illuminating the beach. A man wearing a blue uniform stood near the gate. Either the pilot or the copilot. His complexion was sallow in the artificial light, and his chin was bruised a deep purple. He stared up at Nathan and his brow creased, as if he hadn't expected to see Nathan at all.

The pilot's mouth opened.

In the distance, a wave washed over the beach.

"Ronnie . . . I've come to see . . . Ronnie."

"Jesus!" Nathan lowered the Heckler. "What happened out there? The explosion . . . how did you—"

"Ronnie . . . Ronnie . . . I've come to see . . . Ron . . . *neeeee.* I've come . . . "

The muscles in Nathan's forearms quivered in revulsion. He forced himself to raise the Heckler and aim.

He fired. Missed.

Muddy gray eyes stared into the frosty light. Wide, frantic. The thing waved its hands, wildly signaling Nathan to stop. He fired again, but the shot whizzed over the zombie's shoulder. Hurriedly, it backed off, ripping at its coat and the sweat-stained shirt beneath.

Nathan's third shot clipped the thing's ear just as it ripped open its shirt.

"I'm expected," it screeched. "Expected and I've come to see . . ."

Nathan swore, stunned by the sight of a half-dozen plastic bags filled with cocaine secured to the zombie's chest with strips of medical tape.

Ronnie's mule. Two days dead and still trying to complete its deal.

The thing moved forward. It was smiling now, sure that Nathan finally understood.

Nathan took aim—*"Nathan, stop!"*—but black lights exploded in his head before he could squeeze off another shot. *"You're crazy, Nathan!"* He hit the balcony floor, cutting his left eyebrow on the uneven tile, and his mind had barely processed that information and recognized Ronnie's voice when he realized that the Heckler was being pried from his fingers. *"He's alive, and you tried to kill him!"* He tried to rise and this time he glimpsed the heavy German binoculars arcing towards him.

He had just managed to close his eyes when the binoculars smashed into his bloody brow.

Screaming. God, she was screaming.

She must have realized the truth.

Nathan struggled to his feet just as Ronnie's cries were punctuated by gunshots. He leaned against the balcony and tried to focus on what was happening on the beach.

But they weren't on the beach. The big gate stood open, and the dead pilot was inside the compound, backing Ronnie across a patch of stunted grass. She fired the Heckler and cocaine puffed from one of the packets taped to the thing's chest. She got off three more shots that destroyed the zombie's left shoulder. Its left arm came loose, slithered through its shirtsleeve, and dropped silently to the grass. The thing stared down at its severed limb, confused by the sudden amputation.

Ronnie retreated under the jutting balcony.

The zombie followed her into the house.

Nathan stumbled through the bedroom doorway. Ronnie wasn't screaming anymore. That sound had been replaced by subtler but no less horrifying noises: the Heckler clicking, empty, the zombie whispering Ronnie's name. Dizzily, Nathan reached the top of the stairway just as Ronnie mounted the first stair. He tried to grab her but the pilot got hold of her first and tugged her away.

It stared at her for a moment, still pleading, as if it only wanted her to take delivery, but as it pulled her closer its expression changed.

Its nostrils flared.

It pushed her down onto the stairs and held her there.

Its mouth widened, but no words were left there.

Its eyes were wild, suddenly gleaming.

Hungry.

Dry teeth clamped Ronnie's left breast. She squealed and pulled away, but the thing punched its fingers through her left thigh, holding her down. An urge had been triggered, and suddenly the gut-bucket was insatiable. Its teeth ripped Ronnie's flesh; it swallowed without chewing; it was a shark in the grip of a feeding frenzy.

Nathan backed away, staring at the zombie, glancing at the empty pistol on the hallway floor. Another gut-bucket shambled forward from the shadowy bar. This one had something in its hand, a machete, and Nathan was suddenly glad that he was going to die because he didn't think he could bear living in a world where you couldn't tell the living from the dead, where fucking corpses could talk, could remember, could fool you right up to the moment when they started to bite and tear and swallow . . .

The rusty machete cleaved the pilot's head from his shoulders; the dead thing collapsed on top of Ronnie.

The holder of the machete stared up at him, and Nathan froze like a deer trapped by a pair of headlights.

"Christ, boss, don't worry. I'm alive," Buck Taylor said, and then he went to close the gate.

Buck said he couldn't eat or drink so soon after cleaning up the remains of Ronnie and the gut-bucket pilot. Instead, he talked. Nathan tried not to drink too much Cuervo Gold, tried to listen, but his thoughts turned inexorably to the puzzle of the pilot's strange behavior.

"So the storm was coming down in buckets, splattering every damn inch of soil. Pablo was drinking coffee, and I'd had so much that I just had to take a piss, but it was really coming down—"

The rusty machete lay before Buck on the oak tabletop; his fingers danced over the blade as he spoke. He had once been a center for the Raiders—Good Old Number 66 had never missed a game in seven seasons of play—but Nathan couldn't imagine that he'd ever looked this bad, not even after the most desperate contest imaginable. His bald pate was knotted with bruises, and every time he touched them he looked wistful, like he was wishing he'd had a helmet.

"—so I hacked my way into the forest and got under a tree, that kind with leaves like big pancakes. And I started to piss. And just then I heard the engines. Holy Christ, I got zipped up quick and—"

The twin sixes on Buck's football jersey were smeared with slimy black stains. There was a primitive splint on his left arm, held in place with strips torn from a silver-and-black bandana. The massive biceps swelling between the damp strips of wood was an ugly color much worse than the blue-green of a natural bruise. It reminded Nathan of rotten cantaloupe, a sickly gray color. And the smell coming from the other side of the table was—

"—pissed all over my leg. I ain't ashamed to say it, because the left wing tore off just then and I thought I was dead for sure, with the plane heading straight for me. So I dived—"

Quickly. The pilot had been able to think quickly. He'd ripped off his shirt to show Nathan the cocaine. He'd gotten Ronnie to open the gate. And even though he'd lost an arm to Ronnie's gunfire, he'd acted as if he believed that he was still alive until he got close to her, the first live human he'd encountered since reanimating. That confrontation had triggered his horrible—

"—second thoughts, but there wasn't time. The broken wing flipped around in midair like a piece of balsa wood. No telling where it was gonna end up. Then the 'stream slammed sideways into a big stand of palm trees that bounced it right back onto the landing strip. It rolled and the other wing twisted off. And the wing that was still in the air—"

Came down on the machete. Buck's fingers did. Nathan watched them, and he slid away from the table, eased away from Number 66.

"I could see Pablo in the van. Even through the storm. I saw him trying to find a place to set his coffee. And then the wing hit the van, and the damn thing just exploded."

So the van had exploded. That was why the zombies hadn't been burned. The plane hadn't even caught fire—its fuel tanks were probably near empty after fighting the storm. But the van had had a full tank.

"I'm ashamed about that, but there was really nothing I could do. The fire was so intense. Even the zombies didn't go near it, and by the time it burned itself out there wasn't anything left of the van or Pablo."

Nathan's fingers closed around the pistol. He remembered the pilot ripping open his shirt. He remembered the pilot grabbing Ronnie, the momentary confusion in his muddy eyes, the excited gleam as he surrendered to the feeding frenzy. Buck was in control now, surely he was. But what would happen when he came close to his boss?

Nathan raised the Heckler. Buck grinned, like he didn't quite understand. Nathan looked at Buck's wounds, at the untouched glass of beer in front of him. Good Old Number 66 wasn't drinking, and he hadn't wanted any fried chicken. Maybe he didn't want fried chicken anymore. Maybe he didn't realize that yet, just like he didn't remember what had killed him.

"Buck, I want you to go back outside, back out with them," Nathan said, speaking as he would speak to a child. "You see, risking temptation is the dangerous part. It'll make you lose what's left of your mind."

"Boss, are you okay? Maybe you should get some sleep, stop thinking about Ronnie for a while. Maybe you should—"

Oh, they were smart. Getting smarter every minute. "You can't fool me, Buck. You can fool yourself, but you can't fool me."

Nathan aimed and Buck jolted backward, out of his chair, scrambling now. The first bullet exploded his left biceps, shattering the makeshift splint as it exited, but Buck didn't slow because football instincts die hard. He sprang to his feet, tucked his head, and charged across the kitchen.

His eyes shone with vitality, but Nathan was certain that it was the vitality of death, not life. Buck launched himself in a flying tackle and together they crashed to the floor. Nathan raised the Heckler, and Buck couldn't fight him off because the wound in his left arm was too severe, so he fought back the only way he could. He bit Nathan's shoulder, set his teeth, and tore.

Nathan screamed. White blotches of pain danced before his eyes.

Nathan's finger tightened on the trigger.

A bullet shattered the skull of Good Old Number 66.

Nathan saw it this way:

The crash had killed them instantly. All of them. And when they opened their eyes they found themselves on Grimes Island, just where they were supposed to be, and they imagined themselves survivors. They wandered through the lush forest, across the coral beaches, finding nothing to tempt them, nothing to trigger the horrible hunger.

Trapped in a transition period between death and rebirth they retained different levels of intelligence but were limited by overwhelming instincts. Instinctively, they knew enough to stay out of the sun. It was a simple matter of self-preservation, for the tropical sun could speed their decay. The instinct to devour the living was strong in them as well, but only when they were exposed to temptation. Nathan was sure of that after his experiences with Buck and the pilot. He was also certain that as long as temptation was absent up to the very point that the feeding frenzy took control, the dead of Grimes Island could still function at a level that separated them from the gut-buckets. Oh, they functioned at different sub-levels as he'd seen with Kara North, the pilot, and Buck, but in some cases, they functioned just as well as the living.

Perhaps something in human flesh, once devoured, triggered the change in behavior. Maybe something in the blood. Or perhaps it was the very act of cannibalism. Nathan didn't know the cause, didn't much care.

His wounded shoulder was scarlet-purple and swollen. Five days had passed since Buck had attacked him, and he couldn't decide if the bite was worse or better. Just to be safe, he'd injected himself with antibiotics, but he didn't know if his first aid made the slightest difference.

He didn't know if he was alive, or dead, or somewhere in between.

To clarify his thoughts, he noted his symptoms on the legal pad he'd hidden in his desk after the plane crash. Many were perplexing. He wished that he could consult with a scientist or a doctor, but his first attempt at stateside communications had proved fruitless, and soon he was afraid to communicate with anyone. He didn't relish the idea of ending up as a science project in some lab, and he didn't want an extermination squad invading Grimes Island, either.

The thing that bothered him most was that his heart was still beating. He couldn't understand how that was possible until he remembered that Buck's heart had been beating when he'd shot him—Nathan had felt it pounding against his own chest as they wrestled on the floor—and he was certain that Buck had been dead. Looking at his wounded shoulder, remembering the fire in Buck's eyes when he'd attacked, Nathan was positive of that. There were other symptoms, as well.

He couldn't eat. Every evening he cooked some fried chicken, even though the smell made him gag and the oily feel of it made him shiver. Last night he'd forced himself to eat two breasts and a thigh, and he'd spent the next five hours coiled in a cramped ball on the kitchen floor before finally surrendering to the urge to vomit. And he couldn't keep down Pepsi or Jose Cuervo either. The Cuervo Gold was especially bad; it burned his throat and made him miserable for hours. He did suck ice cubes, but only to keep his throat comfortable. And he'd started snorting the cocaine that Ronnie's mule had brought in, but only because he was afraid to sleep.

Cocaine. Maybe that was the problem. They said that cocaine killed the appetite, didn't they? And he'd started using the stuff at about the same time that he'd stopped eating. But five days without food . . . God, that was a long time. So it had to be more than just the cocaine. Didn't it?

He closed his eyes and thought about hunger, about food. He tried to picture the most appetizing banquet imaginable.

Nothing came to him for the longest time. Then he saw Kara North's mangled hand. The pilot's severed arm. Buck's ruined head.

His gut roiled.

He opened his eyes.

The facts seemed irrefutable, but somehow Nathan couldn't bring himself to leave the compound or, conversely, let the Grimesgirls enter. They were on the beach every night, enjoying themselves, tempting him. Miss November and Miss February sang love songs, serenading Nathan from the wrong side of the glass-encrusted walls. He watched them, smiling his wry smile on the outside, inside despising his cowardice.

He was bored, but he didn't risk watching television, either. If the networks had returned to the airwaves, he would certainly find himself looking straight into the eyes of living, breathing people, and while he seriously doubted that such a stimulus could trigger the feeding frenzy, he didn't want to expose himself, just to be on the safe side.

He didn't want to lose what he had.

So he snorted cocaine and wrote during the day. At night, he watched them. They all came to the beach now, even Teddy Ching. He had no legs; that's why he'd taken so long to cross the island. But Teddy didn't let that stop him. He dragged himself along, eagerly pursuing the Grimesgirls, his exposed spine wiggling as happily and uncontrollably as a puppy's tail. Three cameras were strung around his neck, and he often propped himself against the base of a manchineel tree and photographed the girls as they frolicked on the beach below.

More than anything, Nathan wished that he could develop those pictures. His Grimesgirls were still beautiful. Miss July, her stomach so firm, so empty above a perfect heart-shaped trim. Miss May, her skinless forehead camouflaged with a wreath of bougainvillea and orchids. The rounded breasts of Miss April, sunset bruised and shadowed, the nipples so swollen. The sunken yellow hollows beneath Miss August's eyes, hot dry circles, twin suns peering from her face with all the power of that wonderful month.

Twin suns in the middle of the night.

She walks in beauty, like the night . . . in beauty, like the night . . . of cloudless climes and . . . starry skies and all that's best of dark and bright . . .

And all that's best of dark and bright . . .

Nathan couldn't remember the rest of it. He wrote the words on his yellow pad, over and over, but he couldn't remember. He closed his eyes, and when he opened them the sea was hard with the flat light of morning.

He hurried inside long before the sunshine kissed the balcony.

The beach was deserted.

———

NORMAN PARTRIDGE's fiction includes horror, suspense, and the fantastic—"sometimes all in one story" according to Joe Lansdale. Partridge's novel *Dark Harvest* was chosen by *Publishers Weekly* as one of the best one hundred books of 2006, and two short-story collections were published in 2010—*Lesser Demons* from Subterranean Press and *Johnny Halloween* from Cemetery Dance. Other work includes the Jack Baddalach mysteries *Saguaro Riptide* and *The Ten-Ounce Siesta*, plus *The Crow: Wicked Prayer*, which was adapted for film. His work has received multiple Bram Stoker awards. He can be found on the web at NormanPartridge.com and americanfrankenstein.blogspot.com.

———

He thought he'd learned you could get used to anything,
but then he encountered Susan . . .

Susan

Robin D. Laws

It had taken him until his fifth trip to the loading dock of the old sugar refinery before it finally came to him what the smell reminded him of: alligators. Saint Augustine's Alligator Farm in St. Augustine, Florida. His parents had taken him there when he was a little kid. And, in turn, he'd taken Maggie and the kids during their own trip down there, just three years before The Rising. How could he have forgotten that smell? Thick, damp, loamy. Thousands of alligators lolling around, packed together in mossy water, shitting and pissing and screwing and fighting over chicken carcasses. Grinning up at you as their reek rose into the humid air. Like they knew their stink was going to stay on your skin and hair, root its way into the fabric of your polo shirts and your cut-off jeans and stay there for as long as it could. They might be penned up and put on display, those alligators, but they could still fuck with you. A little last gesture of impotent reptilian malice.

Well, this place smelled like that. It hit you as soon as the guy opened the big corrugated metal door. Forster was glad to have finally pegged the thing that had been nagging at him all this time.

Forster reached for his wallet to pay the guy but Tim, who'd come in behind him, put a restraining hand on his shoulder. The guy waved the two of them through with no payment exchanged. This was a new arrangement. Tim had paid the hundred bucks for Forster last time, but now he seemed to have some kind of comp privileges. It did not surprise Forster that Tim might be providing some kind of quid pro quo service for them. Even if he'd been able to rouse himself to curiosity over this minor detail, he knew better than to ask. If it was interesting enough to come up in idle conversation, Tim might drop a mention of it. Forster had established himself as worthy of trust.

They headed towards the steps that led up to the top level of risers. Tim liked to survey things from on high. Observe the bettors as well as, maybe even more, than the competitors. The first couple of times, Forster had preferred to get his face closer to the action. Now it was fine by him to sit beside Tim. On the way up the stairs, Forster stopped his hand just short of getting a big splinter from the railing. It, like the rest of the bleacher structure, was chunked together from raw, unfinished lumber. The first time it was all fresh and new, like it had been put up the previous day. Now it was starting to get grimy.

"Watch out for splinters," he said to Tim.

"Thanks," said Tim.

They were hardly at the top of the stairs when one of Tim's regulars was on them, panting like a big old sheep dog. Large, wide, bald face distinguished mostly by his big comb-over and silver-framed aviator glasses. He wore a cheap, brown suit, the polyester fabric pilling up at the knees. Matching brown tie, lighter brown shirt. Forster had him down for a government employee of some sort.

"Hecuba's gonna freakin' kick freakin' righteous ass tonight," the regular said. He put extra emphasis on the word *ass*. "I can feel it. It's gonna be her biggest night yet."

Tim leaned his long body casually up against the railing and reached for the cigarette he'd tucked behind his ear. He didn't light it or anything: just played with it, tapping it against his left palm.

"Think so?"

"Know so."

"That kind of certainty . . . I don't know. What kind of odds we want to talk?"

Forster sidled past them towards the usual spot on the third-last bench up. The odds-making process was of little interest to him. He wasn't here to bet. He'd burned out on gambling a long time ago.

He lowered himself onto the hard bench and looked down at the other people. Immediately below him, a white-haired man spoke in a high, flutey voice to a broad-shouldered guy in a plaid flannel shirt. At least a generation separated them and something about the ease with which they sat together said to Forster that they were father and son. Directly over, a very obese young woman with stringy hair and a big white sweatshirt with a picture of Border collie puppies on it unrolled a paper bag and took out a rattling package of cheese doodles. Down front was a row of Tamil guys, all of them in ski vests. The Portuguese, Chinese, and gangbanger delegations were also present in force. They waved fistfuls of hundreds at each other. Forster saw Tim's leather cowboy hat down there among them; he was weaving between the groups, making notes with his stylus on his knock-off Palm Pilot.

The place was fuller than it had ever been before. Word was really getting out. Forster was surprised that the organizers were willing to let so many in. Too many people knew now for this to go on for much longer. The cops would get tipped off and come in the middle of the night with the heavy-duty Gauzner sprayers. They wouldn't bust in during an event, with the bleachers full. Too big a chance of things getting out of hand. As much as they'd like to track down each and every spectator and see them slapped with ten-to-fifteen for criminal facilitation, illicit custody of PMAs, first degree.

Forster closed his eyes. The insides of his eyelids burned. He needed more sleep. He wished he could close his nostrils, too. Identifying the smell had done nothing to make it more tolerable; just the opposite.

He must have nodded off because he started when Tim leaned on his shoulder sitting down next to him.

"Good action?" Forster asked, by way of conversation. Tim nodded. Forster thought maybe there might be a hint of a grin on him somewhere, but with Tim you couldn't always tell.

The P.A. made itself known with a squeal of feedback. Tim shuddered, but Forster did not. Every freaking time they had the mike pointed into the speakers. He'd come to expect it.

The voice at the mike did not trouble itself to rouse any extra anticipation or excitement in the crowd. It was an unconfident teenager's voice, occasionally cracking and inevitably rising towards the end of each sentence. "Everybody get ready for tonight's bout," it said. "Tonight we have the new challenger, Orkon the Eviscerator." The crowd greeted this news with a ritual booing. Orkon was here as meat, just like all his predecessors.

Heavy blue drapes parted down on the left side of the pit, and out came two men in big padded suits, like for attack dog training. Riot helmets made them look like they had bug heads Riot helmets made them look like they had bug heads. They wheeled in Orkon on an industrial-size upright dolly. Six wide leather belts, each with a huge rusty buckle, secured the zombo to it. They had a big fake Viking helmet with tinfoil-covered horns plunked on his head. Orkon looked like he had some fight in him; he hissed and snapped his half-missing teeth at the ring men as they wheeled him to his corner. He wriggled and strained at the belts but there was no give in them. It would be good to start the match when he was still pissed, so they left him in place and hustled it across the ring and through the drapes on the other side.

Forster could see a wave of doubt ripple through the guys nosed up to the Plexi-shielding in the front row. Maybe this one was ready for Hecuba. Some bills changed hands. But then the voice announced the arrival of the previous all-time champion, and the small crowd surged to its feet and was stamping and whistling. They began to chant "He-cu-*ba*, He-cu-*ba*, He-cu-*ba*." Forster half-heartedly chanted along at first, but then left off, not sure who he actually meant to root for.

The ring men came back with the second dolly, this one bearing the shorter, stouter corpse of a woman. Forster had spent a certain amount of time thinking about her, wondering who she'd been before she got bit. There was something about her pear-shaped figure, her wide thighs and the vestiges of sandy, permed hair on the top of her head that, to Forster, said supermarket checkout clerk. Possibly a Wal-Mart greeter. Definitely someone from the lower echelons, like that. Well, she'd found a distinction now she'd never had when she was breathing. More money had changed hands on her in the course of a couple of matches than she'd probably earned in her whole living existence.

Unlike her opponent, Hecuba was not moving at all. Those little lizard-smart eyes of hers were darting back and forth, but that was it. "Conserving her energy for the fight," Forster heard the white-haired dad say to his son, giving him a rib-nudge. The son must have been the newbie; Dad the old hand. Forster had listened to many of the bettors go on about Hecuba, theorizing that she knew exactly what she was doing. She knew she was competing; she had that something extra, that motivation, that made for a champion. Forster had not stirred himself to disagree but had seen nothing in her, other than the usual insensate, predatory stimuli-and-response behavior. She was just faster and meaner than the others, that's all.

The audience was clapping rhythmically, building itself up into a big crescendo. The organizers weren't much in the way of showmen, because they didn't wait for it to peak or anything. The announcer did nothing to build or shape their anticipation. Forster had to admit, though, that this actually gave the thing an air of authenticity, that he would have soured on it even sooner if it had been all faked up. Maybe they knew what they were doing after all.

The ring men casually reached into a toolbox that had been sitting center-ring the whole time, and withdrew from it a pair of plastic Super Soaker squirt guns, one in bright neon green plastic, the other in pink. Both were stained red-brown. Each ring man stepped back, took aim at one of the zombos, and let loose, drenching his target.

The contents would be human blood. Zombos could not, under normal circumstances, be induced to attack each other. They could sniff out live from dead. The only way to make them go apeshit on each other was to spray them with the fresh stuff from a live victim. After his first match, Forster asked Tim where they got it, but Tim refused to speculate. Which answered the question, more or less.

The ring men retreated, and from backstage, one of them hit the remote switch that blew the micro-charges on the belts. Little plumes of smoke rose up from the dollies as the zombos staggered forth. From his struggling with the restraints just a few seconds earlier, a bettor might have put his money on Orkon being first to free himself, and to capitalize on that. But the bigger corpse staggered around, batting at the rising puffs of burnt powder, as Hecuba crouched down, hissed, and made a run at him. She tackled Orkon, knocking him off his feet, and began to claw at his eyes with her jagged, extruded fingernails. Tim leaned forward, biting his lip. One of the Portuguese guys got up on his bench and executed a little dance of exultation. Orkon bucked, squirming out from under his attacker, and flailed wildly at her head. He lunged for the side of her throat and she scrabbled backwards on the particle board flooring. He dived at her. She thrust herself upwards and back to a crouching position. Orkon rose to his feet, too.

The Viking helmet had fallen off in the melee's first moments. As part of the whole warrior theme, the ring men had strapped a belt, scabbard, and sword to Orkon's otherwise naked waist, and for a moment it seemed like he was going to pull the sword and go hacking at Hecuba's head with it. But instead he just tore the belt off and tossed it aside. He threw his head back and shrieked, his gray tongue flopping past his chapped and peeling lips. Hecuba held ground, pawing the flooring with her splayed left foot. Forster noticed there were a couple more toes missing than last time. Hecuba braced for Orkon's charge, and he came at her headlong. She back-swatted him with her hand, the force of which hardly seemed to register with him. He howled again, then thrust a punching hand deep down into her chest. Even Forster couldn't help but wince with the sound of cracking bone. Orkon kept his hand inside her, his shoulder muscles working like he was groping around for something. Another distinct snap followed. Orkon withdrew his bile-smeared arm, holding something long and sharp-ended in his quivering fist. He'd snapped off one of Hecuba's ribs. The room went quiet as the bigger zombo took a step back, raised up the rib like a dagger, and then stepped forward to drive it down through Hecuba's left eyesocket. Leaping from the flooring to put all of his weight behind the blow, the challenger knocked his prey down. Hecuba's limbs flopped like trout on the floor of a boat, then stopped. Orkon pushed his face deep into her gaping chest cavity, to feed. Moments later he leapt back, shaking his head from side to side as he spit chunks of unsatisfyingly dead meat from his jaws.

Then he did the thing every victorious zombo did, the thing that the organizers relied on to control their fighters. He smelled the sweaty, agitated spectators and leapt like a frog onto the reinforced Plexiglas. Blue sparks ran up the metal stanchions separating the see-through panes. Embedded filaments too small to see carried the current to the zombo at its every point of contact with the barrier. Orkon convulsed three, four times, and then fell motionless to the ring's floor, face up and spread-eagled. The ringmen dashed out and rolled their victor into a canvas tarp, which they then pulled tight with what had to be several dozen sets of belts and buckles. By the end of the procedure, Orkon had opened its eyes and was irregularly blinking. The ring men hastened their buckling, and soon it was completely unable to move. They finished off by gingerly wrapping a ball gag around its slowly jawing mouth. A tentative-looking assistant, also fully geared up in padded armor, piloted a gurney onto the stage. The ringmen casually hefted the bagged zombo and flipped him onto the gurney, which they quickly wheeled off through parted curtains.

Forster could hear the blood rushing past his ears. Not a sound in the entire freaking place. He looked at the men across from him, saw their dropped jaws, and checked his own to see if it were also swinging back and forth like the head of a drinking bird. It was not.

The serene expression on Tim's face as he rose to make his rounds through the arena showed that his money had been on Orkon.

Down front, a short, buck-toothed man wearing a fur cap sat staring at Hecuba's opened corpse, tears rushing down both of his capillaried cheeks.

Tim sat across from him in their habitual coffee shop, his arms splayed across the red fake leather covering the backs of the booths. He had laid his hat down beside him, revealing his receding hairline, as accentuated by his habit of gelling his hair tight to his pointy-crowned skull.

"I had opportunity to smell-test Hecuba a couple days back," he said. "Much as they tried to mask it, you couldn't miss the formaldehyde. I mean, just count back the months to her first match. She had to be getting pretty squishy."

"I think I'm bored with this shit, too," Forster said.

"Don't tell me."

"I hardly felt anything at all this time."

The waitress came with their coffees. Tim ordered an open-face turkey sandwich with mashed potatoes. Forster glanced at the menu for the first time, scratched his neck, and said he'd have what his friend was having.

"What has it been? Just six times? And it's already paled on you."

"The process of my beginning to feel nothing seems like it's accelerating. It's the same curve, just faster now. Like I could plot it on a graph." Forster fished a ballpoint out of his coat pocket and began to draw a curving line, like the dorsal surface of a whale, on the diner's all-white place mat. "First is the fear, I feel my heart pumping, and from then I can begin to feel other things: elation, fury, a sense of connectedness to the people around me. Then the fear dies down. Revulsion comes into replace it, and that's fine, too. That's feeling something, after all. I'll settle for revulsion, I think. Then thorough self-loathing. Even more unpleasant, but still feeling. Then this begins to leach away, too, leaving just this sort of flat . . . grayness. Like the people around me are actually a million miles away."

"Present company excluded, naturally." Tim inspected the cigarette he'd been fidgeting with, broke it up into three pieces, and deposited it, unsmoked, in the amber-colored ashtray.

"The drugs were the first, and they lasted the longest of all. There were so many different ones to try. And part of the experience is the people you're around when you're on them, and the things that happen. But the end of that curve was when I couldn't get a buzz off anything. All just maintenance. Big deal. The good time period: that lasted, what, eighteen months? Nearly two years?"

"Sounds about right. Plenty of people party-heartying then."

Tim would know; he'd been Forster's dealer from the start. The two of them had been in grad school together, way back. Now here they were again. Each was the only person the other could fully talk to. Tim had to dumb himself down around the lowlifes he worked with. References to Foucault or Godard strictly off-limits. Forster could share his spiral with no one at the office. The Post-Rising labor market tolerated many quirks, but certain things you didn't discuss in the break room.

"Then the hooker thing," Forster continued, "that overlapped, but all told lasted me maybe a year. Little less."

"Lots of people find that alienating."

"The various fetish scenes—I know you don't want me to get into the details—"

He could see Tim tense up. "Yeah, keep it to vague allusions. That one time I asked . . . "

"Each of those was its own separate curve. Things I never thought I'd ever see myself doing, then quicker and quicker, I was not only doing them but had gone through them, they were dead for me, passé.

"Okay, the S/M scene, that's so all-encompassing. That did last longer than some of the things before it. But still, same pattern. Part of me was hoping that this deathmatch thing . . . It wasn't sexual, it wasn't bodily, it would be different. The spiritual purity of the degradation of it, it would last longer. And the first time—"

"A classic match. Hecuba's first."

"Thought I'd shit myself, I was so scared going in. Scared of a raid. Of it being a scam, of getting robbed and beaten. Of how I'd react when I first saw one of them again. Of maybe one of them getting loose, biting somebody, starting a cascade."

"And jeez, when the head went flying into the crowd . . . "

Forster remembered his coffee and took a big drink of it before it cooled too much. "Yeah, maybe that was part of it. That first one was so . . . so . . . intense that the rest could only disappoint from there. If that third match, that awful drawn-out one where they just wouldn't go for each other—If that had been my first one, if it had built up more, maybe I'd still be feeling a jolt. But the whole time tonight, I kept waiting for it to kick in, and nothing."

"Yeah, that night, that was a classic, all right."

"But tonight, it was all just the same old dull feeling—the same non-feeling. And the people around me, I didn't feel like I was part of them, a member of their race, or even in the same room with them. Like I'm watching via a grainy, black-and-white security monitor. The only thing that got my blood pumping at all was first contact with that smell, and even that was only for the first few moments. You can get used to fuckin' anything, that's what I've learned."

"Ever given any thought to Africa? Or New Orleans?" Tim was referring to places where the syndrome still raged. Most of the Third World still writhed with it; their governments couldn't afford the full array of Gauzner technologies. They had plenty of the bombs but not enough spray units. Various outside funding proposals were snarled in the U.N. for the third year running. New Orleans was still under military quarantine, with only the most determined death's-heads getting through. The whole coastal region of Louisiana kept breaking out and no one was quite sure why. Urban legend held forth on the subject of a Gauzner-resistant strain, but proofs remained elusive.

"They don't interest me. I keep telling you, it's not a death wish. I want to feel the opposite of dead. If I wanted to top myself, I'd just head out to the viaduct and jump. To expose myself to the infection again—you know what that would betray."

"Yeah. Of course." Tim pursed his lips. "I didn't mean to—all I was saying is, the gladiator thing, I was really hoping it would last longer for you."

"Yeah, me, too." The waitress brought the food. Forster stared down at it, unhungrily. Tim dug in. The matches always gave him an appetite.

"Look," said Tim, between oversize mouthfuls of mashed potato and gravy. "I knew this time would come, though not so soon. And you know I sympathize with your malaise. And admire the headlong way you pursue it. There for the grace of god and all that.

"So.

"There's this thing. I been keeping it in reserve for you. I'm only in the preliminary stages of hooking it up. The people who handle this, they're not my usual circle. You'd say they're several circles away, okay? So what I'm saying is it's all chancy. Can't guarantee anything. And if it does go through, these are some crazy, nasty mofos and I can't extend any kind of my usual dispensation. If things go wrong, it's all on you, right?"

Forster sat forward. He felt like his heart had started up again.

"It's really freaking sick, okay? And if this doesn't do it for you, I tell you, my wad is shot. There's no further frontier I'm capable of pointing you towards. But, jeez, if you're into it, it should last you more than six lousy times. Now I know you know the kind of discretion I expect of you. So don't be insulted if I repeat that this has absolutely, in no circumstances, not a word breathed to anyone except for me. This is not like the thing tonight, where they're inviting in half the world and its uncle. Okay?"

"Come on. Tell me."

Tim looked around for eavesdroppers. "Like I say, it's preliminary. It might not come off."

"Come on."

He leaned forward and spoke sotto voce. "How would you like to fuck one of them?"

He walked home from the subway, rock salt crunching under his boots, his breath illuminated by orange streetlights. The very idea of it had given him a hard-on, his first in months. The bitter chill of the air invigorated him. He strode up the concrete steps towards his building's foyer, reaching into his pocket past the Ziplocked supply Tim had sold him, to his keys. As he unlocked the front door, he saw, through its glass, a slim figure wearing a hooded coat. Forster could not see her features, but knew her frame. Sephronia. Her presence utterly deflated him, threw him back into the gray again. He resigned himself and opened the door.

She stepped towards him. "John, I've been waiting for you, hoping you'd—I'm sorry, but this is the only way."

Forster stood before her, paralyzed, not knowing whether to stand there and take it or shove past her wordlessly.

She took another step his way, and lowered her hood, revealing the harsh pink and unwholesome smoothness of the scar tissue that covered her face and entire skull. She'd left off her wig. The gesture was one of remonstrance. Forster knew he should be feeling bad, but had forgotten how.

"I need you to see me," Sephronia said. "To look into my eyes."

He had done this to her, tenderly, over a period of weeks, with a portable acetylene cutwelder. She had consented to the act, sure, but in the expectation that he'd keep her around. That it was a sealing of the permanency between them.

"Please at least say something."

"If I could think of something to say, I would."

She made a third step toward him. He thought he might flinch from her, get backed into the mailboxes, but found himself standing his ground.

"I've been thinking," she said. "That you didn't see the degree of commitment I had ready for you. That you needed to see how far I am willing to go for us."

She pulled back her coat's fake-furred left cuff, to reveal, at her wrist, a freshly cauterized, naked stump. "I did this to show you."

Forster finally found what it took to brush past her. "That's sweet, honey, and I wish I could care." He slid-clicked the lock on the interior door and slipped through. She tried to catch it and hold it open, but he closed it quickly. He headed to the stairs without looking back at her. As he walked up towards his apartment door, he tried unsuccessfully to make himself feel guilt for what he'd driven her to, or, if not that, at least empathy for her state. Most elective amps started with their off-hand, but Sephronia did everything with her left. She'd find someone. The amp lifestyle was one of the fastest-growing out there. She'd get over him and settle down with some young, apprehensive stump-lover anxious to abase himself before her every crippled need. Maybe if he knew she'd end up worse off than that, he'd be able to conjure up the proper remorse.

He looked again at the slip of paper with the address on it. He'd expected another disused industrial site, like the one where the fights were held. But this was an old restaurant with papered-over windows. NEW HARMONY RESTAURANT, said the sign that hung overhead. "DELICIOUS" MEALS— "delicious" in quotation marks.

His hard-on was back, after having deserted him again. The anticipation had made him feel real, for the first couple of weeks. By week three, with still no phone call from Tim, it trickled away. With anyone else, Forster would have concluded he'd been taken in by a line of bull, but he trusted Tim better than that. Tim had made clear that his arrangements might not come through. By the time the call came, Forster had given up on the whole prospect. Yet here he really was, he told himself, really standing in front of the place where he was going to get to fuck a zombo. There were three doorbells, and he'd been told which one to buzz, and how many times to hit it. As he followed his instructions, it occurred to him that the sex of the subject had never been mentioned. He thought it would be better if it were female. Despite his expanded experiences of the aftermath years, he hadn't completely shaken his preference for the woman's equipment.

They kept him standing there for a while, stamping his feet against the sharp cold. Finally a small tear opened up in the butcher's paper that lined the glass door. Dark, heavy-browed eyes appeared.

"Yeah?" said a voice muffled by the glass.

"You got some videos for me to return?" replied Forster, providing the prearranged response.

The door opened. The man behind it was mountainously tall and fat, wearing a food-stained, khaki T-shirt stretched too tight across his belly and man-tits. His long beard and shaggy dark hair were all of a piece. He didn't step aside to let Forster in until Forster took a step towards him. He glowered suspiciously down. Forster understood this as the intimidation necessary to the arrangement. Still, a little talk from the guy could at least indicate what was expected of him next. He looked around at the interior of the building. The restaurant fixtures had been completely torn out. Busted pieces of gyp-rock lay on the floor amid a dusting of plaster. Most of the golden wallpaper had been torn off the walls, but a few pieces remained, and they were stained the color of rust. Could well have been blood; this place might have been a massacre site. This had been one of the city's worst-hit neighborhoods.

Two men appeared, from what would probably have been the former kitchen. One wore a Juventus soccer jersey over gray wool slacks and had a heavy gold chain-link bracelet around his hairy wrist. The other was skinny and looked like he should be working in tech support somewhere, with a white dress shirt, bushy carrot-colored hair, thick-framed glasses, and an overbite.

Juventus-jersey did the talking. "You're Forster?"

Forster nodded.

"Cash up front."

Forster reached casually into his coat, pulled out the roll, and tossed it to Juventus, who plucked it from the air and, without looking at him, passed it back to Tech Support. "Count this," he said. Tech Support rolled away the thick rubber band, dangling it off his thumb as he riffled through the bills nearly as fast as a machine would. Juventus pocketed the entire amount and left the room, going back where he'd come from.

Man-Tits lumbered forward and pointed towards a wooden door, painted white. "She's down there." Forster had been in some pretty brusquely run brothels before, but this was the epitome. It was perfect.

Tech Support evidently felt the lack of amenities and beat Forster to the door, opening it wide for him. He gestured for Forster to precede him down the dark stairs. For a moment, Forster's shoulders tensed up, ready for a conk from behind. But he'd already given up all but pocket change. They had no good reason to conk him.

Forster heard a switch flicked behind him. A utility light hung from a wooden ceiling beam. The staircase led down into a dingy corridor. There were more rusty stains on the whitewashed walls. Under the stairs stood a row of unplugged refrigerators.

"So," came Tech Support's voice, "do you, uh, live in the city, or have you come down maybe from somewhere else?"

Forster was uncomfortable with them even knowing his real last name. The guy had to be fishing for clues they could use in an after-the-fact blackmail operation. "No offense, but I'm not really in a frame of mind for chit-chat."

"Right, sure."

Forster reached the end of the staircase, expecting Tech Support to follow and point him towards the room where she'd be waiting. Instead the guy sat himself down on the second-last step. He brushed some lint off a pant leg. "Look, the others only care about money. For you to do your business and go." He had some kind of subtle speech impediment, but Forster couldn't narrow down exactly what. "But there's a right way and a wrong way to, uh, go about this." He stopped, clearly struggling for the exact right phrase. "Look, you've got to treat Susan in a certain way. You can't assume just because of her condition that she isn't feeling what's happening to her." Tech Support's eyes were watering up. He stuck a finger in past his glasses to rub at an eye. "Try and be—I know gentle sounds funny. It's not the right . . . I guess try and be receptive to her mood, to the kinds of movements she makes." He swallowed hard. "Don't just force yourself and pump, pump, pump. That makes Susan very unhappy, very unsettled for days afterwards. For you, this is just a one-time thing. In and out. Just try to understand and don't be a jerk." He looked searchingly up into Forster's face, presumably looking for a nod of assent or something.

Forster gave him nothing. The guy was creeping him out. He'd felt fine until this. "Which door do I go through?"

Tech Support stood, pulled on his sleeve. "It's not just for her sake I'm asking. It's much better if you let Susan take the lead. You'll like it a lot better, I swear. Really."

"Which door?"

Tech Support pointed to a door at the end of the hallway. Forster walked down to it. Forster looked back and saw Tech Support looking at him forlornly. The guy was draining his jolt. Forster turned around.

"You aren't going to be standing outside the door, are you?"

"Well, uh, I'm supposed to . . . just in case there's a problem."

"But there won't be a problem, will there? Everything is well secured, right?"

"Yes, yes." He started to approach. "I've readied her. You won't have any problems. Just be . . . "

"Because no offense, but I don't want to be aware of your presence. Right?"

Tech Support nodded quickly, up and down. "Right, right." He pivoted and scampered up the stairs.

Forster waited until he heard the upstairs door close shut. He turned back towards the door. He stopped to take a deep breath, to try to refocus himself, to try to get the awareness of what he was about to do surging through his body again. He took a big snort of air like it was coke. And another. He put his hand on the door handle and stepped into darkness. It smelled both like alligators and like formaldehyde. Immediately a noise started up, a low punctuated growl like a cat struggling to choke up a hairball. He reached out and groped for a light switch. Fluorescent lights flickered and then grudgingly went fully on.

She lay face down on what looked like a hospital bed, pastel green paint chipping off its metal frame. They'd spread her out, strapping each leg to one of the bedposts. To accomplish this, they'd twisted both of her ankles severely. Her skin was paler than the specimens Forster had seen at the zombo matches, making obvious a complex of purple bruises around the restraints. As he stepped closer towards her, her growling upshifted into a sort of frenzied pant. He could see her trying to lift and turn her head to see him. A brittle mass of peroxided hair wildly haloed her head, hardly moving as she thrashed. As far as Forster could tell, she'd have been an average-looking woman in life, tall and thin-boned but no particular beauty. The bleached hair was out of character with the rest of the corpse: undoubtedly a post-mortem addition. She shook the bed frame but could not budge it from its moorings; it had been bolted into the concrete floor. There was some give in the bolts, though. He wondered if they knew. He would tell them afterwards. The presence of a little risk made it better.

Forster took another step forward. He slowly moved his fingertips towards the back of her thigh. He left them in the air for a moment before bringing them brushing against her ashen flesh. It felt rubbery and not ice cold, but cool. Her flailing intensified and he pulled his fingers away. He leaned in to study the surface of her skin. White-lines crisscrossed it, and Forster was curious to know what they were. On close inspection, they seemed to be bloodless, open, scabless cuts, perhaps made with a thin blade like a box-cutter's. Maybe they were just artifacts of handling.

A pair of black fake-satin panties had been put on her; they were at least a size too small, and her dead flesh puckered at the waist and leg holes. Forster's hand went out towards them. Then he stopped, and remembered to look around the room for holes in the walls or ceiling. Starting with the places that would afford the best view of his face, he quickly spotted a drill-mark, and checking it out close, a pinhole lens. He withdrew a deck of Post-it notes from his jacket pocket and fixed the gummed edge to the wall, just above the hole. He glanced back at the door, saw that it had a cheap brass slider to bolt it shut. He slid it. Forster turned back towards Susan and her black panties. Without looking too closely, he shoved them to the side. He was rock-hard.

He unclipped his sleek gold-and-silver belt buckle and unzipped his fly. She had stopped her screaming and thrashing. He looked again at Susan. He stepped back. He bit his lip. He checked himself; he was still hard. He zipped up his fly and buckled his belt.

He sat down on the cold cement floor.

Well, Forster thought. Well. Who'd have thought? I've found it. I've found the place. The place below which I will not go.

Well. This has been well worth the money. He breathed in deep. He would remember the air he was breathing. He ran his hands together. They felt real and solid for the first time since the night when it all happened. He ran his fingers over his face. That felt real, too. He felt that he was inside himself. Not above or outside, but inside.

He walked over to Susan and moved her panties back into place. The contact started her to shrieking again. He backed off, startled. He had to look away from her. He sat down again. His chest felt like he was back on speed.

Wow. A place below which I cannot go. Wow.

He unbolted the door and opened it. Juventus and Man-Tits were standing right there, with Tech Support off to one side.

"You didn't take too long in there," Juventus said, expressionless.

"You know what? I've discovered I'm not up to it. I thought I would be but I'm not."

Juventus rolled his tongue thoughtfully under his closed upper lip, his eyes still empty. "Then we have a problem."

Forster felt dampness at the collar of his shirt. He knew that to get through this, he would have to fake the very detachment that had just fallen away from him. "I'm not asking for my money back. I've just decided I don't actually want to fuck the zombie, that's all."

Juventus shoved him back into the room. "You're going to fuck that zombie."

"What? What do you care? You have my money." Juventus shoved him again. He pointed to the Post-it note on the wall.

"You'll excuse me," said Forster, wishing his voice wasn't rising so high, "if I decided I didn't want streaming video on your website of me porking a zombo."

"But you haven't porked jackshit," Juventus said. Another shove. "Raising the question of whether you're a cop. So to prove you're not a cop, you're going to fuck that zombie and I'm going to stand here and watch."

Forster momentarily took his eyes off Juventus and looked behind him, at Tech Support. He looked very unhappy, too. Afraid this would be tough on Susan, no doubt. She was hissing and dry-retching again. Forster glanced down and saw that the bolts holding down the bed were even looser than before.

"You can't just make a guy fuck something. I mean, if you don't got the wood, you don't got the wood."

Juventus smirked. "We got an injection to help you in that area. For twenty-four hours, you'll be a rebar." He made a vague waving gesture; Tech Support opened a plastic case and handed a syringe to Man-Tits.

Forster leapt up to try and grab Juventus by the ears. Juventus punched him hard in the gut and he doubled over. Forster duck-walked backwards and sank to his knees at the head of the bed, gasping. Man-Tits advanced on him. Forster reached over to the belt holding Susan's left hand to the bed post and wrenched open the buckle. She bolted upwards, her freed arm arcing over to the other wrist.

"You crazy motherfuck!" Juventus said, wide-eyed and frozen. "Get the sprayer!" he yelled. Susan ripped the other belt in two and wrenched herself upwards, heaving the bed out of its moorings. It flipped upwards with her and its head-beam clipped Man-Tits on the temple as she lunged for him. She and the bed landed on Man-Tits and shook around. He howled as the bed bounced up and down and blood began to pool out onto the floor. Tech Support was gone from the hallway. Juventus reached for an ankle holster, pulling a small pistol and firing shots into the bed, probably hitting Man-Tits as well as Susan. Then her claws snaked out and grabbed his leg, pulling him off balance and onto his ass. She clawed into his thigh, opening an artery. Juventus groaned and clamped his hands over the wound. Susan slashed away the bindings on her ankles, wriggled from under the bed, and began to gnaw on his crotch. She sunk her fingers into his skull and banged his face repeatedly into the concrete. When Juventus went motionless, she whipped around to face Forster, crouching as Hecuba had.

Tech Support appeared at the doorway, holding a gleaming, unused Gauzner sprayer out before him like an assault rifle. His face was beet red, his nose leaking snot. "Susan!" he yelled. "Susan!" Until she finally turned around.

"Susan, you got to listen to me," he said. She wove in the air before him, like a cobra before its charmer. "Susan, please. I don't want to have to use the sprayer. You do understand the sprayer, right? Just calm down. Everything can be all right. Just us now. No more others. You've taken care of these two. That's all you need to do."

She darted forward and ripped his belly open. She clamped one hand around his jaw-line and lifted him up over her head and against the wall. She banged him against it just like she'd smacked Juventus against the floor. He hadn't died yet and was pleading with her the whole time, though with her grip on his windpipe Forster couldn't make any of it out. She began to keen, almost like she was singing a note. Forster circumnavigated the crumpled bed and Man-Tits' already-shuddering corpse to grab the sprayer. Gauzner designed it to be operable even by a small child in emergency circumstances. Forster pointed it at Susan's back, pulled its big trigger, and watched the blue liquid hit her, slackening and melting the muscles of her back. She fell like a sack. He sprayed her some more, then pointed it under the bed to douse Man-Tits. Then he did Juventus and Tech Support, before they even started moving.

Forster dropped to the floor himself, when it became clear the lot of them were topped. He sat there gulping. He thought about what had happened during The Rising, when the intruder bit Maggie, who then passed it on to the kids. How when they came for him his instincts had taken over, the pickaxe in his hand. How he'd dug it into their skulls, instead of doing what he'd later wished and letting them take him, too.

He'd piece out the exact reasons later, but right now what he knew was he'd come alive again. Silently, he thanked Susan for the resurrection.

The fiction of author and game designer ROBIN D. LAWS includes *The Rough and the Smooth*, *Blood of the City*, and *New Tales of the Yellow Sign*. Robin created the GUMSHOE investigative roleplaying rules system and such games as *Feng Shui*, *The Dying Earth*, *The Esoterrorists*, and *Ashen Stars*. Find his blog, a cavalcade of film, culture, games, narrative structure, and gun-toting avians, at robindlaws.com.

The zombies in this story within a story appear in a teleplay outline—a
simplified version of a real (but never-approved) outline the author wrote
for a certain TV series. Zombies are, after all, fictional.
Monsters, however, we encounter all too often . . .

The Blood Kiss

Dennis Etchison

She had told herself that it might never get this far, all the while hoping
against hope that it would. Now she could no longer be sure which was the
delusion and which the reality. It was out of her control.

"*Chris*? You still here?" It was Rip, the messenger boy who had hung
around long enough to become Executive in Charge of Special Projects.
Whatever, exactly, that denoted. He caught the door as he passed her
office, pivoting on one foot and swinging the other up to cross his knee
with his ankle, the graceful pose of a dancer at rest or the arch maneuver
of a runner pretending that he was so far ahead he no longer had to hurry.
She couldn't decide. She studied him abstractedly and feigned amusement
as he asked, "Aren't you going to the party tonight?"

"Do you care whether I go to the party tonight?"

"Sure." He grinned boyishly, as though forgetting for the moment that
he was thirty-five years old. "The network's going to be there, you know."
He glanced up and down the hall, ducked inside and lowered his voice
to make a joke of his naked ambition. "You hear what we're getting for
Milo?"

"Let me guess," she said. "A belly dancer? No, that was for his birthday.
A go-go boy from Chippendale's?"

Rip imploded a laugh. "You've got to be kidding. He can't come out of
the closet till the third season."

"You never know." You wish, she thought. Closet, my ass. I could tell
you some things about Milo, if you really want to know. But you probably

wouldn't believe me; it wouldn't fit your game plan, would it? Milo the Trouser Pilot. Dream on. "I give up," she said, "what?"

Rip closed the door behind him. "We hired this bimbo from Central Casting. She's going to come in—rush in at five minutes of twelve, all crying that she just totaled Milo's car out front. You know, the white 450 SL? She's so sorry, she's going to pay for everything, *if her insurance hasn't expired.* Milo's freaking, right? So she gets him up to the bedroom where the phone is, she's looking for the number, she starts to break down, she whips off her dress and offers herself—when all of a sudden, surprise! It's a strip-o-gram! Happy Valentine's Day! We're all coming. You got a camera, Chrissie?"

"I'll bring my 3-D."

"What?"

"See you there, R. Right now I've got to retype my outline." What time's it getting to be? she wondered.

"You mean 'Zombies'? I thought it was all set."

"It is. But Milo had some last-minute suggestions. Nothing major. He wants it on his desk tomorrow morning."

"Great," said Rip, no longer listening. "Well, don't work too hard."

If I don't, she thought, who will?

"And Chrissie?"

"Yeah?"

"Have yourself a fabulous evening, stag or drag. Remember, *Don't Open the Door*'s headed straight for Number One—we've got it made! Uh, thanks to your episode, of course. 'Queen of the Zombies' is going to put us over the top!"

"Thanks for telling me that, R."

And don't call me Chrissie, she thought, as he let himself out.

I have it made, you have it made, they have it made, we have it made. . . . I'd like to see them, Milo or anybody else in this production company, do the real work for once: interviewing writers, extracting stories, rewriting all night so there's something more than high concept to give the network. . . . I should have stayed a secretary. At least I'd sleep better.

But then where would they be? And where would *I* be? Back in Fresno, she thought. At my parents'. Instead of here, scuttling around behind the scenes to hold this surrogate family together. If I had a dollar for every time I've saved Milo's tight little ass the night before a pitch . . .

With stories like this one, she thought, shuffling papers.

I finally found the right one. Oh, didn't I. This time, miraculously, it was all there when it came in over the transom; the only real work I had to do was to punch it up a bit and hand it to M for the presentation. The perfect episode to launch the second season. That's what they called it. I wanted them to think it was mine, let's be honest. And it worked. Am I really supposed to give back this office for the sake of an abstraction? Who is Roger Ryman? With the specifics changed it will be all but unrecognizable by the time it shoots—I'll see to that; they'll let me do the script. Who else? And with it will come a full credit at last, Guild membership.... Who will be the wiser? Ryman is probably earning an honest living somewhere, and better off in the long run. He'll never see it. I'll bet he doesn't even have cable.

But what if one of his friends sees it?

Forget it, Chrissie. *Chris.* You're psyching yourself out.

You wanted in this way, admit it. You did.

She removed the last sheet of her latest revision from the typewriter, the one incorporating the changes from today's meeting with. Milo, and began proofreading from page one:

```
        QUEEN OF THE ZOMBIES
                 by
         Christine Cross


1. 24-HOUR SUPERMARKET—NIGHT

Three o'clock in the morning. The market is under
siege—by the walking dead.                        .

Zombie shoppers converge on the produce department,
where the NIGHT MANAGER and a CHECKER, his girlfriend,
are hiding behind the lettuce. He's got to get her out
of there before they spot her. They want something more
than fruit and vegetables.

He makes it to the p.a. system, grabs the microphone,
announces a special on liver as a diversion. The
zombies shamble off to the meat department.

He sends the CHECKER crawling to the front door—but
now zombie reinforcements are pouring in from outside.
She changes course, sidles between the aisles, is
pressed back to the meat department, where the zombies
are busy feasting on liver.
```

One lone zombie arrives at the end of the cold case. All the meat is gone. Rings the bell with thick, jerky movements. No answer. So he climbs up over the counter, grabs the BUTCHER hiding there, lifts him, sticks a hand into the BUTCHER'S abdomen and takes his liver.

As the feeding frenzy continues, the CHECKER is splattered with blood and guts. She screams.

"CUT!"

We see that a movie is being shot in the market. But the GIRL who plays the CHECKER won't stop screaming. As the zombies take off their masks she runs from the set, hysterical.

"Great!" the DIRECTOR says to his FX MAN. "Only next time more blood, okay, Marty?"

He goes off to find the GIRL.

* * *

2. OUTSIDE

In the parking lot, the DIRECTOR comforts her. She wants to please, knows she's not giving him what he needs, but it's too much for her. She's cracking. She's about ready to get on the bus back to Indiana.

The DIRECTOR needs her. She's going to be the Queen of the Zombies. He sends her back to the Holiday Inn. A hot bath, rest—what else can he do for her? He'll even rehearse her later, in private, if that's what it takes.

She put down the pages. Perfect, and so was the rest of it. Now it really moved. Screw the outline, she thought; I could go to script right now, while I've got the momentum, if Milo didn't need to send this version to the network for approval first. A formality. I could keep working—I didn't want to go to that godawful party, anyway. I can have it done ahead of schedule . . . They'll finally realize how important I am to this operation. It might even occur to Milo that he needs an Associate Producer. Why not?

Was he still in his office? She could pay her respects now, beg off for the evening, explain that she's going home to work. That would impress the hell out of him. Wouldn't it?

She clipped her pages together and reached for her purse.

The hallway smelled faintly of disinfectant, and in the distance she heard already the bump and rattle of waste baskets as the cleaning woman moved from room to room in the building, wiping up other people's messes for them and making things right again. As Chris passed the reception area she saw the cart of brooms and cleansers behind a half-closed door, and beyond, through the window in Rip's office, the skyline darkening under a band of air made filthy by another day in the city. It was later than she had thought.

"Good night," she called out.

The cleaning woman straightened and wiped her heavy hands on her uniform, then let her arms hang limp with palms open, as if afraid to be accused of stealing. Her face was flat and expressionless. "Have a nice— nice holiday," Chris added. Well, it wasn't really a holiday. Did the woman even understand English?

Before she went on they exchanged a last glance. The other's gaze was steady and all-accepting, beyond hope and yet strangely at peace. There was a hint of disapproval in the deadpan face; it left Chris vaguely uneasy, as if she were a teenager spotted sneaking in or out of her bedroom. In fact the look was almost pitying. Why? She lowered her eyes and moved away.

She rapped on Milo's door, then entered without waiting for permission.

The room was empty. Of course he hadn't bothered to say good night. Why should he? He never had before. That would change, of course. She had had her office for three days, but it would take awhile for that to sink in for all of them. Things would be different around here soon enough.

She saw the usual signs of a hasty departure. A row of empty Coke cans, a drawer still pulled out for Milo's feet, a flurry of message slips like unfilled prescriptions curling next to the phone, a rat's nest of papers teetering at the edge of the desk.

In spite of herself she found the sight more touching than appalling. He needed someone to bring order to his life, to tidy up after hours each night. He couldn't do it alone. It wasn't his fault, she reasoned; it was his nature. . . . She felt like the sister who corrected his homework for him while he slept, the girlfriend who slipped him answers to the big test, the mother who saw to it that his hair was combed before he left for school.

She was none of these things, she knew, but soon he would recognize her worth. The days of being taken for granted were over.

She smiled as she crossed the office and set her corrected outline triumphantly on the glass desktop, where it would be waiting for him in the morning. He couldn't miss it.

She stacked the message slips, centering her pages between the overflowing ashtray and the rings left by his coffee cup. She positioned his paperweight to hold the pages in place, aligned a pencil on either side to frame them, and started to leave.

The cart was clattering out of Rip's office, heading this way. What if the cleaning woman rearranged things further, slid the pages to the bottom of the wrong pile?

Chris would have to tell her not to touch the desk.

But what if she could not make the woman understand?

She sighed and emptied the ashtray herself, dumped the cans into the waste basket, wiped the glass top and lined up the rest of his artifacts so that nothing on the desk would have to be touched. As she pushed his notepad under the phone and made ready to leave before being caught in the act, the bell within the phone mechanism tolled once, disturbed by the impact. She blinked.

And saw what was written on the top page of the pad.

She blinked again, reread it, her mind racing to understand.

It was in Milo's familiar scrawl, his last memo of the day. She had no trouble making it out. It read:

BILL S. TO WRITE QUEEN OF THE Z'S. WHO'S HIS AGENT?

She stared at it.

She put her hands on her hips, shifted her weight to one foot, then the other, looked out the window and saw nothing but blackness, and read it one more time before her eyes began to sting. The meaning was unmistakable.

Milo had already assigned someone else to do the full script.

She was not even in the running.

She never had been.

She would be lucky to receive a split credit. No, probably not even that much.

Suddenly the scales lifted from her eyes.

She could already envision another writer's name on the screen.

Perhaps Milo's alone. It had happened before.

It follows, she thought. God, does it ever.

And I didn't even see it coming.

Of course she wouldn't be able to file a protest, because that could lead to an arbitration that might reveal the true author whose work she herself had appropriated.

I have, she thought, been had. Again.

But this time I'm not going to settle for the bone they've tossed me. Not now.

This time it stops here.

She picked up the ashtray and hurled it across the room. It smashed into the framed LeRoy Neiman print hanging on the wall. Then she took back the pages and walked out of the office, bits of broken glass sticking to the soles of her shoes and grinding underfoot.

Startled, the cleaning woman stepped aside.

"Not this time," Chris told her through tears of rage. "*Comprende?* I—I'm sorry. Excuse me . . . "

I've made a mistake. A terrible, terrible mistake.

Or someone has.

In her office, she riffled through the file until she found the original draft synopsis, submitted without an agent by an unknown whom she had never met, Roger R. Ryman. He had included both his home and work phone numbers on the title page.

She throttled the receiver, breaking a fingernail as she dialed.

At first he didn't recognize her name. But when she said the magic words, *Don't Open the Door,* he remembered the series and his submission and almost squeezed through the phone to lick her face.

Yes, he would meet her anywhere, anytime.

She gave him Milo's address.

He didn't think it at all odd that she asked him to meet her at a Valentine's party.

3. AT THE HOLIDAY INN

She calls home tearfully. She's getting ready for that
bath, when the DIRECTOR walks in.

Everything's going to be all right. You can do it,
he tells her. He'll work with her personally. He
takes the part of a zombie during their run-through,
touches her, grabs her, enfolding her. She responds

desperately, forgetting the script. She needs him.
And she thinks he needs her.

* * *

4. LATER
She calls home again—but with a different story this
time. Yes, she's doing okay. She's going to make it
out here, after all.

"And Mama? I met a man. Not just any man. He's wonderful,
so kind. He really cares what happens to me . . . "

Great, she thought. Now the only question is, Which one is he?

Bodies of all sizes and shapes streamed past her, arrayed in costumes of one sort or another—heart-shaped hats, dresses with arrows, shoes with cuddly designs, kitschy T-shirts, enameled pins, patterned headbands, pastel jogging suits from the Beverly Center, ersatz camp from Melrose Avenue. Teddy bears lurked in corners with *billets-doux* pinned to their bibs; Mylar balloons drubbed at the ceiling like air bubbles at the surface of an aquarium. She gasped for breath as unidentifiable people bobbed around her, all luminous collars and teeth under the ultraviolet lights, and searched for an opening before the pressure of the music closed in on her again. As she swam against the flow for the nearest door, something like a pincer tried to grasp her thigh, while in the shadows the bears with their shiny black sharks' eyes seemed to move their heads, following her progress.

Another record began to pound, "Waiting Out the Eighties" by the Coupe de Villes, as long-necked men with trimmed moustaches collected around a garish buffet in the kitchen. She had almost passed through when she noticed a huge dyed paté, its top cleaved to resemble the wings of a gull in flight. The center collapsed to reveal a dull, livery interior as the men dipped *hors d'oeuvres* into the mold and made jokes, a thin film of workout sweat glazing their receding hairlines. She recognized the most animated of the conversationalists."

"Rip . . . "

He grasped her shoulder and drew her to arm's length, holding her until he finished his joke, as though she had intruded on an audition. When he finished he threw his head back and laughed too loudly, his Adam's apple bouncing up and down in a vigorous swallowing motion. Finally he turned to her.

"Chrissie, love!" He pulled her closer. "Mark, I'd like you to meet our new Story Editor."

"Rip, have you seen . . . ?"

"No, I don't know where Milo's scampered off to. But I'll bet he's up to no good." He hooked a thumb at the ceiling. "Try topside."

"Rip, if anyone asks for me . . . "

"If I were you, love—" Rip winked. "I wouldn't disturb him just yet."

I'm on my own, she thought. I always have been. The rest was an illusion.

"Never mind." She hoisted a fresh champagne glass, emptied it.

"See you at midnight," she said, slipping through to the stairs.

There were a lot of voices up there. Perhaps that was where she would find what she was looking for. It was getting late, and she had to have everything in place before the fireworks started.

5. MAKEUP AREA—THE NEXT DAY

She's in the chair, getting the coddling she needs from her new family. The MAKEUP MAN is kind, sensitive. She may have left her real family back home, but at last she feels that she belongs somewhere.

When she leaves the chair, the MAKEUP MAN and CREW change their tune. The poor kid's getting to be a pain. She's too nervous, high-strung, dangerously unstable. But it's too late to replace her. Time is running out.

* * *

6. ON THE SET
She breaks down again. The DIRECTOR tries to coach her but it's still not enough. She's too insecure. After take twelve, she pleads with him for the chance to do it again.

"Tell me the way you told me last night. I only want it to be good."

"That's all I want, too," he tells her.

The dim stairway was tricky. A blur of zippy, ironic faces as she ascended: young men without sideburns and casually elegant young women dragged along like camp followers, their made-up smiles fixed and grimly determined. Her wrist brushed something cold and slick. It was a heart-shaped satin pillow, carried as an offering by someone of indeterminate gender. She drew away and hugged the wall as she stepped over sodden paper plates; she made out an imprint of two lovebirds billing and cooing beneath half-eaten potato salad and drooping chicken wings.

"Excuse me," she said.

"Excuse *me*," said the person with the pillow. "Are you the one?"

"I hope so," she said, averting her eyes and hurrying on. Then the words and the masculine timbre of the voice registered. She stopped, looking back.

"I beg your pardon," she said, "but . . . "

Below, a nostalgic sixties strobe light flickered over dancing heads, rendering them all as anonymous as a second-unit crew.

She felt as if she were still trapped in a pattern that had been set decades ago. It would never change unless she did something about it. This was no time to falter. She remembered something her father had said to her before he went away. *When you sit, sit. When you stand, stand. But don't wobble.* The last few hours had brought his words home to her; now she understood.

Where was he? Time was running out.

She scanned the tops of the heads below, but the man with the heart was gone.

She started back down the stairs, panicking. He must not get away.

From the other side of the stairwell, something shiny thrust out to touch her.

"You are," said the man with the satin pillow. "I can tell."

"Thank God."

She pressed him up the stairs to the second landing. A dimmer hallway stretched ahead, cut across by shafts of subdued light from the several bedrooms. She did not remember which was Milo's but knew she must find it before the appointed hour. From below she heard a rush of excitement. Was the girl Rip had hired here already?

"Come with me," she said. "We have to talk."

7. HOTEL DINING ROOM

The DIRECTOR is having dinner with his PRODUCER. The pressure is on to finish in time. But the DIRECTOR

can do it. He's done it before. The last scene is
going to be a killer.

In the scene the GIRL'S boyfriend, the NIGHT MANAGER
from the supermarket, will lead soldiers to a graveyard
to rescue her. There will be lots of pyrotechnics.

Now the GIRL appears in the dining room. She sits
down without being invited, expecting to be warmly
received. She assumes that she is part of the
DIRECTOR'S life now. She waits for his greeting. But
he only looks at her. He takes her aside and tells her
impatiently to grow up. This is real life.

* * *

8. FX TRAILER

The DIRECTOR goes to his FX man for help. The GIRL is
hanging everybody up. He can't let it go on this way.
Nothing is more important than the picture.

What scenes does she have left? They go over the
storyboards: only the Burning of the Zombies.
The NIGHT MANAGER will lead the attack on the
graveyard, shotgunning dummies of zombies behind the
gravestones. Then the National Guard lobs grenades
in—the boyfriend will have to run a careful path
around the explosive charges. Once the dummies are
blown, he'll torch them with a flamethrower.

All they need from the GIRL is a close-up of her as
she receives a blood squib from the shotgun, her
shocked expression as she comes to her senses and
recognizes her lover at the instant he kills her.
Then cut to an exploding dummy.

Is there a way to shoot around her? Long shots,
a better dummy, more blood and effects to cover?
The other zombies will be blown away using dummy
substitutes, but they need her for the reaction shots—
she's the Queen of the Zombies.

MARTY is always one step ahead. He's saved the
DIRECTOR'S ass time and again. This time he's already
made an alginate cast of the GIRL. He's got a full
latex body mold of her ready as a back-up. It is

lifelike to the tiniest detail. It's more than a
dummy—it can be worn by a double, if necessary. Now
they can finish with or without the GIRL.

You're a genius, the DIRECTOR tells him. This is going
to be a bloody masterpiece regardless of actors.
They're nothing but trouble, anyway.

She led him on down the hall. There was a lilting peal of laughter
from the first bedroom; from the second she heard boisterous chatter,
and through the unlatched door glimpsed a pale hand with razor blade
describing furiously in the air above a horizontal mirror. The third was
closed, with a crude sign attached to the doorknob: PRIVATE—OFF
LIMITS. That, she guessed, was Rip's doing.

She pulled the man with the heart into the adjoining bathroom. The
connecting door was ajar; in the bedroom, the soft, filtered glow of a small
lamp. It was enough. "Here, we can be alone . . . "

He stood uncertainly in the middle of the bathroom floor. "I've been
waiting for you," he said.

"I know. I've been waiting for you, too," she told him, and heard giggles
and footsteps approaching in the hall.

"Busted," he said.

"No." She backed up to secure the door. "Not us."

Leaning against it, she allowed her eyes to flutter shut. She waited for
the room to stop spinning so that she could make the speech she had
rehearsed. When she opened her eyes, he had moved closer.

He stood before her and tilted his head quizzically.

"But you don't know what I've got planned, do you?" she said. "I should
explain."

"You don't have to," he said. "I think I understand."

"How could you?"

"I told you. I've been waiting a long time."

"Forgive me. I'm being rude. I don't mean to be. It's just that it's all
happened so fast . . . "

"Take it easy," he said. He withdrew to give her breathing space and sat
on the edge of the tub. "I don't mind waiting a little longer." A reflection
from the tiles glinted playfully in his eyes.

Good, she thought. He's game.

"As long as it's not too long," he said.

In the hall, the footsteps and the giggling drew nearer.

9. ON THE SET

The GIRL arrives with notes in hand, more eager than
ever to please her director.

But he's not in his chair. Somebody else is—a
woman.

The DIRECTOR'S WIFE. The crew is gathered around,
laughing and reminiscing. The WIFE is now the center
of attention. The GIRL is displaced.

She finds the DIRECTOR and tells him off. He uses
people. He doesn't care about anything but blood,
blood and more blood. Why did he lead her on? She'll
tell the world, starting with his WIFE.

He tells her the facts of life. "She already knows."
He doesn't need the GIRL anymore. The relationship
is a wrap.

As she runs from the set, the WIFE observes. How sweet
and innocent the GIRL looks. "I hope she doesn't take
it too seriously. I used to—but now we lead separate
lives. I learned a long time ago that this is his only
real world—making movies. It's all he lives for. Real
flesh and blood can't compete. The only thing he's truly
married to is his capacity for illusion. . . . "

10. GRAVEYARD—THE LAST NIGHT

The crew is working feverishly to rig everything for
the climax.

The DIRECTOR lingers after the rest of the crew
have gone home. At 4 a.m. he finishes checking every
detail. The zombie dummies are propped up on armatures
behind the tombstones, the oil-smoke pots are ready,
the crosses are tilted just so. Nothing left but to
call "action" at dawn. For now, he'll catch an hour's
shuteye in his trailer.

"It won't be long," she said when the footsteps passed.

He shook his head sadly. "It's been such a long, long time," he said at last. "I'd almost given up hope. But you are the one, aren't you? Yes. You are."

"I'm the one," she said. "Now listen . . . "

He waved the stuffed heart. "I've been carrying this around, trying to find the right person to give it to." He made a sound that was halfway between a laugh and a shudder. "But no one would take it."

"You didn't need to do that," she said. Something to recognize him by? She could not remember any mention of it on the phone. It was a good idea, of course; it would have made him easier to spot. Or was it a gift? "What is it?"

He stood and came closer, holding it out. "What does it look like? I wanted to give it away, but there were never any takers. I wonder why that is? But now you're—"

"Yes, of course. There isn't much time. I don't know where to begin. You must be wondering why I brought you here."

"It doesn't matter."

"It does! That's what I'm trying to tell you. I see a lot of people . . . "

"So do I," he said. "Or I did. That's all over now."

Somehow he had gotten across the floor and was now only inches from her. She couldn't see his face; in the shadows he could have been anyone. She recalled a brief flash on the stairs: kind features, pained eyes, a hangdog expression. That only made her feel worse. She forced herself to go on. She could make things right. It was not too late.

Before she could speak, he braced his hands on either side of her head and leaned in to kiss her.

At first she was too dumbfounded to resist. Then she thought, Oh Christ, not at a time like this. Then she thought, What did he imagine when I called him, led him here . . . ?

My God.

"Wait," she said, breaking and turning aside.

But he pressed her and enfolded her mouth again.

At that moment someone pushed on the other side of the door at her back, trying to gain entry. Her front teeth struck his with a grinding like fingernails on a blackboard.

"Sorry," mumbled a voice from the hall.

She spread her hands against his chest. "No," she said, "please, you don't understand. That's not what this is about."

"What *is* this about, then?"

"Will you hurry up in there?" said the voice from the hall.

She was shaken, confused. But there was no time for that. The clock was ticking.

Now there was a pounding on the door.

"This way," she said, and dragged him through the connecting door to the bedroom.

"I wish you'd make up your mind."

"Listen," she said, "my name's—"

"I don't care."

"You sent me a story, right? I showed it to my producer. He liked it. So much that he wants it for next season. *But not to buy it.* Oh, I'm sorry, I'm not making myself clear. It's my fault, too. I'll tell you about that later. But you'd better get down to WGA Manuscript Registry first thing in the morning. File whatever you've got—preliminary drafts, notes, anything."

"Why should I do that?"

"I'm trying to help you! They're going to steal your story. When Milo comes up here, I want you to tell him who you are."

She took the pages of the original version from her purse.

"I had to warn you. Whatever he says, don't back down. We're in this together. Now any minute all hell's going to break loose Regardless of anything, know that I'll stand up for you. I want to make it up somehow. Maybe you'll end up hating me, I don't know. But I've got to try. I'm truly sorry. Believe that."

She inhaled, exhaled, wishing her heart would slow down. In the bathroom a few feet away, someone locked the doors.

The bedroom was quiet, the lighting cool. On the nightstand the contents of a lava lamp flowed together, heated up and broke apart again into separate bodies, endlessly. Her mouth hurt; it was warm and wet. There was a sound of water running.

"What, may I ask," the man said, "are you talking about?"

"I'm trying to tell you that I'm all for you," she said, "no matter what."

Impatience flared in his eyes.

"Make up your mind," he said.

11. AT HIS TRAILER

The graveyard is spooky—he almost feels that he's being followed. He's about to enter the trailer when a ghoul appears. It's the GIRL, in full ghastly makeup.

He tries to get rid of her, knowing she's not really needed. But this time she's coming on differently. Not whining and needful, but happy as a puppy dog and all set to please. See? She's ready, and she's going to be perfect. She's even worked out a little something extra for her moment of death. It's her own idea and she's sure he's going to like it. If she can just try it out on him first.

She seems to have accepted reality. She really wants more than anything else for the picture to be good, after all. The same thing he wants. It's all that matters. She realizes that now.

"You've taught me a lot. More than you know. Now let me give you something back—what you really want. I want it now, too."

12. IN THE TRAILER

She runs through her expressions as he stands in for her lover. She screams on cue. Almost perfect. She needs to try it with the shotgun. She's brought it with her, already loaded with wax blood bullets. She's thought of everything.

"You want it to be real, don't you?" She presses him to take the prop gun. "We have to do it right. I want you to see how much I'm willing to give you. Let's do it all the way. And this time you're going to get everything you want. I promise."

He's reluctant, but he plays it out. When she starts screaming, he fires the shotgun. The look in her eyes is one of peace at last, as blood explodes and she sinks down the wall to the floor. "Jesus, that was great! What a take! If we'd had a camera . . . "

He leans down, shakes her. "Cut. That's it. You've finally got it. Hey, what's the. . . ?"

He touches the wound. **It's real.** When she handed him the gun, it had a live round in the chamber. She had planned it that way.

He cleans up frantically to get rid of the evidence—no one will believe what really happened.

What about the body?

A desperate plan. He'll replace her dummy on the
set with the real thing, propping her up behind the
tombstone like all the other dummies. The evidence
will be blown to hell, then burned to a cinder. When
the flamethrower hits her, the rubber makeup will
burn like napalm. There won't be anything left. He'll
put her into position himself. No one will notice.

"I'm doing you a favor," she told him. "At least that's what I'm trying to
do. If you'll let me."

"Are you the one?" he repeated more forcefully.

"Yes. I mean no." She evaded his grasp once again. "I mean . . . "

"But you said you're the one." He waved the heart-shaped pillow.

"Not like that," she said. "This is about something more important.
Don't you see?"

"I should have known. You're not who I thought you were."

"Yes!"

"Which is it?" he said, angry now.

"Just—not the way you mean it!"

He was about to leave.

"This is very important to me," she said.

"To you," he said. "It always gets down to that."

"And to you! What's the matter with you? Haven't you heard a word I've
been saying? Can't you . . . ?"

He glared down at her. He tapped the pillow into her chest. "It never
changes. You're just like all the rest." He tapped her again more aggressively.
"It's always me, isn't it? *Isn't it.*"

"What do you mean?"

"What do *you* mean?" he said fiercely, directly into her face.

Her scalp began to crawl. Who is this man? she thought. I've made
another mistake, the biggest one of all.

"Wh-who are you?" she said.

"Who are *you,*" he said, "to ask that? Who the fuck do you think you
are?"

She tried to dodge him as he lunged for her, a lifetime of disappointment
igniting his rage. He grabbed her and flung her against the hall door
before she could get it open, pushed himself in front of her. The pillow

thrust up under her chin, forcing her head back. It wasn't soft, after all. It had something dangerously hard inside it. In fact it wasn't a pillow. It was an elaborate, padded Valentine gift box.

He raised it high. She saw the red heart poised to strike her, the satin covering worn, tattered, stained but still a deep crimson, like his face and the roadmap of years there, like the blood that ran from his cut lip. She didn't know who he was. He could have been anyone.

He was a madman.

Suddenly the door rattled. It rammed into her spine as someone tried to open it. She was driven into his arms.

"Huh? Oh. Sorry." Milo's voice through the crack, and behind him the sound of hysterical, theatrical weeping. "Come on. There's another phone down the hall."

"Wait!"

"Have fun . . . "

The man in front of her hesitated. In that moment she made her move and sprang for the doorknob. But he was on her. She twisted around and snatched the heart, heavier than she had imagined, and hit him with it. When he would not let go of her she swung it at his face again and again. She heard a dull breaking sound as she struck bone. The box broke and lumps of candy went flying, shriveled and hard as rocks. He dropped to his knees, a mystified look in his eyes, and toppled forward.

Then other people were in the room, Rip leading the way. Cheerful whispers turned to gasps.

"*What have you done*?" someone said.

"I didn't do anything! He—he was—"

"He was what? What did he do?" A tall woman moved to comfort her. She smoothed Chris's hair, saw the bruised lips, the torn buttons, the wild look. "It's all right now. He tried to assault you, didn't he? I've seen his kind before. The bastard."

"Who is that guy?" someone else said. "Who invited him?"

"I'll call a doctor."

"It was self-defense," said the woman, holding Chris too tightly. "Don't say a word to anybody. Do you understand? You had no choice. Who knows what he would have done to you if he'd had the chance? Something much worse. You know that, don't you?"

Chris had never seen her before. Now she could not remember any of the other faces, either.

She tore free and rushed to the stairs.

Below, in the empty living room, the music had stopped. One solitary young man remained. He stood up self-consciously.

"Excuse me," he said, "but do you know a Christine Cross?"

She stared at him dumbly. She could not think of an answer.

"Well, if you see her, would you mind telling her that I've been looking for her? My name's Roger. I'm supposed to meet her here. Hey, is something wrong? Is that blood on your . . . ?"

Without breaking stride she ran outside, the taste of blood, her own or someone else's, drying to salt on her lips.

13. DAWN

All is ready: backlight through fog, tilted crosses.
Zombies propped up like shooting gallery targets.

The DIRECTOR tells MARTY to use extra-strength
charges. He doesn't want to see anything left when
the smoke clears, not even the animal blood and guts
inside the dummies.

"ACTION!"

The boyfriend, the NIGHT MANAGER, runs like a soldier
through a minefield. Dummies are shotgunned one by
one, then blown up, then torched. All except the
GIRL. She will be the last shot. Where is she for
her close-up?

We don't need her, says the DIRECTOR, winking at
MARTY. She's not on the set? Who knows where she
is—probably on the bus back to Indiana. Who cares?
This is my picture and I say we don't need her. We've
got a perfect dummy. Just blow it up—now.

"ACTION!"

The NIGHT MANAGER advances on her, shotgun ready.
But before he can fire, her head lolls to one side.

"Wait," calls the SCRIPT GIRL. "Her head's out of
position—it won't match."

"I'll fix it," says MARTY.

"No!" The DIRECTOR can't let anyone handle her—they'll discover it's a real body. He'll have to do it himself.

"Watch your step!" yells MARTY.

The DIRECTOR threads a careful path to her tombstone. Tries not to look at her face as he adjusts the head. There. He stands back.

Ready?

"Hold it," says MARTY. Now there's blood running out of her mouth. The shot still won't match.

"Just get it, will you?" says the DIRECTOR. He grabs the shotgun and prepares to fire the blood pellet into her himself. But before he can pull the trigger, her head lolls again as she starts to come to. She's not dead!

He pumps a shot into her, another. But the bullets aren't real this time. Her eyes open and look at him, seeing him there in her moment of triumph. She smiles.

"Die," he mutters, "die . . . !"

She raises her arms, zombie-like, as if to embrace him.

He lunges at her, his hands going for her throat to make it right for the last time. Her arms go around him, pressing him to her in a final paroxysm—and the wires attached to her body make contact, setting off the charge. They are blown up together, married in blood for all eternity.

It's the last shot, the best effect of the film.

<u>END</u>

DENNIS ETCHISON's stories have appeared widely in magazines and anthologies since 1961. He is a three-time winner of both the British

Fantasy Award and the World Fantasy Award. His collections include *The Dark Country, Red Dreams, The Blood Kiss, The Death Artist, Talking in the Dark, Fine Cuts,* and *Got To Kill Them All & Other Stories.* He is also a novelist (*Darkside, Shadowman, California Gothic, Double Edge*), editor (*Cutting Edge, Masters of Darkness I-III, MetaHorror, The Museum of Horrors, Gathering the Bones*) and scriptwriter. In 2002 he began adapting the original *The Twilight Zone* television series for radio, followed by further scripts for *The New Twilight Zone Radio Dramas* and *Fangoria Magazine's Dread Time Stories.* Forthcoming are a career retrospective from Centipede Press's Masters of the Weird Tale series and a volume of new short stories from Bad Moon Books.

Acknowledgements

Special thanks to all the editors who originally commissioned, solicited, and/or accepted these stories and first published them.

"Charlie's Hole" by Jesse Bullington © 2002. First Publication: *The Book of More Flesh*, ed. James Lowder (Elder Signs Press).

"At First Only Darkness" by Nancy A. Collins © 2011. First Publication: *Zombiesque*, eds. Stephen L. Antzak, James C. Bassett & Martin H. Greenberg (DAW).

"The Blood Kiss" by Dennis Etchison © 1988. First Publication: *The Blood Kiss* (Scream/Press).

"We Will Rebuild" by Cody Goodfellow © 2009. First Publication: *Zombies: Encounters with the Hungry Dead*, ed. John Skipp (Black Dog and Levinthal).

"Dead Giveaway" by Brian Hodge © 1989. First Publication: *Book of the Dead*, eds. John Skipp & Craig Spector (Bantam/Mark V. Ziesing).

"Zombies for Jesus" by Nina Kiriki Hoffman © 1989. First Publication: *Strained Relations*, ed. Alan Bard Newcomer (Hypatia Press).

"An Unfortunate Incident at the Slaughterhouse" by Harper Hull © 2010. First Publication: *Sick Things: An Anthology of Extreme Creature Horror*, ed. Cheryl Mullenax (Comet Press).

"Captive Hearts" by Brian Keene © 2009. *First Publication: Hungry for Your Love: An Anthology of Zombie Romance*, ed. Lori Perkins (Ravenous Romance).

"Going Down" by Nancy Kilpatrick © 2006. First Publication: *Mondo Zombie*, ed. John Mason Skipp (Cemetery Dance).

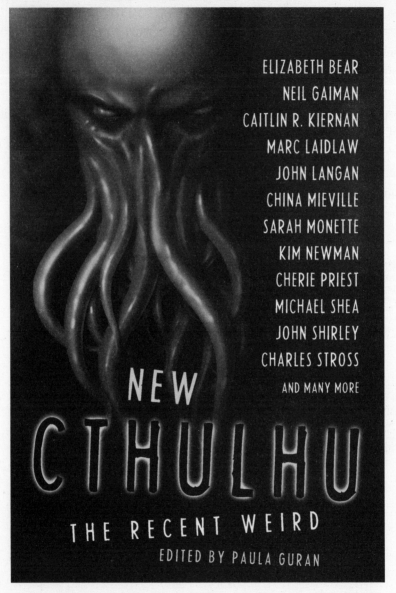